KILL ORDER

KILL ORDER

by
Adam Blumer

Kill Order by Adam Blumer
Published by Lamplighter Suspense
an imprint of Lighthouse Publishing of the Carolinas
2333 Barton Oaks Dr., Raleigh, NC, 27614

ISBN: 978-1-64526-186-5
Copyright © 2019 by Adam Blumer
Cover design by Elaina Lee
Interior design by AtriTex Technologies P Ltd

Available in print from your local bookstore, online, or from the publisher at: ShopLPC.com

For more information on this book and the author visit: AdamBlumerBooks.com

This is a work of fiction. Names, characters, and incidents are all products of the author's imagination or are used for fictional purposes. Any mentioned brand names, places, and trademarks remain the property of their respective owners, bear no association with the author or the publisher, and are used for fictional purposes only.

Scripture quotations are from the New King James Version. Copyright 1982 by Thomas Nelson. Used by permission. All rights reserved.

Brought to you by the creative team at Lighthouse Publishing of the Carolinas:
Eddie Jones, Marcie Bridges, Darla Crass, Shonda Savage, Brian Cross, Kay Coulter, and Jennifer Leo

Library of Congress Cataloging-in-Publication Data
Blumer, Adam.
Kill Order / Adam Blumer 1st ed.

Printed in the United States of America

Praise for *Kill Order*

A positively riveting, un-put-down-able read! Blumer implements an incredible mastery of language, plot, and style in this twist on the cat-and-mouse thriller. *Kill Order* will have you flying through pages to understand the connection between sadistic murders and Landon's displaced memories. A sinister conspiracy at play will keep your heart thundering against your rib cage as you attempt, with Landon, to solve the mysteries of his past to help him, his mother, and his high school sweetheart survive the present. But faulty memories and past crimes have a way of haunting even children of God.

~Hope Bolinger
Author of *Blaze*

Wow, I think I've discovered a new favorite in sci-fi thrillers! Blumer takes us on a wild, rollicking ride of adventure, mixing medical technology, family relationships, and political intrigue, while addressing questions of moral choice and free will. A true tour de force that is better experienced than described.

~David E. Fessenden
Author of *The Case of the Exploding Speakeasy*

With *Kill Order*, Blumer delivers another high-concept, high-stakes thriller. With an expansive cast and an intricate plot, readers will find themselves on a relentless ride that races forward to the final page. Fans of Dean Koontz's thrillers will like this novel. But *Kill Order* offers even more: a look into responsibility and guilt, culpability and fear.

~Aaron Gansky
Author of *The Bargain*, The Hand of Adonai Series,
Who is Harrison Sawyer, Heart's Song, and *Firsts in Fiction*

Adam Blumer has created a story that parallels Stephen King and Ted Dekker's offerings with his own unique voice. *Kill Order*'s inspiration thread is the added spice that makes this thriller unique and satisfying. Blumer's what-if idea is well-researched, and the intrigue and raced for your life moments are well-executed.

~Cindy Ervin Huff
Multi-award-winning author

Already troubled by suspicious blank periods in his childhood memories, Landon Jeffers finds evidence he may be committing violent crimes that he doesn't remember. It's as if something outside of himself were taking control . . . From this premise, Adam Blumer develops one of the premier suspense novels of our time. It's a page turner you won't want to put down till you've devoured the last sentence.

~Donn Taylor
Author of *Lightning on a Quiet Night*

"*Kill Order* is a fast-paced, masterfully written psychological thriller with surprising twists and turns that will keep readers engaged until the very last page. I highly recommend it!"

~Nancy Mehl
Best-selling author of *Mind Games*

"In Adam Blumer's latest novel, *Kill Order*, we find accomplished pianist Landon Jeffers facing one of life's greatest threats. His days are numbered. Cures are in short supply. Negativity and despair mount as an inevitable and premature end to such a gifted life seems too insurmountable. Until a cure is offered, experimental, mind you. No promises are made, but past cases have shown promise ... of death and destruction to those who have been on the wrong side of justice for far too long ... In *Kill Order*, the bad guys could easily find themselves on Raymond Reddington's *Blacklist*.

And Landon Jeffers could easily find himself on the vengeful side of the lawless. A bit mystery, a bit sci-fi, a bit thriller, when the reader pieces these 'bits' together, a story will emerge that will test one's own moral compass."

~C. Kevin Thompson
Award-winning author of the *Blake Meyer Thriller* series
and *The Serpent's Grasp*

Acknowledgments

The book of Ecclesiastes says two people are better than one, but when we're talking about publishing, I think a dozen or more are even better. So many folks contributed to helping me reach this milestone of a third novel. My parents, Larry and Rhoda Blumer, were there during my formative years and gave me plenty of positive reinforcement. My in-laws, Dick and Mary Melzer, have always cheered me on, along with my wife, Kim, and my daughters, Laura and Julia. Beyond those folks, there are almost too many to name, but I'll highlight a few. Special thanks go to the following:

Cyle Young, my agent with Hartline Literary Agency, for taking me on and finding a publishing home. Tessa Hall, his associate agent, gave me excellent feedback on the opening chapters.

Eddie Jones, Marcie Bridges, Darla Crass, and the rest of the creative team at Lighthouse Publishing of the Carolinas for granting me the contract and working with me to achieve the finished product.

My father, Larry Dean Blumer, whose terminal brain cancer journey from 2009 to 2011 gave me the first ideas for this novel and offered an insider's look at what life with glioblastoma multiforme looks like. Several of Landon's symptoms come straight from my father. I miss you, Dad.

My Scribes critique partners at American Christian Fiction Writers (ACFW), several of whom read the entire manuscript and gave me excellent advice. I couldn't have done it without their positive feedback and their enthusiastic support.

Detective Lieutenant Michael Papp, of the Iron Mountain, Michigan, Police Department, for answering my questions.

Christian pianist and recording artist Greg Howlett, whose musical feedback offered authenticity to Landon's life as a celebrity pianist.

Novelists Deb Brammer, Andrea Boeshaar, and Jamie Langston Turner, who have always been there to provide advice and encouragement along the way. Author Kari Fischer deserves special mention for her help with my manuscript.

Novelist Rick Barry, whose evaluation helped push the project over the finish line.

Members of my Facebook street team, who deserve special mention for their help in getting the word out.

Kimberly Delaney, who provided helpful information about ocular albinism.

My wife, Kim, my first reader and the listener of my woes when something in a story is going amiss. Her love of mystery novels has been an asset.

My heavenly Father, for always knowing what's best for me, even with the delays and setbacks in the publishing industry. May He always receive the glory for anything good He does through me.

Dedication

To Dick and Mary Melzer, for being the best in-laws a guy could ask for. Thank you for supporting me and my writing over the years. I think you've sold more copies of my novels through word of mouth than anybody else I know. Your generous and caring spirit has always amazed me.

You cannot change what's over
but only where you go.

—Roma Ryan

A safe but sometimes chilly way of recalling the past is to force open
a crammed drawer. If you are searching for anything in particular you
don't find it, but something falls out at the back that is often more interesting.

—James M. Barrie

Therefore do not let sin reign in your mortal body, that you should obey
it in its lusts. And do not present your members as instruments of unrigh-
teousness to sin, but present yourselves to God as being alive from the
dead, and your members as instruments of righteousness to God. For sin
shall not have dominion over you, for you are not under law but under
grace.

—Romans 6:12–14

Part 1
From the Corner of My Eye

Chapter 1

Friday, October 2
Denver, Colorado

“Landon, you have a brain tumor.”

The truth pressed down, a heavy weight on my ribs. Lying in my hospital bed, I struggled to breathe. Couldn't. I choked out the word, “*What?*”

“Because of the results of the CAT scan, the doctor feared the tumor might be putting stress on your optic nerve.” Amee, my agent, came into focus beside me—head tilted, straight black hair brushing her shoulders. Worry lines traced her mouth. “That's why you're having vision problems, why you didn't see the car when you merged onto the highway.”

The accident. The car coming out of nowhere.

Of course. What else explained this strange blindness in my left peripheral vision? When I studied the ceiling, one-third of the left side of the room vanished as if a black hole had swallowed it. Sweat beaded my forehead.

“You hit your head pretty hard,” she said. “You may not remember everything for a while.”

Squeezing my eyelids shut, I grappled to rewind my memories, searching for any event to explain this strange orientation. Didn't Celeste and I agree to meet after the concert for some drinks?

That's right. Denver Metroplex. The conclusion of my big thirty-city tour.

But why did any of it matter now?

A tumor.

It could be removed and might not be so bad. But that depended on the type.

Events once forgotten flashed through my brain like a fast-paced slideshow—me playing on stage at a grand piano, my backup band pulsing, and the audience cheering beyond the edge of perception. Me playing “Private Island” with my cellist, Kim Ono.

3

Afterward, I'd gone to Celeste's place to hang out for a while, and later I'd headed to my hotel.

I blinked a few times to clear my vision. Turning my head, I scanned my surroundings and waited for my world to come into focus. But it didn't. Colors swirled together and morphed, softening the hard edges nearby into nothing but vague smudges.

My eyes—what's wrong with them?

"There's more. The doctor worried about more serious issues, so he did an emergency biopsy." She hesitated. "Your mom will be here in a few hours. She should be the one to tell you."

The throb in my head crested with each movement, but I pushed through the discomfort. "Tell me what? I want to know."

"I'm afraid it's cancer."

My mind did a swan dive into a dark unknown, into a place where I didn't expect to be. Not at forty-five. Not with so much ahead of me, a Grammy Award-winning pianist.

The news came at me too fast. I needed time—

"It's called glioblastoma multiforme. Stage four."

Whatever that meant. Why couldn't doctors come up with simple terminology for the rest of us? Why not Bad Thing Number Ten in Your Head?

An unseen wound above my right eye pulsed with each heartbeat. Fire shot through the area, and I gritted my teeth. Reached for the wound.

Amee stopped me. "Hey, maestro, you don't want to touch that."

Still lost in the world of thirty seconds ago, when my biggest problem had been only a car accident, I dragged a tongue across parched lips. Precious seconds granted me mere moments to ground myself. "It's bad, isn't it?"

No response.

Not good.

"How long are they giving me? Don't sugarcoat it. Give it to me plain."

"One to three years."

Clamping my eyes shut, too numb to speak, I waited for advice straight from Oprah or Dr. Phil. *Embrace life. Seek out inner strength in the midst of adversity.* Instead, she said, "I'm sure there's something somebody can do to fix the problem—beyond surgery and chemo, I mean."

From my lips burst a derisive chuckle. "I've got terminal brain cancer, Amee, not a broken leg. This kind of cancer doesn't get fixed."

She clucked her tongue, a mannerism that annoyed me to no end. "But I've got some friends in high places who are knowledgeable in the field of alternative brain cancer treatment. A friend of mine in Tucson, Dr. Nicholas Korovin, has been breaking new ground. Folks are calling him a miracle worker."

"Miracle worker, huh?" In my brain flashed the image of a witch doctor chanting while I tiptoed across a bed of red-hot coals. My whole body ached like one massive bruise. I swallowed, mouth parched.

"He removes the tumor and inserts his own specially patented medicinal wafers in the tumor's place. Please, just give the idea a chance. Let me contact him on your behalf and see what I can find out, okay? His services aren't cheap, but hey—you can afford them, right?"

Hmm. Could it be some people died simply because they couldn't afford to live?

My flesh writhed at the thought of something alien stretching octopus-like tentacles into my brain and feeding on it. Yep, the tumor had to go. Pronto.

But cancer supposedly happened to *other* people. Not to middle-aged guys like me who at last had everything I'd ever wanted. A successful career. A dozen best-selling piano CDs to my credit. Hundreds of thousands of adoring fans. A Chicago penthouse condo I already missed.

I bolted upright, awash in dizziness. "Amadeus!"

"Not to worry. I called Miriam at the office, and she found the extra key you told me about. Your cat's doing just fine and having a grand ole time partying with the cats at her place."

Good thing I'd neutered him. Settling against the pillow, I sighed.

"Don't worry about a thing. You and Amadeus can be reunited whenever you want him back. For now, you just get some rest, okay, maestro? Doctor's orders. And don't fret about future concerts or whatever. Every artist needs time off."

Who said I worried about concerts? I'd just finished my big thirty-city tour and could use a break. Well, okay, a certain concert had always been on my bucket list. Maybe I'd never reach the milestone now.

"Maestro, you focus on getting help. Once you're better, we can put that concert in Tokyo on the schedule again."

"You think I'm going to get better? Didn't you hear anything I just said?"

"Didn't you hear anything *I* said? Dr. Korovin has cured stuff like this."

"*Cured* terminal brain cancer? Yeah, right. There *is* no cure for this."

"Landon, think about it. These days you can pretty much buy anything you want if you've got enough cash. Hold off on making any big decisions until I chat with Nick, okay?"

They appeared to be on a first-name basis. A good sign.

She glanced at her watch. "I gotta go. I need to pick up your mom at the airport."

Mom.

Eyelids pressed shut, I dreaded where this journey might take me. After she left, I must have dozed. The ringing telephone on the nightstand jolted me awake.

"Hello?"

"Is this Landon Allan Jeffers?" The words were broadcast from a deep, educated-sounding voice tinged with some type of accent. Russian?

"Yes, it is." I braced myself for the fan who'd tracked me down and wanted to tell me his sob story.

"You don't want to die, do you, Landon?"

Fingers squeezed the receiver. "Excuse me?"

"If you want to live, you'll do exactly as I say."

Chapter 2

Saturday, October 3
Omni Hotel
Atlanta, Georgia

Trina Ellis paid her fare and exited the taxi, slamming the door behind her. Door locks engaged with a click at the same moment the realization hit her.

Wait. The watch.

Whirling back, she waved at the driver when he pulled away. He braked and rolled down his window, eyebrows raised.

"Sorry. I left my bag on the back seat."

The taxi driver tilted his head, one hand to his ear. "What?"

Across the street, due to a concert under way at Centennial Olympic Park, the wailing guitars and heavy bass had drowned out her voice. She repeated herself at a higher volume, and he nodded. A moment later, yellow shopping bag retrieved, she returned to the curb with an apologetic look. "Sorry."

"Loud concert." He motioned toward the park with his head.

Flashing colored lights from the stage lit up the park while the sky beyond eased from dusk to night. The bass throbbed beneath her heels. "So who's playing tonight?"

"Foo Fighters. They're kicker."

The name meant nothing to her. Barbra Streisand was more her style.

Waving good-bye, she headed up the steps to the Omni Hotel and entered through a turnstile glass door. At the reception desk, she requested her husband's room number and asked for a second key card. While the clerk processed her request, she rubbed moist palms on her jeans and rehearsed what she'd tell Ted.

Mom went home from the hospital earlier than expected. She thought it was her heart, but it ended up being only heartburn. Can you imagine that? I got her home, but rather than head to our place, I decided to surprise you. I hope you don't mind. I did try to call, but you don't usually turn off your cell, do you?

7

The clean-shaven attendant handed her the key card. "Have a wonderful evening."

"Thank you."

Her thoughts turned to how Ted would react when she showed up unannounced. He'd been so mercurial during the last few months, not his happy-go-lucky self, but content with her plans to spend the week with her ailing mom. Some of his stocks had taken a hit when the recent bubble burst. Maybe the loss explained his desire to use a few personal days and get away, even without her. Perhaps the pricey watch she'd picked up on the way might cheer him up.

The elevator stopped at the twenty-second floor. She stepped off to behold floor-to-ceiling windows offering a beautiful view of the park below. The concert venue had become crammed to standing room only. Pounding bass filtered through the glass.

Trina scanned the door numbers in her hunt for Ted's room. High-end carpet and furnishings grabbed her eye. He'd paid extra for an upscale suite? The hotel he'd booked for their anniversary trip six months ago had been a dive compared to this place.

The pounding *rat-a-tat-tat-tat* from the type of gun she'd observed only in movies shoved her toward the wall.

A quick head check confirmed nobody in the hallway.

Where had the popping sounds come from? Maybe concert fireworks were to blame.

Gunfire went off again, unmistakable this time, so loud the blasts reverberated in her chest. Could a gunman be in the hotel? Maybe on this floor?

Following the number sequence, she dashed down the hall. Rounded a corner.

2217.

The card swiped, and the door's mechanism released. Shoving her way in, she closed the door with her back pressed against it, a sigh on her lips.

More shots. Her body jerked. So close. A long barrage of rounds rattled off with barely a pause, then ceased.

The stench of something burning filled her nostrils and the otherwise-palatial suite.

"Ted?"

No answer.

Straight ahead stood a glass and chrome side table. Taupe walls and a purple rug. The edge of a large wall TV gleamed on the far left, but the wall to her right obscured the rest of the room. When she peeked around the edge, her jaw slacked.

Across the room, Ted knelt beside the open window, huddled over some sort of black military-style gun on a tripod. He pulled the trigger, and the rounds pounded in her chest again, the gun eating up an ammunition belt. Metal casings spiraled and bounced, the stench of gunpowder strong.

The gun pointed beyond the dark open window and balcony toward the park below, the scene of the rock concert and so many people.

Trina backed away, trembling. Her gaze strayed to other guns scattered around the room, all with extended barrels and large gun magazines. Numbness seeped through her limbs.

The shopping bag slipped from her fingers and slapped the floor.

Ted swung his head around. Bloodshot eyes widened. "What are *you* doing here? Get out!"

"Ted, wha-what's going on?"

He ignored her. Resuming his place at the gun, he pulled the trigger again.

Acid burned the back of her throat. With the staccato of each round, images flashed in her mind of bullet-riddled bodies lying in bloody piles.

Something untamed rose inside her. Two steps bridged the distance to Ted's side and the gun. She kicked the tripod, and the gun fell. It spewed bullets across the balcony before Ted righted it.

Cursing, he glared at her and cocked his fist. The stinging impact twisted her head around. Her feet collapsed beneath her.

The stranger in her husband's skin rose and towered above her, his hair askew, dark circles around his wild eyes. He swept a gun off the floor and pointed it at her face, the barrel jittering. "Go! Get out of here before I shoot you too."

She scrambled to her feet and fled. A barrage of rounds blasted inside the room like a series of explosions in her limbs. They punched the wall above her head. Yanking the door open, she barreled into the hall and collided into a man wearing a security uniform. He grabbed her upper arms.

"In there! He's got a gun." Sobs erupted from her mouth, and her legs gave out. She slid against the wall.

The man yelled into a walkie-talkie, something about a shooter on the twenty-second floor.

Another man, a cop, grabbed her arm and helped her up. He moved her farther away and muttered something about ensuring her protection.

9

She complied in a stupor, barely cognizant of the men in SWAT uniforms storming past her.

More gunfire.

An explosion rattled her teeth. The hallway filled with smoke.

Then eerie silence.

No one needed to say a word. Something inside told her Ted wouldn't be coming home.

***

"Don't look at the cameras. You can just look at me." Ashlee Toyer from CNN gave her a comforting smile from the beige easy chair. A vase of red roses, mixed with sprigs of baby's breath, perched on a table to her right.

Sitting across from Ashlee, Trina untangled the tissue wrapped around her fingers. She'd applied a fresh application of lipstick, which she seldom wore. But one made concessions when going on TV.

Her mind flailed, and she sought to steer it somewhere beyond the studio and cameras, to the trip she'd take with her grieving kids after all the interviews. At least she still had them.

"And then in your own words," Ashlee said, "just say what we talked about. You remember. About your husband not being himself."

"Now?"

A nod. "Sure. Whenever you're ready."

Don't look at the cameras.

"Okay." Trina exhaled and licked her lips, suppressing the flutter in her stomach. "Ted and I were married for twenty-three years, but that night—that terrible night when I walked in on him—I didn't even know who he was."

The TV anchor glanced down at her notes and looked up. "You didn't recognize your husband?"

"No, I did, but he just didn't seem like the person I married. I mean, Ted never even drove over the speed limit. To do something like this—I mean, it's crazy."

"Why do you think he did it?"

"I wish I knew. People wonder if he had connections to ISIS or some other terrorist group. But that's ridiculous. Ted wasn't a member of any-thing, unless you want to count Sam's Club."

Ashlee cocked her head. "But if he didn't seem like your husband, who *did* he seem like?"

"This is going to sound crazy, but it was almost like"—Trina swallowed—"like somebody else had entered his body."

She pushed aside memories of a smiling Ted handing out gifts at Christmas, of Ted kneeling on one knee, even in the snow, to propose to her. She dabbed at her tears with the tissue. "This wasn't the man I married. I hope when they do the autopsy they find something wrong with him."

"Like what?"

"I don't know. I guess something must have gone weird in his head. How else can you explain his killing seventy-three people?" She shrugged. "He had no reason to do that."

"So you think something was wrong with his brain?"

"Oh yeah." Trina's fingers twisted the tissue again. "I mean, he must have had a brain tumor or something to explain his odd behavior. It was like—I don't know—like something broke inside his head."

Chapter 3

Two months before
Wednesday, August 5
Chicago

*D*o *what we ask, or you and your girlfriend will die.*
A blood-freezing chill stuttered through Ray Galotta's bones as
he read the text message. He paused on the front steps of his town
house and white-knuckled the railing for support.

No, not another threat. Not when he appeared so close to being free.

At first, he'd assumed the texts must be a stupid joke. But the threats
had escalated over the last few months and left a trail of death in their wake.

Trembling fingers combed through his thinning russet hair. The bitter
truth soured in his mouth and almost drove him to his knees.

Three people are dead because of these sick monsters.

If only he'd called the FBI right away instead of shrugging off the
anonymous texter's instructions. Maybe the dead might still be alive.

Breathing. Living. Enjoying life.

He kept reading and scrolling.

They'd texted him the address, following the protocol of the last two
times, and ordered him to terminate the man by noon tomorrow. Daniel
Meyers, the name attached to this latest kill order, lived in Rolling Mead-
ows, perhaps on a sprawling estate, an executive he hadn't met. Most likely a guy with business connections—that detail appeared to fit the pattern.

The first threat had been similar, except they'd gone after Marcus, a
classmate from years ago. Ray had assumed the text must be a prank until
his friend turned up dead. The second threat had provoked a more serious
response, but investigators hadn't moved fast enough, and a former girlfriend, Leah, had died too. A bullet to the temple.

No.

He wouldn't stay and let it happen again, not to those he cared about.
Especially not to Sylvia. He'd call Daniel and warn him in the same way
he'd done for the others. Then he'd run.

But how could he be ready? And what about Sylvia?

It didn't matter. Did they have any choice? At least if they ran, they had some sort of chance. Staying here invited a death sentence.

Ray shoved the key into the lock and pushed his way inside his town house. Slamming the door closed, he pressed his back against it. He dropped the cell phone—his direct connection to evil—to the floor and stomped on it, pulverizing it into a thousand tiny pieces. Plastic skittered in multiple directions.

How many people carry cell phones around every day, not even considering the potential?

Ignoring the mess, he grabbed his jean jacket and hurried through his too-silent home one last time, finding the wad of cash in the cookie jar, grabbing essentials, tossing them into a messenger bag, turning off lights. Saying goodbye. With a tightening throat, he headed outside, pulled the locked door shut behind him, and took in the ambiance of the crisp evening. On any other night, he would have paused to delight in the moment.

Would he ever be back? Would *they* ever let him?

He descended the steps to the sidewalk, vigilant and wary. Keeping his focus fixed straight ahead, Ray did his dead-level best not to let on what he'd detected.

Across the street a man in a brown shirt and jeans leaned against the brick wall of another town house. He not so secretly studied Galotta above the top of his sleek, silver tablet. Probably video-recording him and doing other cloak-and-dagger stuff he got paid to do.

Why should I be surprised?

Someone appeared to be watching—always watching. But when had the watchers ever been this bold?

Turning on his heel, Ray strolled away from his home and from peace he'd once known. As if he didn't care.

But of course he did. Would he ever find such peace again? Maybe if he evaded the watchers and got out of this godforsaken town … and reached Sylvia—

The watcher followed, the smack of his footfalls cracking like gunshots through the cool-but-getting-colder air. He made no pretense of making his pursuit covert.

Realization sent adrenaline coursing through Ray's veins. Though they'd given him a deadline, something must have changed this time. They appeared to be coming for him *now*. Did they intend to kill him?

Why the difference this time?

He'd gotten the fake IDs and passports a week ago, thanks to a privileged authority in the police department. In preparation, he'd also been withdrawing small amounts of cash from his paycheck over the last few months. It had to be enough for now. More time to plan his exit strategy in greater detail would have been ideal, but he lacked that luxury.

Breaking into a jog, Ray pushed himself into dark alleys and traversed busy streets. A breath-snatching pinch in his side throttled his lungs and almost made him trip and kiss the cement.

The pounding of the watcher's pursuing footsteps receded in the distance. Had he lost the guy? He hoped so, but he better keep a sharp lookout.

In the shadow of a busy McDonald's, he found a phone booth, thrust in several quarters, and brushed the stinging sweat away from his eyes to read the numbers well enough to dial them.

God, please. Let her be there.

Her velvety voice answered. "Hello?"

"Hey, it's me." Sucking in air, he forced himself to slow down, though his hands trembled.

"Ray, you're out of breath. Are you okay?"

He peered out the smudged window, probing empty sidewalks and deceptive shadows. "No, I'm not okay. Sylvia, it's time for us to run."

"What?"

"We gotta go. Now. Remember what we talked about, what I told you we gotta do?"

He'd been prepping her for weeks via text messages from the prepaid phone, planning ahead for this scenario.

"Of course, but—"

"No buts. Just leave. Walk away. Now."

"But—but I can't. I—"

"You *have to*. I just left the town house, and a watcher's after me. They aren't waiting for the deadline this time. I think they're coming for both of us *now*."

She cursed.

He decided not to share the text message. The threat against her life would've been too much for her to take in right now—it might shatter her. Maybe he'd tell her later. Panic wouldn't be helpful, but he couldn't deny the importance of urgency.

"Look, you've got"—he checked his watch—"maybe a half-hour lead time. Probably not much more than that."

15

Tension stretched the taut silence like the slowing heartbeat of a dying man. He searched the perimeter of the phone booth. Still no sign of the watcher, but he must be nearby. Time to move.

"Meet me at O'Hare in half an hour. Kiosk for Hallmark cards."

He told her he loved her, clicked off, and scrubbed his hands across his sweaty stubble. Determined to pull himself together.

Everything's gonna be okay. We can both pull this off. There's still time.

Now with the phone booth behind him, a probing gaze burned a hole in his neck. He swung toward the street.

Nobody. At least no one discernible. But he'd learned the hard way that these men wouldn't hesitate to use means beyond standard detection to find him.

His friend Eddie had learned this fact better than anyone—one of the first, dead because of him. His name squeezed Ray's heart and stung his eyes.

He'd made the mistake of asking Eddie for help. Working with the computer crimes unit, Eddie might have established the identity of the unknown texter of the second threat, the one dooming Leah. But his techie friend must've gotten too close to the truth. Now his children wouldn't know their father.

Gulping in some fresh air to begin the next leg of his journey, he pictured Sylvia grabbing her purse and racing out of her music studio.

God, please keep her safe. Please let her reach me before somebody else reaches her.

Chapter 4

Landon
Monday, October 5
Tucson, Arizona

Out of the darkness loomed the longest corridor I'd ever seen. Unsmiling, fast-trotting people in suits and ties swept by, not glancing at me or saying a word. As if a boy trudging along in a suit and shiny shoes couldn't be anything unusual. A much younger and smaller version of me clutched Mom's hand and looked up at her, unsure whether I wanted to go any farther.

"M-mom?"

"It's okay, Landy. I'm here with you." She smoothed down my stubborn cowlick.

"But do we have to—?"

"Yes, we do. This is for your own good. Remember what I told you?"

Be a good boy. Jesus is watching.

We came to a shiny, burgundy door. Mom opened it and nudged me inside. A man seated behind an enormous desk yawned and looked at me. He leaned forward in his chair to give me the once-over, elbows on the desktop, fingers steepled in front of him.

"So this is"—he glanced at a folder on his desk—"Landon Jeffers, huh?" Lowering thick, black-framed glasses, he studied me over the top. Halted the progress of another yawn.

Unsure what to say, I nodded. Reaching toward me, he squeezed my fingers in a strong grip. I worked hard not to grimace.

A tuft of gray hair wrapping the sides and back of his head reminded me of a piece of ancient, dirty carpet. But the top of his head shone bubblegum pink.

He cocked his head. "Your mother told you what this is all about, hasn't she?"

"Yes, sir." But I didn't understand any of it. Someone wanted to evaluate me, but why? Because I liked to play Mozart on the piano and had gotten my picture in the paper for winning a regional contest?

His thick glasses magnified his eyeballs several times their ordinary size, reminding me of an owl. "You realize you're a special boy, don't you?"

"Special?"

"Not like other kids. Not like your friends. We're going to see how special that is. That's why you're here, okay?"

"Okay." Licking my parched lips, I peered at my polished leather shoes.

Big mistake.

If I hadn't been admiring my penny loafers, I would have seen the knuckle side of his hand coming without warning, without reason, out of nowhere. It smacked me hard across the cheek and toppled me off my feet.

I landed on my side, smacking my head on the floor. My ears throbbed.

Something jolted me awake in the hotel room. For a moment, I couldn't recall what I was doing here.

The memory or dream—whatever it might have been—perched on the edge of my consciousness. For a split second, the man's slap still stung, his words echoing.

Special. Not like your friends.

What an odd dream. Or had it been something more?

I glanced at the clock.

The phone call from Dr. Korovin had set many details in motion. After the flight to Tucson, my mom and I checked into the Holiday Inn Express, the adjoining door intended to put her at ease in case I needed anything. Now, while she got settled, I slumped on the bed and raked fingers through my hair.

Why, God, why? Why did you do this to me?

A sudden desire hit me to find a piano and pound out "Sorrow," a depressing song I'd written for myself years ago. For those rare days when life really stank to high heaven. Why did this have to happen to *me*?

The curse dropped from my lips without conscious choice, releasing pent-up frustration. After all, I didn't have anyone else to blame. And if God was in control, as my mom had told me countless times while growing up, wasn't *he* responsible?

Exhausted and sweating, I clamped my eyelids shut, making the blindness complete this time. As if on cue, Mom knocked on the adjoining door. I whipped it open.

"Are you okay?" she said. "I thought I heard you call out."

The lie slid off my tongue. "I'm fine."

She entered, her big-hipped form swathed in one of those flowery dresses she always wore. Long, gray-streaked black hair hung limply on either side of her face, resembling drab curtains that begged for a vigorous wash. Her oval face had nice muscle structure, but her cheekbones would have stood out more if she'd worn some blush.

The thought of giving her a fifty and instructions to head to the nearest salon tempted me—that is, if they had any salons in this godforsaken town. Then again, she had beliefs about wearing too much makeup. Convictions for just about everything. No doubt that invisible straitjacket constricted her life just as much now as it had when I'd been a naïve kid.

She reclined on the edge of the bed and tilted her head. "We should grab something to eat."

"I'm not hungry."

I looked toward the left window I could make out only by looking at it head-on. The tumor had damaged part of my optic nerve, and now I suffered permanent blindness in my left peripheral vision. During a stop for my prescription at Walgreen's—steroids to reduce brain swelling and prevent seizures—I'd had to turn my head to the left to see the full price tags.

I might not drive again—a real invalid. Okay, driving may not seem to be a big deal in the scheme of things, but there's no denying the male ego.

"Landy, you've gotta eat something. You'll need your strength for the procedure tomorrow."

The procedure.

During the call with Dr. Korovin, we'd discussed my options. Beyond the vision problems and off-kilter balance, I suffered weird memory lapses. Some periods in my past had vanished.

Either way, the tumor had to go—at least what he could remove without damaging healthy tissue. I had the money to pay extra, so the decision had been simple. And if Dr. Korovin wanted to throw in mysterious medicinal wafers that would supposedly heal me, why not give his therapy a try? It couldn't hurt, and I preferred it over radiation and chemo.

So surgery and follow-up therapy from Mr. Miracle Worker appeared to be my next destinations on this highway to hell. But just the suggestion of a neurosurgeon boring into my skull with a drill tomorrow gave me the shakes.

"Landy, please. You need to eat something."

"I don't *want* to eat." Though a large bag of salted pistachios might have roused a hint of an appetite.

19

Could this be an ideal time to argue about the diet? During the flight here, she'd lectured me nonstop. No more red meat, no more junk food, not even Mountain Dew, which I'd survived on daily for years (but didn't tell her).

She bit her lip as if she were about to cry and struggling not to. "I know this is hard, but our dear heavenly Father only does what's best and—"

"Best? You seriously think this is best?"

She recoiled like I'd struck her. "Landy, didn't you hear anything I taught you over the years?"

Of course. I'd heard every cliché and platitude so many times I knew them all by heart. Then I'd graduated from college with a music education degree, attempted to teach music to sixth-grade psychopaths who refused to be taught, and come to the realization that all my mom's wise sayings, straight from the Good Book, must be nothing more than empty words.

That God wasn't there to help me—not through any of it. And if God hadn't been there for me during my first disastrous year of teaching, why should I trust him to stand by my side now?

But of course, I didn't say any of this. How could I? Where else might a bachelor like me go? I didn't even have a significant other to take care of me; Celeste and other women in the cities where I toured had been convenient for drinks and company, but I'd entertained no serious intentions with any of them. Who remained but ole, faithful Mom, whose words at the Denver hospital drifted to me with perfect clarity.

Don't you worry about a thing. I'll take you home after the surgery and take care of you until we figure out what to do next.

We?

Now my problem had become hers, too—a realization I wrestled with. Apparently, I would soon return to Michigan's Upper Peninsula and be her little boy again. I'd be back in the ramshackle A-frame house on E Street in Iron Valley, Michigan. Trapped in the embarrassing past I'd fled from.

Perfect.

What mattered now required biting my tongue and keeping the peace, but how could I live with her when her every breath came out like a sermon, an accusation?

I mustered all the goodwill I could scrounge up. "Of course, I remember, Mom. You taught me lots of wonderful things. I know you did."

"Just showing you the love of Jesus."

The cliché nearly choked me.

Think kind thoughts, Landon. Be positive.

Maybe if I kept this charade going, I'd keep the peace, and this impossible scenario might just work out.

Before leaving, she kissed my forehead and admonished me not to worry. On top of the nightstand, she'd left the Iron Valley newspaper behind in case I wanted to check out the latest community happenings.

I flipped through the small-town newspaper with the original title of *The Daily News*. Thankfully, my ability to make out words had improved. The front page featured the story about a meth lab discovered in somebody's basement—common fare in this part of the country. That and snowmobile accidents in January.

An article on page five snagged my attention. A private citizen had purchased the old historic building that had once provided the facility for my alma mater, Iron Valley Christian School, which had closed about a decade ago due to low enrollment. The buyer planned to convert the building into a community center for the performing arts.

Built in the early 1900s by a community drunk on the wealth of an iron ore boom, the ornate Victorian redbrick building had appeared outdated when I'd been a child. Drafty and cavernous, it bore ornamental wooden moldings everywhere and high ceilings that had no practical use beyond looking pretentious and raising the heating bill.

At the sight of the black-and-white photo of the familiar place, something clicked in my brain like someone had pushed a button. My throat itched. Without warning, white-hot fire blazed in my forehead, stealing my breath away.

Scrunching my eyelids closed, I cried out. Fingers crinkled the edges of the newspaper, pulling it into fists.

The image of the school flared in that strange blindness occupying the left side of my vision. Resembling a black hole, the emptiness sucked me down ... down ...

... to a dark, cold place where the wind howls and freezing fingers wrap around my arms and pull me—screaming—straight down. As if yanking me to my awaiting grave.

Out of the blackness of night looms the redbrick of the school; its walls, lit by a distant streetlight, rise before me in full color with white block letters centered on one blank wall: IRON VALLEY CHRISTIAN SCHOOL.

Running hard, I gasp as if someone pursues me. My legs work hard to move me through several feet of snow. Calves strain. When I pass the building, dashing I know not where, I catch the reflection of a much younger version of myself in the window.

Reaching the playground, I slow and stuff freezing, numb hands into my pockets. A bone-chilling wind lashes snow, gritty like sand, against my cheeks.

I stop and look around, heart hammering. Steaming breath bursts from my mouth as the sight before me tightens the muscles in my body.

Not three feet away, two men lie facedown in the snow, blood pooling around them. In fact, the blood is so fresh the steam rises toward the wind-shrieking night.

My stomach clenches, and I know I need to flee. Because someone is coming.

Coming for me.

But my legs, seemingly frozen to the ground, refuse to move. I grab ahold of them and work to pull them free, but they don't budge.

The wind howls, numbing my face. The snow releases me, and I fall to my knees in the whiteness. Crying out for help, I cradle my head in my arms, and ...

... when I opened my eyes, I found myself back in the hotel room. The agony in my head vanished as if a vacuum had sucked it right out of me. But my teeth still chattered from that terrible, dark place. Clammy sweat bathed my body, and my chest rose and fell, rose and fell. My lungs sought to catch up while air mercifully rushed in.

A wave of nausea rippled through me.

Where could the wastebasket be?

There. Across the room.

But if I moved, the sickness would only worsen. Biting down hard on my lower lip, I struggled to keep my gorge back.

Take deep breaths.

While I waited out the queasiness, I puzzled over where the vision, or whatever it might have been, had come from. I'd never been yanked into a dream in the middle of the day before.

Forcing myself to lie still settled my stomach and made me grateful I hadn't been stranded in the cold after all. Had I really cried out, or had that been part of the strange dream too?

Might this be a side effect of my brain cancer? Maybe I'd had a seizure; the doctor in Denver had warned me I might. Brain swell due to the tumor applied pressure to blood vessels, possibly interfering with normal brain function. But supposedly the steroids in my bloodstream lessened the odds of seizures.

I rubbed my forehead where the invisible knife had sliced into my head mere moments ago. The pain had been agonizing, but now nothing remained but the conviction that what I'd just witnessed hadn't been a dream but something else.

The windows had reflected a younger version of me.

Could the brain cancer be messing with my memories? Had I just re-lived a scene from my past? In fact, an event so terrible my brain had once locked it away, never expecting one day I'd find the key?

Chapter 5

Two months earlier
Wednesday, August 5
Chicago

Ray Galotta took a taxi most of the way, then hopped out and jogged. Fire blazed in his calves and thighs, and a knife dug into his side, but he didn't let up. He reached the airport in twenty minutes.

But could he be free? Maybe even in Chicago's O'Hare International Airport, getting lost in the crowd—lost from the men who wanted to use him or kill him—might be easier said than done.

After buying two tickets using his fake IDs and passports, he strolled away from the counter and glimpsed the nearest TV screen. There a news anchor rattled on about a recent string of murders of business movers and shakers.

The sound had been turned down too low to hear, but he didn't need to be a lip-reader to discern the contents; the graphics gave them away. He probably grasped more about the story than the anchor did. Several names were recognizable, and a disturbing fact chilled him to the bone; all the people Ray had warned had still wound up dead.

Eight victims total. No, nine by today's count. And he and Sylvia would be next if they didn't get out of the country. Now.

Sweaty clothes clung to him, chilling him. While he lingered near the kiosk for Hallmark cards, his gaze raked across the faces of strangers, searching for watchers. Meanwhile his nerves did a hellish ballet in his stomach. He glanced at his watch.

C'mon, Sylvia. Where are you?

If she'd taken him seriously, she would have been here on time. But maybe that was the problem.

She must think I'm crazy.

"Ray?"

The cadence of her velvet-soft voice spun him around, a wave of disbelief crashing into him that she'd come and sneaked up on him so easily when he'd been trying to stay alert. Coiffed blonde hair brushed the tops of her shoulders above the trim purple business suit. Delicately arched eyebrows hovered over sparkling blue eyes.

Wow, she'd made it, and she didn't even seem out of breath. She'd actually believed him when he'd been on the brink of giving up hope.

He pulled her close and kissed her, a cloud of her exotic perfume tickling his nose. "I didn't think you'd make it."

"I didn't either." That voice of perfection had sung the mezzo-soprano in Handel's *Messiah* last Christmas and brought the mesmerized crowd at the United Center to their feet.

"But you have voice students this afternoon. How did you arrange it?"

"I canceled my lessons and walked away … just like you told me to." She studied his outfit. "I see you left in a hurry too. Did you just leave a shift?"

"No. I—" He wagged his head. "It doesn't matter." He'd foolishly worn his police uniform under the jean jacket, thinking it might lend extra protection. What it really did was make him an easier target. These people weren't beyond killing a cop, as Eddie's death had proved.

Her clothes weren't exactly inconspicuous either. Perhaps they could both find some new duds and stop standing out.

He searched her porcelain-smooth face, stunned that she'd really do this for him. Just walk away from her life. Like something actors did only in movies.

She'd brought nothing but her purse. He jerked his head toward it. "You didn't pack."

"You told me not to. You said they could be watching."

Good. She'd remembered their texts.

With the nudge of her elbow, he eased her away from the kiosk. "We've been standing here too long. Let's move." Lowering his arm, he gripped her hand. He'd never let her go. They'd have to kill him first.

Ray quick-stepped his way across the busy terminal, and she matched his stride. All the while he scanned the crowd, looking for anything or anyone out of place. But nothing aroused his suspicions. He surveyed only impatient businessmen on their way to important meetings and families on vacation with noisy children. Incongruous laughter echoed across the busy terminal, making his tight shoulders relax a little.

On a nearby TV screen, a headline flashed. "Mass shooting in Detroit." Images flashed of an ambulance, of paramedics carrying bodies on gurneys. Atlanta had been the worst yet. Not another one. Would the madness never end?

She grabbed his arm. "What is it?"

"Nothing for us to worry about." He swallowed, and they resumed their stroll. "The last time we talked, you said I was being paranoid."

"I believe you now."

"So, what changed your mind?"

"Haven't you heard?"

He stopped. Studied her face. "What?"

"Stevenson, that reporter—she's dead."

Ice water flushed his heart down to his knees. No, not nine victims. Ten. And there would be twelve if they didn't get out of here ASAP.

He'd called Rachel Stevenson at the *Chicago Tribune* from the prepaid phone, sharing everything he knew about the murders and their connections to his kill orders. She'd apparently come too close to the truth, and now she'd been killed too.

When is this madness going to end?

The news stories he'd pieced together truly comprised part of a grand design; the conspiracy couldn't be just a whim of his imagination. And now that Rachel had died, they were perhaps the only ones beyond the conspirators who knew the truth.

Such knowledge could guarantee a ticket to an early grave, but he had tickets to somewhere else in hand.

"Wait." She faced him, desperate eyes searching his. "So what do we do now?"

"I already told you."

"Leave the country."

His family would later assume they'd eloped, just like he'd teased they might. Then again, maybe he really would marry her. Do everything proper. And why not? If they'd found freedom, they could do anything they wanted.

"I already bought us tickets to Paris, just like we talked about. The flight leaves in about an hour. Then we'll disappear somewhere in Europe. Change our identities."

"Disappear together." An impish grin curled her lips. "I love the sound of that."

Later, he'd somehow contact his financial adviser, drain his bank accounts, and transfer the funds to some offshore account. Who could say how long they'd be living off the grid? Weeks? Months?

He squeezed her hand, and they threaded through the crowd toward their gate. In nine hours they would be free. The thought teased him.

Too much to hope for?

Chapter 6

Monday, October 5
Tucson, Arizona

There are three types of people in this world: those who don't care when something traumatic happens, those who overreact in a crisis, and those who master the correct response to any given situation. My mom fell into the second category.

Minutes ago, she'd heard me cry out and rushed into my hotel room, wondering if I was okay. When I told her about the sudden headache and the bizarre vision, she'd freaked out.

Now she rushed past me, in search of her purse, a breeze following her wake. "I need to get you to the hospital. You need—"

"Mom, haven't you heard a word I've said? I'm telling you, I'm all right."

She faced me, conflicting emotions warring on her face. "But this could be early signs of a stroke or an—an aneurysm. I'm calling an ambulance." She marched toward her room, probably in search of her room phone since she didn't believe in using cell phones.

Sheesh.

"No, Mom, please don't. I'm … I'm okay. The mind trip, or whatever it was, is gone."

No answer.

The curse word leaked under my breath. Groaning, I hauled myself to my unsteady feet. Where had that blasted cane she'd gotten me run off to? No sign of it anywhere. Grabbing onto furniture aided me in crossing the room, and I eased across her threshold to face her.

Mom turned, corded phone in hand, about to dial. Seeing me on my feet steadied her. "You can walk."

"Of course, I can. I'm not a total invalid. Please, for Pete's sake, put the phone down. I'm fine. Besides, I'm having surgery in the morning, remember? It'll probably fix whatever's going on now."

Obeying, she embraced me and held me tight, her body shaking in my arms. We parted. "But I'm scared," she said. "Something's wrong with you."

"Mom, didn't you get the memo? I've got brain cancer. Of course something's wrong with me. But isn't something wrong with all of us?"

Smearing tears away, her expression softening, she appeared more at ease. Perhaps I embodied the security of having a man around the house, something she'd lacked for years.

She brushed past me and opened her purse. Rummaged through it, searching—for what, only heaven knew. Constant activity always equaled her remedy for stress.

"Want some coffee?" she called over her shoulder. "I sure could use a strong cup right now."

"Sure, that would be great." Her version of a strong drink made me smirk. A Jack Daniel's would have hit the spot right now, but coffee would have to do.

Saying she'd grab some coffee from the lobby, she headed out the door. Five minutes later, we sat across from each other on my bed, hot cups of the robust brew warming our hands under the glimmer of a nearby lamp.

"I would have preferred the Alterra Dark Sumatra I make at home," she said, "but for hotel coffee this isn't half bad."

The grimace reached my face before I could mask it. When I reached for a sugar packet, she stole it away from me.

"No more refined white sugar for you, remember?" She dumped in a packet for herself, a gesture that smacked of cruelty. "Sugar feeds cancer."

Here we go again.

Junk food explained why I found myself in this mess, she would say. Didn't I realize all the terrible things "they" pumped into that stuff? They. The enemy. The grand conspirators of the paranoid. Yada yada.

For years Mom had been preaching at me about the evil men who poisoned the world's populace through the food industry. Now she had just the fodder she needed to say she'd been right all along, and she didn't disappoint. For several minutes she lectured me as if I'd missed this speech the last dozen times and professed that she'd get me healthy.

"Okay, so what am I supposed to do?" I said. "Drink my coffee black?"

"Of course not. I grabbed you some honey packets." She handed them to me.

I opened my mouth to protest but stopped. Reconsidered. Honey had never been my first choice for coffee sweetener, but why not try it? Besides, she did appear to be going out of her way to be helpful.

Squeezing some of the golden stuff into my coffee, I stirred it around, and taste-tested it. "Not bad."

She swung her spoon toward me as if wielding a pointing tool. "If I'm going to help you get well after your surgery, we can start now by making some simple diet changes, but I need your cooperation here, okay? And I don't care what that doctor in Denver said. Your time's up only when the good Lord decides it's up and not a minute sooner."

Could all this diet talk be her way of avoiding the topic I wanted to discuss more than anything else?

"What?" Her unblinking gaze probed me. "Don't you want to get well?"

"Of course I do."

"Then what's on your mind?"

"What's probably on yours too, only you don't want to admit it. My memory of the school. I can't help thinking about the shooting."

She'd given the best thirty years of her life at Iron Valley Christian School, serving as head secretary and staying many years after the incident nobody liked to talk about. Including now.

Her gaze skittered to the mop of my curly, black hair, then to my open-collar, aqua Henley. "Landon, you've got a brain tumor. The cancer's probably messing with your memories, and that's why you had the vision—or mind trip—or whatever you want to call it."

Mom paused for another sip. "You know, the brain's a mighty mysterious thing for weighing only three pounds. I started doing lots of reading when I heard about your diagnosis. One author's hypothesis, in particular, has really got me thinking. He believes our brains record *every single moment* of our waking lives from birth to death in 3-D and stereo surround sound. Sure, we have memories, he says, but we've lost the connection to the master recording. But what if we could get it all back? Just imagine all the amazing things we've forgotten."

And maybe some events we really don't want *to remember.*

An interesting hypothesis for sure, but she excelled at changing the topic. "I'm not talking about the mysteries of the brain here. I'm talking about the shooting at the school when I was twelve."

She grimaced like she'd swallowed wrong. "You know very well why we don't talk about that."

True. The topic had been verboten for years, and persistent probing had never gotten me anywhere, so I'd eventually stopped asking and done my own research. The local newspaper archives had told me nearly everything I'd wanted to know. But now with this cryptic trip down memory lane, I couldn't let the topic go so easily.

"But I just saw a memory about it, Mom. About an event I haven't been able to remember for years."

"How can you be so sure that's what you saw? Even if you remembered something about the school, that doesn't mean it was on *that day*."

"But there was blood in the snow—and I saw the bodies of those two men."

Her eyes squeezed closed, one fist clenched. "Please, Landon. I don't want to talk about—"

"But we've gotta talk about it. I need to remember."

She leaned closer, coffee strong on her breath. "Why?"

"Because it's part of my past, part of who I am. I want to understand it better, especially now that my days may be numbered. Maybe there's something important I missed."

"Believe me, you didn't miss anything worth remembering." She peeked into her cup as if peering into mysterious waters best left undisturbed. "Besides, sometimes forgetting is a blessing. Perhaps the doctors were right. Maybe your repressed memories are a gift from God."

I shook my head. Imagine losing up to five years of recall because of an event so traumatic that the brain locked them up and threw away the key.

She pursed her lips. "Believe me, Landy, you don't want to go down this path. You might not like what you find."

"If I'm going to die sooner than later, I don't want to go without knowing the truth."

"The truth?" Her glance sharpened into a glare. "You make it sound like I've been lying to you all these years. You already know what happened. What good would it do to rehash it all now?"

Why had I been standing in the snow with the bodies at my feet? That detail from my mind trip didn't jibe with what I'd been told or what the newspapers had reported. Articles said I'd been found after the shooting in one of the classrooms, lying in a fetal position, unconscious.

Could there be more to the story? Because of the tumor, might my brain now be setting those captive memories free?

But if I went through with the surgery, would the operation wipe those memories clean? Dr. Korovin had mentioned the possibility of some memory loss.

Wait.

What could I be thinking? In no way could the surgery be negotiable. The tumor had to go.

Mom shook her head. "I don't know why you want to bring all that up now. Don't you realize how it hurts me to remember? Memories of that terrible day only remind me of what happened to your father." Her face had turned haggard as if the topic had wrestled her to the floor and wrung out any strength she had left.

Knowing I'd get nowhere now, I let the topic of the school shooting go. "There's something else I was wondering. When I was little, did you ever take me somewhere for some special testing? You know, like for advanced readers or something?"

She averted her gaze, refusing to look at me. "Special testing? I don't know what you mean."

"Experts who wanted to evaluate me, to determine if there was something special or unusual about me."

"Not that I can recall."

Could the dream about the man smacking me across the face when I'd been a boy be a lost memory too, though Mom wouldn't admit it? What if other memories wanted to resurface? Imagine all the unknowns I might discover about my past. What assurances did I have that the surgery wouldn't pull the plug on every one of them?

If it did, I might never discover what really happened on the day of the shooting.

My cell phone went off, and I grabbed it.

Amee.

"Hey," she said. "Just checking on how you two are doing."

"Fine." I eyed my mom's displeased expression. "We're both fine."

"I'm just down the hall if you need anything."

"Thanks, but we're good."

"No second thoughts about tomorrow, huh? Remember, Dr. Korovin said if you weren't absolutely sure—"

"Actually, Amee—"

"You *are* having second thoughts." Incredulity ebbed from her vocal cords.

"Some of my repressed memories appear to be coming back. You know, from the day of the shooting when I was a kid."

Silence.

My mom bowed her head. Shook it from side to side. As if unable to grasp where this phone call might be heading.

My concerns about losing the repressed memories forever poured out of me.

Amee listened to my spiel without comment. Then: "There's absolutely no reason for you to think the removal of this one tumor is going to wipe all your memories clean."

"Well, I didn't mean *all* of them. Just the ones from that day." The cigarette I'd secretly smoked in my room hours ago (window open so Mom wouldn't detect it) had shaved off the edge of my nerves but didn't seem to be helping now. My hands trembled.

"At the same time, there's no guarantee all the repressed memories you have *the potential of remembering* will be there later."

"But see, that's my concern."

The moment stretched thin before she spoke again.

"Let me just remind you of what Dr. Korovin told you could happen if he *doesn't* remove the tumor from putting pressure on the optic nerve. Do you really want to go blind? And if the tumor spreads, you could lose the use of your hands. Those are very real possibilities."

Sudden heat prickled the back of my neck, and I stared at my fingers. Without my piano, I'd be a nobody. A loser. My fame swirling down the drain.

But unless a miracle happens, isn't your career over already?

Who could guarantee any of the miracles this guy boasted about would even come true?

What might be more important? Retaining a bunch of repressed memories I may not recall anyhow? Or living another day without fear of suddenly losing my sight or the use of my hands?

I blew out a breath. "You're right. Let's do it. I want to go ahead with the surgery."

"You're sure about this?"

"Absolutely sure."

Whether I ever learn the truth or not.

Chapter 7

Two months before
Thursday, August 6
Somewhere in France

The farther they traveled from Chicago, the more those steel fingers squeezing Ray Galotta's fear-sick heart began to loosen.

Enjoying their newfound freedom, they did some quick sightseeing in Paris, taking in the Louvre, but lingering in the city made him uneasy with street cams everywhere. The less they appeared on the grid, the better. He couldn't ignore the nagging voice muttering in his head that a watcher could be trailing them, even across the ocean.

They had to find a way to disappear. Unfortunately, he hadn't planned that far ahead. How exactly did one vanish in Europe? He grasped enough not to use credit cards, but the rest appeared to be guesswork.

A cab took them several hours from the city. Deep in the French countryside, they chose a charming hotel situated beside a picturesque lake. But a restful night wasn't to be.

Sometime in the wee hours, a hand clamped over his mouth, grinding his lips into his teeth. Synapses in his brain fired in a frenzy. He flailed his arms in the dark, trying to hurt his attacker and free himself.

A fist slammed into his stomach. He bent over, the agony snatching his breath away.

A bedside lamp flicked on, and he squinted.

Three masked men in black lingered beside Sylvia, where she cowered in bed.

An adrenaline overdose pushed his heart into overdrive, but he didn't have time to bargain with them. Two held him down on the bed, gagged him, and tied his hands behind his back. The third hauled Sylvia to the floor and tied her hands too.

"Please! Please—don't hurt me!" Her musical voice edged toward hysteria, but the man stretched duct tape over her mouth. Her gorgeous body, swathed in a delicate nightgown, a souvenir from Paris, shuddered with panicked sobs.

Her terror-filled gaze searched his. Their eyes met, and he shared the look of realization while straining at his bonds, mind flailing. Unless a miracle happened, their lives would be over.

One of the men yanked the power cord off one of the lamps, wrapped it around Sylvia's creamy neck, and began strangling her.

The men wrestled Ray's head around so he wouldn't miss a second of her final, desperate moments. He sweated and fumed, wanting to save her but finding himself powerless to do so.

C'mon, Galotta. Do something.

She kept her wide, terrified eyes locked onto his as if acknowledging their last connection. With his eyes he told Sylvia how much he loved her and begged her to forgive him before her spasming body stilled.

He stared at her, the silence stretching and teasing.

This can't be happening. Somebody, make it stop.

Hot breath tingled against his neck. "You were told what would happen if you didn't do what we said. You'll never run again, will you?"

Sobs wracked his body, and he found himself unable to think, unable to fight. Hope had died on the floor with his dear Sylvia. Why didn't they just kill him too?

He gaped at her lifeless body, at her sightless eyes widened in shock, until her image rippled in his tears. His stomach folded in on top of itself, and he would have thrown up if not for the gag. Acid seared his throat.

Never would they be man and wife. All their hopes for mutual happiness had been destroyed. They'd been fools to think they could escape from these sick monsters.

The watchers had tracked him all the way to Europe. He could hardly believe it. But how could he be so important?

Restraining hands let him go and removed the gag. Ray Galotta slid to the floor and wept over her lifeless body, her skin still warm to the touch.

A strange buzzing swelled in his ears. Someone had plugged in a razor and began shaving his head; russet locks rained down on Sylvia's gown like so many flower petals fluttering into an open grave.

What now? Could this be some new method of torture?

He shot a look toward the bed. One of the men had opened a black case and methodically laid out various-sized scalpels. Another prepared a syringe.

Could his worst ordeal still lie ahead?

Skin on the back of his neck puckered.

God, do something.

"Please ... please don't kill me. I'll ... I'll do whatever you want."

"Yes," Sylvia's executioner said. "We'll make sure you do."

Chapter 8

Tuesday, October 6
Tucson, Arizona

You may never wake up, Landon. This could be it.
Lying on my back in a paper-thin gown, I drove fingernails into my palms, an electric razor's buzzing filling the room. Behind my right ear, the nurse cut off a section of those blasted black curls that had been impossible to manage anyhow.

I resisted the urge to yell. Even to curse. Curse everything and everybody.

Attention fixed on the bland ceiling tiles, I struggled not to think about the reality that threatened to steal my breath away.

This can't be happening, God. Why don't you stop it?

Somebody was about to crack my head open like an egg and mess around inside. Wasn't there a TV commercial like that? Some type of gizmo that scrambled an egg while still in its shell?

God, please. Wake me up from this nightmare. I'll do anything.

A wave of panic swept over my head. I struggled to inhale, clenched my fists. Scrunched up my eyes.

"Landy? Hey, Landy!"

The sound of her voice resembled hot syrup splashing down on a warm pancake, melting the butter along with my anxiety. Fingers eased, unclenching my fists.

"Mom?"

Her face hovered in my line of sight—that weak jaw, the double chin she hated. The way her hazel eyes peered down at me offered a panacea. "Hey, calm down, Landy. I'm here. It's okay. Soon you'll fall asleep, and you won't remember any of this."

But I wanted to remember. All of it. Everything I'd missed when a child and so wanted to remember. Didn't she understand that?

Landy.

She made me feel like such a child—nobody else used that boyish name. Perhaps because I remained a child in so many ways.

Perhaps this could be my wakeup call. Possibly I could make a bargain with God like people did in movies. Maybe I'd promise to change if God would give me a second chance. And maybe, just maybe, he'd even listen.

"I'm going to pray for you now. Is that okay?"

I gave a small nod. Sure, why not? What could it hurt? But why would God even listen? Let her have her way and her God—and pray as well if she felt like it would do any good.

But redemption must be too late for me. I'd walked away from my faith long ago. God supposedly gave second chances to the penitent, but surely he knew that if I suddenly turned to him, it would be nothing but a ruse. A ploy for my mom's sake. If it hadn't been for the cancer, would I even be thinking about God right now? Did I really think I could manipulate the Creator?

She began, and I folded my hands together in a mere formality, a gesture of compliance that meant nothing more. I'd forgotten the true heart gesture of worship long ago, if I'd ever known it to begin with.

"Dear heavenly Father, we bring Landy before you now …"

For perhaps the last time I treasured the long, strong fingers that had made me a legend. I worshipped them and hoped I'd be able to use them later. That is, if I even woke up.

"… and give him peace now as he goes into surgery. Perhaps we aren't supposed to understand, Lord, but we *are* supposed to trust. Help Landy to trust you at this time, even though he may not understand …"

Would I ever play those songs again under bright stage lights, under the gaze of my adoring fans? Without my piano, what would I do? In what would I find fulfillment in life? I'd been somebody only because of my piano talent, and now this monster called cancer threatened to gobble that away like a demonic Pac-Man.

"… your strength, guide the surgeon's hands to do the work they need to do. Help them to remove as much of the tumor as they can. And if it's your will, Lord, would you lift Landy back to his feet and help him to be whole again? It doesn't matter what the doctors say. You are the Great Physician. You can do it. I know—"

The nurse to my left vanished, swallowed by the blindness in the left corner of my eyes. Why would I be surprised? I should be used to this handicap by now. Closing my eyelids tight, I envisioned the school where the fateful event from my past, the day I still couldn't clearly remember, had occurred.

Why so fixated on the school? An unseen voice whispered back.

Because your mind knows you need to go back—that's why. Time to take care of unfinished business, Landon.

But what odd timing. Now that memory's gate had opened a crack, releasing memories from this period I couldn't recall, might it now be slammed shut again? Irreversibly? For all of time? Would I never discover the truth?

But what could I do now? I'd been rendered powerless and placed where I hated to be above all else: no longer in control.

My mother said "amen," her warm lips brushing my forehead.

"Landon, can you hear me?" the nurse said.

"Yes."

"Great. I want you to begin counting backwards from one hundred. Can you do that for me?"

My throat had turned dry, my mouth pasty. My voice trembled. "One hundred … ninety-nine … ninety-eight …"

I never reached ninety-seven, but I did remember.

Chapter 9

Landon
Tuesday, September 14, 1982
Iron Valley, Michigan

Someone was yelling in the playground out by the slide.

The girl's shout drifted through the window, which had been propped open to let the breeze in. In sixth-grade study hall, seemingly chained to my desk, I'd grown weary of the algebra I knew had nothing to do with my future. Raising my hand, I asked Mr. McCrosky if I could use the restroom. He barely looked up from his fantasy novel and gave me a distracted nod. On the cover a bronze-muscled warrior gripped a glowing sword.

I took off, quickly using the bathroom and then studying the playground through the bathroom window. Sure enough, Myles Cochran and his buddies, the bullies my friends and I called "the posse," had gathered in a circle around a small, blonde-haired girl.

Striding toward the scene, I hoped I could help. I could get in trouble for not returning to study hall right away but not if I had a valid excuse. After all, I *had* heard someone shouting and feared she might be in trouble.

Jade Hamilton, the new girl, lived with her dad, an auto mechanic, in that yellow, rundown house on the corner. He'd opened a repair shop just two blocks from the school. According to rumors, her mom had run off with the mailman, but the story changed weekly. The last I'd heard, she'd joined the circus and did amazing feats on the high wire that made the crowd gasp.

The taunting voices of the posse drifted toward me on the breeze. "Ping-Pong eyes! Ping-Pong eyes!"

I neared their tight circle but held back, deciding to assess the situation first. No need to engage in a fight if one wasn't necessary. Not that I'd invite one anyhow. Truth be told, I'd long been a coward.

"You're just a bunch of bullies." Jade bracketed her arms across her chest, muscles cording her neck. "You don't bother me."

"Ping-Pong eyes! Ping-Pong eyes!"

"Let me pass, you morons. I need to go inside now."

Five of them lined up, shoulder to shoulder. Whenever she moved, they shifted like one virtual wall on feet. They engaged in their initiation ritual, determining whether she presented a threat to their control. I recognized the drill—they'd done the same to me once.

"Ping-Pong eyes! Ping-Pong eyes!"

Why the trouble? She had the prettiest blue eyes I'd ever seen—so light they appeared to be almost white. Though she had a small frame, I suspected she had a heap of gumption hidden away.

I wasn't mistaken. Without warning she charged into Myles and his buddies as if to tackle them all singlehandedly. But they were bigger and weren't letting her through the chain of their arms. Myles shoved her, and she lost her balance, sprawling on her back with a grunt.

Several items toppled from her pocket to the scraggly grass. Several dollar bills, two York Peppermint Patties, and the wallet-size photo of a woman I didn't recognize.

"We're in charge of this playground!" Myles perched his hands on his hips, elbows wide. "And don't you forget it. When we tell you to get off the seesaw, you get off when we say so. Got it?"

Jade glared at them, arms still folded across her chest. Neither confirming nor rejecting. Myles wasn't finished.

"Give us trouble, and you'll be seeing us again." He and his henchmen withdrew, nearly stampeding me as they marched away.

"Hey, leave her alone!" I called to Myles's back, but he ignored me. He'd already had his fun, and there wasn't anything I could do to turn back time. I'd managed to be conveniently late. Again.

Not that I would have gotten involved anyhow. Myles and his buddies had threatened to break my fingers if I ever interfered. *Then your future on the piano will be over, loser.*

I offered Jade a hand. She grabbed it, stabbing me with a look of annoyance while I pulled her to her feet.

"Hey! You okay?" I said.

"Of course I'm okay." She straightened her skirt, a brown, frilly thing with bright-red flowers. "I didn't need your help, by the way."

I reached down to collect her stuff, but she moved more quickly. She snatched up the candy and money in a flash, stuffing them back in her pocket, but she'd overlooked the full-color snapshot of the blonde-haired woman.

Snatching it from the lawn, I studied it. The beautiful woman resembled somebody I might have seen in the Sears catalog, the one with the pages I faithfully dog-eared to mark what I wanted for my birthday or Christmas. Her mysterious blue eyes flashed, complementing the mischievous smile on her bright-red lips. She resembled a movie star, certainly not somebody from Iron Valley.

Jade snatched the photo out of my hand. "Hey, that's mine!"

"Sorry. I was just—"

"Some help you were against those losers." Shoving the photo away, she met my eyes, and the reason for the teasing became clear. Her pupils, fixed on my face, darted side to side as if two tiny guys were playing Ping-Pong with her pupils inside her head.

Wrenching my startled look away took effort, but something in my breeding told me not to stare. "That woman in the photo—is that your mom?"

"That's none of your business."

"Sorry. Just trying to be friendly."

"Why?"

"Why?" The Ping-Pong game snagged my attention again. "Well, you're new, right? Probably don't know very many kids around here."

Her chin rose. "I'm doing just fine by myself, thank you very much. I don't *need* your help."

Fine. If she intended to be ungrateful, she could do so all by herself. Shaking my head, I turned to stalk away.

"Thank you," she called to my back.

Stopping, I looked back. "You're welcome. I'll try to be quicker next time."

"And I'll try to be more grateful." The faintest of smiles tugged at her lips. "Hey, you're Landon Jeffers, the piano player, aren't you?"

She'd apparently heard about my geekiness. "And I take it you're Jade Hamilton?"

She nodded. "I'd love to watch you play sometime."

I puffed out my chest, flattered that I apparently had a fan before she'd even sampled my repertoire. "Well, okay. Sure."

"I can't play a hoot on the piano, but I'm taking flute lessons. I sure do love music."

"I play on the gym stage during lunch hour after I eat and then at the end of the day before my mom's done working in the school office. But then I usually use the old piano in the storage room because of basketball practice."

"Sounds good. Well, I gotta go." She turned.

The big man on campus rose inside me. "Hey, if Myles gives you any more trouble, you just tell him to come and talk to me."

Jade giggled and sauntered away like she knew I didn't have the guts to do any such thing. But soon she would need protection—real protection—and I'd have to rise to the occasion. Would I be ready?

Chapter 10

Present day
Tuesday, October 6
Iron Valley, Michigan

"It's perfect," Ray Galotta said. "I'll take it."

The plump woman with the thousand and one tattoos lingered and studied the surgical scar on his head, her expression begging to know what had happened to him. She'd have to die curious.

"I'll need a security deposit upfront as well as the first month's rent," she finally said as if snapping out of it.

He studied the window, curious about the view he'd find beyond it. Based on his research, it had to be the right one. "So how much do I owe you?"

She told him.

Pulling out his checkbook, he wrote her a check while she watched, jaw working at a wad of bubblegum. She offered little appeal, but of course, no woman could compete with Sylvia.

He tore off the check and handed it to her. Somewhere downstairs a child wailed. Forlorn and pitiful.

She frowned at the check. "Galotta. Is that Polish?"

"Nope. Italian."

"Okay, we're all set here, Mr. Galotta. You got good references. I bet you'll be a great renter."

You better hope so, lady, because you have no idea who I am.

From the middle of the room, he studied the open doorway and the hallway beyond. Above them, the house creaked, and the wind rustled in the attic, like a living thing, lungs wheezing. Hot water heat made pipes tick and pop, as if somebody lived in the walls, paid to keep up the act of motion and noise in a place where nothing important or exciting ever happened.

His presence promised to change all that.

She cocked her head. "You know, I have several larger rooms that are still empty. I could give you the same price if you prefer one of those."

"Nope. Like I said, I want this one." His gaze lingered on the window, never straying.

"Suit yourself."

He sampled the empty space—walls, floor, ceiling—and considered what he would do to fill the space. And the time. He sought not to imagine what Sylvia, once an avid Home and Garden Channel fan, would have done in a room like this with just a little paint and plenty of genius.

His new landlord left, stairs creaking, and he closed the door of the small bedroom and zoned in on the only item of interest. At the old window, he pulled out his binoculars and zeroed in on the backyard of the Jeffers residence. Landon's bedroom window fell into his sights.

Excellent.

So much to do while Landon remained out of town, but he chose the wise path of waiting until nightfall before he dove in. Soon he'd have an even better view.

From inside the house.

Say goodbye to life as you know it, Jeffers.

Part 2
Memory Trips and Daymares

Chapter 11

Saturday, October 24
Iron Valley, Michigan

"So how did the surgery go?"

"Better than expected," I said. "The surgeon removed about ninety-five percent of the tumor. I'll be having checkups every month to see if the cancer is still growing. Now at least the tumor isn't putting pressure on my optic nerve, so I don't need to worry about my vision problems getting worse."

"That's great, Mr. Jeffers."

"Please, call me Landon."

"Oh, sorry."

Janet Fillmore, a gawky teen with overly large glasses, didn't look a day over sixteen. Amazing how young beat reporters could look these days. We chatted on the front porch swing on an unseasonably warm autumn day, just a week shy of Halloween. Freshly fallen, multihued leaves blanketed the road and swirled like little dust devils when the wind got up its dander.

A better interview location would have been on lawn chairs in the sun, but Dr. Korovin had advised me to stay out of its harmful radiation.

"I understand you're doing alternative therapy." Janet peered up from her notepad, where she furiously recorded my words. "Could you describe what you're doing for diet?"

"Mostly an alkaline diet of lean fish and chicken, raw fruits, and vegetables. No refined sugar, dairy, red meat, sodas, or junk food. Oh, and I eat a lot of grapefruit."

"Grapefruit?"

"Yeah. It's a good thing I like it. I eat tons of that stuff."

And yes, I've lost just shy of twenty pounds in the last few weeks.

"What else do you do for your health? Beyond your diet, I mean."

"Aside from practicing the piano, I mostly avoid stress. I go for long walks every day in the fresh air." Now that most reporters had left town, the treks were doable. But I usually took my cane along since my balance still evaded me sometimes. "I'll be doing physical therapy every week, and then I plan to get lots of sleep and hope God doesn't call my number."

A smile touched her lips. "Hope this interview isn't giving you too much stress."

Actually I hoped *she* wasn't too stressed. She'd appeared pretty nervous when she arrived—her handshake clammy, her every few words a stammer. *It's not like I get to interview a Grammy Award-winning pianist every day, somebody who's actually played for the president at the White House.*

Rising, she told me the story would appear in next Tuesday's entertainment section and thanked me for taking the time. It was a small-town newspaper, after all, and I probably had a few other, more important, interviews to do.

True. There had been more than a few, mostly for *Rolling Stone, Billboard*, and *Entertainment Tonight*. All the reporters had asked the same question. Can we expect more music from Landon Jeffers?

I'd wanted to shout the answer from the rooftops after that uncertain moment when I'd sat down at a keyboard for the first time after the surgery. Yes, I could still play the piano as well as ever, I'd told them, and I didn't plan to stop making music unless the cancer took it away. Even Amee and my producer had an idea for a new extemporaneous CD called *Songs from the Living Room.*

My mom had consented to the remodeling of an unused, main-floor bedroom into a piano studio for practicing and recording; I wouldn't have to go anywhere to be productive. Even now the pounding of workers' hammers and the buzz of their saws drowned out the gentle cadence of leaves scudding down the street.

As Janet headed toward her car, something about her profile reminded me of someone I hadn't seen in years. Who could it be?

Mom stepped onto the front porch, the screen door squeaking in protest. "How did it go?" She'd accompanied me on my journey toward good health and shed a few pounds herself; she'd never looked better.

"Fine, I guess."

Janet sped away in a blue death trap, leaves swirling.

"Seems awfully young, doesn't she? You'd think, given your fame, that they would have sent someone more … I don't know …"

"Experienced?"

"Yeah."

I hadn't expected to do the interview with someone who looked like she might be writing a high school paper on "Famous People I've Met." On the other hand, Iron Valley was about as small town as you could find. But by small-town standards, I was about as famous as you could get.

Certainly an interview from the managing editor—an exclusive, in fact—would have been more appropriate. But perhaps a certain angry woman on a mission from my past had poisoned the staff toward me, even now after all these years.

"Sharon Bartholomew is still in town, isn't she?" I said.

"Yep. Some people just never move away, do they?"

"In more ways than one."

Sharon had never forgiven me for her son, Joey's, death. Not that I'd been responsible, of course, though I'd been there that day when he fell from the cliff overlooking an old sunken mine not far from where I stood right now. Amazing that I could remember that much, given how generally hazy my memories had become these days.

"Want some more freshly squeezed lemonade sweetened with stevia?" Mom said.

"No, I'm good." Hesitant feet trudged toward the porch swing, and I reclined, gripping the armrest and deciding not to divulge that my balance appeared to be worse today. Why worry her? Dr. Korovin had been amazed that I hadn't had any seizures or headaches given the malignancy of the walnut-sized tumor nestled in the cerebral cortex behind my right ear. In short, walking issues couldn't be anything to complain about.

Though I'd had only good news for Janet, the truth of my health situation still confronted me with questions I couldn't answer. Dr. Korovin had promised miracles, but what if he couldn't keep them? What if my number was indeed up in three years? Waves of heat rolled up my chest at the thought. I felt great today, but I would have been a fool not to admit that things could quickly change. Now I could start dreading that date on the calendar for my next checkup and MRI.

Mom reached for my shoulder and squeezed it. "Tomorrow I'm going to Marquette to spend a few hours with your father at the psychiatric ward. Why not come along? He'd be so thrilled to see you."

Just the mention of that sterile, colorless place made my skin crawl. "Thrilled to see me? Last time I went there with you, he didn't even know who I was." Bitterness colored my tone, but it was too late to take it back.

"Okay, so maybe his memory isn't so good. But don't you want to see your own father?"

53

I looked away, not meeting her eyes.

She took the wicker chair, placing herself so she occupied the center of my attention. "It's hard to see him in a place like that. I know that's why you don't like to go."

Nope. Definitely not easy to see Dad lying on his back, drooling like a vegetable. "That's not it."

Her brow creased in a network of wrinkles.

Why not just get it all out? Be honest.

Meeting her gaze head on, I said, "He wasn't there for me all those years, Mom. I don't feel like I really know him."

"Don't be silly. Of course, you know your own father."

"Do I really, Mom? You seem to forget I was only thirteen when he went to prison."

"Of course, I haven't forgotten. But for you to say—"

"He wasn't there when I was growing up, when I needed him most. It was like … like I didn't even have a father." Sampling the air between us, I measured her angst and chose to press on. "That's why I don't like going to see him. It only reminds me of what I missed."

She shrugged. "I suppose you're right. Forgive me for not looking at the situation from your point of view. It must have been hard for you with him locked up all those years."

Hard didn't even begin to describe it. My friends had talked about their fathers constantly. They'd played ball with them, fixed old cars with them, gone to football games with them. How could I have countered that?

My dad's pickling away in a prison cell somewhere.

I'd had no one else to fill that fatherly void, and no remedy existed— he would never be coming home. Few memories lingered of the warm-hearted guy who'd tromped all over the neighborhood, delivering the mail with a smile and a kind word, with the biggest calves I'd ever seen. Or the train nut who'd schedule his Saturday errands based on when a particular train passed through town so he could park, watch, and embrace the thunder vibrating through his every fiber.

But that man had vanished, his remaining years spent in a psychiatric ward after a prison beating that left him with brain damage and blindness in one eye, in a life few would have described as more than existing. He couldn't stay in prison with injuries like that. The judge showed leniency and agreed for him to be moved to a secure psych ward in Marquette, Michigan, about an hour from my mom's house.

Though no longer in prison, in a lot of ways he remained there. Doctors said he'd never improve. He might as well have been dead. For all practical purposes, he already was.

I leaned forward and wiped my eyes. The event had happened so long ago. So why this sudden swell of emotions when I rehearsed this period in my past?

Because you lost your father, Landon. Because life was never the same again.

Mom made a displeased sound, something between a disgusted grunt and a growl. "Well, it wasn't like your father could *help* not being there for you."

Holding in my exasperation required herculean effort. So Dad couldn't have helped doing what he did to put himself in that hellhole of a place? No, he couldn't be responsible for anything, could he?

"Mom, he pulled the trigger. Nobody made that decision but him."

"Yes, but your father's actions kept people alive. Remember?"

What could she be talking about?

Shortly before Christmas in 1982, two men had gone to the school where my mom worked as secretary and robbed the safe. My dad had showed up with a hunting rifle, Rambo style, and shot them. Killed them both in cold blood. That's what I'd understood based on the newspaper articles and tidbits people around town had told me over the years.

Perhaps she referred to the fact that the men had been armed and dangerous. But nothing in the newspapers had said anything about my father's heroic actions keeping others safe, though I could imagine a defense attorney saying something like that. Because the burglars had guns too, some of the shooting on Dad's part *had been* self-defense, but the jury didn't see it that way. Not when forensic experts said he'd shot them both in the back when they'd been running away.

She rubbed her hands together. "But of course the jury missed the truth thanks to those …" Hunting for a sanctified expression, she tightened her lips. "Those crooked prosecutors." Punching her thighs that way must have hurt. "Sorry. You shouldn't have gotten me started."

Looking up, she studied me. "Will you come and see him? Let bygones be bygones?"

Yeah, sure. Let's kiss and make up and act like nothing ever happened to put those men in their graves.

My head wagged. "No, I don't think so. But you go ahead. At least he'll remember you."

55

Did she even have a clue?

Rising, I headed toward the door, but she grabbed my arm, forcing me to face her. Her voice quaked. "Landon, please. He's your father! Give him another chance."

I wrenched my arm away. "Sorry, Mom, but I'm not ready. Maybe some other time."

Though childhood friends had never taunted me about my dad, I'd known what they whispered behind my back.

Poor Landon, the son of a murderer.

Truth was, I couldn't stand the sight of him.

***

In the afternoon Amee called and asked about my status. After hearing my health report, the queen of ADD changed the subject and talked about sales, something that never left her mind, even at a time like this. Which right now appeared rather in poor taste, but I cut her some slack.

My CDs had begun flying off the shelves the moment the cancer news reached my fan base, and the sales of my latest CD, *Private Island*, had taken off. Nothing like brain cancer to wring sympathy, in the form of cash, out of even the coldest of hearts.

I'd given generously to several cancer charities in the past, so fans appeared to be even more sympathetic. Probably from Amee's perspective, though she didn't dare say so to my face, my cancer presented a godsend in some ways. I'd probably never seen brisker sales, and my story dominated the entertainment news.

"Did you get a certain something in the mail?" she said.

"Yep. I've got the greeting card here." Handwriting in various penmanship and colors crammed the inside. "Thank you. That was sweet."

I surveyed the multitude of well-wishes and greetings and familiar names scrawled in penmanship representing each person's personality. The girls in the office who handled publicity. Angie, my makeup guru. Kim Ono, my cellist. The members of the band. Even Ted, the bass player I'd frequently butted heads with.

My throat tightened, and I regretted seeing the card. Another reminder of the prosperous life I must now turn my back on. Possibly forever.

"They all signed it," Amee said. "They're all so sorry you're sick."

"And you didn't force them at gunpoint, huh?"

A chuckle leaked out. "No, it was completely voluntary. Everybody misses you so much, and they hope you get better soon." As if I had nothing worse than a twenty-four-hour stomach bug.

She sounded so much like my mom. Why couldn't anybody accept the fact that I'd probably die soon? That is, unless Dr. Korovin truly had the hands of Jesus.

Her words, I supposed, had real meaning behind them. If he didn't cure me, they'd all be looking for new jobs. What would Amee look like without the backing of my wealth?

She always effused an upscale professional appearance, just as she had the last time I saw her: silk baby-blue Armani blouse, black business slacks. Coifed brown hair with blonde highlights brushed the tops of her narrow shoulders, her subtle Asian features artsy and refined. Everything about her spoke of wealth, sophistication, and the cutting edge of style.

That was Amee with a little bit of my wealth thrown in. Impeccable as always.

What would she do without me? That is, if I didn't survive.

If only I knew what to expect.

***

That night I tossed and turned, still reviewing Mom's words and mine, searching for subtext, for the answer to the grander mystery that had made me a lost, fatherless boy.

Smearing moisture away from my eyes, I puzzled over what might be up with me lately. I'd been overly emotional ever since …

Ever since you've realized you're no longer in control of your life, that you're in the hands of a God you hardly know or understand. Now you're supposed to trust the Almighty, even though you have no idea what his purpose could be in all this.

Around midnight I rose and took a melatonin pill for a helping hand. The western wind rattled the windows, pushing in storm clouds. Raindrops tinkled against the window.

Insomnia had never been an issue for me, but the pain of fatherlessness had risen to the surface, a scab torn loose, the wound raw. I longed for the bleeding to stop. Maybe these emerging childhood memories would help.

I had no idea that something even more disturbing would pay me a visit during the night.

57

Chapter 12

Sunday, October 25
Iron Valley, Michigan

I awoke and rubbed my eyes to see through my brain fog, my body tangled in the sheets and blankets. Through my open window drifted birdsong, the sigh of twilight, the chuckle of autumn leaves. The rising sun peeked just past the edge of my blinds and cast a yellowed, warming beam on the far wall. God's probing flashlight.

The alarm clock announced 7:23, earlier than normal, but I'd slept well. Lifting my hand, I studied it. It didn't shake like it had the day before. I decided to get up, but when I swung my legs to the hardwood floor, I nearly planted my feet on …

A hammer?

Grabbing its wooden handle, I lifted it off the floor, studying it. Where on earth had the hammer come from? And why had it been left here, of all places? I hadn't had any use for—

A stabbing throb above my left eyebrow harmonized with a blinding flash of light in my peripheral blindness.

I squeezed my eyelids closed and gasped for breath, hands drawn into fists. Crying out, I dropped the hammer on the bed and cradled my head in my arms. My mind leaped into …

… a dark night blessed with evil deeds. Leaves rustle in the heavily treed backyard.

The distant glimmer of a streetlight offers enough illumination for me to glimpse the backdoor of the small bungalow, which is barely visible in the capering shadows.

I wedge the hammer claw against the jamb and give the handle one more pull. The door springs open, giving me access to the basement. Licking my lips hungrily, I know what I'll find inside. And then …

The cranium-twisting headache faded at the speed in which it had begun. Awareness delivered me back to the small bedroom on E Street, with me sitting on the edge of the bed. Gasping and sweating and fighting a wave of nausea.

Gaping at the hammer, I puzzled over where the bizarre vision—or whatever it might be—had come from. Acrid morning breath soured in my mouth while my gasps petered off. I blinked and wet my Sahara-dry lips, my heart slowing back to normal speed.

What could be going on? Had this strange vision been only the remnant of a bad dream? And why had the sight of the hammer triggered it?

In my dream a hammer had been used to pry a door open.

A pounding rattled my bedroom door. "Landy, are you okay?"

My head swung around, seeking a hiding place for the hammer. But what did I have to sense guilt about? I hadn't done anything wrong. I returned the hammer to the floor, and a swift kick sent it skidding under my bed and out of sight.

The pounding became more insistent. "Landy?"

"I'm fine, Mom. I just had a nightmare. That's all."

Or rather a daymare. Wasn't that a type of nightmare during daylight hours?

The door filtered her voice. "You need to move those lazy bones if you're coming to church with me this morning."

Why had I let her talk me into going? Because I hated to disappoint her. After all, she'd done so much to take care of me and adjust her life so I could live here comfortably.

"Okay, Mom. I'm coming."

No time now. Dealing with the hammer would have to happen later.

I rose on unsteady feet, reached for my cane, and hobbled to the bathroom for a quick shower.

Chapter 13

Sunday, October 25
Iron Valley, Michigan

On the way home from church, Mom's hands strangled the steering wheel. "Landy, what were you thinking? How you played that hymn—" She wagged her head, her voice high and tight. "That was completely inappropriate and embarrassing for me. I hope you realize that."

I kept my attention fixed on the road. "I'm sorry you and your friends didn't like the way I played the song, but I was just being myself."

"Being yourself?" Due to the loss of my left peripheral vision, I must have missed her glare.

"Your worship leader should have done more homework before asking me to play. Doesn't he realize I've been playing jazz and pop piano almost exclusively for the last five years?"

"That's no excuse. You can't expect everyone to keep up to date on your career as well as I have. You got your start as a classical pianist, remember? Then you played hymns for a while."

Yeah, that had been a real bore—and with no money in it. I would still be stuck in that old, stinking apartment if I'd chosen to keep playing Chopin and the grand old hymns of the faith for the rest of my life.

An industry expert had advised me to research what people wanted and play that instead. Companies did it every day—going to consumers, researching what they wanted, and delivering the goods. It was called good marketing.

"My point is, you grew up in this church, Landy, and you should know better. Isn't knowing your audience and being sensitive to it the first rule in being an effective communicator?"

Score Mom.

"We're a bunch of old fogies who like our hymns played the old-fashioned way. You obviously weren't thinking of anybody but yourself."

Out my window, the woods blurred past.

Her words stung me to silence, and I assumed the posture of a chastened little boy again. Yes, they'd expected me to play a hymn that couldn't match the dryness of Pastor Mayhew's sermon. Well, I didn't regret what I'd done. "Crown Him with Many Crowns" with some pop rock rhythms and a dose of the blues thrown in had been just what the doctor ordered.

She turned silent, perhaps realizing she'd said too much. After clearing her throat, she said in a gentle voice, her anger burning itself out, "I'm sorry. I should have kept quiet, but you know I like to speak my mind."

Isn't that the truth?

"But there's a bigger issue at stake here, Landy. I'm concerned about where you are with the Lord."

Oh boy. Here we go.

In a few minutes she'd break into the Romans Road and conduct an altar call right here in the car. "The Lord and I are just fine, Mom."

"You are, huh?" Her gaze probed me, but I avoided it. "You're not the Landy I used to know. You've … changed."

"Of course, I've changed. I've grown up. I'm a man."

"That's not what I mean. Look, I don't want to argue with you—"

Yes, you do. You love every blessed minute of it.

"—but I'm concerned about where your life is headed. I can't help wondering if maybe the cancer is … well … maybe it's more than just cancer."

"What's *that* supposed to mean?" I glared at her and clamped my teeth together so hard my jaw ached. "Just say it. You think God's punishing me for not staying on the straight and narrow."

"Not punishing you, no. If you're God's child, you're beyond his punishment. Jesus took that punishment in your place, remember? But sometimes God … well … sometimes he chastens us to get our attention, to nudge us back on the path when we've strayed."

"So this is God's wakeup call. That's what you're saying."

She studied my face but said nothing and everything at the same time.

"So what does he want me to do? Get on my knees and shed crocodile tears?"

"I'm not saying that."

"Then what *are* you saying?"

"I'm saying—" She hesitated, attention back on the road. "I'm saying that if I were you, I'd spend some time in quiet reflection and evaluate where my life is heading. I'd ask myself if God is at the heart of it. Because if he isn't, then I'd be afraid."

"Afraid?"

"Afraid of going my own way, of thinking I can live my life on my own terms. Because if I'm a child of God, there's no better recipe for a miserable existence than trying to live my life without him in the driver's seat. You were bought with a price, Landy. You are not your own."

Of course, I knew what verse she referred to. I'd memorized it and dozens of others like it during Sunday school years ago.

"Landy, has it occurred to you that your piano playing is a gift from God?"

"Of course."

"Then hasn't it also occurred to you that what God has given to you … he can just as easily take it away?"

I bit my bottom lip almost hard enough to draw blood. Hadn't this been my fear all along—that I'd lose the use of my hands? That everything I'd achieved up to this point in my career would just vanish away?

My battle against the cancer had the upper hand today, but what about tomorrow? Unless Dr. Korovin proved to be the miracle worker he claimed, I was a dead man walking. But first I'd lose the use of my hands. Making beautiful music and bringing crowds to their feet would be nothing but a memory.

You're going to die, Landon. In fact, you'll probably go before she does.

Throat tight, I said, "Why would God do that—take my gift away? What good could that possibly do anyone?"

"The purpose could be his getting your attention. His reminding you of who you used to be."

"Which is?"

"A child of God—that's who you used to be. Or so I thought." Our eyes met, her face stricken. "But what happened to you, Landy? Where did you go?"

Chapter 14

Sunday, October 25
Iron Valley, Michigan

I longed for strong drink. Ached for it. But of course, not a drop could be found, not in this God-fearing, booze-eschewing place. So I resorted to a cigarette beside the open window instead, one I'd hidden away in a carton under my mattress. The nicotine at least put a Band-Aid on that hollowed-out feeling in my soul until Mom called through the door that lunch was ready.

We mostly ate in silence, chicken from the Crock-Pot with rosemary, carrots, and potatoes. I didn't look at her. Instead, I kept my attention on my food or out the window at the gently spiraling leaves.

Mom deserves some credit. She tried to make conversation—oh, how she tried—but I proved to be merciless and didn't budge an inch. How dare she question my faith? How dare she preach at me like that?

Okay, so I'd strayed a bit. My church attendance hadn't been regular in years, and I wasn't the naïve kid I used to be. But she didn't know my heart. She couldn't say I didn't love God or have faith in him just because I'd jazzed up "Crown Him with Many Crowns."

Because I did love God. Of course I did.

True. My piano playing was a gift from God, but my gratitude hadn't vanished. There. A flicker of thankfulness warmed my heart. So where did we go from here?

Hasn't it occurred to you that what God has given to you … he can just as easily take away?

Her voice sliced through my thoughts. "Landon, are you okay?"

No, I'm not okay. I'm a shallow sinner who let fame go to his head. I thought I was truly somebody, but now I'm a nobody. A big fat zero. I'm stuck in this pathetic place when I'd rather be doing a concert in Tokyo. In a few years, I'll be dead. Then who'll even remember who I was other than diehard fans who'll reminisce about the guy who used to *play a mean piano? Or kids who'll pick up my used CDs at the local Goodwill and look me up at Wikipedia?*

"I'm fine," I lied.

Her probing eyes chased me, and I fled. To say anything else might have gotten her preaching again, and I couldn't bear any more of her sanctimony. Small doses went a long way, and she'd exceeded her daily—maybe even weekly—allowance.

Another sermon and I'd remind her that I could easily pack my bags and head back to Chicago in a taxi within the hour. My wealth could hire a nurse if need be. Did she want that?

While I ate, Mom mentioned that she'd taken a few weeks off from the day care. She asked if she could do anything to make my stay more comfortable. Could she pick up something for me at the grocery store? I told her I couldn't think of anything.

"Have you changed your phone number yet?" I said.

"I called AT&T. They said they'd get the number changed soon."

Ever since my arrival, the downstairs phone had been ringing nonstop; more often than not, a news-starved reporter occupied the other end. The paparazzi from *People Magazine* and *Star* must have gotten word that I'd moved in with my mom. They'd never let up now that they had a big story. Nothing like a celebrity's brain cancer to boost newspaper sales. They sickened me.

But even with the number change, I wouldn't be able to look out the window anytime soon without some bottom-feeder with a camera spying on me. Maybe in time they'd get the hint and leave me alone.

Not wanting to say anything to encourage another journey down the Romans Road, I said, "I was surprised to see Jade Hamilton at church this morning. She's still in town, huh?"

"Yeah, but that wasn't her plan. After medical school, she wanted a job in one of the cities. But then her dad didn't want her to go—you know how close they are—so she made the tough choice to stay in Iron Valley."

During the opening hymn, her glance had angled my direction. Shoulder-length blonde hair had been pulled away from her face and pinned in the back, light-blue eyes tinged with disapproval. A moment later, she shifted her scowl back to her hymnbook, which she shared with a little boy with matching blond hair.

Had that been her son, Henry? The offspring of that unsavory boyfriend who'd walked out on her like a coward, abandoning her while pregnant with his child?

The reason for her displeasure puzzled me. Why so unhappy to see me back in Iron Valley after all these years?

"Now she's a home health nurse here in town," Mom said. "In fact, she'll be by tomorrow to start your therapy."

The carrot between my molars nearly choked me. "What?"

Two little penciled-in arcs lifted since her eyebrows had disappeared long ago. "Dr. Korovin's orders, remember? He said you may eventually experience more difficulty walking, and I see you leaning on that cane more and more. She's just going to check you out, suggest ways to keep you limber and on your feet. Who knows? Maybe she can even help improve your balance. Sometimes the brain can relearn skills it's lost."

Stabbing a piece of meat, I sought to shove aside my uneasiness about seeing Jade again. We'd been a couple once long ago, while still in high school. Before I'd moved away and turned my back on everyone in this town, including her.

Did she still play the flute? She'd once shared her dream for us to travel across the country and make beautiful music together. Problem was, her flute playing stank, but I'd never had the heart to tell her.

With a sigh I chose not to think about Jade right now. Too many people appeared to be unhappy about my return to Iron Valley, and I didn't understand why.

"So what's this I hear about a neighborhood theft?" I said. Pastor Mayhew had mentioned it in the context of a prayer request.

Mom pressed her lips together in a tight seam. "It happened to Millie West, one of our elderly shut-ins. You see, her husband was an old-coins dealer. When he passed, he left her a rare collection. It was all the investment she had left in the world. Well, now somebody has stolen it."

In my daymare I'd broken into somebody's house with a hammer, but the connection to Millie, of course, strained logic. It had been only a dream. "And she kept it all in her basement? The coins, I mean."

"Uh-huh. Locked away in an old safe with a combination. I kept telling her to put those old coins in a safety deposit box, but she doesn't trust banks and wouldn't listen to me. And now they're all gone. Probably at the hand of some sick druggie needing funds for his next fix."

I shoveled in more chicken. "So where does Millie live anyhow? Anywhere nearby?"

"Only a couple of blocks away."

Perhaps I'd passed her house during my around-the-block hobble with the cane, but of course, I wouldn't have known which one belonged to her without someone pointing it out.

Mom cleared her throat, a characteristic gesture that meant she desired to ask me something. "Landy, did you sleep okay last night?"

"As far as I know, yeah." My gaze connected with hers for the first time, her soft hazel eyes heavy with regret; she knew she'd said too much in the car. I accepted the apology by meeting her look head on. "Why do you ask?"

"Oh, no reason really. I just thought I heard you wandering around the house last night. That's all. As you know, the floorboards have a distinctive creak. I figured maybe you were—I don't know—restless or something. Once I thought you must have taken the stairs down to the basement."

Mom still kept Dad's tools and his train memorabilia stored down there. Surely the hammer, the one hiding under my bed, had come from there. "N-no. I don't think I was up in the night, but my memory isn't so great these days."

"Dr. Korovin says that's to be expected. Perhaps you were up and just don't remember."

My fork skewered another carrot. "I don't like the idea that I might be wandering around the house like a sleepwalker and not realizing what I'm doing. And then there's these weird memory trips and daymares I told you about."

"You mean, you've had another one?"

"Oh yeah. Several. Some nights they come when I go to sleep and sometimes during the day when I least expect them. If anything, they're becoming more frequent than ever, like I'm remembering events I'd forgotten."

"I think you should call Dr. Korovin and tell him. I hate to say it, but they could be caused by ministrokes. Those steroids you're taking are supposed to help prevent seizures, but maybe you need something stronger."

"Part of me wonders if there's another reason for them—other than my brain problem, I mean."

"Like some hidden purpose only God could understand?"

"Yeah. Something like that."

She tipped her head. "Who knows? Some people put a lot of stock in their dreams and try to discover the hidden meaning. Others see dreams as only a way for the subconscious to rid itself of what's troubling it. But who can really say for sure? Certainly, we find lots of Bible stories with characters having dreams for important reasons, but does God really work that way today?" She shook her head. "I doubt it."

She rose to her feet and began clearing the table.

I peered out the window into the backyard—at the temperature gauge on the old oak tree, then at the old red shed where Dad had kept the lawnmower and other odds and ends. A sudden inexplicable desire to visit that backyard of my boyhood nearly overwhelmed me. Maybe I'd stroll out there later.

My gaze swept across the kitchen, still orange with country decor and seventies ceramic touches, even after all these years. As if the place might be trapped in some sort of time warp. Expectantly, I waited for Jan from *The Brady Bunch* to march in and whine about Marcia's popularity at school.

Sheesh.

Getting up, I headed to the sink. I'd suggested years ago that Mom get a dishwasher, but she'd insisted—true to character—that she didn't need one. Said she enjoyed watching the birds and the changing seasons through the window while she scrubbed her pans. But I suspected she might be hoarding my monthly check.

Mom claimed she never had the money for new stuff, though I'd been sending her generous monthly checks for years. I hated to see her living in such a museum, but really, she loved history more than most things.

When not at the day care, she tracked down the mysteries of the Jeffers family at countless genealogy websites. In fact, she so excelled at such research that a church friend had recently paid her to discover whether a distant uncle had died at the Battle of Gettysburg.

I pressed a hand to the small of her back. "I think it's my turn."

She looked at me, wide eyed. "What?"

"You need a break once in a while, and I hate to be a burden."

"Landy, you're no burden. I've been lonely clunking around in this big, old house by myself for all these years. Having you here, in spite of the circumstances, is a wonderful blessing for me. I *like* taking care of you. Please believe that."

Maybe a little too much.

"Even still, I want to do this."

"Okay, fine. Whatever you say." She flopped the warm dishcloth into my hand and chuckled. "Lord knows we butt heads once in a while, don't we? But be assured that you're always wanted around here, Landy. Always."

Once she moved out of the way, I took her place and contemplated how best to spend my afternoon. My fingers itched to play the recently tuned piano in the almost-finished music studio, but Mom would be taking her ritualistic nap. Until workers finished the soundproofing, my playing would almost certainly keep her awake.

As if reading my mind, she patted my arm. "When you're done, why don't you go lie down and rest, too? God made the body to rest one day out of the week."

"You know I've never been one for naps."

Already she treated me like an invalid, and it irked me. But maybe she could be trying reverse psychology. The more I detected she might be babying me, the more I'd work to prove I could do tasks on my own.

Returning to my chore, I allowed my focus to wander to the old sandbox, where I'd once created countless castles and used the garden hose to create a terrible flood for the intruding ants. Amazing that someone hadn't gotten rid of that old sandbox by now.

The sandbox.

The back of my throat itched. A flaming dagger sliced into my head, stealing my breath away.

Stumbling, I dropped the pan I'd been scrubbing with a *clang*. Clutched the countertop to counter my buckling legs.

I clamped my eyelids closed, and the daymare flared to life. An image, at first tiny, sparked in the corner of my eyes and mushroomed until its expanse filled my vision.

Chapter 15

Sunday, October 25
Iron Valley, Michigan

*M*y hands. *I'm clawing at the cool, moist, gritty soil in the sand-box.*

It is nighttime, little more than smothering darkness. The kind that makes my chest tighten as if the next breath might never come. In the distance echoes the endless mantra of the whippoorwill. Frog song surrounds me.

In spite of the cool air, I'm warm. Hot, in fact. My shirt sticks to my chest while I dig in the sandbox with aching fingers.

My heart races. I must hurry. I must finish before someone sees—

Mom's hand, fingers tight around my arm, brought me back to the kitchen and the present. The staggering universe found its balance. Righted itself.

I panted like I'd sprinted a mile at full tilt.

"Landy, are you okay? You look like you've seen a ghost."

Sweat slicked my clammy skin. Black dots swirled in my vision. Was I going to pass out?

Holding onto the counter appeared to be my wisest course of action. The headache eased and faded until it disappeared altogether.

Mom gripped my arm again. "Are you all right?"

I straightened tentatively. "Yeah. I think so."

She put an arm around me. "C'mon, I think you better sit down."

But I didn't care to at first. Move too quickly, and I might lose my lunch. Easing across the room, I returned to my seat at the kitchen table, legs weak, head woozy.

She stationed herself across from me, brow furrowed, gazing over a flower arrangement in the table center: daisies and golden iris and Virginia bluebells. A silk manifestation of garden treasures she'd never had the time or patience to try raising on her own. Mainly because she spent too much time tracing which cousin, twice removed, claimed George Washington as a forebear.

71

"What happened?" she said.

Should I tell her about the sandbox?

"I don't know. I had a sudden, terrible pain in my head, as if someone was hammering a nail into it. But it's gone now." My fingers rubbed my forehead where the pain had been most intense. Now everything appeared to be the way it should be.

Lips pressed together in that familiar look I'd seen before, she rose and reached for the telephone. "I think we should call Dr. Korovin right now. He said you might get some terrible headaches, that they might precede seizures. Maybe that's what you just had."

"No, Mom. I'm okay now. The headache's gone. Besides, it's Sunday. I doubt you're going to reach him."

"But remember, he said to call anytime, day or night. Why else are you paying him the big bucks?"

She had a point. Some facilities required patients to live on the premises for therapy and close monitoring. But Dr. Korovin believed that patients showed the best recovery and were most comfortable in their own homes and that technology, when used correctly, brought people closer together. Every other day I stationed myself in front of my laptop, turned on my webcam, and had an interview with Dr. Korovin to assess my status.

"Look, I'm supposed to have a video conference with him tomorrow at two. I'll mention it to him then."

She gripped me with her gaze, brow furrowed. "Okay, but you be sure to tell him what just happened here. If you don't, I certainly will."

***

I lingered in my bedroom, unsure what to do with myself until I could be certain Mom must be taking a nap. Then I became a man on a mission.

Because she might hear me on the basement stairs, like she had the night before, I left the house through the front door and circled around back to the external basement door. After I'd returned the hammer to its customary place on the pegboard—sure enough, that must be where I'd gotten it—I headed back outdoors by the way I'd come in, careful not to let the basement screen door slam shut behind me.

Before returning to the house, I paused, focusing on the sandbox. A nearby truck rumbled down the city street. A few houses away, a dog barked.

Of course, Dr. Korovin's fiddling around in my head to remove as much of the cancer as possible could be to blame for these strange daymares. No mystery there. Presurgery Landon was clearly not postsurgery Landon, nor would he ever be. On the plus side, memories appeared to be more vivid now than they'd ever been before—so maybe, just maybe, I might reclaim the repressed memories I'd lost.

But now, for the third time without warning, I'd had an unnerving daymare so real that I'd felt transported to the actual time and place.

But what could these daymares be all about? Memory or fantasy? And how could I tell the difference?

If they proved to be rehearsed memories in full color and stereo surround sound, what had I been burying in the sandbox? But to concede that the event depicted in the most recent daymare could have taken place meant I'd possibly broken into somebody's house with a hammer. Mom had heard me prowling around—I must have been up in the night. But why no memory of the event? The questions perplexed me.

A nippy breeze peppered my arms with goose bumps and carried the faint scent of burning leaves and chrysanthemums. I should have brought a jacket, but what I'd decided to do wouldn't take long.

Of course, my mission must be absurd—I hadn't visited the backyard in years.

I scanned my surroundings. To my right the neighbor's blue ranch house rose just beyond the chain-link fence; to my left rose a privet hedge and an alley beyond. Straight ahead, only feet away, a pile of multihued leaves from maples and birches shedding their summer glory had nearly buried the old sandbox.

My sweeping gaze froze. The skin between my shoulder blades prickled.

Wait.

I *had* been here, and not long ago. But how could that be?

Kneeling, I swept away the moist mat of leaves and forked my fingers into a mound of cold, gritty sand, which appeared to have been recently disturbed. My chest quivered. A trowel, its tip upended in the sand by several inches, proved to be more effective than my fingers.

As I worked, the cool breeze brushed the patch of stubbly hair behind my right ear, which had been slowly filling in since the surgery. Blocks away sirens wailed. I trembled and clenched my jaw.

The trowel clanked against something metallic. My breath caught in my throat.

Casting the tool aside, I clawed at the bottom of the hole until my aching fingers unearthed cloth. When I cleared more sand away, a shape emerged. A brown bag.

Moments later, the bag came loose, heavy in my hand, its mouth tied closed with a leather strap. My chest heaved with my panting. My mind flailed, unable to grasp what I must be seeing.

Even before looking inside, I suspected what I would find. Thousands of dollars' worth of old, valuable coins.

Chapter 16

Sunday, October 25
Iron Valley, Michigan

God, what's going on? How can this be happening to me?

Lying in bed, sucking the life out of a cigarette, I couldn't dismiss the questions. How could I have broken into Millie West's house and taken her coins without remembering what I'd done? Even more bizarre, why would I have broken into her house in the first place? I didn't even know Millie, and at the time I'd known nothing about her valuable coins. Or even the combination to her safe. Even if I *had* known about the coins, I never would have knowingly stolen them; as a matter of fact, I'd never stolen anything in my life.

Bottom line: the scenario had to be impossible.

Could this be somebody's idea of a sick joke? Or might my messed-up brain be to blame?

I needed to tell Dr. Korovin. Maybe he could explain all this.

Massaging that tender spot over my left eye, where the headaches had flared, I rolled onto my side and spotted the alarm clock.

2:34.

Mom must be up from her nap by now. The creaking floorboards pinpointed her location; she worked in the kitchen, probably fixing a mug of hot lemon-ginger tea before settling in the living room and enjoying reruns of *I Love Lucy*, her favorite TV show.

Sitting up, I rubbed my eyes, mind feverish with conflicting thoughts and emotions. I eyed the bottom dresser drawer, where I'd shoved the bulging bag of old coins, hidden under some underwear and out of sight so I wouldn't have to think about it.

But I needed to think about it. I had to come to terms with what I'd done and what this development meant.

Landon, what have you done?

My mom's Uncle Eddie had suffered Alzheimer's for years before his death. One day, without realizing what he was doing, he'd strolled into

75

a supermarket and pulled down his pants for all to see. Thankfully, he'd been wearing boxers.

Would I now be doing mindless stuff like somebody with Alzheimer's? No, that didn't make sense, because this hadn't been mindless activity. Purpose had been behind it. But how could it be mine if I had no motive?

Landon, what is going on? What are you doing to yourself?

My hands cradled my head. So where could I go from here? Should I turn myself in to the police? But why do that if I hadn't intended to harm anyone? Then again, maybe I *had* been in control of my actions and intentions, but I'd merely forgotten what I'd done. After all, my memory wasn't so super these days.

Perhaps.

But if I proved to be guilty of the crime, then I should sense some guilt. But I didn't. Instead my mind-set was … well … baffled.

And betrayed. Betrayed by myself.

Could someone be pulling a prank on me? Framing me? Trying to make me lose what little of my precious mind I had left? But who and why?

I didn't know the safe's combination—I couldn't have. But what did it matter? I had the coins and the memory of taking them, so I must be responsible. What other option could there be?

In the short term, I'd take the most logical steps. Return the coins before anybody could be the wiser. But how would I do so without being discovered? Mom had her eye on me practically all the time, worried about a fall or seizure. And I couldn't tell her the truth. She'd make me go to the police. No question.

Another question, this one more sobering, descended on me. Could I ever again lay my head on my pillow at night without fearing what I might do in the dark? How could I ever trust myself again?

***

That night, unable to sleep and wanting to get my mind off my troubles, I found an old box of photos, mostly of me when I'd been a kid and had fun in the neighborhood, the sun sprinkling freckles across my nose.

And Jade Hamilton—her presence dominated so many photos. At birthday parties. At youth group events. At the annual church trip to the amusement park.

One picture widened my eyes. A picture of me, Jade, and Tyler Acorn at the old treehouse. With the help of Tyler, another playground misfit, we'd built a treehouse in the woods behind the school. Actually, Tyler's dad, a construction worker, had done most of the work and added a door and a sign. NO BULLIES ALLOWED.

Jade's dad had taken the photo and later made a copy for my scrapbook.

Lost in a world of so many years ago, I fell asleep with my fingers wrapped around the photo. That black hole in the corner of my eyes sucked me into days neglected but still remembered in some long-abandoned, forgotten place.

Like a thunderclap, the darkness smothered me and pulled me down. Down.

Into the well of memories.

Chapter 17

Saturday, September 25, 1982
Iron Valley, Michigan

"Skinny, fat. Skinny, fat." Jade Hamilton squished a gummy bear between thumb and forefinger, making the little bear obese one minute, tall and thin the next. She plopped it into her mouth with a smirk.

"Very funny." I chuckled, plucking at weeds in the lawn. "Why do you always have so much candy?"

She blew blonde bangs away from her face. "Didn't I tell you? My mom's family owns a candy business."

I wagged my head, not taking her seriously.

We'd met behind the school on a hot, breezeless fall day. Joey Bartholomew, the aviation nut, had invited us over to his house to play Atari, but we'd grown weary of his hogging the game time.

A white cast embraced one of Jade's arms; she'd recently decided to be Nadia Comaneci, the Olympic star, on the monkey bars. Unfortunately, I hadn't been quick enough to catch her. My mom called Jade "accident prone." She rarely looked before she leaped.

"So," Jade said, "I really want to know. Why did they have to take *The Bionic Woman* off the air? My dad and I loved that show."

"Beats me."

"But there's something about it I just never understood."

"Yeah? What's that?"

"If Jamie Wagner could run so fast because she was bionic, why did they always show her running in slow motion?"

"Hm. Good question."

Jade picked at a scab on her knee. "Did you know that human blood is actually blue until the air hits it?"

"Did you know you can change the subject faster than the speed of light?"

Jade ignored me and pressed a sticky hand to my forehead. "Are you feeling better now?"

"Of course. I'm fine." I'd taken a tumble off the swing a while back, and Jade liked playing nurse as usual, ever since her trip to the hospital for the broken arm.

She popped a bubble, and it nearly caught her nose. Must have been her favorite Bubblicious. She especially adored "Island Squeeze." Perhaps that explained the source of the sickly-sweet aroma wrinkling my nose.

She said with concern, "Must have hit your head pretty hard when you fell, but you'll be okay, though you must have a slight case of ambrosia. Why don't you try to sit up?"

Of course, she meant *amnesia*, but I chose not to correct her. Claiming my feet, I checked my bearings. I was fine, but she pressed her small fingers to my wrist anyhow.

"Hmm. Pulse is still pretty fast, but I guess mine would be too if I pulled a stunt like that. Good thing you didn't break a wrist or something. That wouldn't be so great for your piano playing. You need to be more careful next time."

Yes, Mother. Of course, Mother.

Since she'd brought up the topic of piano, I told her about my teacher, Mrs. Riddle, who had a dozen cats, and how annoyed I became when she did little more than criticize everything I did and rarely spoke a word of praise.

"Well, don't listen to her," Jade said. "I think you play just great. Definitely better than anybody I know. I'm so glad you're my friend."

I licked my dry lips. "Are we friends, Jade?"

"What a tomfool thing to ask. Do you really think we'd be here together at the playground so often if we weren't friends?"

An awkward silence plugged the hole between us. I had no idea what to say. Sometimes the right words didn't come out, no matter how hard I tried. It appeared to be the perfect time to pull out the locket. She accepted it, face brightening.

"Sorry I missed your birthday." I shrugged. "I thought it would be nicer to give you something a week or so later, after everybody already gave you all the good stuff."

"But this *is* the good stuff. Landon Jeffers, this must be the nicest gift anybody's ever given me."

Huh?

How could this cheap gift from the Sears catalog compete with the bicycle and the Ping-Pong table? "Look inside the locket. I bet you'll be surprised."

"Hey, it's us, at Cedar Point. That must have been just before we went on the Corkscrew, and then I threw up." For all her tomboy exterior, she was all girl inside.

"I just love it, Landon." She embraced me with her smile, her wide-eyed gaze bursting with admiration. Not used to such attention, I glanced away, cheeks sizzling. Before I could prepare myself, she planted a big kiss on my cheek, jumped up, and dashed away. Full tilt across the playground as if the very demons of hell nipped at her heels.

"Jade?" I lurched to my feet, attention riveted to her retreating back. Should I go after her? "Jade?"

But she didn't turn or even indicate she'd heard me. She just sprinted, blonde hair fluttering behind her, like she might be embarrassed, and I puzzled over what I'd done to make her flee like that. After all, she'd been the one doing the kissing.

The throb of abandonment swelled in my chest. Right then I swore I'd willingly give my life if somebody even touched a hair on her head. But I had no idea what that promise, made on a warm September day with no hint of the future, might lead to.

Chapter 18

Present day
Monday, October 26
Iron Valley, Michigan

When I crawled out of bed the next morning, the room swam as if I'd stepped off a merry-go-round. I paused to gain my bearings and searched for anything amiss. From what I could tell, no hammer or other implement of violence lay carelessly discarded on the floor for me to trip on.

At the memory of Jade's reaction to the locket, a smile teased my lips. I could still sense her kiss on my cheek, planted by young lips that had never touched a guy's cheek like that before.

Why did she dislike me so much now? If only I could remember.

While I headed to the bathroom for a shower, the unsolved problem of Millie West came back to haunt me. Priority one must be to return the stolen coins to the sandbox until I found a way to sneak them back to Millie's. But how could I evade Mom's eagle eye?

At breakfast, she served me two fried farm-fresh eggs on whole-wheat toast, buttered with coconut oil. I began squeezing my halved grapefruit into my juice glass, just like Dad used to do, when the doorbell rang. While Mom went to see who it could be—probably a kid selling magazine subscriptions to support local athletics—I downed the juice and cleared the table despite still being a little wobbly on my feet.

Mom appeared, voice heavy with apology. "Sorry, Landy, I thought the appointment was this afternoon, but I must have made a mistake. She's here. Now."

She?

"She wants to evaluate you for physical therapy."

"You mean, *right now?*"

"Uh-huh, she's in the living room as we speak."

And of all the people God could have chosen, he'd selected Jade Hamilton. The awkward situation couldn't have been more perfectly arranged.

We'd once been joined at the hip, but the romance had soured, and I'd fled town, turning my back on everyone, including her.

Oh, this should be priceless.

***

Diminutive Jade wore her healthcare uniform: a pastel-blue blouse with pink swirls, navy slacks, and white sneakers. Her blonde hair, once wispy and unruly as a girl, was now coifed and brushed her tiny shoulders. As always, that lithe frame and that long, skinny neck made her appear vulnerable, as if she were a little girl who'd lost her puppy.

The look had always roused my manliness, made me sense like I needed to protect her somehow. As if she were perpetually in danger. Which she wasn't. But there it was.

All dirty looks in the church auditorium had vanished, and only a professional smile greeted me. After all, this was business. Her paycheck ensured that she help others, and I appeared on her list of patients.

My mind tripped back to a hot summer day, the monkey bars, and her broken arm, the beginnings of her fascination with all things medical. In a strange way, it might have been a good thing that I didn't catch her that day. Perhaps she might never have become a nurse if I had. Amazing how so many of life's events were connected, a small ripple that ringed a larger pond.

"Hello, Jade."

"Hey, Landon."

She still had that familiar Southern lilt in her voice as if she'd grown up in the Old South. The truth was, she'd lived in Michigan all her life, but her "Daddy" had been born and raised in Georgia. Since her "Mamma" had run off with another man, she'd grown up with only her dad, the two of them inseparable—partners on numerous fishing, hunting, and camping trips. If I ever got lost in the forest and needed somebody to blaze a trail to safety, I knew who to call.

"I'm here to evaluate you," she said in a matter-of-fact tone, "to see what's up with these balance issues you've been having."

"But how did you know?"

She met my gaze: solid, unflinching, not even a clue of feeling. "The network notified Dr. Korovin that I'd be your home healthcare nurse. Then I called him, and he filled me in."

Her probing stare went even deeper as if she could peer into my head and analyze the damage left behind. That old jitter remained, her pupils rocking back and forth in a steady, soothing cadence. Almost mesmerizing. Like she could hypnotize me if she wanted to.

With a grim but brave face, she said, "I felt so bad when I heard the news. I have a pretty good idea what you're up against, Landon. Once you lose mobility, things can go downhill pretty fast. The important thing right now is keeping you moving."

She asked me about my routine, and I filled her in on my daily habit of walking around the block a few times, and I described my diet and the steroids I took.

"That's good," she said, "but I still need to see what's goin' on. If you're having balance issues, then there's something wrong."

Well, of course something's wrong. Otherwise you wouldn't even be here.

She must have realized her blunder. With a determined look, she said, "I'll be honest: sometimes the brain can get so messed up, I'm afraid it's a tangle only God could unravel. Other times it can be retrained to work around what went wrong, to find a new path. When it can, exercises can help. We'll just have to give 'er a try and see, okay? Hopefully, your problem is the untangle kind."

"So where do we begin?" My palms had moistened.

"Well, first, I'd like to assess the extent of your balance problems. And then we'll go from there. Sound good?"

I'd always admired her determination to get through medical school and make something of herself. Most people didn't know about her struggle with ocular albinism, a genetic condition that primarily affects the eyes. Long story short, she couldn't process details in the distance. For example, if she peered across a farmer's field, she might recognize the farmhouse and the colors of the siding and roof, but she'd be unable to make out any windows or doors.

Physical traits that accompanied her albinism included lighter skin and hair color than anyone in her family; thankfully, her eyes were dark blue, not the stereotypical pink. Oh, yeah, and the jitter in her eyes—that condition is called nystagmus, a big part of the albinism too.

Her condition didn't require her to take any medication, and her only aid were reading glasses. Probably her most annoying limitation was that she couldn't drive, so she used a taxi service. Her inability to drive had been perhaps her biggest embarrassment in high school. She'd felt so left out when all her friends had taken driver's training.

Jade asked me to do various tests: Holding out my arms horizontally from both sides and resisting her force when she pushed down on one arm. Keeping my arms out and trying to stand on one foot while she pressed down on one arm. Losing my balance, I had to step out.

I laughed nervously while doing these acrobatics for her. "Boy, this makes me feel like an old man."

"Well, you've got brain cancer, Landon. That would mess with anybody's head, not that you haven't always had weird ideas messin' with your head anyhow."

That sounded more like the old Jade teasing my memories.

Next, she asked me to stand straight, keeping my arms extended horizontally from either side "as if you were Jesus hanging on the cross." Then she said, "Now, using your right hand, touch the tip of your nose with your index finger. Good. Now do the left side. Okay."

She studied me like a specimen under a microscope. "Yeah, I'm seeing some definite awkwardness on your left side, which should be no mystery since your tumor was on the right side. Unfortunately, it did some damage to your coordination before it was removed."

Perhaps making conversation might distract me so I wouldn't be so self-conscious. "So how's life been treating you, Jade?"

"Can't complain, I guess. None of us really can, if you think about it. Every day we're not in hell is a good day, right?"

Every Saturday her daddy camped out on the corner near Trotsky's Bar and preached to the drunks when they stumbled out. Naturally, she had the same mentality, having been told all her life that everybody was doomed for hell unless she opened her mouth and told them about Jesus. I couldn't forget her preaching at me while a kid on the school monkey bars until the day I shared the disappointing news that I'd already prayed the sinner's prayer.

Her cell phone went off, the simple ringing of an old antique telephone. She excused herself, easing toward the door leading to the front porch and speaking in soft tones. Twenty seconds later she returned.

"Sorry about that. I always forget to turn the blasted thing off. And wouldn't you know it would ring when I'm busy with a patient." She paused. "Isn't it sad how we let all these gadgets run our lives?"

I nodded.

"You wouldn't believe how much Kasi, my cousin Wade's wife, talks on her cell phone. I think she burns something like four hundred minutes per month."

"I'm sure there's counseling for a problem like that."

Jade grinned mischievously. "You wouldn't believe what Wade did to her. It's top secret, so you gotta promise not to breathe a word." Wade was the stereotypical science geek. I didn't know him very well, but I could probably pick him out of a police lineup: messy blond hair, chubby cheeks, thick glasses, a pallor due to lingering indoors at his computer too much.

"My lips are sealed."

"Well, he went online and secretly purchased one of those cell phone signal jammer contraptions. Lately, when he decides she's had enough phone time, well, he just turns on the jammer, and she loses her signal. It drives her crazy. She thinks something's wrong with her phone." She chuckled.

"When's he going to tell her?"

Her eyes widened like I'd struck her. "Why would he do such a tom-fool thing as that? He's having way too much fun."

As if remembering her reason for being here, Jade bent low to check my knees and test their flexibility. When she did, a golden necklace slipped from the folds of her blouse and dangled free.

Something akin to an electrical shock jolted me. Could that possibly be the same locket from my memory trip? The one I'd given her on her twelfth birthday?

She asked me to lower my arms to my sides and appeared oblivious to my discovery. I decided not to say anything.

Next, she shot a glance toward the kitchen to ensure we wouldn't be overheard. Rising, she peered into my eyes, pupils jittering. Those tiny tennis players engaged in a ferocious battle right now. "I guess I'm a little surprised to see you back in town, especially after what happened to Joey."

Joey Bartholomew, the high school classmate, had fallen to his death at an abandoned mine. Obviously, I still grasped the basic facts, though particulars remained a bit fuzzy. The connection between Joey's death and my being in town evaded me.

"Well, I'm not exactly here by choice, Jade. Frankly, this town is one of the last places I'd choose to live, but in case you haven't noticed, I've got terminal cancer and only my mom to look after me."

She moved closer, her volume a tic lower. "But we promised, remember?" A pause while waiting for confirmation. "We agreed that you'd move away and never come back because of … you know."

"What happened that we would make a promise like that?"

She edged closer to me, the aroma of strawberries filling my nostrils. If I'd forgotten her beauty or why I'd fallen for her once, I had no problem remembering now.

Cocking her head, she said, "No fooling. You really don't remember, huh?"

I shook my head.

A sigh-whistle blew between her teeth. "The brain cancer must have short-circuited some of your memories. They still blame you, you know, even after all these years."

They.

Joey's mom, Sharon, and anybody else who listened to her bitter rantings and were swayed to her side. She'd probably seen the newspaper interview, boiling mad that I'd returned to town.

Blame me? "Good grief, everybody knows it was an accident." Just remembering how far Joey had fallen that day still made me break into a cold sweat. In fact, I'd been afraid of heights ever since. "He got too close to the edge, slipped, and fell."

"You're kidding me, right?" Her eyebrows hiked. "Dr. Korovin told me you've suffered some long-term memory loss, but I didn't think it could be *this* bad."

After another quick look at the doorway to ensure my mom wasn't nearby, she nailed me again with those amazing, jittery eyeballs, her voice almost a whisper. "You forget that I was there that day and saw everything. And I've kept our secret all these years, just like you asked me to. But I suppose you've forgotten all that too."

What secret? What could she be talking about?

Just then recall flashed back that this issue of what had really happened at the mine that day had driven us apart years ago. I'd eventually left town, especially since practically everyone, led by Joey's mom, blamed me for what had happened. Everyone, that is, except my mom, who'd stood by me and refused to believe the lies.

How could I have possibly forgotten so much? The event resembled the school shooting. The details of that day remained fuzzy too; perhaps like the tragedy at the school, my mind had blocked details of Joey's death too. And maybe now the memory trips would slowly unveil the truth, like peeling the layers of an onion.

Before I could probe further, Mom strolled into the living room with a tray bearing a pitcher and tall, ice-filled glasses.

While Mom poured Jade a glass of lemonade, Jade's gaze flicked a question my direction. Clearly matters remained unresolved between us, but this wasn't the right time to lay them out in the open. When would we be able to talk again?

Chapter 19

Tuesday, October 27
Iron Valley, Michigan

Troubling dreams swirled in a confusing tangle of fantasy and memories, slapping me hard across the face and jolting me awake from the dead of sleep. I lurched up in bed with a shout, panting. Puzzled by what had awoken me, I peered through the dark at my raised hands.

They were covered with something … wet.

Hands shaking, I turned on my lamp, fearing what I might see.

A substance resembling blood appeared to be everywhere. On my hands. On my T-shirt and shorts. Smeared all over my sheets and blankets too.

Gasping, I leaped from my bed and shrank away from the sight. The coppery aroma filled my nostrils, nausea crawling up my throat.

Wake up, Landon. Wake up. You must be dreaming.

But I wasn't. This was real.

Back pressed against the opposite wall, I took in the macabre scene, blood whooshing in my ears. It looked like a murder had taken place in my bed, but there wasn't a body anywhere.

Just me. Alone.

Taking deep, measured breaths, I sought to wrap my mind around what had happened. But none of this made any sense.

I must have been up in the night again—that much appeared to be obvious. But what had I done this time?

Scrambling to my knees, I searched the floor for any sign of a weapon. Last time I'd used a hammer. A knife would have caused this much blood, but to my relief I didn't see one anywhere.

Had I been wounded and didn't know it? I didn't sense any pain, but sometimes shock can deaden the mind to injuries.

A quick search of my arms, legs, and torso for wounds revealed nothing. If I'd spilled that much blood, wouldn't my wound be obvious? Unless …

A moan seeped through my lips.

Had I hurt someone this time? Killed someone without remembering what I'd done?

Might it be possible? Did I have a split personality like Dr. Jekyll and Mr. Hyde? Could I be a good person when awake? Someone evil when I slept?

Against the dresser I leaned, chest heaving, hands shaking. There had to be a logical explanation.

God help me. What's going on? What have I done?

A pounding rattled my bedroom door. Next came Mom's frantic voice; she must have heard my shout. "Landy! Landy, are you okay?"

Relief pulsed through my veins. At least I hadn't hurt her.

Enough with the secrets—I couldn't keep them anymore. I stumbled toward the door on shaky legs and wrenched it open.

Mom recoiled at the sight of blood on me. "What did you do? Did you hurt yourself?" She grabbed my arms, searched my wrists.

My heart wrenched at the realization. "No, Mom, I'd never do something like that. I just woke up, and the room was like—like this. *I* was like this."

She shrank away from my bloody hands as if reality had slapped her hard across the face.

My teeth chattered. Cold—oh so cold. "Mom, I don't know what happened. I don't know whose blood this is. It isn't mine. But I didn't hurt anybody. I swear I didn't."

Her voice suddenly became cool, efficient, and businesslike; she'd tucked the emotional part of herself away, out of sight. "Come with me."

"What? Where?"

"Landy, you're in shock and about to pass out. Go take a shower and warm yourself up. You need to wash that blood off anyhow. Then we can talk."

Yes, take charge. She'd always been great at that. Long lacking my father's leadership, she'd learned to step in and get the job done.

At least she'd decided not to call the police right away. That at least gave me some hope. I envisioned myself locked up in the jail and protesting my innocence despite somebody else's blood splashed all over my bedroom. A jury wouldn't need even five minutes to convict me.

Afterward, I dried off and returned to my bedroom, a towel cinched around my waist. In my brain fog I'd forgotten to grab a change of clothes.

Still cleaning up, Mom wielded rubber gloves and balled my bloody sheets and blankets, stuffing them in a black trash bag.

The unemotional get-it-done side had taken over, making her mechanical, businesslike. "Give me your clothes."

I handed them to her, and she added them to the trash bag. She met my gaze with a look of wariness edged with disbelief. "C'mon, I'll make us some strong coffee." Once again, making strong coffee became the first logical step when facing any problem.

But soon, cradling a steaming mug in my hands, I had to admit the joe offered an excellent start. The caffeine swept the cobwebs away. At least now I could process the event, but what was I supposed to think?

Mom studied me from across the kitchen table. "We've got a problem here, Landon."

No kidding, Mom.

"If that blood isn't yours, somebody else is hurt pretty bad or maybe even dead."

I didn't begrudge her for stating the obvious. Sometimes coping simply means repeating the truth to yourself, no matter how obvious it may seem at the time, until it sinks in.

"While you were changing, I headed outside with a flashlight, hoping to find a blood trail. Did you realize you left your bloody sneakers parked outside by the front door?"

My heart thudded. "I did? Did you find a trail?"

"Nope. Nothing."

But somebody's still out there somewhere. Hurt bad. Shouldn't we call an ambulance?

Maybe Mom had already done so but hadn't told me. She appeared to be managing the event pretty well without my help. What would I have done without her?

She flicked on the radio for the local news at the top of the hour. Not a word about anyone being assaulted in the night, but of course that fact shouldn't be surprising if I'd hurt someone only hours ago. Hanging my head, I longed for a Jack Daniel's.

What's happened to you? Where do we go from here?

Turning the radio off, she began pacing the room. "Either way, Landy, whether you can explain what happened or not, we need to go to the police."

"But Mom—"

"Now hear me out. I've got a garbage bag full of bloody clothes and blankets. We can't just ignore them."

But we could burn them.

Her eyes narrowed as if surmising my thoughts. "Besides, somebody could be lying in a pool of blood somewhere and need help. The police need to be looking for that person."

True. There might even be time to save whoever had been hurt.

"C'mon. Let's go," she said.

In her van I raked my fingers through my hair. "Mom, I have no idea what happened. If I hurt someone"—*or killed someone*—"I have no memory of any of it. I don't even know how I did what I did ... or who I did it to ... or why I did it."

Driving, she pressed a warm hand to the side of my face as if checking me for a fever. "Oh, Landy, what's going on inside that head of yours? I suppose the cancer could have messed with the part of your brain related to judgments and choices."

"But if I did something without deciding to, am I really responsible?"

For the first time I could recall, she didn't spout off any pat answers. "Ask someone who snores the same question. Sure, we can do something without realizing it and still be responsible. It's like having a dream, I suppose."

"Dreams are beyond our control."

"We may not intentionally *plan* to dream what we do, but dreams still come from what's inside us. We're still evil inside, Landy. Remember what the Bible says."

Here we go. Buckle on that Bible belt.

"'The heart is deceitful above all things and desperately wicked.' What comes from inside us defiles us and makes us needy of God's grace. The first step is to take responsibility for that wickedness. Then we have to realize our helplessness to deal with it in our own strength. It's why Jesus died for us on the cross. He did for us what we couldn't do for ourselves."

I *was* an evil, wicked sinner—no need to twist my arm about that. But she didn't launch into a plea to repent, kneel at the altar, or wring tears from my cold heart. Instead, she asked, "Have you ever been angry and did something stupid on impulse, without thinking about it? Without *planning* to do it?"

Once I'd lost my temper and kicked my booted foot through a plaster wall, but I wasn't about to tell her *that* story. I shrugged.

"Well, there you go. People hurt or kill other people every day without intending to. When they're late to work and run a red light, they don't *intend* to kill the pedestrian."

"I believe they have an expression for that, Mom. It's called involuntary manslaughter."

That would be my criminal charge because there didn't appear to be any motive. I hadn't been negligent or mad at anyone, from what I could recall. Why couldn't I remember what happened?

Because you have brain cancer, you moron. Your brain will never be normal again.

She cleared her throat. "Look, when they understand about your brain cancer and realize your brain could be triggering involuntary actions, maybe they'll show leniency. Dr. Korovin could even give testimony on your behalf. Maybe we could use an insanity defense."

Clearly she'd been doing some thinking since I awakened her, all bloody, in the dead of night. Leaning forward, I cradled my skull in both hands. Why not do an insanity defense? I *was* going crazy, wasn't I?

I pictured Amee going ballistic when this PR nightmare hit the fan. The banner headline flashed in my mind: GRAMMY AWARD-WINNING PIANIST LOSES MIND, ARRESTED FOR MURDER. My career would be finished, but, of course, wasn't it already?

Drawing in a deep breath, I let it rush out of me. I dreaded telling Mom about the theft of Millie West's stolen coins, but since the two events appeared to be connected, did I have any choice? When I finished, she gaped at me. "Landy, why didn't you tell me about this earlier?"

"I don't know. I was embarrassed. I—I thought maybe if I returned the coins somehow, everything would be forgiven and forgotten. I just hadn't come up with a clever way to return them yet."

"Returning the coins is simple enough—I'll help you—but tell me more. How did you know it was you?"

I told her about the daymares and described recovering the coins from the sandbox.

She blew air out of her cheeks. "You may have strayed from God—goodness, we all stray sometimes—but this is something else. You've never been a thief before, have you?"

"No. In fact, how could I have stolen coins I didn't even know she had?"

"What?"

"This is what I mean, Mom. Something's going on here that doesn't make any sense. I've never met Millie in my life. I don't even know where she lives. I didn't even know she kept rare coins in a basement safe with a combination until you told me. In fact, I don't even know the combination, so how did I get the safe open? Does any of this make sense to you?"

Her face morphed into a picture of bewilderment.

"Now I wake up with blood all over me. It's almost as if—" I straightened, overcome by a new train of thought.

"What, Landy?"

"It's like someone else is controlling me."

Chapter 20

Tuesday, October 27
Iron Valley, Michigan

After nearly having a heart attack when she recognized me from the tabloids and gushing about my latest CD, the ponytailed female police officer at the Iron Valley Police Department blushed and became businesslike. "Sorry, guess I got a little carried away there. Was there something I could help you with?"

I couldn't believe I was speaking the words. "I may have—um—some information about a possible stabbing. I'd like to talk to one of your officers, please."

Her smile went on a sabbatical. "No problem. Why don't you take a seat. Somebody will be with you shortly."

When I took a chair beside my mom, the receptionist picked up a phone and talked in hushed tones, watching my every move.

Five minutes later a cop in his mid-thirties lumbered toward us. I expected a guy in uniform, but he sported khakis and a baby-blue polo. He wore short, neatly combed russet hair and a matching soul patch. Suspicion and something smelling of wariness or a general distrust of people glinted in his black eyes. Short but barrel chested, he probably pumped iron when off duty to compensate for his vertical deficit. Few qualities are more important for a police officer to exude than power.

His strong-gripped handshake enforced the intimidation factor. "I'm Ray Galotta, the detective lieutenant."

"Nice to meet you." I stayed seated and introduced myself and my mom. His narrow, ferret-like eyes expressed neither recognition nor surprise. Apparently, celebrities didn't impress him.

He rubbed a hand across a stubbly face that had once seen its share of acne. "The receptionist said you have information to share about a possible stabbing?"

"That's right."

Poker face. "Okay, why don't you follow me?"

Mom rose to come along, but, tired of being treated like a child, I patted her arm. "No, you stay here."

Officer Galotta studied me. No doubt he puzzled over my attachment to my mother, given my age. The situation was complicated.

He led me out of the lobby, through a door, and down a seventies-style, wood-paneled hallway flanked on either side by closed doors. I assumed they were interview rooms like I'd seen on TV, but I wasn't here for any high-pressure interrogation. The facts were straightforward, and I had no plans to be evasive. In Mom's trunk lay a trash bag filled with bloody linens and clothes. After the results of DNA tests, Galotta would surely arrest me once he heard what I had to say.

But the detective didn't lead me into any of these rooms. Instead, he pushed open a glass-paneled, rear exit door and shot a glance back as if to remind me to keep up, face expressionless.

I followed him outside to the employee parking lot. "Where are we going?"

Galotta's right hand brushed the holstered pistol on his right hip. "That's not important. Just come with me, please."

Something didn't smell right here, but what could I do?

He led me past a row of navy patrol cars, lined up side by side like a perfect set of Matchbox cars, until we reached an old navy Chevy sedan parked at the end. Galotta circled to the front passenger door and opened it for me. "Get in."

Peering in at the black interior, I hesitated. "Where we going? Weren't you going to ask me some questions?"

"Just get in."

Once I complied, he slammed the door behind me as if I were unable to do the task for myself. Lingering traces of secondhand cigarette smoke burned my nose.

Galotta slid behind the steering wheel and started the engine. The radio blared Berlioz until he quickly switched it off. *Symphonie Fantastique.* Interesting. I wouldn't have pegged the cop as a classical music fan. He appeared to be more the Bon Jovi type.

He slipped on shiny, gold-framed aviator sunglasses and pulled out of the parking lot, turning right onto Main Street. Which proved to be oddly empty.

The hum of rubber tires kissing cement only magnified the unnatural silence in the car. The officer finally said, "So you're probably wondering where we're going."

"You could say that."

"If anything seems familiar, just speak up."

I shot him a glance. "I don't understand."

He met my eyes. "You will, Landon. Just give it some time."

"Weren't you going to ask me some questions?"

"Why ask you questions when I already know the answers? Now that would be a waste of time for both of us, wouldn't it?" His expressionless face gave nothing away.

We must be playing some kind of mind game, right? "Well, if you already know the answers, maybe you wouldn't mind sharing. I'm still pretty much in the dark here."

"All in good time, Landon. All in good time." He braked at a vacant four-way stop, then pressed the accelerator. "So how have you been feeling since the surgery?"

He must have seen the newspaper article about my return to Iron Valley. "Pretty well other than some dizziness and a few memory issues."

"Cancer's a tough thing. I know. My kid sister died of leukemia when she was seven."

"I'm sorry."

"Why should *you* be? It wasn't your fault."

"I know. I was just—"

"Having any awareness issues?" He paused. "Let me guess. You're doing certain deeds, but you don't remember doing them, right?"

I studied him. He kept his focus on the road, giving nothing away.

"Like I said, Landon, all in good time. We've got a lot to talk about."

My mind stuttered. How could Galotta know about my memory issues? It appeared almost as if he'd *known* I would visit his office today. But how could that be possible?

Minutes later, he pulled alongside a curb and stopped. Leaving the car idling, he exited and circled around to open my door. I grabbed my cane. Stepped into autumn sunshine on shaky legs. Looked around.

LaRosa Boulevard lay maybe five blocks from my mom's house. Someone nearby must have been burning leaves—the comforting aroma filled my nostrils.

Galotta motioned me across a patch of struggling lawn to the sidewalk. A leafless tree rose to my right. Scraggly grass and weeds in dire need of mowing rose in a tangle around its trunk.

The officer gestured toward the street. "Anything coming back to you?"

Coming back to me?

We stood in an older, less prosperous part of town. Ramshackle two-story houses with postage-stamp yards flanked both sides of the street and rose together as if seeking comfort in mutual misery. Old, banged-up cars, some "repaired" with duct tape, rusted away in the dim morning light.

Then it happened.

The flapping sound drew my attention to a stretch of sidewalk only a dozen feet away. Crime-scene tape outlining a section of sidewalk danced in the breeze. Even from here the blood stood out on the cement.

The blood.

My mouth watered.

Cold fire sliced into my forehead like someone had thrust a knife into the bridge of my nose without the blessing of sedation. I gasped and bent at my waist, arms cradling my head. Barely able to grab a breath, I gritted my teeth and waited for the agony to pass.

God, help me.

Could I be having a stroke?

The barrage of memories slammed into my chest. When I clamped my eyelids shut, the daymare flared in the corners of my eyes, replacing the pain. There flashed the image of …

… a woman jogging down the sidewalk. Pretty, young, affluent. Not from around here. Maybe she's from out of town, visiting family.

Short, blonde hair has been pulled away from her face in a girlish ponytail. Black designer sunglasses hide her eyes above prominent, model-status cheekbones. Navy yoga pants stretch across narrow hips that haven't yet known childbirth.

A hot-pink T-shirt hugs her shapely torso. An MP3 player is clipped to a pocket on her hip, and a tangle of black wires dangles from matching pink earbuds.

The music is so loud she can't hear me. Doesn't realize I'm coming up behind her with the knife.

She's the mark, and I instinctively know what I must do.

I raise my arm. Slash downward.

She jerks her head around. Screams. Crumples to the ground.

Blood is everywhere: on my hands, on my clothes.

For a moment I can't move, a strange buzzing filling my ears. She lies there like a broken Barbie doll. A choking sound gurgles from her open mouth.

I run and ...

... the past hurtled away from me. Like the memory and all sensations associated with it had been sucked out of my head and bottled for future reference, leaving me feeling sucked dry and disoriented. Present reality rushed into the void, simulating a drug hitting my bloodstream.

My eyelids snapped open to the autumn sunshine—and to the cop watching me with a peculiar look. Fascination? Revulsion?

I searched my hands, awash in nausea, ready to throw up. But the blood had vanished—this fact stemming the tide.

Gasping, I straightened and dropped my arms to my sides. Blinked and looked around, my clothes again drenched in sweat. Though exhaustion claimed me, the pain had vanished. Another daymare come and gone. Could they be getting worse?

Galotta eased closer and grabbed my arm, apparently to steady me. "Do you remember now?"

***

Back in the cop's car, I leaned my head back against the headrest and took deep breaths, eyelids clamped shut, glad to be away from the horror of the tape and the knife and the blood.

What have I done? This so can't be happening.

Freezing and shaking at the same time, I folded my arms across my chest.

"Maybe this will help."

I opened my eyes. Galotta offered me coffee in a thermos cap.

"No thanks." My stomach revolted with sickening spasms.

"Really, I think you should drink it."

"No, I'm okay." My tongue dragged across dry lips.

"You don't look okay. The caffeine might—"

"I've had these episodes before. They pass. I'll be fine."

"Fine. Have it your own way."

My heart banged like a kettledrum while the truth seeped in.

The blood on my hands. The memory of the attack.

It must have been her. And it must have been me.

And somehow—don't ask me how—Galotta knew all about it.

But how could I have done this? I didn't even know the woman's name.

From the driver's seat: "Are you going to tell me what you remember?"

"What's the point? Don't you know already?"

Neither confirming nor denying, Galotta sipped the coffee I'd declined. I'd been mistaken; the joe's aroma made my mouth water. Apparently, the sickness had passed.

I swallowed. "Is she okay? The woman, I mean."

"She might live. The next twenty-four hours will decide." He removed his sunglasses and folded them, surveying the quiet street. "But see, that's the point." He swiveled his head, eyes boring into me like his gaze could pierce straight to my scar tissue. "She was *supposed* to die, Landon."

Chapter 21

An ice cube slid down my spine. "What—what are you saying? What do you mean—she was *supposed* to die? Was *I* supposed to kill her?"

Galotta remained silent. While the planet continued to slide, derailed from its orbit, he put the car in gear, and we moved again. Once he'd driven well out of town, down dusty country roads, he pulled off to the shoulder amid weeds that scraped the car's underbelly and squeaked to a stop.

He shut off the engine. "Get out of the car."

"Why?"

"Just do it."

Weary of this riddle, I opened my door, gripped my cane, and pushed myself out on wobbly legs, leaning against the car for extra support.

Galotta headed to the trunk and opened it, fiddling around inside beyond my view. He closed the trunk and bridged the distance, thrusting a manila folder into my hands.

I eyed it. "What's this?"

"Take a good, long look—in case there's anything you're not putting together."

Opening the folder, I pulled out its contents. My heart, my breath, my life—everything froze. Hands tremored when I stuffed the photos back into the folder and thrust it back at him.

The pictures—I'd been captured in all of them, stabbing her. He had photographic proof that I'd done the unthinkable, and Mom possessed bloody evidence in a garbage bag. What else did he need to put me away for a very long time?

Then it hit me. How could someone have been on hand to photograph the assault? A passerby? Perhaps not so strange. Didn't everybody have cell phones with cameras these days?

Didn't matter. Either way, my life had just come to a screeching halt.

Galotta tossed the folder into the car through an open window and faced me without expression.

"I guess you better arrest me," I said.

"No." His dark eyes glittered. "I don't think so."

"I don't understand."

"No, but you will. That's why we're here, Landon, so all your questions can be answered." The cop folded his arms across his thick chest. "Your first impulse will be to run. Don't even think about leaving town. I have these pictures. I also have your DNA. I'll match it to the DNA found at the crime scene, and just like that, I'll have your arrest warrant."

"I didn't *intend* to hurt anyone. I don't even know who that lady is."

He shook his head. "Don't you get it?"

"Someone else was controlling me—that's what you're saying, right? That explains why I hurt her when I didn't mean to."

Galotta threw his head back, arms raised to the sky. "Finally, Landon grows a brain." He smirked at me. "I'm gonna have to lead you down the primrose path step by step—I can see that now. You were chosen because of your amazing brain ability, but now I'm starting to wonder if they got the wrong guy."

I have been chosen?

A slow ache began to build in my temples, accompanied by a vision that graced the backs of my eyelids. A long corridor. An office with an unsmiling, gray-haired man.

You realize you're a special boy, don't you?

Special?

Tests. Experiments. When I'd been a child.

Could they explain this oddball memory I couldn't place? Had someone been watching me since I was a kid? Might that same person, or persons, be behind this nightmare unfolding before me now?

The words somehow squeezed out. "But—but how could someone be controlling me?"

"Didn't you recently have surgery?"

"A brain tumor." But of course, Galotta already knew about that, just like he had knowledge about everything. "Dr. Korovin removed most of it."

"When Dr. Korovin was messing around inside your head, he didn't just remove the tumor. He inserted something in its place. After all, you know what they say. 'A mind is a terrible thing to waste.'"

Moisture had been sucked from my throat. "Dr. Korovin said they were medicinal wafers to keep the cancer from returning."

"Well, guess what? Korovin lied." Reaching out, he rapped on my skull before I could pull away. "He put something in there, all right. An implant, a microchip—call it whatever you like. Either way, it does its job. It controls your brain. And whoever controls your brain, controls you."

The truth sank into my bones. I'd become like one of those drones used to take out the enemy in Afghanistan.

My gaze flicked back to the dusty road, the rustling trees around me, and the searing sun made my eyes ache. So I hadn't chosen to do these evil actions—at least that truth brought a measure of relief. But who could be the puppet master pulling my strings?

Korovin? Galotta? Or someone else?

Could that person be watching us even now?

No longer was I an award-winning pianist. I'd become a thief and an assassin, programmed against my knowledge and will. Someone had stolen the most important things about me—my identity, my reputation.

My free will.

Now I'd become a slave. A slave to a terrible agenda. And powerless to break free.

I gripped my cane to still my trembling hands.

"The theft and the stabbing—those were just a dry run," Galotta said. "We've got bigger plans for you."

"We?"

He ignored me.

"What plans?"

"All in good time, Landon. All in good time." A faint smile touched his lips. Being in control obviously turned him on.

"But tell me why. Why was I supposed to kill her?"

"Because she killed her mother."

"What?"

"Doesn't matter. Her time was up—her name was on the list for termination. She was your mark. That's all you really need to know."

A list implied others in a queue. Waiting for me? On some kind of high-tech crime network? My breath lingered in my lungs, eyes on the tree line, before I released it.

Las Vegas. Atlanta. Could so many mass shootings be somehow connected?

Think, Landon. Think. This is either the most elaborate joke anybody has ever played on you, or it's the most outrageous scenario. Keep asking questions.

"Why are you telling me all this?"

"You were just supposed to quietly do your kill order, clean up the mess, and not remember any of it. But something went wrong. You're not like the others, but it's time for you to be the person you're meant to be."

Others? How many other drones could there be?

"You're malfunctioning. Remembering things you shouldn't. Not disposing of evidence like the implant tells you to."

The hammer. The bloody shoes, clothes, and sheets.

But how could Galotta know?

If someone could control my brain, perhaps my eyes served as cameras. Maybe the puppet master could see everything just like I did. In real time.

"Why are you making me do these things?"

Galotta pressed hands to his chest. "Me? You think *I'm* in control? No, I'm just the janitor sent to clean up your messes."

"But if it isn't you, who's doing this to me?"

"That's not important."

"Then can you at least tell me the purpose behind it all? If someone is making me do things beyond my knowledge and will, I think I at least deserve to know why."

"Because some people are rich enough to get anything they want. Yep, that's right—*anything*. And thanks to current technology, there's no reason for those in control to get their hands dirty."

"But why me?"

The cop sniffed, glanced at his watch. "Look, every day people get brain cancer, Landon. And what's the brain if not a CPU that explains everything we do? Hack into that computer, and I could make you do anything. Jump off the nearest tree like you're Superman. Even strangle your own mother."

He chuckled, but I didn't find any of it funny. "Lots of people get brain cancer, and let's face it—most of them are going to die anyhow, right? Why not extend their lives and give them some value before they pass on? In some ways those in control should be thanked. They actually give their little lives some meaning before they make their final exit."

They. How many people could be involved in this conspiracy?

"Then when those folks are no longer useful or compliant," he said, putting emphasis on the last word, "we just let the cancer do its business and find somebody else."

Like disposable paper cups. Used, crushed, and tossed into the trash.

The craziest scheme I'd ever heard of. Any moment somebody would wake me up from this insanity.

"Do you know the real reason I brought you here?" Galotta said. "I was originally supposed to arrest you and terminate you. You're a big risk. But apparently the head honchos still have important plans for you. They asked me to help you better understand the game plan to ensure future cooperation."

Galotta eased closer until his acne-pitted face came practically nose to nose with mine. "Because you *will* cooperate, Landon. Oh, yes, you will. That is, unless you want those you love to end up on that termination list I told you about."

Somehow I kept my face expressionless.

"And don't even think about telling anyone. Not the FBI. Not nobody. Remember, I'm with the police department. I have eyes everywhere. Besides, nobody will believe your story anyhow. You've got brain cancer, and you've been doing some mighty strange things lately like sleepwalking and playing strange games in the night."

Beyond him I focused on the trees, rising tall and straight. Impregnable. Like prison bars.

"Don't think about telling your mom either. If you do, she'll die in the worst way imaginable … and at your hand."

Yeah, I'd like to see you try.

Galotta's breath reeked of stale coffee. "They can make you do it. Don't think they can't. That would be matricide, Landon. Can you even imagine what that would be like to kill your own mother?"

My throat had turned so dry I could hardly swallow. I shook my head.

"What? You don't believe me? You think you're the only one?" Galotta's voice broke, the first sign that his tough-guy facade bore weak spots. "Imagine killing someone you love. Imagine seeing yourself do it when the whole time you don't want to."

Clamping my eyes closed, I resisted the sick fantasy.

"Look at me."

I refused. He didn't know me like he thought he did.

He slapped my face. Hard. "I said, *look at me!*"

Cheek stinging, I glared at him.

"I know, Landon, because I've been there. I didn't believe any of this either, not at first, so they killed Sylvia, the woman I loved, right before my eyes." He paused, jaw locked tight, eyes moist. "And then, after cutting my head open, just like they did to you, they made me do something completely evil, something totally beyond my control."

I found my voice, though it sounded strained. "*Made* you?"

"Get in the car, Landon."

"Where are you taking me now?"

"You don't believe me—I can tell. So I guess I'll have to show you."

"Where are we going?"

"To my mother's grave."

Chapter 22

Tuesday, October 27
Iron Valley, Michigan

Back in the lobby, Mom rose and faced me, worry lines creasing her forehead. "You were gone a long time. What happened? They didn't arrest you?"

I struggled to keep my voice calm. "No, I'm free to go."

"But how could that be? Don't they want to see the bloody clothes and sheets?"

"Officer Galotta said he'd be in touch if he had more questions." I hated to lie, but what could I say to get her out of this place? And far away from Galotta?

"But doesn't he want to test the blood for DNA?"

"Nope." Well, at least that part rang with truth.

"But that doesn't make any sense."

"Sorry, Mom. I know—it's all pretty weird. I don't know what else to say."

She just looked at me with a baffled expression. Of course, she didn't buy any of it, but what else could I say? I had enough to sort through in my throbbing head without worrying about saying too much and endangering her life. Could someone be watching us even now?

My mind tripped back to the cemetery, to the bouquet of silk white lilies and the slab of gray-veined marble with Lucinda Galotta's name engraved on it. The stomach-clenching truth of what Ray Galotta had done to his mother repulsed me. So he'd grown up in Iron Valley before moving to Chicago to be a cop. Or had he been lying to me?

Touching Mom's elbow, I eased her toward the door. "I'm not asking any questions, and I don't think you should either. Let's just go, okay?"

Mercifully, she fell silent and said little the rest of the way home. When she pulled into the garage, I complained of a headache and said I needed to lie down.

"You need to call Dr. Korovin, too," she said. "Tell him about what's happened."

Dr. Korovin had gotten me into this mess. He was the last person I wanted to talk to right now.

Later, I sat on my bed, knees pulled to my chest, temples pounding. I studied the corners of my room, searching for tiny cameras and listening devices. But they didn't need cameras, not if my eyes *were* the cameras. Galotta's departing words echoed in my skull.

Don't try anything stupid. They can see and hear everything you do.

What? They can read my thoughts?

Not exactly. But until you find a way to amputate your head, you're pretty much stuck.

I crawled under the covers, stunned and lost, my mind drifting away like a boat lost at sea. And somehow, in spite of all the stress and overwhelming knowledge drowning me, I peered past the darkness of my life and glimpsed an even greater darkness, the blackness of the past. And something I didn't understand told me Jade would soon be drowning in it.

The impending sense of dread nearly overwhelmed me. The phone would ring, and somebody would be there. Not talking, just breathing hard, breathing hard. And waiting for the right time to go after her—

A pounding on my door jolted me awake. I rubbed my eyes, surprised that I'd actually slept.

"Landon, are you okay? It's late. You need to eat something. I've got some homemade minestrone on the stove."

I fumbled with my blankets, tangled around me like constraints. Thrashing out of them, I pulled myself free, panting and sweating. Understanding too well how a trapped animal must feel.

Earlier I'd been freezing. Now I was scalding, my T-shirt and shorts soaked. Could this just be the stress getting to me, or had I come down with the flu on top of everything else?

"Landon?" Mom's voice betrayed more insistence this time.

"I'll … I'll be there in a few minutes." I gently rubbed puffy, tender eyes with the heels of my hands. Before drifting off to sleep, my mind had worked away at my problem. But so far the solution evaded me, and I was trapped. Paralyzed. Unable to work my way free.

Whoever controlled my brain could apparently see and hear everything I did, but they couldn't know my thoughts. At least I had those to myself and would closely guard them. A private oasis.

How those in control manipulated me didn't rise to the importance of *when*. When would they send me on my next assignment? Galotta had said they had big plans for me. But what could those be?

No. I wouldn't hurt anyone else—I wouldn't let myself, even if I had to chain myself to my bed and give my mom the key.

Nighttime appeared to be when I did my darkest deeds. Perhaps I could consume large amounts of coffee and keep myself awake. But I would need some sleep to maintain good health. And on top of everything else, I still lived with my brain cancer.

I sought to dodge the wave of despair, but it crashed into me anyhow. My head bowed in a rare moment of reverence.

God, I know we aren't exactly best buddies, but I need your help here. There must be a way out of this. Would you please show me how? I have to find a way out without hurting my mom.

Based on what I'd learned, none of my loved ones would be safe. But could the puppet master get to Dad? Probably not while he lived in a high-security psych ward.

In an odd way, I envied him. Of any of us, Dad must be the safest of all.

***

Over lunch—grilled turkey breast and organic goat cheese on whole wheat—I determined to act normal, but I hated keeping secrets from my mom, especially after my confession about Millie West's stolen coins.

"Landon, are you okay?"

"No, I'm not okay. I think I might be sick. I threw up earlier." She didn't need to know the reason.

Reaching across the table, she pressed a warm hand to my forehead. Though she was babying me again, I didn't mind it so much this time.

"Oh, Landy, you're burning up. I think you should call Dr. Korovin. Tell him about what's going on."

Galotta hadn't said anything about *not* calling Dr. Korovin, and I did have an appointment. And now that I'd had time to think, I figured the good doctor must somehow be at the heart of the matter. But perhaps he was a marionette too, swinging at the end of so many strings.

Later, I booted up my computer and called Dr. Korovin's office. A pretty woman who sported obviously dyed red hair answered my call. Moments later, Dr. Korovin appeared on camera, friendly and smiling. Always in a suit and tie. Slicked-back black hair. Matching unblinking eyes.

"And how have you been lately, Landon?"

"Not so good. Something's wrong with me."

"Oh, I'm sorry to hear that." He arched an eyebrow and folded his hands on his desktop. "Why don't you start at the beginning and tell me everything?"

So I did, except the part Galotta had forbidden me to tell anyone. I talked about the memory trips, the daymares, and the theft of Millie West's coins. After all, Galotta hadn't specifically forbidden mentioning *that* part of the story.

"I guess I'm"—I hesitated—"I'm doing bad things without knowing or remembering that I did them. Does this have something to do with my brain cancer?"

The smile remained plastered to Dr. Korovin's lips. Could his face even be real? "Well, Landon, the brain is a very sensitive organ we may never completely understand, and the cancer *did* invade some healthy tissue. There is no denying that some brain damage occurred, particularly affecting your eyesight and balance. In a secondary way, your memories have been affected too."

The smile vanished. "But Landon, I think you know very well why you are behaving this way."

"I do?"

"Officer Galotta spoke to you earlier today. In fact, I observed the entire exchange."

My scalp tightened. The police car must have been rigged with cameras.

Or maybe he observed everything through your eyes.

Dr. Korovin's pleasant expression morphed into something hinting of stunned sympathy. "You must not care very much about your mother's welfare to be calling me like this. What an impulsive and foolhardy thing to do. Officer Galotta's warning was not to be taken lightly."

Anger shoved the words into my mouth before I could think. "You have no right to do this to me."

"No, I have every right. Remember, I told you my techniques were experimental and that I could neither promise recovery nor guarantee how your body and brain would respond to them. Your brain has responded ... well ... unpredictably. You were warned about possible eventualities and gave your consent. Do you not remember?" His head gave a little jerk. "Oh, that's right. Silly me. It is very likely you cannot remember."

"You're not going to get away with this!" My teeth clenched. "This is my life we're talking about here. You have no right to—"

"An unfortunate outcome is perfectly within the parameters we discussed. It was a risk you said you were willing to take. Do you not remember, Landon? You signed on the dotted line." He held up the application I'd signed. His camera even zoomed in on my signature.

I flushed. "But you lied. You said you were putting medicinal wafers in my brain to fight the cancer. You didn't say you were going to transform me into a killing machine at someone else's beck and call. This isn't what I signed up for, and you know it! What did you put in there? A microchip that can tap into my vision and alter my decision-making capacity?"

His face, void of emotion, had become unnervingly robot-like. "I am sorry if the procedure hasn't lived up to your expectations, but no, I did not lie. Yes, there *is* a medicinal implant in your head, but it does more than fight cancer. I told you I can't promise complete healing for everyone in every case, but there is a difference between being healed and staying alive."

Sucking in measured breaths, I sought to maintain some control. "I'm listening."

"The implant is there for a reason—to ensure your condition does not worsen. And like I said, you might even get better in some ways. But future health is actually *your* choice. Follow the game plan Officer Galotta described, and you will not only spare the lives of those you love. You'll preserve your own."

"What are you saying?"

"I am saying that if you cooperate with the program, the implant can keep the cancer at bay, Landon. You could lead a productive life for many years to come. You may even learn to walk without your cane. Remember, we have plans for you. You cannot very well be useful to anyone if you are confined to a bed or dying."

But how could I believe anything he said? He'd lied before. Why not now?

"You can actually *keep me alive*?"

Korovin lifted his chin. "Certainly you read the testimonials in our brochure. No, those people were not lying. They were not paid actors."

But they must be murderers-for-hire—all those smiling cancer survivors. And weren't there supposedly *thousands* of them? Multicolored pins dotted a map somewhere, in a highly secured office, equipped with computers and tracking devices. And people like Korovin giving them assignments.

Kill orders.

My mouth dried. How far might people be willing to go to stay alive?

Dr. Korovin's smile returned. "Now you understand better. There is a reason why some of my patients live and others die. I can only assume, Landon, that you number among those who wish to survive."

"But I have to be willing to … to kill other people."

"Actually, being willing doesn't have anything to do with it, but your compliance to the, um … game plan … would certainly make life easier for everyone—don't you think? And really, *kill* is such an ugly word. *Terminate* is such a … well, I have always liked that term better. And remember, you would only be terminating those who deserve it."

"Deserve it. What do you mean?"

"Forgive Officer Galotta. He did his best, but he left a few key points out of his presentation." He grabbed a deep breath. "Look at it this way, Landon. Our justice system has been broken for decades—wouldn't you agree? Murderers go free almost every day. Justice is no longer about who is guilty but who can afford the high-priced attorneys. You're now part of a network that applies justice where it has been … uh … negligent. Not even the wealthy should be exempt from paying for their sins. Wouldn't you agree?"

I nodded.

"So, if a murderer goes free, why not give justice a helping hand?"

So rational. So pragmatic. So seductive.

Undoubtedly he'd made this presentation many times before. I could sense his clever words, his well-thought-out persuasion, drawing me in. Like a coffee addict into a Starbucks. But I discerned the deception for what it was. This was nothing but sugar-coated murder, but he made it all sound so harmless, so righteous. So Kumbaya.

"No, I won't do this. You're not going to make a murderer out of me."

Korovin spoke as if repeating a script. "We do our best to ensure the satisfaction of our customers. If you have a formal complaint, you can always go to our website and submit one. Just click—"

"You're not going to get away with this. You—"

"Landon, if I were you, I would check on your mother."

His image flickered and died.

Chapter 23

Tuesday, October 27
Iron Valley, Michigan

Irushed into the kitchen, where Mom used her KitchenAid mixer to combine ingredients for some sort of natural foods version of a cake. She jerked up, startled. "Heavens, Landon! You're all flushed. What's wrong? Did your call go okay?"

My pulse thrummed in my ear lobes. "Uh, yeah. I'm fine."

The mixer wasn't even close to the sink, so it couldn't possibly electrocute her. Out the window the backyard heralded no signs of impending peril. No men in black descended from helicopters and stole across the lawn toward the house, rifles clutched in skilled hands.

Swiping at a drop of sweat slinking down my cheek, I gave myself a mental shake. "He said ... uh ... He said ..." A quick glance into the living room put me at ease. Certainly nothing there inspired fear or harm. "He said the symptoms are normal and ... and nothing to be concerned about."

She thrust a fist to her ample hip, mouth twisted to one side in dimple-inducing disgust. "No way. He actually said that? Why, that's ridiculous."

"He said if I keep going along with—with the plan"—her hand wasn't even close to the mixer; no threat of harm there—"then things will be fine. I may even walk without my cane someday."

"That's great to hear." She gave me her back, attention on her recipe. "And as far as this morning, well, you reported the situation to the police and now told your doctor. So I'd say you've done your civic duty. Not much more you can do than that."

She turned and surveyed me, concern-tinged eyes probing. "Why don't you lie down? You look a little—I don't know—not like yourself."

But I didn't want to lie down. I didn't know for sure whether the puppet master could watch everything through my eyes. I longed to search the house, to be sure little cameras weren't watching our every move. To ensure her safety.

Ambling into the living room, I peered out the large picture window. There were no signs of life, not even squirrels, as if even they knew the world was out of whack today. Not even Walkie-Talkie, the power-walking brunet who constantly babbled to herself while she pounded the pavement.

I meandered into the dining room and eyed the chandelier suspended over the cherrywood table. Prism-like shards dangled from golden bowed arms. Nothing unusual there.

You've been watching too many movies, Landon. Do you really think—?

Wait.

A black dot clung to one of the adjacent ceiling tiles.

A dot? Or a hole?

Probably a beetle had lucked out and fled the cold outdoors for the warmer, cozier interior of the house. But the more I studied the dot, the more suspicion grew that it must be something else.

Standing on a dining room chair, balance wobbly, brought the black dot up close and personal. Skin tingled between my shoulder blades.

A clean, round hole stared at me. But a hole leading to what?

C'mon, Landon. Now you're just being paranoid.

I had to know for sure. But just when my fingertips began to loosen the tile, icy fire shot through my head. I gasped, knees buckling, and lost my balance. Fell. Slammed onto my side on the carpeted floor.

Barely able to breathe, I attempted to call out to my mom—I even reached for her—but I couldn't make a sound; something had paralyzed my vocal cords.

My fingers fumbled, trying to grasp whatever sharp object had entered my skull, but of course there was nothing there. I lay in a fetal position, praying for the pain to let up.

Where could Mom be? Hadn't she heard me fall? Perhaps not over the whirring of the mixer.

The agony vanished in concert with the kitchen's ringing phone. I pulled myself to my knees, panting, sweating, shaking. What on earth had just happened? I'd had nail-in-the-head headaches before but not ones that prevented me from calling for help.

Mom's voice drifted from the kitchen. "Sure, hold on. I'll get him for you."

I rose unsteadily to my feet, sweat lathering me in a thin sheen, when she strode into the room. Hands pressed to the tabletop for support, I took a deep breath and righted myself.

Phone in hand, she eyed the overturned chair. "Are you okay?"

What could I say? "Yeah, I'm fine."

"There's some man on the phone asking for you. Sorry, I asked, but he wouldn't give me his name."

"Thanks." Watching her retreating back, I pressed the phone to my ear. Classic timing to get a cold-turkey call from some determined fan who'd somehow tracked down my mom's unlisted number. "Hello?"

"Whatever it is you think you're doing, Landon, just stop."

The man's voice, lower than Galotta's or Korovin's, was heavy with a New York accent. How large could this crime network be?

Heading to the living room, I crossed to the picture window. Searched the sun-blessed world for anything or anyone amiss. "Who is this?"

"How we're watching and listening isn't important. Just accept it."

Evil breathed on the other end, and it was talking to me. I shivered. The sweat was doing its job. "But how do you—?"

"You really don't get it, do you? You think we're just playing games?"

"No, I don't."

"Sure you do. You think we're just full of—"

"No, I don't."

"Part of you wonders if this is all some elaborate joke, right? Some big prank. Admit it."

A pause. "Okay, I admit it."

"You want proof this is for real, don't you?"

"No." Well, that wasn't exactly true.

"Yes, I think you do. Fine. If proof is what you want, I could hurt your mom real—"

"No! Please." Heat swelled in my chest. "Please don't hurt her!"

"Maybe her hand could get caught in that mixer she's using in the kitchen *right now*."

"No!" I spun and marched toward the kitchen, still on the tether of the cord. Mom had her back to me. She appeared to be f—

"Not a step closer, Landon!"

I froze, breath trapped in my throat.

He's watching every move you make.

"One step closer, and she dies. *Right. Now*. Don't think I won't do it."

Holding my breath, I glued my eyes to her back. The seconds screamed at me. I think my heart even paused beating.

It appeared unlikely that anyone could kill her in a split second, unless we had an intruder with a gun, but why test the waters? I loved her too much to risk her life.

"But you still don't believe me," the voice said. "Do you, Landon?"

Backing toward the living room on weak legs, I gasped, hungry for air. "Yes, I believe you."

I glanced back at the hole in the ceiling tile. Could that be the source of a camera? Had to be. But if cameras watched me, that meant he couldn't see through my eyes. A relief, at least.

"No, I don't think you do. You still need proof, don't you? Maybe your mom could slip and fall in the bathtub. Hit her head. Did you know drowning can occur in as little as two inches of water?"

He's playing with you, Landon.

"Please don't hurt her." My thoughts veered to Lucinda Galotta's tombstone. White lilies swaying in the breeze.

"But you want proof, don't you?"

Surveying the world beyond the picture window, I swallowed. "No, really, you don't have to—"

"But I have to hurt someone. If I don't, you'll never believe I mean what I say. And it's very important that you're a believer, Landon. It's critical that we develop some sort of circle of trust here."

Like I'm ever going to trust you people.

"Just give me a name. Any name. Maybe somebody you can't stand. I'll show you how easy it is to get what you want. It'll be a free kill on me."

A free kill?

I made the connection. *Strangers on a Train*, a movie by Alfred Hitchcock. One man commits a murder on behalf of another, then expects the returned favor.

I eyed the kitchen doorway again. "No, I don't want you to hurt anybody."

"I could always choose someone for you. Maybe Ted, that bass player you don't get along with."

He knows everything about you, Landon.

"No, please don't." Sweat trickled into my eyes, stung them.

"But you need proof." The man sighed, weary of our game. "Fine. Then I'll give you something small but irrefutable."

A swing back toward the window. "No, please—"

"Here's some proof for you to chew on—pun intended. You know Mrs. Bradeen, that sweet, old lady across the street?"

A clamp tightened around my chest. "Please don't hurt her!" Mrs. Bradeen's husband, in the nursing home down the street, suffered from Alzheimer's. Every day she shuffled down the street to visit him.

"Don't worry, Landon. She isn't who I had in mind. But her dog is being terminated *right now.*"

The screech of tires jerked my head toward the street, and I bolted to the window. A black van hurtled past, going too fast. Its wheels screeched, and it careened around the corner.

A small, brown spaniel I'd seen countless times lay broken and un-moving in the middle of the street. I spun away, nausea clawing at my throat. Mom had often said the dog's days must be numbered the way Mrs. Bradeen let it wander the streets without supervision. But how could the killer have known about that?

Don't you get it, Landon? They know your neighborhood. They know your house. They know everything. About. You.

Too late I considered that I should have gotten the license plate number. Should have written the numbers down. But then, why bother? Who would I call? Certainly not Galotta.

"Landon? Landon!"

The tinny voice, repeating my name, sounded miles away. I'd forgotten about the phone and numbly pressed it to my ear. In almost a whisper, I said, "I'm here."

"Do you understand now that we mean business?"

"Yes."

"We're not playing games here. So you might as well relax and just accept your new normal. Accept that we're in control now."

Accept that you'll crush me like a Dixie cup once you're done using me?

"No more funny business—got it? Next time it'll be more than a dog lying in the street."

The line went dead.

I collapsed on the couch and ran fingers through my hair, spent and ashamed by my sweating, by my shaking. And angry that I couldn't do something more, finding myself powerless and unable to fight back. And humiliated that the man on the phone could crumble my defenses so quickly and push me into begging mode.

Through the window seeped Mrs. Bradeen's wail. She'd made the grisly discovery. With her husband in the nursing home, that dog had been her constant companion. Her only source of love and support. I clenched the phone in my lap.

How dare they!

This situation was unacceptable. No one should have this kind of power over anyone. I couldn't live like this. There had to be a way of escape from this trap, but what could I do?

Getting up, I headed to the dining room, eying the hole in the ceiling tile.

You like to watch? Fine. I'll give you a good show you won't forget. You can't read my mind, but that's precisely why you'll fail. Because you have no idea what I'm planning.

So, Landon, what are you planning?

I had no idea. At least, not yet.

Part 3
Way of Escape

Chapter 24

Wednesday, October 28
Iron Valley, Michigan

The gray-headed, stooped man at Peking Gardens helped Mom with her chair. "You have wonderful time here, yes? We happy to have you today, famous Mr. Jeffers."

"Thanks, Mr. Chen." I took the chair at the small, round table across from my mom and ignored the stares and whispers. "We'll both have the buffet, please."

"Very good, yes." Mr. Chen bobbed his head and pressed both hands together as if offering a prayer to his ancestors. Would he next kiss my shoes? "So honored to serve Mr. Jeffers today. Would it happen to be Mr. Jeffers's birthday?"

"No, nothing like that."

Mr. Chen spread his hands, eyebrows hiked. "No special occasion?"

"No, I'm just taking my mom out for lunch."

His serious expression softened and gleamed with approval. "Ah, so. Very good. We very honored." When Mr. Chen smiled, his whole face split in half. "Too bad we have no piano. Mr. Landon could play for his lunch, yes? Play piano much better than he wait on tables."

He burst into laughter, his whole body shaking, caught up in the mirth as if he'd told the funniest joke in the world. Which it wasn't.

I'd been a waiter here years ago back when I'd needed a summer job between years in college. No need to be a spoilsport. I gave Mr. Chen my biggest smile—and wished he'd go far, far away. "Yes, I'm much better at playing the piano."

Mr. Chen backed away, and a pretty Asian waitress took our orders and asked what we wanted to drink. We chose water with slices of lemon, though I ached for a Mountain Dew or something much stronger. After she left, we filled our plates from the steaming, fragrant buffet; I let Mom tell me what I could and couldn't eat and returned to our table. Mom prayed the perfunctory blessing over the meal.

Immediately after the prayer, I sensed someone at my elbow. A teen girl, her face an invasion of acne, asked for my signature with a pleading expression. While I acquiesced and signed a napkin, of all things, she prattled on and on about how much she loved my music. I thanked her for being such a loyal fan, and she backed away, like I was a king and she couldn't show me her backside.

Being a celebrity isn't what people think. It means being interrupted at all hours by well-meaning people who want to grovel in your presence, like you're some kind of god who could sprinkle the pixie dust of success on them if only they'd stoop a little lower. I had no patience for this kind of attention today. If this proved to be only the prelude to greater things to come, we'd get our food to go and enjoy it at home.

Except we couldn't leave today. Not if I wanted my plan to work.

"It sure was thoughtful of you to take me out to lunch today." Mom cocked her head with a pleasant look. "It's not even my birthday."

"I know, but sometimes it's important just to get out and enjoy a treat once in a while."

She patted the wavy, black hair she'd curled just for the occasion. The brown dress with the fancy, white embroidery around the collar set off the dark, hazel hue of her eyes. Burgundy diamond earrings dangled from her tiny lobes. She looked prettier than I'd seen her in years; Dad would have been pleased.

Truth be told, I was famished but not for steamed veggies and baked salmon on a simple bed of wild rice. I eyed her Szechuan beef and General Tso's chicken, my mouth watering. Surely an MSG fest awaited whoever sank his or her fork into the delicacies, but on days like this one, I simply didn't care. Maybe if I could think of a reason to encourage her use of the ladies' room, I could snatch a morsel.

Oriental music serenaded us from pinhole ceiling speakers. Skimming the crowd, I searched for anyone unusual, anything out of place. Might someone, beyond celebrity stalkers, be watching us even here? Someone must be, but I didn't see anything or anyone out of the ordinary to arouse my suspicions.

"Mom, you deserve it after welcoming me back into your home and taking care of me," I said. "Treating you once in a while is the least I can do." In fact, I considered with a stab of guilt, I probably should have taken her out sooner.

She patted my hand. "It's not really like you need much taking care of, Landy. You're doing great, all things considered."

True. Other than balance issues and the cane dependence—I could live with the loss of peripheral vision—I had much to be grateful for. But Korovin's threat still hummed in my brain. If I didn't cooperate with the game plan, the puppet master could turn the cancer valve back on.

A day had passed since my unsettling visit with Officer Galotta, and nothing but virtual memories had disturbed my sleep. The windows of my bedroom hadn't been disturbed, and the door had been locked from the outside (thanks to my mom's help). From what I could tell, I hadn't been up for any nocturnal missions, at least not lately.

But surely this relative peace couldn't continue, not with the puppet master's plans for me lingering on the horizon. What did he have in mind? Blow up the Pentagon? Assassinate the president of the United States? I didn't intend to just wait around until I did something worse than stab a jogging stranger, which had been bad enough. Time to go on the offensive.

In fact, I couldn't help glancing at my watch and feeling like time must be running out.

Mom graced me with concerned eyes. "Do you need to go somewhere?"

"Sorry, just a bad habit. Where do I need to be? Nowhere." I had no concerts. No career. No life. I forced a smile. "I'm fine."

"Well, you've hardly touched your food, Landy. And honestly, I think it would be okay for you to have some of that roast chicken on a stick. Monosodium glutamate is definitely not on your friend list, but I doubt it would kill you to have a little bit occasionally."

But what I'm about to do just might get both of us killed.

Did I have the nerve to go through with my plan?

"Well, we're all going to die eventually anyhow, right?" I forced a chuckle, something I did only when the nerves got to me and I didn't know what else to say—and she knew it. The laugh must have sounded even hollower in her ears than it did in mine.

The worry lines around her mouth deepened. "Is everything okay? You haven't been yourself for a few days. You seem worried about something. Are you feeling sick?"

Ah. My cue.

"Actually, I've been having a few … um … regularity issues lately. In fact, I need to use the men's room, if you'll excuse me." Rising, I reached for my cane.

She rose to help me, but I held out a hand. "No, Mom, I'm good. Enjoy yourself. I'll be right back." I hobbled away and waited until I'd passed beyond view before brushing aside the sweat that stippled my forehead. I'd been trying so hard to pretend everything must be okay, but Mom knew me too well. I was a pianist, not an actor. How much longer could I keep up this act?

I also couldn't help feeling guilty. Of course, I loved my mom, but taking her out for lunch hadn't been the altruistic gesture she might have supposed. Then again, if this worked out, I might be able to keep her safe.

Maneuvering toward the bathroom, I took a quick detour into the familiar, smelly kitchen. The chefs, too busy arguing in Chinese and trying to keep up with the noonday crowd, didn't notice me. I slipped into the familiar walk-in freezer.

Amid rows of boxed teriyaki sauce packets and bags of frozen chow mein and shrimp, I pulled out the pad of paper and hurriedly scribbled down two versions of the same message.

If the puppet master controlled the brain implant wirelessly, the freezer's steel plate, stainless-steel panels, insulated with polyurethane foam, would surely block any signals. Which meant I would be virtually undetectable by GPS, Wi-Fi, or anything else that might track me.

Hurry, Landon. Move.

I had only minutes before Officer Galotta or one of his thugs received the emergency phone call that I'd disappeared from the grid and needed to be tracked down.

Just shy of the last few symbols, a girl, not a day over thirteen, rushed into the walk-in freezer, presumably on a mission for more ingredients. She gasped, eyes rounding.

I flashed her a smile. "Oh. Hello."

She hustled out of there.

Great. Time to move.

Finishing, I slid the copies into their predetermined locations and headed out of the freezer, nearly colliding with Mr. Chen. The scared girl slunk at his elbow.

"Landon?" His expression revealed more confusion than condemnation. "What you doing here?"

I slung an arm across his shoulders like we were old buddies. "Just taking a look at my stomping grounds. Just remembering old times."

The tension evaporated, and Mr. Chin smiled. "Ah, so. Old times. Good to remember, yes?"

***

Mom had been good friends with Jade's dad for years, so it wasn't unusual for her to drop by their house with a basketful of goodies, including some of Mom's favorite jams. That was our next stop after lunch, but I questioned whether we would reach our destination when we nearly collided with Officer Galotta on our way out of Peking Gardens.

"Hello, Mrs. Jeffers. Landon." He tipped his head with a warm smile like he'd momentarily stepped out of Mayberry. But the comparison ended there.

Every muscle in my body tightened at the sight of him and the memory of our last meeting. His horrifying words. His mother's headstone in the cemetery.

"I'm sorry to interrupt your day," he said more to my mom than to me, his voice slathered in politeness. "Just wondered if I could chat with Landon for a minute … privately."

Mom lingered by the van, expression wary, while I followed Galotta down the sidewalk toward the dumpster behind the restaurant. When we'd slipped beyond eyeshot, Galotta pressed his hands against my chest and shoved me until my back slammed into the building. My cane clattered to the cement.

"What are you up to, Landon?"

I kept a poker face. "What do you mean?"

"That was an interesting trip to the men's room. Problem is, you never even went in there. Nice little detour to the kitchen's walk-in freezer. What were you doing in there?"

The fact that the freezer had worked and that Galotta didn't know my secret only emboldened me. "What—you guys don't know? I thought you could see everything I—"

His fist plowed into my stomach. I gasped and doubled over, for a moment unable to breathe.

Galotta muttered a few colorful words. "I knew the first time we met that you were going to be trouble. This going-rogue business has gotta stop."

Hands on my knees, I feared I might lose everything I'd just eaten. Then the pain eased up, but when I straightened, Galotta whipped me around and slammed my torso against the building, yanking my arms painfully behind me. Something cool pressed against the back of my head. The nose of his handgun?

127

"What. Were. You. Doing. In the freezer?"

During our last encounter, he'd crumbled my defenses. He wouldn't be so successful today. I fought to keep the panic out of my voice.

"What are you going to do? Kill me in broad daylight? My mom knows I'm back here."

A jab of the gun's cold steel against my skull made me wince. "I could easily kill you and then her too."

"You'd draw a crowd. Everybody would know you did it. Then I'd be dead, and so much for your friends' big plans for me. You really want to be in the newspapers as the cop who killed Landon Jeffers in cold blood?"

Rage sizzled in his voice. "Answer my question. Otherwise your mom has a heart attack in five minutes. Don't think I can't do it."

Telling him the truth wasn't an option. This proved to be my only way of escape—no plan B existed—so I had to stay calm and think my way out of this one.

Could he really cause Mom to have a heart attack? Doubtful. Unless Mom had become a drone like me. But she hadn't.

"Like I told Mr. Chen—and as I'm sure you overheard—I was just remembering old times. I used to be a waiter at—"

"For two summers between years in college—yes, I know. Have you forgotten we know everything about you?"

No, not everything.

Galotta growled impatiently. He knew he couldn't shoot me. "Okay, put your hands on the back of your head. Spread your elbows."

When I complied, he jammed the gun into my back with one hand while his other searched my pockets. He yanked out my wallet, my comb, some breath mints. The important piece of paper crinkled in his hand.

"Well, well," he said. "What have we got here?"

Remaining silent, I waited.

Hot breath crawled down my neck. "What do these symbols mean?"

"What—a guy can't even doodle?"

Galotta cursed. "Turn around."

I faced him, though my chest quivered.

His eyeballs resembled dead things somebody had dug up from a grave. He thrust a finger in my face. "Stop jerking my chain. Do you understand me?"

Nothing but empty threats, just as I'd expected.

Imitating his stone-cold expression didn't prove too hard. I had a good teacher.

Weary-faced, like he knew he'd been beaten, Galotta returned everything to me except the doodle paper. He handed me my cane with care—such a gentleman. "Okay, you can go. No more funny business, Landon. Don't forget—we're watching."

Scare tactics. Nothing but intimidation. And I'd called his bluff. He couldn't kill me, not if the puppet master had big plans. Do that, and he'd be dead too.

When I turned to leave, he said, "By the way, your mom's life doesn't mean diddly to us. How much does it mean to you?"

Chapter 25

Wednesday, October 28
Iron Valley, Michigan

"What was *that* all about?"

"Nothing, Mom. Can we just go?"

In the van she started the engine but didn't put it in gear. Instead, she just stared at me. "Landon, what on earth is going on? What did Officer Galotta want with you?"

Of course she'd be a problem—no question. She'd ask one too many questions and get herself killed. "I—I can't tell you."

I fiddled with my right penny loafer until my foot was firmly planted in it again, and I clutched the slip of paper, the second copy. There hadn't been time to check the van, but it had probably been bugged like the house. What could I tell her without hurting her?

"Something *is* going on, isn't it?" she said.

"I'll explain later. I promise."

"Why can't you tell me now?"

I studied the busy highway through the windshield. "Please, Mom, just let it go. Believe me, it's for your own good. When I'm able to explain what's going on, I'll let you know."

She relented. Five minutes later—five minutes of unnatural silence while she processed the situation—she pulled in front of Jade's dad's house.

The place had been stamped in my memory: the dirty, yellow siding; the white shutters; the front porch that sagged to one side like someone had fallen and lain there far too long. Except what I glimpsed didn't resemble the ramshackle place at all; somebody had poured some cash into the place, and it appeared pristine. I pondered whether somebody had also cleaned out that old attic where Jade, Tyler Acorn, and I used to play. Used to engage in secret missions with G. I. Joe dolls, secret codes, and a nearly all-powerful nemesis lurking somewhere in the neighborhood, determined to stop us.

131

Lately, old photos had brought more of those days back to me. Oh, the fun times we'd shared. Carefree. Void of any real danger.

The question was, would Jade recall any of that chapter of our lives? A lot depended on her memories, which I hoped might be better than mine.

I offered to take the basket to the front door. The task would have been easier for Mom, but we'd both agreed that I should live normally when possible, even though errands like this one took more time and effort on my wobbly legs.

Perhaps if I acted fast and kept my gaze fixed on her face, whoever kept an eye on us would never see me slip the second doodle note, the one from my shoe, into the basket. A risk I had to take if there was any prayer of this plan working.

Jade must have had the afternoon off because she waited at the screen door long before I arrived. "Hey, this is a pleasant surprise. I see you took my advice about getting your exercise."

"Yeah, well, it keeps me moving and on my feet." I held out the basket. "This is for your dad."

"Of course. How sweet." She opened the screen door to accept the gift.

At the moment she reached for it, I changed my mind. Instead of slipping the note into the basket, I placed it directly into her hand but kept my focus on her face. Kept those cameras, if they existed, pointed where they would cause the least trouble.

"What's this?" She glanced down, the door levered against her hip.

Eyeballs still glued to her face, I said, "Oh, you know, fancy jams and some cranberry bread, your dad's favorite."

"No, I mean this." She held up my folded note.

Stiffening, I refused to look at it. "A note from my mom to your dad, of course, but you'll need to translate it for him." I silenced her *What do you mean?* look with, "You know, seeing you again after all these years has brought back a lot of memories of when we were kids. Remember the old clubhouse in the woods?"

My deflection worked. She nodded with a half-smile, apparently not puzzled by my abrupt shift in topic. "You mean that old treehouse that would have fallen apart if Tyler's dad hadn't repaired it?"

"Yeah. And Joey Bartholomew and his friends had their own treehouse on the other side of the woods. Remember our pretend battles? Us against them?"

Jade leaned against the jamb, arms folded, a smug grin teasing her lips. I'd forgotten how stunning her blue eyes could be in the right light. "I'm not so sure how *pretend* they were. Getting shot in the rear end by a BB gun doesn't exactly tickle, you know."

"But remember, that wasn't my fault. Did Tyler tell you it was? He said the BB gun wasn't loaded. I was just supposed to swing it around and act tough. I had no idea it would go off in your direction."

The corner of her mouth rose. "Hmm. But it was *your* BB gun, if I recall correctly. *You* were the one who was supposed to make sure it wasn't loaded."

Excellent. She mastered the memories well enough to surprise me.

I chuckled. "Remember all our secret slogans?"

"You mean like, 'I smell something rotten in Denmark' from Shakespeare?"

"Yep, that's *exactly* what I mean. And don't forget our secret code." We locked eyes for a meaningful beat.

Her reminiscent look morphed into one of puzzlement. "Landon?"

"Well, hey, gotta go. Been fun chatting with you." Turning, I began hobbling down the sidewalk toward the van, cane clattering.

"Landon, is everything okay?" she called to my back.

"Just fine," I called to her. "Don't forget to read that note to your dad, okay?"

"Of course." Uncertainty hovered in her vocal inflection. "Be sure to tell your mom thank you."

"I will. See you at therapy tomorrow. It is tomorrow morning, right?" Glancing back, I caught her nod. "And Jade"—I did a full turn and held her gaze, just long enough for a hummingbird to dash lickety-split to one of the feeders before zipping away—"something is definitely rotten in Denmark."

***

That night, two text messages awaited me. The first came from Celeste.

> Hey, u doin ok? Haven't heard from u lately. Give me a call. Miss u.

Why couldn't she take a hint? I wasn't interested. Amee's text came next:

Hey, maestro! Dan likes three out of the five songs from that demo you sent for Songs from the Living Room. Are you doing okay? The piano playing is always great, but … well, I'll just say it. These are some pretty depressing songs on here. There's a difference between sentimental and I'm-going-to-go-slit-my-wrists. Sorry if I'm too blunt. Give me a call and think HAPPY thoughts!

Oh brother. Of course my latest songs were … well … a bit different from my normal stuff. I had a lot on my mind these days.

Hugging the pillow, I waited for the two sleeping pills, provided by Mom, to do their business. Perhaps I'd experience another uneventful night—a blessing from God, as Mom put it, with the windows and doors locked.

What would the puppet master require of me next? Each day brought me closer to another inevitable march toward my next mission of violence. What more could I do until I found the keys of freedom but maintain the status quo? Until either the puppet master or I took the next step?

I intended to be first in line.

The message I'd written to Jade in secret code flared in my mind. She'd scrawled the symbols, based on *The Lord of the Rings*, in so many old notebooks that she couldn't have forgotten them. In the message I'd told her not to call me, and she hadn't. Surely she'd deciphered the rest by now. Otherwise she would have called, confused.

Tomorrow held the key. If Jade comprehended my note, then the morning would change everything.

Staring at the ceiling, I prayed to a God I wasn't even sure I understood. But perhaps he knew me.

God, you will help see this through, won't you? If not for me, for Jade and my mom at least. I hate putting them in danger, but what choice do I have if I want to keep them safe? I can't do this on my own.

Talking to God gave me a funny feeling. At least I could talk to him, and the puppet master couldn't hear. This knowledge filled me with glee.

That night, no moon gleamed outside my window. For quite a while, I drifted on a restful eddy of nothingness. Even the small movie screen in the corners of my eyes remained pitch black as if a light had gone out deep in my soul.

But then the slightest change occurred there, as if God had said, "Let there be light." That pinprick grew and swelled, filling my vision until it glowed as hot and bright as the noonday sun. It became blinding when it enveloped me. Forcing me to squint, turn my face away, and glide more deeply into the past than ever before …

Chapter 26

Monday, September 27, 1982
Iron Valley, Michigan

For weeks I'd been practicing *Clair De Lune* for my next competition piece. It was Jade's favorite song, someone had told me, and I wanted her to be the first to hear it. But where could she be?

Mom hovered in the doorway of the storage room at school, weariness etched on her face. "C'mon, Landon, we gotta go. It's late."

"But she was supposed to be here. She promised."

"Sometimes people can't keep their promises. Maybe something came up to prevent her."

Something like what? Had her father gotten hurt or killed?

I rose from the piano and grabbed the sheet music. Following her to the parking lot, I glanced to the west. A spectacular sunset shimmered on the horizon, countering the uneasiness that pickled in my gut. "Can I call Jade when we get home?"

Mom agreed, but later when I called the Hamiltons, no one answered. After supper, I grabbed my bike and arrived at Jade's house in five minutes, a cop car parked in the driveway. Something *was* wrong.

A mustached policeman answered my knock, his expression solemn. "Yes?"

"Is Jade Hamilton home?"

"Son, this isn't really a good time. Maybe if you—"

Someone or something must have interrupted him because he disappeared and left me standing there, unsure what to do. After a murmur of voices from inside, he returned, gave me an apologetic nod, and opened the door to let me in. Jade must have given the okay, said I was a friend.

I edged into the living room, where she and her dad occupied the couch, her face downcast. Thank God he was okay. But if her dad was fine, what could be the problem? When would someone tell me?

Two cops, one of whom had let me in, brushed past me on their way to the door. Had I interrupted them? The air in the room hung heavy like a humid summer day just moments before a refreshing thunderstorm. I couldn't shake my uneasiness. Maybe I shouldn't have come. I didn't wish to intrude, but if Jade was in trouble …

Her dad clutched her hand, and she stared at the Kleenex box on the coffee table with a blank expression, not even acknowledging me. There were no tears. No hysterics. Just pure numbness. A fly buzzed against the window, unable to find its way out.

Someone tell me what's going on!

Jade rose and strode toward me, head bowed. The aroma of strawberries filled my nostrils. She wouldn't look at me. "I'm glad you're here, Landon."

"What's going on?" I whispered.

She reached into her pocket and handed me the photograph of a woman, the same snapshot I'd found in the grass at the playground on the day we met. The blonde woman's bright-red lips stretched in a mischievous smile.

Jade sniffed. "You're right. This *is* my mom."

"What's wrong? Did something happen to her?"

She didn't answer. Or couldn't. Her hand flew to her mouth, and she whirled, rushing away down the hallway. A door slammed, echoing through the house.

I turned to Mr. Hamilton, a tall, big-boned man with reddish curls and the largest Adam's apple I'd ever seen. He slouched on the faded green couch, his numb expression looking right through me. I perched on the chair across from him.

Somehow I sensed he needed me. Who wants to be alone at a time like this? Whatever had happened, it must be bad.

Not until now did I observe the wall plaque and the many service medals on colored ribbons dangling from it, glistening in the half-light, honoring his war service. He'd seen his share of death in Vietnam, I'd heard, but even still, something terrible had slammed into him now, and he was trying to hold onto … something. He gripped a black Bible with gilded pages in both hands, knuckles white, like he drew strength from its contents through the leather.

"Mr. Hamilton, what's wrong? Did something happen to"—I almost said, "your wife," but even at my young age, I sensed it would be a mistake—"Jade's mom?"

His Adam's apple bobbed. Licking his lips, he focused on the wall behind me. On a place of nothingness that distanced him from the question reflected in my face. Moisture edged his eyes. "Somebody broke into her house while Jade's stepdad was on a business trip. And the police … they—they found her … and …"

He shrugged helplessly, closed his mouth, opened it. Couldn't seem to get the words out. His hands, gripping the Bible, began to tremble, like he might lose control and throw it somewhere … at someone …

"What do you mean, they found her?" I said.

His glistening eyes met mine. "Son, somebody murdered her."

Chapter 27

Present day
Thursday, October 29
Iron Valley, Michigan

"Landon? Landon, wake up."

I pushed away the probing hands and rolled over, embracing the comforter, seeking to return to the bliss of ignorance.

The annoying hands jostled me again. "Landy, you've been asleep too long. I never should have given you those sleeping pills."

Rolling onto my back, I groaned. Sunshine from the window thrust needle-sharp pinpricks of light at me. I squinted and twisted my face away. If I kept sleeping, I didn't need to worry about what might go wrong today. About how my plans could fall apart and hurt those I loved.

"Landy, you need to wake up. You've slept the morning away, and Jade's here."

Jade.

Recall swept over me: her face pinched with shock when she grappled with news about her mother's murder. The past so fresh from my dream I could almost taste it.

"What? She's here now?" Heavy eyelids blinked, unmoving like sludge. My head must have spent the night in the washing machine, spinning around and around and—

"Your physical therapy. Don't you remember? Jade's here for your appointment."

Sitting up, I scrubbed my hands across my whiskery face. "What time is it?"

"It's after ten a.m., and she's waiting. *Now.*"

Wow. I'd overslept big-time. At least I'd gotten my rest; I'd need it today. "Okay, I'm getting up."

"That would be nice."

"Tell her I'll be right there."

She departed.

I scanned the room. No blood. The Dr. Jekyll and Mr. Hyde syndrome had granted me another night's reprieve. Maybe I'd soon be free of these shackles for good.

Swinging my legs to the floor, I gauged my questionable balance. Ready or not, it was game time.

***

Jade rose from the couch, her face pale with droopy eyelids. She must have translated my note just fine. Confirmation appeared in the green gym bag stationed on the floor beside her tiny shoes; she'd brought what I requested.

"Landon is so sorry he's late this morning." Mom aimed an apologetic look at Jade. "He doesn't usually oversleep like this."

"That's okay." Jade eyed me. "Sleep is good for you, but you haven't even eaten your breakfast yet. Should we reschedule?"

"N-no, that's okay," I said, our eyes locking. If my plan had any hope of taking place, it needed to happen now. But I rather felt like Bilbo Baggins, about to set off on a grand adventure without even my handkerchief.

Breakfast, at least, would have been nice, but there simply wasn't time … because as soon as Jade entered the room, she'd unknowingly wound a ticking bomb.

"It's okay," Mom said. "I'll just fix him some eggs later."

Jade nodded. "Eggs are healthy, though actually"—she nailed me with a meaningful glance—"I'd rather eat lasagna."

The oddness of her words jolted me, but then the memory rushed back. We'd once used that line from the cartoon character Garfield as another secret code. It meant things were okay but could be better.

Translation: She'd worked out the meaning of the coded message. If whatever I had in mind needed to happen now, she was on board.

Not intending to sleep so long, I now felt rushed to execute my plan—and rushing rarely proved to be a good idea—but it had to be now if we had any prayer of escape. I only prayed my mom would accept my startling news, so suddenly coming out of the blue. But first I had to be sure.

"Did you bring your cell phone?" I said to Jade. In response to her nod, I said, "Why don't you test it? Try to call someone. Anyone."

Mom lingered at my side, eyebrows raised. "What's going on here?"

"It's okay, Mom. Remember when I told you I'd explain what had happened with Officer Galotta yesterday? I'm about to make good on my promise."

Jade punched in the numbers and pressed the phone to her ear. "Nothing. I just get dead air."

The wireless signal jammer I'd asked her to borrow from her techie cousin must be working. But I was still taking a risk. According to my theory, if the jammer blocked cell phone calls, it would also stop whatever the puppet master used to connect to my implant.

Galotta's past words echoed back. *Until you find a way to amputate your head, you're pretty much stuck.*

Not quite. If I blocked the controlling signal, amputation became unnecessary. This plan might work after all.

But one important problem remained. If I'd somehow evaded the puppet master's observation and control, then he surely knew by now I'd gone dark—which meant we had mere minutes to get out of here before Galotta or somebody else in the network showed up.

"Mom, I have a surprise for you."

"Well, what is it? I can tell something strange is going on." Her gaze bounced between us, waiting for the punch line, a fake smile frozen on her face.

"More than anything else," I said, "I need you to trust me right now."

"Of course, Landy. I've always trusted you."

A deep breath filled my lungs. "We need to go on a road trip. We need to get in your van and drive away. Now."

Mom blinked. "And go where?"

"That's part of the surprise."

"For how long?"

"I don't know." I decided to tell her the truth. "We may never come back."

"What!?" She ogled me like I'd slid into the waiting arms of insanity. *Stink!*

I should have waited until we were well on our way before delivering the punch line. "Look, I can't explain right now. There isn't time. You just have to trust me."

She backed away, lips pressed together. "What if I don't want to go?"

This was the response I'd feared. "You don't really have a choice. If you stay, they could hurt you to try to get to me."

"They?"

My watch shouted at me. How many minutes had passed since Jade showed up with the jammer? Three minutes? Four?

I nudged Mom toward the door. "I can explain everything while you drive."

She gave me a slow nod while reaching for her purse.

Compliance supplied all I cared about at this point. Turning toward Jade, I reached for the gym bag. "Thanks for following my instructions and bringing what I requested. You'd better call a taxi. I wouldn't stick around here if I were you."

Jade's eyes rounded. "You mean, this isn't some kind of joke?"

"Um, no joke. I'm dead serious. I wish I could explain, but there isn't—"

"If you're in some kind of danger, then I'm coming too."

"What?"

"When those looking for you find out I helped you get away, won't they come after me too?"

Later, she'd surely change her mind. "All right. Fine. I'll explain everything on the road. Then you can decide if you really want to come along. Besides, don't you have to work today? And what about Henry?"

Her son, the blond-headed boy at church.

"I can always take a few personal days, and my dad can look after Henry when he's not in school. He does that a lot anyhow."

Mom swung toward the hallway leading to her bedroom. "I need to pack."

My fingers clamped around her arm. "Mom, there isn't time. We have to go right now! That cop—Officer Galotta—he's not who you think he is. He's probably on his way here right now to stop us."

Mom's eyebrows pinched together in a frown. "But he's the police. We shouldn't run from the police."

I grabbed her arms and forced her to face me. "Mom, I don't think you understand. He killed his own mother. Is that what you want him to do to you?"

Chapter 28

Thursday, October 29
Iron Valley, Michigan

Like he did each morning, Ray Galotta surrendered to his death wish. He rose at the first blush of the rising sun, stood at attention before the full-length mirror in his T-shirt and boxers, and raised the Magnum 357 to his right temple. He neither trembled nor broke a sweat when he pulled the trigger.

Click.

Of course, nothing happened, but he'd attempted it anyhow. Just like he'd tried so many times before. Maybe someday the unexpected would happen, and he'd experience the blessed release he'd long been seeking.

Maybe I'll see Sylvia again.

Sinking to the edge of the bed, he closed his eyes. Pictured her lips brushing his, her arms pulling him close, her love taking him far, far away from this pointlessness. Which exactly described his life now.

While enjoying a late breakfast on his morning off, he contemplated his impossible situation. Sometime in the night, those controlling his brain had awoken him and made him remove the bullets from the gun before wiping his memory clean of the event, something akin to an eraser kissing a chalkboard.

He'd reloaded the gun just before bed—he knew he had. But the pattern repeated itself each morning, thus being cheated from death. This hindrance from being set free from this nightmare he called life.

They won't even let me kill myself, for crying out—

His eyes widened. Pupils dilated. An alert flared across the message center of his central nervous system. He needed neither a phone call nor a text message to know.

Landon Jeffers had disappeared from the grid. That meant only one thing.

He's making a run for it.

Galotta smiled.

Let the hunt begin.

Chapter 29

Thursday, October 29
Iron Valley, Michigan

Mom climbed behind the wheel of the Chrysler Town and Country, expression dazed, and cranked the engine while I rode shotgun and Jade took a seat in the back. The garage door rolled up, and Mom backed out. Dark windows peered at us like sad, lifeless eyes, as if the house acknowledged we were abandoning it.

Mom hit the brakes hard. "The coffee maker! I think I left it on."

My fingers encircled her arm. "Leave it. We have to go. Now."

She backed out the rest of the way and poured on the gas. The van shot forward.

Sucking in a deep breath, I let it linger in my chest. Would we ever come back to this place? To my new music studio? Already I longed to touch those ivory keys.

I studied the silent, deserted street. It was almost as if everyone knew evil was coming and had chosen to hide behind locked doors and drawn drapes. The sky seeped a strange color of foreboding slate gray; the forecast promised rain—lots of it. In the distance, a fork of lightning zigzagged to earth.

In the rearview mirror, the house receded in the distance. I told Mom to take us to the bank. "I need to withdraw some cash. Think they'll let me take out a hundred thousand?"

Her head whipped toward me. "Maybe in cities you can get away with doing that, but local banks don't have that kind of cash on hand."

"We'll need to live on cash for a while."

She braked and started turning around.

"What are you doing?" I said.

"Remember all those checks you used to send me? Well, I'm sorta like Millie West. I don't trust banks either, so I cashed them and—"

"Don't tell me you've been keeping that money under your mattress."

She flashed a sheepish grin. "Should have a pretty nice nest egg by now but not a hundred grand."

Pulling alongside the curb, she raced inside the house with her purse; back in three minutes, she hit the gas, and we were on the move again.

Soon the place would be crawling with cops, trying to track me down after Galotta released evidence about the stabbing and made me a wanted fugitive. Then he'd tap into whatever resources he had, which were considerable, to track me down.

If only we'd left immediately and not wasted precious minutes on explanations and the cash grab. We could have been miles away by now, but at least part of the burden had been lifted off my shoulders. At least at this moment, the first time in a long while, I experienced the sensation of being a free man.

And I had friends to help me. I didn't need to carry this burden alone.

As we sped farther away, the tightness in my chest loosened by degrees. No trace of Galotta or other police anywhere. But something didn't sit right. Our exit had been too neat, too easy. Would they really let us slip away without resistance?

Jade sat ramrod straight on her seat. "Um, Landon, your note left a lot of unanswered questions. So somebody's trying to track you, like, for real?"

"Yeah, for real."

"Okay. And are you sure they can't track you now?"

"No, but the last time I deviated from their plan, they gave me a headache so bad it knocked me to my knees. I'm good so far."

"Mmm, okay, but how could they give you a headache? You need to help me out here. I'm not sure I—"

"Well, it's a long story." Reaching for the gym bag, I unzipped it. A bright-green light glowed from a walkie-talkie-looking contraption inside. "So this is supposed to jam all wireless transmissions, huh?"

"That's what Wade said. And not just wireless. GPS, Wi-Fi. All of it. There's a second one in there too. That way one will still work if you need to switch batteries."

Smart.

I said, "If what Wade said is true, then it's also blocking any signals from the surveillance devices in this van."

Fear scurried across Jade's face like she'd been violated. "What are you talking about? You mean to tell me—"

"I'm pretty sure they bugged this van, too. They've been monitoring me at all times."

"Then why are we in here now?"

"Because we had to take this van—there was no other way to make a run for it." My gaze swept the van's interior, mind abuzz. "Do you mind giving me a hand? Let's look around and see what we can find."

Her eyes widened, fingertips pressed to her temples. "Um, Landon, this still isn't adding up for me. Why don't you start at the beginning."

Sometimes I'm single focused to a fault.

I left my seat, crawled into the back, and began searching without her help. "I thought at first that the puppet master must be looking through my eyes, but that didn't explain the camera I found in the dining room. If he was looking through my eyes, he wouldn't need cameras in the house, right?"

Jade sighed. "Landon, what *are* you talking about?"

I met her eyes. "So what exactly did you tell your cousin?"

"Just that I needed to borrow his jammers for a few days. That's all."

"You didn't tell him anything else?"

She gave me a pointed look. "No, Landon. I followed your instructions to the letter, just like you asked me to. I'm not stupid."

"Sorry, I didn't mean—"

She leaned closer until we were practically nose to nose. As usual, she smelled like strawberries, even after all these years. "Okay, enough already. I want to know what's going on. Why would a cop be coming after you? You'd better start talking, Landon, because I want some answers, like now."

"Well said, Jade." Mom nailed me with her eyes in the rearview mirror. "Start talking, Son. I want to know why I just abandoned my home of more than forty years to drive off to who-knows-where. This had better be good."

"Oh, it is, Mom. Believe me, it is." I held up a small, black device, about the size of a quarter, that had no reason to be hiding behind the side stereo speaker. While they stared at me, I dropped the surveillance device to the floor and stomped on it.

***

I told them everything, including my bizarre meeting with Officer Galotta, at least what I could remember with my spotty memory. The news proved to be too much to take in—I could tell that right away. Mom and Jade just stared at me, mouths open.

"You've gotta be kidding me," Mom said.

Jade raised her eyebrows. "This is some sick joke, right?"

"No, Jade, it isn't. I saw that black van speed away after running over Mrs. Bradeen's dog. I saw the photos of me stabbing that woman."

Jade shook her head. "I still don't get it. How could you possibly stab someone without knowing it?"

I splayed my hands. "Call it some kind of mind control. I don't know what else to say."

"It's your brain." Mom kept her focus glued to the road. "If somebody knows how to control it, they could make you do almost anything." She huffed. "Oh, I can't believe we trusted that Dr. Korovin. You mean, the whole time we thought he was operating on you and removing the tumor, he was really just putting something in your head so someone could track and control you?"

"No, Mom. He removed the tumor, all right. But he put something else in its place."

Air rushed out of her lips. "Oh, this is criminal. We should go to the police. Then again, we already tried that, didn't we?"

"We need to find somebody we can trust," I said, "somebody far away from this situation to help us. Maybe the FBI—I don't know."

Mom slammed her hand down on the steering wheel. What a sight to behold when she was ticked off. "Amee recommended Dr. Korovin. Do you think she's in on this too?"

Amee? I hadn't even considered her involvement. She *had* said Dr. Korovin could be trusted—and look at what had happened.

"I don't know. It doesn't matter." Now that I found myself on the run, I had no reason to contact Amee, unless she could help us somehow. But this suspicion didn't exactly make me brighten to the idea.

"You know," Mom said, "this whole thing reminds me of an episode of *I Love Lucy*. See, Lucy gets an intercom system and accidentally listens in on one of Ethel's private conversations. You bet it causes a lot of trouble. I guess that's the same sort of thing these bad men are doing to you."

"I guess so, Mom." Could it be she wasn't taking our situation seriously?

At the bank, I went in and returned five minutes later, one of the signal jammers protruding from my back pocket.

"Sure enough." The grin proved nearly impossible to suppress. "Their Wi-Fi was down the whole time I was in there. Should have seen those clerks scurrying around, trying to figure out what was wrong with their Internet connection."

Mom eyed the gym bag I'd taken with me. "What have you got in there?"

Unzipping the bag, I gave her and Jade a glimpse of the cash. "Do you think fifty grand will get us by for a while?"

Mom whistled. "Yeah, Son. Added to what I grabbed from under my mattress, which was about thirty thousand, that should be plenty." She steered the van out of the parking lot.

"From now on, we don't use credit cards. We live on a cash-only basis." I studied Jade, who peered out the window.

She started and looked at me with a hint of embarrassment as if I'd caught her napping. "What?"

"This is your last chance to get off this roller coaster. We can swing by your house and drop you off on our way out of town." But even as I said the words, what Galotta had told me about his fiancée, Sylvia, drifted back.

Jade turned back to the window as if ignoring me, but I knew better. She was taking it all in, all right, maybe a bit too much.

"Jade, this isn't one of our childhood games at the tree house with BB guns, okay? I don't want you getting hurt."

"I know." Front teeth came down on her bottom lip.

Would Galotta harm Jade if I let her go home? Or could she be putting herself in more danger by sticking with us? If only I knew the right path to take.

"Umm, Landy," Mom said, "where are we going? Right now we're heading east out of town."

The window resembled a picture frame of the city flashing by. I craned my neck. We were on Highway 2. A sign up ahead announced that US 141 South was fifty miles away.

No, Jade would be in greater danger by staying with us. Besides, her dad would be there to protect her, and he was more than capable. I swiveled back to her. "You should go home. Really. You can just tell them you didn't know what the jammer was for, which is true—you didn't. They can't possibly know how much you know."

She nodded reluctantly.

"Mom, we're taking Jade home."

But minutes later, when we cruised down her street and rounded a familiar bend, Jade groaned. "Oh no! We're too late."

Two police cars had parked in the small driveway in front of the Hamiltons' house.

Chapter 30

Thursday, October 29
Iron Valley, Michigan

L ightning zapped the tops of distant trees. Galotta raced to the Jeffers place and parked on the curb. The house stood dark and silent, seemingly deserted. Even as he rushed to the front door, he discerned he must be too late.

No one came to the door, not even Landon's mother.

He's taken her away for her own safety. Like a good son.

Which, he accepted with a stab of irony, embodied exactly what he would have done if only they'd given him the chance.

It was his day off. If he'd been monitoring the police frequency, he would have known, as he now guessed, that fellow cops had already come and gone. The moment Landon vanished from the grid, he'd released the photos and DNA evidence connecting Landon to the woman's stabbing. When his colleagues discovered Landon wasn't here, they'd begun looking for him elsewhere.

Galotta slid on gloves, pulled out a key for emergencies, and entered the deserted house. He paused in the silence of the vestibule and discerned only the perfunctory murmurs of an unoccupied house: the hum of the refrigerator in the kitchen, the tick of the grandfather clock in the corner of the living room.

The acrid aroma of something burning tainted the air. He strolled into the kitchen and turned off the coffee maker, the pot's bottom black. They'd been gone for a while.

Had he told Landon too much? Perhaps he shouldn't have mentioned what they'd done to Sylvia, what he'd been forced to do to his own mother. The information had made Landon only more desperate to run.

The famous pianist had shown himself to be more resourceful than he expected. He'd somehow found a way to block the wireless signals, which meant he must have some smart friends.

Landon had fled—but where?

What would I need if I were on the run?

Galotta ignored the police radio—too early to blow his cover just yet. He pulled out his cell phone and hit the speed dial. Susan, his personal grunt, picked up. He didn't waste time on pleasantries.

"Landon Jeffers. Freeze his assets. Now."

Fingernails clicked on a keyboard. "Too late. He just withdrew fifty grand."

His curse rent the silence. Landon displayed some smarts, but he could be smarter. "Jeffers's immediate family members—I want to know where they live. I want everything you've got."

"I'm already on it. He has no siblings." She listed aunts, uncles, and cousins living in Colorado Springs and Toledo.

"I want surveillance on all of them. ASAP."

"You got it."

"What about his father?"

"He's in a high-security psych ward in Marquette, Michigan. I didn't mention him for obvious reasons."

Of course, but wasn't his father part of all this? Could he help Landon? Impossible. He couldn't even tie his own shoes.

"Anybody else?" he said.

"No, sir."

"Any clue yet on how Landon went dark?" Galotta said. "He must have had help." There'd be a full investigation before heads rolled, but these things took time.

"It's too early to say. All video and audio surveillance footage is being reviewed now. One interesting tidbit. He had a physical therapy appointment around the same time we lost his signal."

"Who's his therapist?"

"Jade Hamilton, a friend for many years. The police are looking for her too. She's also missing."

Ah, yes. Jade.

They had a rather thick dossier on her; her connection to Landon and his family was by no means small. Who else would Landon turn to but a childhood friend?

"I want surveillance on her family too."

"Beginning the process now."

He told her to be on standby for further instructions and clicked off, his gaze roving the backyard through kitchen windows.

Yes, Landon, run. Run as fast as you can. But you'll soon discover that it's never far or fast enough.

He drew in a deep, calming breath. In a way he couldn't help admiring the celebrity pianist and his heroic escape. At least he possessed noble motives; trying to save his mother aroused a pang of envy.

Then came another reason to admire him. If Landon got away and worse came to worst, he, Galotta, would be guilty of gross negligence. He'd no longer need to play Russian roulette each morning. When they terminated him, he'd have his one-way ticket out of his mess.

This living at the end of a very tight leash would be over. He and Sylvia would be together forever. Wasn't that what he wanted more than anything?

Yes, God, please. Just end this.

If free, he'd never need to eliminate another innocent man or woman on the run for dear life again, like Landon attempted to do now. Goodness, how he'd watched them run. Right into their awaiting graves.

But no, not yet. He still had a few chips to play in this game before it was all over. And if he made the right choice, he might actually come out ahead.

Chapter 31

Thursday, October 29
Iron Valley, Michigan

When Mom braked, I said, "No, no. Just keep going. We don't want to attract attention."

Mom eased down on the gas, and the van continued rolling down the street just like any other passing vehicle. Nothing to see here. At the Hamiltons', the cops were probably grilling Jade's dad and looking for answers he couldn't give. But they'd surely be on the lookout for me too.

Jade's voice quaked. "How could they possibly know about me?"

I kept my head down—no time to be careless. "I don't know. Maybe Galotta saw me pass you that note with the secret code. Maybe they were suspicious all along. Then when you arrived at the house and they lost my wireless signal, you were the logical link."

Now that we'd driven well past the house, I straightened. "Jade, you can still go home. We can drop you off at the next block, and you can walk the rest of the way. Just tell them the truth. You didn't know anything."

She wagged her head. "Nope. I'm staying. I don't turn my back on friends when they need my help."

I wasn't going to argue with her, though I wasn't sure how she could help our situation. But I knew her pretty well by now. Once she made her mind up about something, good luck changing it.

My tense shoulders and neck relaxed more the farther we eased down the street. So far so good, but could we really get away so easily? Surely Galotta knew our only possible means of exit had to be my mom's van. Wouldn't everyone be out looking for it?

We had to ditch the van and find something else in a hurry. The longer we stayed in this vehicle, the less chance we had of getting beyond the city limits.

"Uh, Landy, we might have trouble." Mom peered into the rearview mirror, face stricken.

I spun. In the distance, a police cruiser pulled out of Jade's driveway and steered toward us, maybe twenty car lengths away, but still …

The painful jab of Galotta's gun pressed against my head leaped to mind.

"Just stay calm," I told her. "Drive like you normally would."

Her voice wobbled in a higher range than normal. "But he's going to see the license plate. He's going to recognize the van."

"No, he's too far away. He may not even realize who we are." I sucked in some air despite the brace clamped around my chest. "Okay, take a right at the next stop sign. Slowly. Don't do anything to attract attention."

She followed my instructions.

"Okay, now go faster but don't break the speed limit."

The twenty-five-miles-per-hour speed limit was unnervingly slow. My gut screamed at us to get out of here, but speeding away would have been the worst thing my mom could have done.

I searched for the cruiser in my side mirror. It hadn't yet reached the stop sign. "Now quick. Take a left onto the alley behind G Street."

She obeyed, all the time gasping and staring out the windshield in a daze. "Oh my goodness. I can't believe I just did that. I've never evaded the police in my life."

"Great job. Keep going." I patted her arm and shot a look back just in time. The cruiser flashed past in a navy blur, heading somewhere fast. What could be more pressing than finding us?

The van lurched to a stop in the middle of the alley. Mom shoved the gear into park and buried her face in trembling hands. "Landon, you better drive. My nerves can't handle any more of this."

Jade's eyes narrowed. "But you're not supposed to drive."

I ignored her. While the van idled, I got out to switch places and surveyed the alley, the autumn breeze refreshing my face. Had anyone who mattered spotted us? Didn't matter. We wouldn't be here long.

Taking Mom's seat, I stared out the windshield at the cracked cement. Could I safely drive the van without my full peripheral vision? Safety wasn't at the top of our list, but getting out of town certainly was.

"Landon, what are we going to do?" Jade said. "They'll still be looking for us."

"I know, I know. I'm thinking."

Three houses down, someone had parked a large boat in a roomy driveway. A large, gray cover shrouded its bulk. The cream ranch-style house with burgundy shutters appeared to be immaculate. I'd never seen a hedge so expertly contoured into a perfect rectangle. The place must belong to retirees. Who else had the time to be so meticulous?

Jade followed my gaze. "Oh, that's the Stellabrini place. They've been family friends for years. Just headed to Florida for the winter. My dad checks on the place while they're gone."

Rubbing my morning whiskers, I said, "Do you think they'd mind if we borrowed their boat cover?"

"Better yet, the garage is empty, and I know where there's a key."

Chapter 32

A half hour later, after abandoning the van in a stranger's garage, I sped down the highway in a green, ten-year-old Chevy Malibu. The scrawny teen guy with the wiry black hairs sticking out of his chin had happily accepted the $8,000 for the used car. He'd been asking only $5,000 but upped the price to $6,000 when he recognized my identity.

I paid the extra fee and tossed two grand into the pot, requesting his silence about seeing me. The bonus was worth every cent to get out of this town and keep his trap shut.

Now I eased up on the gas and set the cruise. The rock lodged in my chest, the embodiment of my tension, softened to human flesh. Leaning back against the head rest, I let my aching neck relax. For some reason, tension usually settled there, and tension headaches quickly followed. Unfortunately, sitting in a car for several hours wouldn't help.

"You shouldn't be driving, Landon," Mom said from the backseat. Jade rode shotgun.

"No, you need to rest." How could I forget her shaking hands? She'd never seen so much excitement in one morning. None of us had.

"But you're the one who should be resting. Keep an eye on him, Jade. He can't see the middle stripe."

"I'm fine. I can see the shoulder on the right side. Based on that, I have a pretty good idea where the middle of the road's supposed to be."

"I think you're driving just fine," Jade said.

I aimed a calculated look at my mom in the rearview mirror. "See, Mom. Nothing to worry about." My attention returned to the road. "What's important right now is just getting far, far away."

"Unless you get us all killed first." Mom huffed.

"Staying in Iron Valley would have gotten us killed, all right?" I gestured with one hand.

"Just keep both hands on the wheel and both eyes on the road," Jade said in a tight voice, "if you don't mind."

Silence enveloped us. I suspected what they must be thinking because I couldn't get the same nagging thought out of my head. We were officially fugitives now, on the run from the law, like something in a movie. Our circumstances had become too weird to comprehend.

"That was clever," Jade said, "using that secret code to tell me you needed the jammer."

"Not too hard to remember, was it?"

"Naw. I'd written it down in several old notebooks."

"So we fudged the elvish a bit. Not sure Tolkien would have approved, but hey, it worked."

Roadside trees raised skeletal limbs toward a leaden sky, their summer glory long shed. Clouds burst, and rain hammered down without mercy.

"So, Landon, where are we going?" Mom hadn't been a happy camper to part with her van, even though I'd explained that it wasn't gone, just in safekeeping in case we ever returned to Iron Valley.

"I guess we need to talk about it." I gave Jade a sideways glance. "Any ideas?"

Her eyes smoldered with incredulity. "You mean to tell me … we just drove away from—from our lives"—she gesticulated grandly with both hands—"and you don't even know where we're going?"

"Well, the point wasn't to *go* somewhere but to get *away* from somewhere. Thanks to your help, we succeeded. I figured we could decide our destination while we traveled."

Jade blew out a sigh. "Wow, talk about a road trip without a clue."

Smiling, I said, "But aren't those usually the best kind?"

"But we still need a destination, Landy," Mom said. "We can't just drive around randomly for the rest of our lives."

I gritted my teeth, having forgotten what a terrible backseat driver Mom could be. She lived by to-do lists and schedules. If life hadn't been carefully planned down to the minute, she stressed out. Well, maybe I exaggerated but only slightly.

"We need to decide what *to do* next," Jade said. "That will tell us where to go, right?"

"Okay, so let's decide." I nodded. "I mentioned the FBI earlier. Know anybody we could call?"

Jade shook her head, pretty face downcast. I wasn't sure who would win the blue ribbon for being the unhappiest about our predicament—Jade or my mom. Jade probably had her mind on Henry, the cute kid she'd left at home with her dad. I'd given her every opportunity to ditch this ride, so why would she be pouting now?

"Maybe we just need to stay out of sight," I said, "until I can tell my story to somebody who can work on my problem behind the scenes."

"You mean *our* problem." Mom's tone vibrated with irritability. "You forget we're all involved in this now, whether we want to be or not."

Sheesh.

The eye roll came on involuntarily. "Yes, Mom, it's *our* problem. I'm sorry I had to drag you into this mess, but now that you understand my— our—problem, don't you see I had no other choice?"

Mom shrugged her reluctance. Then her face brightened. "I know. Your cousin Rob." He worked as an attorney near Toledo. "He'd probably know what to do."

Probably laid it on a bit thick. Rob, most likely too young and inexperienced to know how to deal with anything this big, might know those who had the right connections. I agreed that he qualified for our list, which Jade kept on a small notepad. But so far the page appeared pretty blank.

"Wait." Jade tapped the pen on the pad. "My uncle Jed's a senator in Washington, DC. I bet he'd be interested in your story."

A glance her way. "So exactly how long were you going to wait before mentioning this guy? He's exactly the person we need."

"Sorry. I didn't think of him until now."

"Got his phone number?"

"Yeah."

"Excellent."

Her wary eyes studied me. "I better talk to him first—you know, to sorta set the stage. I'll also need to call my boss about work and my dad to discuss his watching Henry." She pulled out her cell phone.

"Remember, cell calls won't work with the jammers," I reminded her. "We'll have to find a pay phone somewhere."

"Landy, we still need a destination," Mom said. "Where are we going to sleep tonight?"

"Let's just keep heading east and make a decision when we stop for lunch, okay?"

"If we find a restaurant with a pay phone," Jade said, "I could make those calls too."

Any calls to Jade's dad could lead Galotta to the restaurant, but did we have a choice? Soon we'd be hours away from Iron Valley; by the time

Galotta tracked down the restaurant, we'd be long gone. Though Galotta would know we were heading east, he wouldn't know our destination any more than we did.

"But what if someone recognizes you?" Mom said. "I'm not sure this is a good idea."

"I'll do my best to keep a low profile. What do you suggest? Maybe I could shave my head."

Jade shook her head. "The whole idea is *not* to stand out. Maybe we could stop at a gas station along the way and buy you some camouflage hunting gear. Then you would fit right in like a real Yooper."

Did my chuckle sound forced? When had I ever intended to look like a Yooper? Not a bad idea.

Conversation tapered off, and my focus became glued to the road. The countryside flashed past in a blur. In my rearview mirror, Mom sagged to one side and appeared to fall asleep, mouth hanging slightly open.

I glanced at Jade. "I'm glad you're here."

She kept her eyes on the road. "I'm glad you're glad."

"I think Mom appreciates it too."

"Not sure if you knew, but your mom and I have become pretty close over the last few years. Guess I've been sort of a surrogate daughter for her, not to mention that we're prayer partners at church."

"Glad to hear it."

"Your mom"—she lowered her voice and peered into the rearview mirror to ensure Mom slept—"she's had some rough times with your dad being gone and everything. Now there's this situation. I'm glad I could be there for her."

Dad had been gone, leaving Mom alone to fend for herself all these years. Remorse wrenched my heart for being out of touch.

The moment passed, and I cleared my throat. "You know, I've been wanting to talk to you about something, but I'm almost afraid to."

"We didn't finish our conversation about Joey Bartholomew's death, did we?"

"Nope. And not just that. I wanted to ask you about the school shooting too."

Her head whipped toward me, eyes widening. "Why would you want to talk about that?"

I told her about the memory trips, particularly the memory about the school shooting that didn't fit the popular narrative. "After the shooting, I was standing in the snow outside the school, but that's not what I was told or what the newspaper printed."

She twisted a golden lock around her finger. "Okay, so you've had a few vivid dreams. But how do you know what you saw in your mind was what really happened?"

Vivid hardly described my dreams. How could I make her understand?

"How exactly do you know these mind trips, or whatever you want to call them, depict accurate memories?"

"I guess I don't other than a gut feeling. Jade, these are more than dreams. It's like … like I'm really there, living the moment for the first time in 3-D and stereo surround sound."

"Well, I certainly hope you've got more to go on than that. Even if they are more than dreams, memories can become distorted over time."

"That's partly why I'm glad you came along. You could fill me in on what really happened. By comparing notes, I'll know whether my memory trips are accurate."

Her brow furrowed. "But maybe you have repressed memories for a reason. Maybe you aren't *supposed* to remember. Have you thought of that? Besides, your mom told me that reminding you of the past may not be such a good idea. She said you almost had a stroke once."

"She was exaggerating."

"She thought you were having a seizure. She was about to rush you to the hospital, she said."

"She was making a mountain out of a mole hill." But even when I said the words, I acknowledged that I shouldn't be too hard on her. Hadn't I entertained similar fears?

"I'd feel terrible if I reminded you of something that pushed a button in your brain and caused a seizure. I guess it's good that I came along. If you had a seizure, I'd know what to do."

A moment of silence. "But I really want to recover the memories I've lost. I want to understand."

"But the memories are already coming back, right? That's what you said."

"Bit by bit." I just wished they'd hurry up.

"Then maybe God should be the one to lift the veil in his time. Please, Landon. I don't think I should be the one to reveal something if you're not ready to hear it. When God knows you're ready, he'll show you what you need to know."

***

Lunch presented a quandary. Sedans and trucks crowded the small parking lot at Janie's Café, a sure sign the food had a good reputation, but how could I keep a low profile? A crowd meant being overlooked might be easier, though it also presented more eyeballs that might recognize me. Though I could eat in the car and play it safe, in the end, I decided to risk it. Besides, my backside reminded me that I'd been sitting in the car far too long.

A polite but weary-faced woman in a blue apron, who looked like she should be home cooing over her grandkids, led us past the crowded bar, where a TV broadcasted a football game on ESPN. She stationed us at a small, worn wooden table in a dark corner. The abundant shadows would work in our favor.

The camouflage baseball cap we'd purchased at a gas station on the way would help. My curly black hair was part of my trademark, and the hat kept most of it out of sight. Keeping my nose in the menu, I didn't look at the waitress when I ordered. I concluded with, "And a Mountain Dew as well, please."

Mom glared at me, not wanting to make a scene, but I ignored her. I was in no mood to bandy words with her, especially in front of the waitress. We needed to fit in, not draw attention to ourselves, and my hands were shaking. Believe me, I *needed* some Jack Daniel's, but Mountain Dew would have to do. To keep her happy, I ordered a side salad to go along with my sandwich.

The waitress finished with our orders and sauntered away.

Jade beelined to the cashier for change and headed to the outdoor pay phone. Our food arrived in her absence, but Mom and I decided to eat our chicken fillet sandwiches while still hot; they'd been topped with melted bleu cheese and onions. Mighty tasty.

We also discussed our travel destination but wanted Jade's input before making any decisions. Besides, the results of her phone calls could influence our plans.

When Jade returned, Mom said, "How's your dad?"

"Worried but okay." Something about Jade had changed; her manner broadcast something more serious, more subdued, now. Maybe the reality of our new normal had settled in. She barely touched her burger and fries.

"So, what did he say?" I said.

"The police asked him a lot of questions and then left. Since he didn't know what was going on, there wasn't much he *could* say."

"You didn't tell him anything about our wanting to contact your uncle, did you?" I said.

"No."

"How's your boy?" Mom said.

A wave of emotion rippled across her face. "Henry misses me, but he's fine. I told my dad and my boss that I'd only be gone for a few days."

"But how can you go back?" Mom sipped her hot tea. "Aren't the police looking for you too?"

"They were at first, Dad says. Now the cops only seem to care about finding one person: Landon."

"Well, that's good," I said. "That means you can call a cab and go home anytime you want to."

She smirked. "Yeah, right. You seem to need about as much help as you can get. And if you get any health issues along the way ... well, it's a good thing I'm here."

"Excellent point," Mom said. "So did you call Uncle Jed?"

"He wasn't in, so I left a message, but he can't exactly call us back. I did reach his wife, my aunt Marianne, though." Her eyes lit up. "At least I know where we can spend the night and maybe a few days if we need to. I'll tell you all about it on the way."

When we finished, Mom agreed to pay at the cash register while I handed her a fifty and ducked out of there. Jade and I loitered by the car, chatting, when Mom hightailed it toward us. If lions had been nipping at her heels, her pace wouldn't have been quicker.

She grabbed the keys from my hand. "Hurry. Get in. We've gotta get out of here!"

My eyebrows shot up. "What's wrong?"

"I just saw your face on TV. You're in the news, Landon, and somebody there might remember seeing you."

Chapter 33

Why do so many people live in cities, given that the least-populated areas of this world are the most beautiful?

Trees rose everywhere. Tall, mammoth pines, higher than telephone poles, scraped the clouds. Sometimes they covered the roadside in neat rows beyond what I could see. The dirt road wound through the woods on the way to Pike Lake like the surveyors had been heavier on moonshine than on common sense. But if the road delivered us to our destination, I couldn't complain.

The rain finally stopped, and the clouds broke apart, revealing blessed sunshine and pristine skies. Great blue swatches of the lake glimmered every now and then through breaks in the trees. Small, weatherworn signs announced exotic destinations including "Almost Paradise" and "Lake Haven." Nothing but cabins and summer homes, apparently. Who else but vacationers or retirees would put up with the forty-five-minute drive back to civilization in Newberry?

"In the middle of nowhere" didn't exaggerate, but this was exactly what I'd hoped for. An out-of-the-way spot where we could hang low for a few days, make a few landline phone calls, and decide on a game plan.

"We used to come here for a week each summer," Jade said in a voice thick with reminiscence. "We'd swim in the lake, catch fish for supper, get sunburned on the beach, and go for long walks in the woods with the mosquitoes and pick wild blueberries. But then Aunt Marianne got sick, and we stopped coming after that. Nobody's been back much since, though one of my cousins comes out every once in a while to mow the grass and make sure everything's as it should be."

"And it has power and a telephone?" Doubt dripped from Mom's voice.

"No power unless you want to count a generator. But yep, there's a landline telephone."

I shook my head. "So telephone lines but no power lines. That doesn't make any sense."

"It does if you want to limit your clientele," Jade said, "if you don't want a bunch of city slickers trashing the wildlife."

I counted the worry lines in my mom's forehead. She embodied no roughing-it type, but this bivouac should last only a few days, right? And then what? An FBI safe house? That's what I prayed for, but a small voice in the back of my head told me not to count on it.

"This is it." Jade pointed. "There's the driveway."

Gravel crunched under the Malibu's tires when I turned off the road beside a sign announcing PINES PALACE and followed two-wheel ruts between more trees. Ferns, quack grass, and other weeds scraped the car's undercarriage. Apparently Jade's cousin had slacked off on the maintenance lately.

The driveway wound up a small rise and abruptly ended only feet from a quaint, if not rustic-looking, log cabin, perched atop a fern-covered hill. A beautiful blue lake shimmered through the greenery below.

I parked, glad to be on my feet after our five-hour drive. Stretching my back, I inhaled the strong, sappy aroma of the deep woods. A cool breeze whooshed in the treetops, and mosquitoes spiraled in a whiny buzz around my head, no doubt sniffing my blood. And here I'd hoped I'd be free from pursuit in this out-of-the-way place.

Popping the trunk, I reached for full paper bags. After the restaurant scare, we'd stopped at a mom-and-pop convenience store and grabbed toothbrushes, toothpaste, deodorant, body soap, and anything else we anticipated would be useful for an extended stay.

"That was smart, grabbing so many extra batteries," I told Jade when I handed her a bag. In fact, we'd completely cleaned out the stunned proprietor, an elderly guy with wiry gray hairs growing out of his leathery ears.

"Well, there's no telling how long we'll need those signal jammers."

True. And there was no way of guessing how many batteries we'd go through if we intended to keep the jammers on 24-7. But what else could we do until we knew for sure we'd found safety?

Mom had suggested we drop by one of the rare Walmarts and grab some extra clothes, but I'd disagreed. Walmarts are filled with security cameras, inside and out. Galotta would know not only what we purchased but also the vehicle we drove—color, make, and model. We'd just have to keep wearing the same clothes for now. Jade had suggested we wrap ourselves in towels and wash our clothes in the lake. Wouldn't Mom have loved that?

While Mom and I waited and slapped mosquitoes, Jade stalked off to retrieve the key; it was stored in a magnetic box hiding under the green propane tank, which hulked under distant scrubby pines. We'd need the generator working if we desired electricity and hot water, and the water pump for using the toilet and taking showers. Jade had been camping most of her life and had no aversion to roughing it, but Mom would be pretty adamant about that shower.

Jade returned with the key, led us up rickety wooden steps to the front door, and unlocked it. Stale air greeted us when we ventured into the cave-like interior. Opening the shades and windows revealed decor both primitive though not unwelcoming. Old fishing nets dangled from wall-mounted canoe paddles that hadn't seen water in years, and ceramic deer peered at us with black, lustrous eyes.

Mom and I followed Jade down a pine-paneled corridor to two bedrooms and a small bathroom. The ladies decided to share one bedroom and let me have the other one to myself. Fold-down stairs led to a loft, a low-ceilinged dwelling where kids or Hobbits would be more at home.

In the other direction, the corridor opened to a spacious great room with a dining area and a small, open-concept kitchen. All were situated under a peaked cathedral ceiling of golden pine beams and matching, crisscrossed rough-hewn logs. The place had a certain charm to it. I could almost hear bluegrass music playing softly in the background.

Dust motes danced in slivers of light leaking past the edges of large, draped windows. Jade opened the drapes, creating a cloud of dust that made her sneeze. Smudged glass patio doors overlooked a rear deck and provided a breathtaking view of the lake. Jade opened the doors, slid open the screen, crossed the deck, and headed down wooden steps, built into the hillside, toward the lake.

I eased toward the screen door and peered out. Nothing but nature sounds embraced me. Never in my life had the sound of so many frogs and crickets filled my ears. Or maybe I'd simply forgotten.

If I'd been on vacation, I might have delighted in the sight of this beautiful place, but little could dispel the tension digging its talons into my shoulders. Finding this out-of-the-way spot relieved some pressure, but unsettling facts remained.

We'd become fugitives of the law, and I had no idea whether Uncle Jed could help get us out of this mess. We'd also found refuge at a new, foreign place. I preferred the security of the old and familiar, but right now that proved too dangerous. I longed to sit down at a piano and lose myself in music for a few hours. But in lieu of the piano, a Jack Daniel's would have been nice right now.

Hmm. Maybe Uncle Jed had a secret stash somewhere. Or was he a teetotaler?

While Jade went to work on the generator, Mom wandered across the great room and checked out the black woodstove, the rocking chair, and the L-shaped blue sofa in the far corner. Nothing but Clive Cussler novels crammed the bookshelf.

An old-fashioned corded phone perched on the kitchen counter, and I checked it out. The welcoming sound of a dial tone reminded me that we weren't completely cut off from civilization.

Now that we'd found a place in no-cell-phone-reception country, I could probably switch off the jammers and save the batteries. But I wasn't completely sure how the jammers worked or how the puppet master had controlled me. Until I knew otherwise, playing it safe appeared to be wise.

I lowered the receiver. Jade had Uncle Jed's phone number and wanted to talk to him first. At least she could let him know she was staying here with guests and prepare him before I told him my unbelievable story.

With the contact of Mom's hand on my shoulder, I turned. Her hazel eyes had glazed over with that unsettled look I'd seen only on rare occasions, such as the day when she'd received word of my dad's beating at the prison.

"How long are we going to stay here, Landy?"

"I have no idea." I pulled her into a hug, and we embraced in the middle of the room, enveloped in the silence and strangeness of the place.

"God will take care of us." She pulled away, turning her gaze toward the patio doors. "He must have a plan for good in all of this."

Pressing my lips together, I remained silent. So far, I hadn't seen any grand hand of divine Providence in our situation. If anything, the reverse appeared to be true. God had abandoned us, and that fact offered the worst feeling of all—being left to our own devices, which appeared to be far from adequate for the task.

If only God made more sense … then I'd find a reason to believe.

And trust.

Right now, I just felt trapped.

She wandered over to the kitchen cabinets and snooped around. "You should see all the canned goods in here. If civilization crumbled tomorrow, we'd be fine for months."

We also had wood for heat and plenty of water in the lake—not to mention fish, if Jade's fishing stories weren't exaggerated. If worse came to worst, I could look for venison, though I'd never hunted a day in my life.

Until now, I hadn't even considered weapons for self-defense. We should have purchased a handgun or two along the way, but perhaps the necessary documentation would have left an electronic trail for Galotta to follow. Maybe Uncle Jed had some weapons stashed away someplace, just in case. The rifle hanging on the far wall shouted "antique," but maybe it could save our lives if necessary.

The sight of the firearm triggered something in the web of my gray matter, and a burning sensation, at first only warm and then hot enough to boil my blood, funneled in between gaps in the web. I bent at my waist, cradling my throbbing head in my arms, when a fresh memory leaped to my mind in full color. Against my retina flashed …

… an overweight man in jean overalls with a sweaty face and brown, caterpillar-like eyebrows hovering over giant brown eyes. Those eyeballs betray an absence of clear reason. He gestures to me, and I follow him through a doorway and into a kitchen.

"C'mon, L-L-Landy. Come and s-s-see what I g-g-got."

Pans hang from the ceiling on hooks. Stainless steel sinks, two stoves, and a refrigerator surround us.

He turns, and I nearly slam into him, this obese man who smells of Vicks VapoRub. Though he can repeat dialogue from each episode of the original Star Trek *series word for word, he's never been in school past the sixth grade.*

"You c-c-can't t-t-tell nobody, g-g-got it?" He narrows his eyes in a feeble attempt to appear mad.

"I won't, Louie. I promise."

"It has to be our s-s-secret. But s-s-since you like hunting, I th-th-thought you'd like to see it."

I nod, and he leads me to the dark corner of the pantry, which is crammed with canned fruit and vegetables. And there it is on the bottom shelf, where he's been hiding it.

Half covered by a hand towel, but shiny when he reveals it, lies a rifle.

My mom's hand on my back brought me back to the cabin, and I gasped for air as if I'd been swimming underwater and just broke the surface. Disoriented, I blinked and straightened, the accompanying headache and burning sensation vanishing. Sapped of strength, I staggered toward the couch and collapsed onto it.

These episodes were becoming an annoying habit.

"Landy, are you okay?"

Nodding, I waited for the nausea to pass. Nothing like finding yourself planted in one world while your brain is stranded in another.

Ballooned cheeks expelled a blast of air. "Just another memory. I'll be okay."

"Are you sure?"

"Yeah."

"If something happened to you while we were out here in the woods, miles from a hospital, I'm not sure what we'd do."

"I'm fine. Really. Besides, Jade would know what to do, right?"

"I sure hope so."

"Mom, do you remember the janitor at Iron Valley Christian? A big guy named Louie?"

Mom sank into the rocker across from me. "Why, sure. Louie Clover. Died of a heart attack about a decade ago."

"For some reason I just remembered him. I don't know why."

"He wasn't too bright, but he sure could clean."

I'd seen Louie's rifle hidden in the pantry at the school. For the first time after all these years, I'd glimpsed it in a lost memory. But what did it mean? There must be a reason for the release of this memory now.

Maybe.

Maybe not.

Perhaps this would confirm another important moment in this jigsaw puzzle of my past. If I waited long enough, the truth of those hidden years might finally come to light.

From the open patio doors drifted the sputter, then steady drone, of a distant engine, reminiscent of a tractor; its invasive sound echoed through the trees. Jade must have gotten the generator running. And the propane tank should still be pretty full, she'd said, so we would have fuel for months.

Not that I had any intention of staying here that long, but given our circumstances, who could say? At least we'd found shelter. But could we be safe here? Would the signal jammers really hide us from the puppet master? Or had he simply let us go so he could play games with us? Like mice released in a laboratory maze.

If Galotta shows up here, Landon, where will you go? How will you get away?

Now that we'd hunkered down in an isolated spot, he could surround us. Cut the phone line. Close in. Terminate all of us in the dead of night.

The kill order would be clean and efficient. Without anyone knowing. Without a chance for any of us to call for help.

A sliver of ice slid down the small of my back.

Real comforting thoughts, Landy. How does this help anything? Remember what Amee suggested. Think happy thoughts.

Getting up, I headed toward the door, immersed in the coolness seeping through the screen, and sought to see the beauty in our situation.

Maybe Jade's phone call to Uncle Jed would provide some answers.

Chapter 34

Thursday, October 29
Iron Valley, Michigan

During a quiet evening in his apartment—photo albums on his lap, pictures of Sylvia surrounding him, embracing him—Galotta's phone rang. He picked up. "Yeah, what do you got?"

"You asked about locations where Jade Hamilton has been in the last five years. I may have a lead," Susan said. "The girl's uncle, Senator Jed Hamilton, has a private lake house in Michigan's Upper Peninsula. Closed up for the winter. Jade used to go there for a week each summer."

"And?"

"There's a landline there, and there's been some recent phone activity. Calls to the senator and one call to a private residence in Iron Valley, Michigan."

"Well, the senator wouldn't be calling himself, now would he?"

"And it isn't his wife. She's been in assisted living for several years now."

Galotta took a deep breath. A private lake house situated in the isolated woods—he liked the sound of that. "I assume you engaged heat imaging from one of our satellites."

"Yes. Somebody's definitely staying there, but family members may do a time-share thing or even rent the place to friends. It could be anybody."

He thrust his tongue across his molars, searching for remnants of the roast lamb. "No, it's him and the two women."

"You don't know that."

"Yes, I do."

Because I know how far a trapped animal will flee. And besides, what other safe house could he possibly find so quickly?

Galotta moistened his lips. "To be sure, track down the whereabouts of all family members. We'll find out by process of elimination. If it's not any of the family, it has to be them. Also put a tap on the landline there—incoming and outgoing."

"Already taken care of."

"Let me know what you discover. Knowing who they call will also tell us who they are."

"Done. Anything else?"

"If all family members are accounted for in other locations"—he hesitated only a heartbeat—"request a kill order and send in three operatives."

"Three?"

"One for each fugitive. We can't take any risks. They need to be terminated immediately before this situation goes any further out of control."

"But, sir, even if you eliminate the senator's family, you can't possibly know—"

Galotta slammed his fist down on the photo album. "Just do what I say."

A pause. "Samuels will need to approve this first." A slight tremor in Susan's voice.

"Excuse me? You need to get with the program. Samuels gave *me* clearance to use *whatever means necessary* to eliminate Jeffers, including those aiding and abetting him. Got it?"

Almost a whisper. "Yes, sir."

"Do you have any idea what this means for both of us if Jeffers somehow escapes our net?"

"I'll be in touch."

"I expect nothing less. And you better have good news."

Chapter 35

Thursday, October 29
Near Newberry, Michigan

While sunset smeared the sky with otherworldly colors, we ate in silence around the fire pit down by the lake, seated on lawn chairs Jade had found in the boathouse. Normally, the bugs would still be pretty bad until the first freeze, Jade said, but the roaring fire kept them at bay.

We heated canned beans with bacon in a pot perched on the grate and enjoyed mandarin oranges out of individual-sized cans. Continuing with my special diet was out of the question, given our limited food options, but I wasn't about to complain.

For a while no one spoke, each lost in his or her own thoughts. The silence rolling off the lake unnerved me; I couldn't recall ever being in a quieter location.

We'd made the important phone calls, but I'd held off on discussing mine until we'd filled our stomachs. Finally, Jade asked, "So how did your talk with my uncle go?"

"Not so good. If you hadn't prepped him and told him I was a good friend, he probably would have hung up on me."

Her jaw dropped. "No way!"

"I can't really say I blame him. It's a crazy story, but at least he heard me out."

"And?" Jade said.

"He agreed to make some inquiries."

Jade stared at me. "And that's it?"

"Yeah, that's it." I didn't try to hide the defeat in my voice. "Okay, yeah, I was hoping for more, but at least it's something."

"Did he offer any protection?" Mom said.

"Nope."

"And you told him about that cop—Goyolla or whatever his name is?" Jade stabbed a mandarin orange, expression incredulous. "You told him about how he threatened you?"

"Oh, yeah. He knows as much as you do. But think about it: it's a lot to take in. I mean, mind control? A crime network using brain implants? You can't make this stuff up."

I scraped the last of the beans from my paper plate and licked the savory, smoky flavor off my fork. At least the comfort food didn't disappoint. I couldn't recall the last time I'd supped on savory pork and beans around a blazing fire.

Jade rose and flung her empty plate into the fire. "Well, this is just … why, it's completely unacceptable. He's my uncle, after all. I tell him we're in danger, and he's not, like, gonna believe me? I'm gonna go call him back and make him see reason."

She turned as if to stomp back to the cabin, all cylinders firing, but I reached for her arm. "Jade, wait. Give it a rest until morning, okay? I was on the phone with him for more than an hour. Maybe he just … just needs time for things to sink in."

She flopped down on her chair with a huff. "What on earth is there to sink in, I'd like to know? We need help—like now. I'm in danger, too—his own niece—and he doesn't give a care?"

Crushing my orange can under my foot, I sighed. "Look, we've all had a long, confusing day. Maybe things will look clearer in the morning. Maybe he'll call us back."

"I'm sure you did the best you could." Mom's gaze appeared lost in the flames. "Thanks, Son."

I inhaled deeply through my nose, sucking in the comforting aroma of pines wafting on the gentle breeze. The blazing fire heated my arms, baked my face. "I thought he'd at least offer us protection while others investigated this mess. Maybe in a safe house somewhere."

Mom tilted her head, looking beautiful in her own special way. "But isn't that what this place is—a safe house of sorts?"

Our eyes met, but I remained silent. She thought we were safe here? If Galotta pulled into the driveway, we'd have no choice but to flee into the wilderness. Without food. Without shelter.

"The fact is," I said, "we don't really know for sure." *It could be a death trap.* "And we're exactly where we started—alone and without help. And I've still got this stinkin' implant in my head that makes me do bad things—and nobody but you two and Galotta believe me."

From across the lake drifted the mournful call of a whippoorwill.

Jade folded arms across her chest. "So where do we go from here? What's our game plan?"

"What if Uncle Jed decides not to help us?" Mom said.

I swallowed. "Then we find someone else who'll listen. Admit it. This is way too big for any of us to handle on our own."

"But what if *nobody* listens?" Jade shook her head. "Then what?"

I'd mulled over worst-case scenarios, uncertain about voicing my radical ideas. Maybe the time had come. "Well, we do have a few options."

Mom raised an eyebrow. "Such as?"

"Well, for starters, let's think about what we *do* know instead of what we don't. They say knowledge is power, right?"

Jade shrugged. "Okay, so what do we already know?"

"We know the identity of two people connected to our problem: Dr. Korovin and Ray Galotta."

Jade's nose wrinkled. "Oh, I hate crooked cops."

"Crooked doctors are just as bad," Mom said, "and Dr. Korovin seemed like such a nice man."

"We also know where this whole business began," I said. "We've even been there."

"Korovin's clinic in Tucson." Mom eyed me. "You're not suggesting we go back there, are you?"

I lifted my hands in a helpless gesture. "Right now we're just brainstorming. No negative feedback allowed, okay? Let's just get all our ideas out there before we do anything else. You're both as much a part of this problem as I am. I want to know what you think. Jade, you got that notepad from earlier?"

"I'm ready when you are."

The moment of silence eased into the night. Small waves lapped gently on the shore of Pike Lake's sandy beach, now cast in shadow while the sun slipped beyond the earth's zenith.

"Okay," I said, "what else do we know?"

"Amee recommended Dr. Korovin," Mom said. "She could be involved."

"My thoughts exactly," Jade said. "I'm writing her name down. She could be part of this mess."

Silence came next. I said, "Okay, what else do we know?"

Mom frowned at me like I'd morphed into the enemy. "You've still got that … that thing … in your head. And as long as it's still there, we can't be one hundred percent certain what you'll do. No offense, Landy, but you've hurt innocent people. Will you try to hurt us too?"

"It's a fair question," I said.

"But you were acting under the control of others," Jade said. "As long as we stay here and use the signal jammers, you should be beyond their control, right?"

"Theoretically. We don't know exactly how the puppet master was controlling me, but so far, all evidence points to the jammers doing their job."

More silence and encouraging nods.

Mom cleared her throat. "Can we stay here?"

"Galotta might dig into your life"—I aimed a look at Jade—"and make an educated guess about where we are. This may not be the safest place after all."

"But we can't leave yet." Jade bit her lip. "We need to give my uncle more time. Besides, the landline is the only way he can reach us."

I shook my head. "We can always find a pay phone and call him from the road. And as much as I'd like to stay here for several days, I'm uneasy about staying in one place too long."

Jade remained silent, her disappointment obvious. No mystery how much she loved the woods.

"Okay, so we leave, never stay long in one spot, and keep using the jammers." No uncertainty about where my mom stood.

"Do we just keep running, hoping Uncle Jed will help us eventually?" I said. "Is there something else we could do to fix the problem ourselves?"

"We need to find a brain surgeon who'll take that hideous thing out of your head." Mom glared at me like I'd become the enemy again.

"We already know one in Tucson," Jade said.

"That may solve *my* problem," I said, "but it won't solve the bigger issue of evil people in charge of some sort of crime network. Now that we know about it, we gotta do what we can to stop it, right?"

"But we need to be realistic." Jade caught my eye. "Besides, you just said this problem is too big for the three of us to solve on our own. Right now *you* have to be our priority. Maybe we *should* go to Tucson."

Mom threw up her hands. "And do what?"

"Find Korovin and make him take out that … whatever that thing is in your head," Jade said.

Mom burst into laughter. "That's like something from a movie. Kidnap Korovin? How would we even go about it?"

"I didn't say *kidnap* him," Jade said in a defensive tone. "But he's responsible. If he put the implant in, he knows how to take it out, right?"

Mom nodded slowly, grudgingly accepting a truth she'd rather avoid. "So there's one concrete idea. Go to Tucson and somehow get Korovin to remove the implant."

They looked at me now, waiting for answers. More so, they sought leadership.

"I agree, Mom. Trying to get Korovin to do what we want might work for some made-for-TV movie, but it's too dangerous. He's probably expecting us to try that. One wrong step, and he'd catch us in his lair right where he wants us. Home court. Then he'd kill us and hush it all up. Nobody would ever discover the truth."

"Even *if* we somehow found Korovin," Mom said, "how would we make him do the surgery? Put a gun to his head?"

"How would we know he wouldn't kill you on the operating table?" Jade's voice had turned high and tight as if stressed. "That's just crazy."

I remained silent. If we kidnapped his wife and put a gun to her head, he'd do whatever we wanted. But were we prepared to be evil like he was? Make him do things against his will? Just like the puppet master had been doing to me?

Part of me liked the idea, but that's what scared me. Oh, the tantalizing attraction of pragmatism. Beat the enemy by being evil like him.

"Either way, that implant is still in your head," Mom said just when it dawned on me how dark the sky had become. "If I were you, I'd want it taken out."

"And there *are* other brain surgeons," Jade said. "Who says Korovin is the only guy who can do the job?"

"But maybe freeing me from the implant shouldn't be our top priority," I said. "Maybe what's more important is finding someone powerful who can shut down this crime network before more people get hurt. Once the bad guys are caught, then this implant problem becomes obsolete."

"So we're back to Uncle Jed." Jade wagged her head with a sigh. "He *needs* to be a believer."

"We need irrefutable proof." Mom fixed a knowing look on me.

I tracked her. "We need a third party, a medical expert, to confirm what's in my head."

"He could remove the implant and confirm what it is." Jade scribbled down our words. "That would be physical proof. What more would we need?"

Cringing at the mention of another surgery, I said, "Maybe brain scans would be enough."

"Either way, we'd need a brain specialist," Mom said. "Somebody completely unbiased. Someone we can trust." She shot a look at me. "But who?"

I lifted my shoulders. "Maybe Uncle Jed could recommend someone. Maybe we'll have a clearer idea in the morning—that is, if he calls us back."

"Oh, he'll call us back, all right," Jade said. "He'd better, or I'll give him a talking to."

We finally agreed to sleep on the matter. Maybe the morning would cast our problem in a whole new and better light.

Maybe.

Now that the conversation had died out, we watched the flames while the calming silence of the lake crept in. Leaning my head back, I peered at the stars.

Never had I seen so many. In one sky. Ever.

The beauty took my breath away.

When I reached my bed, sleep didn't need any encouragement. And neither did my dreams.

Chapter 36

Tuesday, October 5, 1982
Iron Valley, Michigan

After my piano lesson at Mrs. Riddle's house, the place overrun by more cats than could be wholesome, Mom swung by Evergreen Cemetery near the edge of town. We arrived fifteen minutes late, but that made it easier. Because of the crowd, I knew exactly where to go. Yet still I hesitated.

What do you say when your friend's mom has been murdered?

Mom smoothed hair on the back of my head that refused to lie flat. "Want me to come with you?"

"Naw, that's okay. I need to do this on my own. I won't be long."

I studied the newspaper clipping on my lap.

SCHWEITZER CANDY FORTUNE HEIRESS FOUND STRANGLED

Jade had told me her mom's family owned a candy business, but I hadn't taken her seriously. Uncle Andrew sent our family a box of Schweitzer chocolates every Christmas, but I knew next to nothing about Schweitzer candies other than that their caramel-filled chocolates were amazing.

Candy fortune? So Jade's mom had been rich? If she had died, how might that fact affect Jade?

I couldn't imagine someone strangling my mom. Even now I visualized big hands wrapping around Jade's mom's neck. Tightening, squeezing …

A fly batted against the window, snapping my mind back to the car.

"Okay, Landy." Mom sighed. "I didn't drive clear across town for us to just sit here. Get a move on."

My hand reached for the door lever, and Mom gave me the small bouquet of flowers we'd grabbed from the florist along the way. Daisies were Jade's favorite. Maybe they'd cheer her up.

When I stepped out and faced the crowd, making an appearance didn't seem like the smartest idea. What if I said something stupid? Then my mind skipped back to Mom's parting words—that I was here for Jade.

I strolled past plenty of headstones, silk flower arrangements, and smiling stone angels. By the time I reached the shiny, brown coffin and the small knot of people gathered around it, the pastor in the gray suit was drawing his prayer to a close. Jade stood next to her dad, who wore a navy suit, his arm wrapped around her. She wore a long, purple dress, her golden hair pulled back in a single braid slung across her back, tissues clutched in her hand.

After the pastor said "amen," people lined up to give Jade and her dad hugs, spoke in reverent tones, and milled around before dispersing. I eased closer, feeling awkward in my jeans and polo. The attire didn't appear to be appropriate given the occasion.

But Jade apparently didn't care. Her eyes lit up, and she barreled toward me, crushing me in a massive hug. I'd rehearsed the few words I should say—"I'm so sorry for your loss" and "I'll be praying for you"—but I hadn't expected this. Should I hug her back? My face burned while I waited for her to release me.

She finally pulled away, her voice thick with grief. "I'm so glad you came, Landon."

"I'm so sorry," I said. "Here, I brought you these." I handed her the daisies.

She accepted them with a murmured thank-you.

"I wish I knew what to say."

"What *is* there to say? Nobody can bring her back."

"I'm so sorry." Not knowing what to do with my hands, I shoved them deep into my pockets.

Oh, what a dumb idea. Now what was I supposed to do? Mom had told me not to ask her anything about the murder, but now I didn't know what else to say.

Mr. Hamilton thanked me for coming and reached for my hand, giving it a wince-inducing squeeze. I'd heard lots about the Vietnam vet who checked his yard's perimeter nightly—with a loaded shotgun, some said. If the war had left him with anything, it was a bad case of paranoia.

"Jade has told me so much about you." His warm, friendly eyes twinkled. "Thanks for bein' her friend through all this."

"I'm so sorry." Aware that I'd just repeated myself, I closed my mouth. Then an appropriate remark came to me unbidden. "I'll be praying for you during this difficult time."

"Yeah, she'll be needing your prayers, all right," said a sarcastic male voice behind me. I didn't recognize it and spun around.

A teen guy with an acne-covered face and a smug expression watched us from only a few feet away. He edged toward Jade and her dad, hands balled into fists. He wore blue jeans and a black T-shirt with the graphic of some heavy-metal rock group airbrushed on the front.

Gerald Hamilton tightened his protective arm around Jade. "Who are you? And what's this all about?"

The guy jabbed a finger toward Mr. Hamilton's face. "Now just hold your horses, gramps, and I'll tell you. In fact, that's why I'm here—to say my piece." He spoke loudly as if not caring who heard. Thankfully, most folks had left by now.

I lingered at Jade's side, unsure what to do. Months ago I hadn't protected Jade at the playground like I should have. Maybe I'd found my chance to redeem myself.

Thick, black hair fell into the teen's eyes until he swung the locks away with the quick jerk of his head. "What's this all about?" He swung the accusing finger toward Jade. "*She's* what this is all about!"

"I don't understand." Jade eyed the stranger. "I don't even know who you are!"

"But that's what's so sad, isn't it? You don't know a thing about me, but I know *all* about you! I guess I might as well introduce myself. I'm Lucius Brandon Schweitzer III, your stepbrother."

Jade's eyes widened. "My ... my *stepbrother*?"

"Certainly you knew about me."

"Of course, but I don't believe we've ever met."

Lucius studied the coffin, face solemn. "She was my mother too, you know." He swung his attention back to Jade. "Don't you ever forget that."

"I'm sorry." Jade swallowed. "I know this is hard for everyone."

Lucius's lips trembled. "She never stopped talking about you, you know. About how much she missed you. About how she never should have run off with my dad because she loved *you* so much."

Mr. Hamilton raised a hand. "Now, just calm down, son. This is a funeral."

I was glad he'd said something. If he hadn't, I would have been tempted to.

Lucius ignored him and swung that black hair out of his face with another jerk of his head, his glare fixed on Jade. "It wasn't fair! And it's all your fault."

"What do you mean?" Jade said. "What did *I* do?"

"You're the reason why she never … never had any room for me."

Jade shook her head. "I'm sorry. I didn't know."

Lucius took two steps toward Jade until he stopped only a foot away. I'd never seen such hatred on someone's face. Mr. Hamilton tightened his arm around Jade as she faced her brother.

"I've always hated you," Lucius said, "and now that I've seen you face-to-face, I hate you even more." His cheek twitched, his voice hovering somewhere between anger and insanity. "So what do you think about that?"

Veins pulsed in Mr. Hamilton's neck, and he advanced forward, hands balled into fists. "That's about enough, son. If you can't let your stepsister mourn in peace, you're not welcome here."

Lucius's eyes flared, and he puffed out his chest, daring Mr. Hamilton to lay a finger on him. What would happen if Lucius started a fight? Would I join in?

We didn't have time to find out. A husky man with a bull neck in a navy suit headed straight toward Lucius without hesitation. "That's enough, Lucius. It's time to go. Now."

Lucius ignored the muscular hand planted on his shoulder and kept his eyes on Jade, a smirk teasing his lips. "You'd better watch your back, sis. You haven't seen the last of me!"

In a flash the man with the bull neck wrestled Lucius to the ground as if he were a secret service agent. He pinned the teenager facedown in a classic wrestler's move, putting Lucius in a headlock. Lucius's face flashed a bored expression.

"Are you going to stop?" The man tightened his hold until Lucius cried out.

"Ow! You're hurting me."

"*Are you going to stop?*"

"Yes!" Lucius's face crimsoned. "Now let go of me, you"—and he added a word or two that made my ears burn.

The man released Lucius, grabbed him by the arm, and hauled him to his feet, practically lifting him off the ground. He marched the red-faced teen away from us and toward the parked cars.

While they retreated, I studied Jade, not knowing what to say. She visibly trembled.

She frowned. "Wow. He's hated me all these years, and I never even knew it."

"Some way to meet your stepbrother, huh?"

Her gaze fixed on Lucius and the man; they neared a black limo.

"Who on earth was that guy in the suit?" I said.

Jade's nose wrinkled. "Oh, that's Jake, my stepdad. More like a bodyguard, don't you think? But I guess he has to be to handle somebody like Lucius."

The moment of humor broke the nervous tension, but I couldn't shake off Lucius's hateful words. From now on I'd be keeping a more vigilant eye on Jade. My sixth sense told me I hadn't seen the last of Lucius Schweitzer.

Chapter 37

Present day
Friday, October 30
Near Newberry, Michigan

In my dream, Jade and I rode a roller coaster and screamed our lungs out, hands in the air. She grabbed onto my arm as we careened around a turn and plunged toward a sidewalk, where folks looked on from below. One watcher stood out from the others: an acne-faced teen with an evil smile. He jerked black hair out of his face.

Lucius.

Suddenly, he sat on the roller coaster, twisting around from the row of seats in front of us. He reached for Jade, grabbed the chain bearing the locket around her neck, and tightened it until he began choking her.

She screamed, and I woke with a shout in the cabin bedroom deep in the Michigan woods. Heart pounding and breath panting, I detected I wasn't alone.

A human-shaped shadow darted across the moonlit room. Approached my bed.

The man-sized shape jumped on top of me, his weight crushing me. One arm shoved under my chin, cutting off my air.

You're dreaming, Landon. Wake up. Wake up.

But I wasn't.

Whoever had landed on top of me—a man?—grunted and gasped; he pressed his forearm harder against my windpipe. With both hands, I fought to push his arm away so I could breathe. Something silver flashed in the darkness from the man's other hand.

Moonlight blazed through the blinds, glinting off a shiny, metallic surface.

At the moment the arm came down, I twisted away. The knife sliced into the mattress, harmonizing with the man's grunt.

I grabbed the knife-wielding arm with my left hand. With my right, I struck at the shadow. My fist connected with a jaw, and I pictured the head snapping back.

The intruder groaned.

Gasping, I held onto the wrist of the knife-wielding arm. The man cursed and grunted like a feral animal. Sour breath, stinking like moldy cheese, gusted in hot blasts against my face. I fought the gagging reflex.

Moonlight, nearly bright enough to be day, shimmered across the wrinkled, crazed face of a man not much older than I. Luminescent eyes glowed with hate. In the shadows loomed a bald head with a long surgical scar zigzagging across the milky-white scalp.

I stared.

Another brain cancer patient. Another drone just doing what he's programmed to. Sent to kill me.

Though I hated to hurt the man, the drone wasn't giving up without a fight.

The knife arm came down again while I struggled against it with both hands. The tip inched toward my chest. Gasps exploding out of me, I pushed with all my strength.

The man possessed amazing strength. Could I match him?

The tip inched closer to my chest. Grunting, he closed the gap.

Two inches. One inch.

God, please!

I yelled for help.

The room's overhead light blazed when the tip danced a mere fraction of an inch from my heart. The man cursed. Another whiff of the foul breath blasted me.

And then a clang.

The man rolled off me. Crumpled to the floor beside the bed.

Mom hovered over me with a triumphant grin. She clutched the handle of a massive frying pan in both hands.

Scrambling to the small dresser at the foot of my bed, I rifled through the gym bag stuffed with money, toiletries, and other odds and ends.

There.

The lights on both signal jammers still glowed green. They still worked.

But the puppet master had found us.

How?

"Landon, who is this man?" Mom's voice quaked. "Why was he trying to kill you?"

I spun toward her, T-shirt damp with sweat. My mind sorted through options of what I could say, but I'd grown weary of deception. "He must be a drone."

"A what?"

My gaze strayed to the wide-open window. To the torn screen. My chest sucked with a slow, penetrating burn. "That's what I call them—the assassins. The puppet master must have sent him to kill us."

Starting with me.

Over Mom's shoulder, Jade appeared in the doorway, sleepy eyes blinking and coming awake. When she spotted the unconscious man lying on the floor, she shrank back. "W-what's happened? Who's he?"

Mom told her.

Jade's eyebrows lifted. "But—but how could they know we're here?"

My fingers raked through my hair. "I don't know. The wireless jammers are working fine, so the puppet master must have found some other way. Maybe he traced the phone calls."

Jade's startled eyes fixed on mine. "But if he did that, then they must know I called my dad."

My mind whirled. "No, you called him from the restaurant."

"But I called him again later. From here."

"You did?"

She nodded.

What could I say? I'd brought Mom along for her safety, fearing the worst. Gerald Hamilton, a strong and capable man, could surely handle the police. But if the puppet master had traced the calls and connected the dots …

Jade pressed her hands to her face. She brought them down to cover her nose so only her eyes showed, owlish in their fear. "Landon, we gotta go back and help them. Remember what Galotta told you, what he said about his girlfriend."

I regretted that I'd ever told her. "I'm sorry, Jade. We can discuss this on the way."

When I turned away, she got in my face, steely fingers tight around my arm. Worry and anger coalesced into a blazing flurry. "They go after family members—that's what you said. They go after those we love to get what they want."

She'd become hysterical. The last thing we needed right now.

I grabbed her arms to steady her. "Jade, first you just need to calm down. We can discuss this on the way, okay? Second, we've gotta get out of this place."

A check of the drone confirmed his still-unconscious state. Grabbing the knife he'd intended to use to filet my heart, I cut the cord off a nearby table lamp.

"I don't understand," Mom said to my back in a dazed voice. "We're leaving? Now?"

"We have no choice." I wiped stinging sweat out of my eyes and glared at the drone. Waited for him to sit up like the classic killer in any horror flick. "Mom, we can't stay here. If this drone failed, I bet others are on their way."

Turning, I checked the clock. 2:39. I rolled the unconscious man onto his stomach, eying the wedding band on his finger. The cord served well, and I secured his wrists together behind his back.

Rubbing my forehead, a sharp throb pulsing over my eyebrows, I considered our status. How could any of this be possible? The signal jammers were supposed to stop the signals. What had gone wrong? Maybe thinking we'd found freedom had been a mistake all along.

But if so, why had Galotta let us run? Why let us find this place deep in the woods?

To trap us.

My scalp prickled. Knots secure, I rose to face them. "There isn't time to debate this. We gotta get out of here. Now."

"But where are we supposed to go?" Mom pressed a hand to her neck.

"I don't know, okay? Just—just away from here!" The words exploded out of me more forcefully than I'd intended. The buildup of several days of pent-up fear and frustration had lit a powder keg. I'd hoped for at least one night of undisturbed rest after the nightmare of the last few days. But we'd discovered a crime network, sure enough, and now our names were on the list for termination.

I pulled Mom close. "I'm sorry. I didn't mean to yell at you. It's just—"

"It's okay, Landy. You've been under a lot of stress lately, and it's been a long day for all of us." We pulled apart, and her eyes glinted with understanding. "But you know how to get things done, don't you? You remind me so much of your father."

My father? I had no idea what she could be talking about. I turned to hide my confusion and reached for the gym bag, stuffing my things inside. Trying not to think.

But I needed to.

What lay ahead while we waited for Uncle Jed to take us seriously? How long could we run without help? Where could we go to be safe with this stinking GPS in my head? Especially now that the jammers appeared to have failed us.

Wait.

Maybe the drone had been programmed *before* he came within range of the signal jammers. Yes, that might explain it. Once the drone had come within range, maybe he'd become a kamikaze.

I groped for a reason to keep trusting the signal jammers. Could we really be on our own without protection? I had no time for these jumbled thoughts and questions.

Turning to Jade, I said, "Could you pack up as many of the food supplies as you can? Let's try to get out of here in five minutes."

With a quick nod, she disappeared down the hallway toward the kitchen.

"Can you round up the batteries?" I asked Mom. "As many as you can grab?" She hustled after Jade.

Nope. I wasn't willing to throw away the signal jammers. Not just yet.

Facing the room and the man who'd wanted me dead through no fault of his own, I rubbed a hand across the beginnings of a beard. I'd decided to grow one to make me less recognizable.

Mercy granted me only a solitary moment of peace to collect myself before …

The floor creaked from the cabin entrance.

We were not alone.

Chapter 38

Friday, October 30
Near Newberry, Michigan

Toward the window, climbing through the torn screen, we scurried into the night.

I hefted the backpack over my shoulder, heavier now with the supplies Jade and Mom had managed to grab in their haste. A dozen yards into the trees, we crouched amid dancing ferns and peered at the cabin. On the way, I'd been tempted to grab the rifle off the great room wall, but Jade had warned it didn't work, was too old.

So now we have no weapons. That's just great.

The cabin blazed with lights from the two bedrooms and the hallway leading to the kitchen and the great room. Darkness shrouded the rest of the structure, hiding our intruder in shadow.

Somewhere nearby, an owl hooted. A spider of fear crawled up my back.

"Who is it?" Mom panted hard. She hadn't had this much excitement or exercise in years.

After sweating only moments ago, now I shivered in my light jacket. "It's another drone. Come to do the puppet master's dirty work."

"You don't know that," Mom said. "Maybe a neighbor heard the ruckus and came to investigate."

"A neighbor would have knocked first," Jade said.

A human-sized shadow glided across lighted windows, eclipsing them. It resembled a feminine silhouette to me, a female drone. Had to be.

But we were forty-five minutes' drive from the nearest town. Where had the woman come from? Had she driven to get here? Coming on foot seemed implausible.

"Oh my word!" Jade grabbed my arm. "That's Mrs. Reynolds from the other side of the lake. Sometimes she'd give us bait. I didn't realize she had brain cancer."

So they send locals. Those closest to the kill zone.

It made sense. I visualized a national database and a director finding Mrs. Reynolds and sending her here. Maybe he'd roused her from sleep at the push of a button for a mission she'd never remember in the morning.

Something pricked my neck. I slapped at the mosquito and brushed my fingers against my jeans.

Mrs. Reynolds, an overweight woman with short hair, paused at one of the great room windows in full view. She appeared to be wearing a pink nightgown and holding something just beyond sight, her sweeping gaze searching the place. Then she turned, possibly compelled by new information, and headed toward other parts of the cabin as if looking for our blood.

My skin prickled. A cocktail of nerves and adrenaline surged through my veins, making me heady, ready for action.

Maybe Mrs. Reynolds felt the same way. Perhaps the puppet master had given her a jolt of adrenaline, maybe an extra burst of other chemicals too. Could this possibly explain the man's superhuman strength in my bedroom?

Could someone really control others that way, at just the push of a button? But we're all drones in a way, aren't we? Controlled by something?

Mrs. Reynolds reappeared in the great room and did a slow turn, watching, listening. Now she moved into full view, a gun in her hand.

I tensed. Did Mrs. Reynolds really know how to use a gun? Didn't matter. The combination to Millie West's safe had been beyond my knowledge too.

The puppet master programs the necessary knowledge. We truly are puppets.

"C'mon," I said. "We need to get out of here before she comes looking for us."

"I only had time to grab a few of the batteries," Mom said. "Maybe we should try to lure her out of there so we can get more."

The curse word slipped out under my breath; I didn't care whether Mom heard. "I'm not going back in there, but you can if you want to."

There proved to be no takers. If the jammers didn't offer the protection we desired, maybe batteries weren't so important.

"Look," Mom said. "She must have untied the man who attacked you."

Sure enough. The guy made a showing with a knife he must have grabbed from the kitchen because I'd stuck his weapon of choice in my back pocket just in case I needed it. He pulled down the fold-away stairs to search the loft.

"Hey." Jade pointed. "There's a third one."

We couldn't mistake the loping gait of another woman; she trudged up the driveway, at first little more than a bobbing shadow in the moonlight. She clutched what appeared to be a rifle. The front door creaked, and she entered the cabin, lost in shadow. Then she reemerged in the great room.

"She looks pretty old," Mom said.

"Old or not," Jade said, "I'd rather not cross paths with her."

"Besides," I said, "we're outgunned."

"Not so fast." Jade shot me a knowing look. "Remember Y2K? Uncle Jed was a big believer, and at one time this place was like a fortress. He stashed some handguns away in case of an emergency. Follow me."

She led us into thick shadows, through tall weeds, and over fallen logs. How she knew her way so well in little more than moonlight amazed me. Because of her albinism, she missed details in the distance, but perhaps that meant her vision became laser sharp when objects were close in limited light.

Crickets lifted their song in a mighty chorus. A dark shape rose before us. The squeak of the generator shed door made me wince. Maybe the drones, too busy searching the cabin, wouldn't notice.

Bottles of antifreeze and motor oil littered the small, shadowy room. The musty, stale air oppressed me; I pressed a finger under my nose, resisting the urge to sneeze.

Jade flicked on a small twelve-volt light in the windowless room. She substituted two upended paint cans for a stepladder and reached toward the rafters. If I hadn't looked up, I would never have seen the gun cases stored above our heads.

"See?" Jade said. "Now aren't you glad I hung around?"

"But we can't take these," Mom said in a half whisper when Jade handed her the gun case for a 22-caliber Ruger pistol. "This is stealing."

"Mom, that man tried to kill me. Once they figure out we're not in the cabin, they'll be out here, looking for us."

"Uncle Jed put these here for self-defense," Jade said in a calm voice. "Once he has all the facts, he'll understand. Do you really want to argue about stealing at a time like this?"

Mom quieted.

Jade hefted down a grocery bag with a grunt. "Here's ammo." She handed the bag to me and focused on my face, pupils jittering like a large number on the Richter scale. "Okay, what now?"

"We make a beeline for the car and hopefully get out of here the same way we came."

That is, if we can get to the Malibu without a confrontation.

I studied Mom; her eyes had rounded, mouth puckered. If we found ourselves in a gun battle, she wouldn't be much help. She'd never handled a gun in her life.

Jade led the way back into the night, where moonlight frosted each tree trunk and blade of grass with silver. Ferns and small tree branches slapped against our legs, arms, and faces. The forest pulsed with night sounds.

I didn't need to tell Jade to avoid the driveway and the exposed parking area. She chose a circuitous route, bringing us up behind the parked car. There we crouched, and I stared.

The Malibu's hood had been raised, like one of the drones had tinkered around inside before joining the others.

Eliminate our means of escape and then come after us in the dark. Clever.

"Should we even bother trying to start it?" I said.

Jade snorted. "Wouldn't waste my time."

"Oh no," Mom whispered. "You mean, we're stuck here?"

"Not so fast," Jade said. "There's an old Ford stored in the pole barn."

My face jerked toward her. "Pole barn?"

"Yeah, we passed it before turning onto the driveway. It's easy to miss."

"Does the car work?"

"The last time I checked."

"Which was when?"

"Don't ask."

"Do we have any other options?"

"Not that I'm aware of."

"Then lead the way."

The pole barn rose thirty feet in the trees to our right. Creeping through tall pines toward it, I shot a glance back at the cabin.

All lights had been extinguished, eliminating any signs of life, like the drones had vanished. But we weren't stupid enough to fall for the ruse.

Were they searching the woods for us? If they weren't in the cabin, where else could they be?

Together, Jade and I pushed the barn's large front doors open; they whined on the unlubricated track, making me grit my teeth. Only blackness yawned inside. Mom had wisely grabbed a flashlight from the house, and its illumination revealed an old silver Ford Monte Carlo parked in the middle. Storage shelves and everything from old lawn chairs and rakes to flower pots and sawhorses flanked the sedan on both sides.

Jade opened the driver's side door and fiddled around inside. Moments later, she straightened with a triumphant smile, a key chain dangling from her finger. Mom, who'd anticipated that she'd be driving, accepted the keys and got in. Jade slid into the back, and I decided to ride shotgun. I handed the bag of ammunition to Jade. Of any of us, I figured she instinctively knew what to do with it.

So far so good. But where could the drones be?

They'll know where we are soon enough.

Mom turned the key in the ignition.

Rrrrrrarrr. Rrrrrarrr. Rrrrrrarrr.

The engine failed to catch, the battery low on juice. If she kept trying without success, she'd only drain whatever power remained. In the process, she'd trap us in the barn, and the drones, alerted by the whining starter, would surely be on their way.

Maybe I could switch batteries with the Malibu. Did I have time? Doubtful.

I had an idea. "Turn on the headlights. Sometimes that warms the battery a bit. Let the car sit for thirty seconds or so before trying again."

Headlights blazed a path into the darkness between the open barn doors.

Mom shrieked.

The three drones confronted us in the doorway, whitewashed in the beams, weapons at the ready.

Chapter 39

"Lock the doors!" Jade cried.

I did. But what use would locked doors be against a shotgun and handgun?

"Uh, Landy?" Mom's voice quaked.

"Try the engine again, Mom!"

Rrrrrarrr. Rrrrrarrr. Rrrrrrarrr.

The engine sneered at our hopes of resuscitation.

The drones advanced a step.

"Um, Jade." I fought the panic rising in my voice. "If you want to load those guns, now might be a good time."

"Working on it as I speak," came the calm reply.

"What am I supposed to do?" Mom said.

"Again, Mom! Try to start it again!"

Rrrrrarrr. Rrrrrarrr.

The engine caught. Sputtered. Coughed.

The stench of burning oil from the long-unused engine burned my nose. Exhaust smoke billowed around the car's exterior, reducing visibility and creating a sort of screen. Maybe it would buy us some time.

The old woman raised the shotgun toward the windshield, but with the thick cloud, her aim could be only a guess.

Mom's voice rose an octave. "Landy?"

"Duck!" I pushed her head down and ducked under the dashboard.

BAM!

Thunder boomed in my chest. My ears rang.

I peeked over the dashboard. The old woman dropped the shotgun and clutched her shoulder, which blossomed red.

The gunfire hadn't come from the drones. I whirled.

Jade was leaning out the open window of her rear passenger door. She clutched a pistol in both hands, elbows locked, one eye squinted. Ready to shoot again if necessary.

Amazing.

Mom raised her head. "Landy?"

"Give the car some gas, Mom!"

The engine revved, but we went nowhere.

The bald guy rushed the car, knife in hand. If we chose to flee on foot, he'd be there waiting for us. We had only one way out of this mess.

"Put it in gear, Mom! Go, go, go!"

The air rushed out of me. Mrs. Reynolds filled the open doorway, feet spread apart, handgun gripped at arms' length. She pointed it at Mom.

Mom ducked and stomped on the gas. The car lurched forward—first false starts and then leaps—like a bucking bronco.

The gun bucked in Mrs. Reynolds' hands. A hole punched the windshield between Mom and me.

The Monte Carlo raced toward Mrs. Reynolds. She leaped out of the way.

We careened past her. The pole barn spat us out into the night. Headlights whitewashed skeletal tree limbs while we blazed toward them.

Mom wrestled the steering wheel, and we swung away just in time. Down the gravel driveway we sped, the engine growling like a hungry predator.

At the end of the driveway, Mom took the right turn too fast. The car fishtailed, and we swerved onto the main road. I clutched the armrest. The tires found purchase, and we raced down gravel back roads, the headlights carving our path through the dark.

Mom whooped. The little adventurer inside, long dormant, had finally come alive.

The road stretched before us, a narrow swatch of tan hemmed in on both sides by menacing trees and encroaching shadows. But they could do nothing to stop us now. They could only watch us speed into the night.

On the run once again.

***

Forty-five minutes later, well after three o'clock in the morning, we stopped at the nearest open-twenty-four-hours-a-day gas-and-groceries joint for supplies. Mom headed inside with a crisp one-hundred-dollar bill.

While Jade slept on the backseat, oval face illuminated like an angel's, I filled the tank. Returning to my seat, I slouched and kept my head low, collar up, like somebody on *America's Most Wanted.* The fall evening had turned chilly.

Mom returned while peeling off plastic blue gloves and tossing them in the trash. I'd forgotten. Mom never, ever touched receipts. Something about them bearing nasty chemicals certain to obliterate the human race.

She slid into her seat. "I grabbed the last two four-packs of AA batteries they had. We'll need to find another source for batteries soon. Oh, hey, here's your change." She dumped some bills and coins into my hand.

Because of my insecurities at the cabin, I'd left the wireless jammers on and burned six batteries during our brief stay. With only sixteen left, we had enough batteries to last at least another twenty-four hours. Until I knew for sure, I had to believe the jammers helped us somehow, though my faith had been shaken.

Mom had also grabbed plastic cups, a half-gallon of milk, a sixteen-pack of bottled water, snacks (mostly pretzels, Mom's favorite), bananas, and raspberry jelly-filled doughnuts for breakfast. She'd apparently let up on her dietary restrictions for me. Tall cups of dark Colombian coffee, filled at the refreshment oasis, finalized her purchase.

"The coffee's fresh." She handed me mine. "The guy made it special just for us. Seemed glad I gave him something to do, poor kid."

"No salted pistachios, huh?"

Grinning, she pulled out a can, doing a little dance with it right before my eyes. "Of course. I'm not a total dummy." She appeared a tad giddy considering that we could have been killed not so long ago.

I snatched the pistachios. "Wow. Thanks, Mom."

"You're welcome." She focused on her coffee, licking her lips. "I grabbed mostly necessities, though I was a little naughty getting those doughnuts. But I figured you deserved them."

Forget doughnuts when I had salted pistachios.

"I can't believe the prices at places like this." Her nose wrinkled. "Makes me feel sick when I think of all the supplies we had to leave behind at the cabin."

My mom, the eternal penny pincher. If she'd won the lottery (not that she'd ever be caught dead buying a ticket), she'd still be buying deodorant from the dollar store.

The scalding coffee burned my tongue, but it proved to be a small price to pay; I mellowed the strong and smoky brew with some half-and-half and Sugar In The Raw. I'd been trudging through a chemical low after the adrenaline rush at the cabin. Now the caffeine sharpened my senses while we lingered in the comforting silence, softly illumined by the gas station lights.

Mom half turned toward the backseat, Jade's coffee in hand. "Oh, I didn't realize she was asleep, the cute thing. I hate to wake her, but it'll get cold if—"

"We'll have to split it. She doesn't drink coffee."

"Oh, that's right."

"Her dad never let her drink it when she was growing up, so she never got a taste for it."

"Guess I forgot." Mom flashed a toothy grin. "Fine. More for us."

For a moment we communed in silence, lost in our own thoughts and coffee bliss. Then she said, "We need to find a grocery store." She reached for the bag of pretzels. "This kind of food isn't good for you, Landy. We need some vegetables."

Great. Carrot sticks. Just what I wanted.

Not.

"Sorry, Mom, but eating healthy isn't even on my radar right now. Staying alive is a little higher on our priority list, don't you think?"

"So what exactly *is* our priority? Where are we going next on this scavenger hunt from you-know-where?"

"Where Galotta will never expect us. We're going home."

Amazing that she didn't strain her neck the way she whipped her face toward me. "*What?*"

"Jade's dad and her son—I never intended to put them in danger. We've gotta go back and check on them. Take them to a safe place."

Wherever that is.

Her eyes widened. "That seems pretty risky. You're serious?"

"As serious as a heart attack."

I scrunched my eyes closed for only a millisecond, but it proved to be sufficient. Images jumped out: Jade's son, Henry, mouth covered in duct tape, tears streaming down his face.

No. I couldn't live with myself if Galotta used Mr. Hamilton or the boy for bait just to get to me. No way, no how.

My stomach quivered at the potential of the boy being hurt, the lad who could have been mine if things had worked out differently with Jade years ago. None of it made sense now. Why had I left town? What had caused the rift between us? Then the tragedy at the mine leaped to recall, and Jade's recent words echoed in my mind.

You forget that I was there that day and saw everything.

But what had Jade seen? Why couldn't I remember? And why wouldn't Jade tell me? Her worry about brain seizures had been a convenient excuse not to be forthcoming.

There's something she doesn't want you to remember.

But what?

Mom interrupted my speculations. "Okay, so we go get them. Then what?"

"We keep contacting Uncle Jed and hope he comes through by providing help."

"And that's it? Those are our only options?"

"Appears to be."

"Isn't there someone you're forgetting?" Her dramatic pause made me tense. "God can help us too, you know."

The sigh came unbidden. "Mom, please—"

"No, you listen to me." She ignored her coffee for a moment and faced me. "Our sovereign God has a purpose for every event under heaven, whether you believe that or not."

"Actually I *do* believe that."

"Well, if you believe that, then I've got something else for you to chew on."

I waited.

"If you're a child of God, Satan can't control you. Only God can."

Her words sank in by degrees, understanding dawning. Or at least to the level I wanted it to.

"Landy, surely you remember all the sermons you've heard on this topic. If you've trusted Jesus as your Savior, the Holy Spirit lives inside you. And if the Holy Spirit lives in you, he also controls you. And if you submit to him, guess what? Nobody else can control you to do evil. Not the puppet master. Nobody."

Her gaze embraced me, apparently waiting for me to burst into a hallelujah. When I said nothing, she continued.

"Okay, I'll say what you won't. Signal jammer or no signal jammer, Landy, you don't have to do what these evil men want. Sin no longer has the power to control you. Even without the batteries to block the signals, you *can say no.*"

Her words hung in the air between us, and I tasted them, unsure. "But they can control my mind, Mom."

"But not your soul. Don't you see? Your soul is spoken for. It's forever beyond Satan's reach now … if you're a child of God."

If you're a child of God.

Those words echoed in my mind like a mantra.

Sure, I believed in God. Couldn't that be enough?

A Bible verse leaped at me out of nowhere. "Even the demons believe—and tremble!"

So if simple belief in God wasn't enough, what more did I need? And hadn't I settled this decision of trust long ago?

A puzzle piece of recall clicked into place, a Sunday school lesson when I'd been a kid. The teacher used a chair as an object lesson, sitting on the chair to demonstrate trust.

Until we sit on a chair, we haven't shown our trust in it.

Are you sitting in the chair, Landy?

If I sat in the chair of trust in God, the puppet master couldn't dominate me. That's what Mom meant.

My mind diverted to Jade's dad's sad tale. Back home from Vietnam in the late seventies, plagued with nightmares of searching tunnels as a "tunnel rat" and not knowing what he'd find around the next corner, he'd turned to harmless NyQuil to cure his insomnia. But when the NyQuil no longer did the job, he reached for vodka and slid into full-blown alcohol dependence … until the day he gave in to Jesus and surrendered to God's control.

That explained why Jade didn't drink coffee. While on a crusade against NyQuil and vodka, Mr. Hamilton had banned anything that might become habit-forming. Some might call him extreme, but the method behind his madness made sense.

He'd submitted, and God had taken control. And God's control had overruled the vodka's control.

Gritting my teeth, I let the thoughts spin around in my malfunctioning brain, my pride rearing its ugly head. Of course, I acknowledged what Mom wanted from me. She desired to have an altar call right here in this car because she surely doubted my faith like I did. Well, I wouldn't give her that satisfaction, so I changed the subject and talked about our trip back to Iron Valley.

Mom didn't preach anymore after that. Maybe she found contentment in the fact that she'd given me plenty to think about.

I'd grown accustomed to her well enough to realize the coffee wouldn't keep her, or any of us, awake for long. We needed to find a safe place to sleep, especially after the exhaustion of the last few days. But a hotel would be too risky.

Ultimately, she drove until she found a dirt road winding deep into the woods. When it dead-ended, she braked to a stop and shut off the engine. And there we locked the doors, closed the windows, and chose to rest. Drones or no drones.

Exhausted beyond reason, I leaned against the door and crashed. Dead to the world. Not caring about anything but sleep.

This time a knife-wielding drone failed to disturb my slumber, but the night didn't promise the most restful sleep either. My unsettled past still beckoned.

Chapter 40

Thursday, November 18, 1982
Iron Valley, Michigan

The telephone rang, but I ignored it. After supper and homework, I wrestled through the middle of Chopin's difficult Scherzo no. 2. Oh, those sixteenth notes! No matter how hard I tried, my fingers wouldn't cooperate with the timing.

Seconds later, Mom stood in the doorway, phone muffled against her shoulder. "It's Jade. Something's wrong. She sounds petrified."

I grabbed the phone. "Hello?"

She spoke in a half whisper. "Landon, I think there's a robber in our house." Fear chased her panting. "I can hear him. He's making all kinds of racket. He's probably gonna—gonna steal Daddy's new stereo."

"Slow down, Jade. Take a deep breath. Where are you?"

"In Dad's study, hiding under his desk."

"Where's your dad?"

"He's got jail ministry tonight. I'm here all alone, and—and I don't know what to do."

"So call the cops."

"I already did. But by the time Sheriff Bartholomew gets his rear in gear, the stereo system and TV'll be history."

"Hold on. I'm on my way." I hung up.

Filling my mom in on the way to the garage, I climbed on my JC Penney ten-speed.

"Landon, are you out of your mind? You don't want to interrupt a burglary. You could get shot."

"But Jade needs my help! She already called the police. Could you call them again? Tell them to get over to Jade's house right away. Mom, she's in danger. I have no choice."

Before she could utter another word of protest, I tore off down the street, wishing I'd grabbed a heavier jacket to ward off November's chill. The sun had set hours ago, and there was no traffic in sight, just night shadows reaching malevolent fingers toward me, seeking to claim me for their own. My bike chain rattled, threatening to wake the dead; I stopped pedaling to shush it.

Two blocks away, I glimpsed Jade's house. Darkness claimed every window, the place appearing like a lifeless shell. A beam of light slashed across one window, then vanished.

Anxiety plucked a string deep in my chest. I hoped whoever prowled inside the house hadn't hurt Jade.

Reaching the front lawn, I ditched the bike under some trees and hustled toward the backyard. I stuck to the shadows and wished I'd brought a flashlight. Leaves crunched underfoot. I crouched below what I estimated to be a window of Mr. Hamilton's study. I eyed the white lattice.

Maybe I could climb up to the window, knock on the glass, and check on Jade to be sure she was okay. Perhaps I could even persuade her to climb down.

But I had no time to decide. Just then someone opened the window.

"Jade?" I whispered.

No reply.

The shadowy window belched out a dark shape, somebody who apparently had the same trellis idea.

"Jade?" I called again.

When the descending figure still didn't answer, fine hairs rose on the back of my neck, and I backed away. The adult-size person leaped to the ground and drove an elbow into the side of my head.

Lights exploded behind my eyelids, and I sank to the grass in a daze, head throbbing. Along with my disorientation drifted the overpowering aroma of aftershave. Everest by Avon. I recognized the scent because my mom had gotten the aftershave for my dad.

The police found me lying on the grass, clutching my head and moaning. Before I could explain, two of the heftiest cops I'd ever seen threatened to tackle me if I even twitched.

I didn't.

After one of the cops led me into the house, Jade confirmed my story. At least the burglar hadn't harmed her. Though exhausted and a bit disheveled, Jade appeared to be fine.

My gaze swept the immaculate living room, and I suspected I'd missed something. If the burglar had ransacked parts of the house, he'd clearly skipped this room.

When the police sat us down and started asking questions, Jade cried, "I know who did this! It was my stepbrother, Lucius Schweitzer."

The larger of the two officers, the one with no neck, jotted the name down in a small notepad as Jade spelled it. "Why would he do this to you?"

"Because he hates me, that's why. Let me show you." She led us down the hallway. Everything appeared to be untouched until she flicked on the light in her bubblegum-pink bedroom. A bomb must have gone off inside.

And because I'd gone along for the ride, I happened to hear everything—everything I didn't know about Jade's odd family, her mother's murder, and her conviction that Lucius must be responsible.

Her mother's murder was still an open case, one of the cops told us, and the Chicago police weren't any closer to figuring out who'd strangled her. At first, the police had suspected her murder might be part of a burglary gone wrong until they discovered expensive jewelry lying around the place, untouched.

While Jade tackled the questions only she could answer, I called my irritated mom to assure her that Jade and I were fine. Mr. Hamilton arrived, enraged that some stranger had trespassed on his perimeter. The police wanted to talk to him too.

Later, my head still buzzed with questions when Jade and I sat on the living room couch and peered out the picture window at the silent street beyond. Before they left, the cops had searched the house and canvassed the neighborhood, looking for clues about the burglar's identity. The intruder had to be long gone now, the cops said. But if that was the case, why did I still sense that someone watched us now?

"He hates me," she said. "That's what this is all about. It's a personal attack on me."

Her ransacked bedroom proved her point. But the fact was, as the police had pointed out, they had no concrete evidence of Lucius's involvement. Neither of us had seen his face. We had nothing to go on but gut instinct and my memory of Everest cologne.

"Why does he hate you so much?" I pressed a wet hand towel, wrapped around several ice cubes, against my swollen temple. Then the foolishness of my question dawned on me. Of course, I hadn't forgotten Lucius's bitter rant at the funeral.

"It's all about the money."

"The money? What are you talking about?" I played dumb about her wealthy mother.

"My mom was a multimillionaire. A few weeks after her death, I found out she'd divided her fortune equally between her second husband, Jake—the guy you saw tackle Lucius at the funeral—and me. That doesn't even include her life insurance. I get some of that too."

I swallowed. Did this mean she'd be moving away? Too afraid to ask, I remained silent. Surely with her dad here, she considered Iron Valley her home.

"Promise me you won't say anything about the money to anyone." Her eyes connected with mine. "Not even your mom."

I hesitated. Never had I kept secrets from my own parents.

She leaned closer until we were almost nose to nose. "Landon Jeffers, if you breathe a word of this to anyone, I'll break your fingers one at a time. You'll never be able to play Chopin again."

Her face betrayed not a hint of humor. She sounded too much like Myles Cochran, the playground bully, for my taste and didn't appear like herself.

"Okay, fine. I won't tell anyone—promise. You can trust me. But why all the secrecy?"

"I don't know. I guess … I just don't want people treating me differently, that's all. And they would, too, if they knew about any of this. People always act weird when there's this much money involved."

She paused. "Well, it's not really *my* money, at least not yet. My dad says it's being held for me in some kind of trust until I turn eighteen. At that point, I can do whatever I want with it."

The twinge of jealousy pounced before I even had a chance to identify it. I'd always wanted a shiny, black grand piano, something I could only dream about. What would she do with her share of her mom's wealth? Live in a big house with butlers and ride around in a fancy car?

I put the pieces together. "So Lucius is mad because your mom gave the money to you instead of to him? I mean, even madder than he was at the funeral?"

She nodded. "I don't understand it, though."

"Why not?"

"I was pretty little when my mom abandoned my dad and ran off with Lucius's dad, Jake. I was, like, seven years old. Dad turned into a religious fanatic, and Mom couldn't take any more of him. She chose to say good-bye to him and me after taking me on this wonderful trip to Disney World.

"She told me she was leaving my dad and had found a new boyfriend. She wanted to know if I wanted to live with her and Jake. I had a choice, she said. Well, it wasn't really a choice. I mean, how could I leave my dad all alone?"

She paused, her voice almost a whisper. "Anyhow, that was a long time ago. I hardly remember anything about her except riding horses with her at the family ranch. In fact, she seemed pretty mad when I chose my dad over her. Yet she loved me so much that she wanted *me* to have the money."

"That doesn't seem so strange to me. Remember what Lucius said at the funeral?"

She nodded, focus lost in the flickering candle on the coffee table.

"Sounds like your mom talked about you all the time. She must have loved you very much, even though she hadn't stayed in touch."

She wagged her head. "But she never called. She never wrote. I assumed all these years that she *didn't* want anything to do with me. Then I find out she missed me all this time, that she meant for half of the money to come to me all along."

Recalling Lucius's rant in the cemetery, I bit my lip. A new idea dawned.

Maybe she was protecting Jade.

"Could I have misjudged her all these years?" Jade said.

"Hey, we all make mistakes sometimes, right?"

"Not about something like this." She paused and sniffed; her nose had begun running. "Oh, Landon, I forgot to tell you. I searched my bedroom with the police, looking for anything stolen. And can you believe it? Everything appears to be there except one thing. Your locket—the one you gave me on my twelfth birthday. Lucius stole it. I know he did."

The full meaning of her words struck home.

Inside the locket was a photo of the two of us, taken at Cedar Point. Just after we'd gotten off one of the tallest roller coasters in the world.

Jade didn't appear to be the only one in his crosshairs.

"As far as the cops and I can tell," Jade said, "the locket appears to be all he stole. But you realize what that means, don't you? It wasn't really a burglary."

"Well, if it wasn't a burglary, what was it?"

Something that should never appear in the eyes of Jade Hamilton, something starved of hope, glinted. "It's personal. He wants to scare me to death."

Before I could downplay her concerns, she clutched my arm, stark fear flashing in her eyes. "Landon, if anything should happen to me—"

"What could possibly happen to you?"

"—tell the police it was my stepbrother, Lucius."

"What are you saying?"

She hesitated. "I think he might really try to hurt me next time."

"Why do you say that?"

"I should have told you this before now. He's been doing other stuff too. The police know all about it, but I haven't told anyone."

I waited, unsure whether I wanted to hear but knowing I had to now.

"They say there's no proof that it's Lucius, but I know it is. Has to be. Nobody else hates me as much as he does."

"Proof of what? What did he do?"

"A few months ago, I was sleeping when a noise woke me up. It was one of those really hot nights, and both windows were wide open. When I looked at the window closest to my bed, somebody was standing there—I could see his shape. He was right there, just on the other side of the screen, watching me."

"What did you do?"

"I screamed, and the person ran away. My dad called the police. I told them I thought it was Lucius, but they said it couldn't have been him. He lives in Chicago, many hours away, and he supposedly has friends who say he was with them at the time. But I don't believe it—it *was* him. He's been doing prank calls too."

"What?"

"Someone calls and just breathes really heavy on the other end. When I ask who's there, the person doesn't answer. He just hangs up. One time someone with this deep voice called and just kept repeating my name over and over again. I could tell it was Lucius trying to talk really low. But then last week, it happened again, but this time the voice finally said something other than my name."

"What?"

She peered into my eyes without flinching. "He said he's going to kill me."

Chapter 41

Present day
Friday, October 30
Near Newberry, Michigan

"Hey, Landon, this is your morning wakeup call." Jade sounded way too spunky given what we'd endured last night. But then it occurred to me that of any of us, she'd probably gotten the most rest.

I rubbed my morning whiskers. Didn't budge. Considered that the textured edge of a seat belt had probably become permanently etched across my cheek.

The memory of my dream blazed across my mind, and I flirted with the temptation to ask her about Lucius, but—

"Landon, wake up." Mom waved a jelly-filled doughnut under my nose. Maybe she thought the temptation of a potential sugar high would achieve what she couldn't.

"Rise and shine, lazy bones." Jade grinned. "It's after seven thirty. We need to get moving. We're at a gas station, and your mom just filled up."

Accepting the doughnut, I sat up too fast, and my head pounded. Dr. Korovin had warned me about possibly severe headaches—like I could trust anything he'd told me. I scratched my head, mouth tasting like a sewer smells. Took a bite. "Okay, I'm moving."

But not by much. I ached everywhere. Even my eyelids hurt.

"Hey, impressive work with the gun last night, Jade." I squinted into the morning light. "Where'd you learn moves like that?"

"Did you forget? *The Bionic Woman* used to be my favorite TV show."

"Oh, yeah." Rubbing my eyes again, I still didn't move.

"Hey, I called Uncle Jed," Jade said from the seat next to me, "and he's doing more research on his end. He sounded more encouraging this morning."

"Well, that's good to hear." Mom handed me some hot coffee and said it might help me wake up.

"He's also going to find a brain surgeon he can recommend for some scans or possible surgery," Jade added.

"Excellent." I nodded.

Jade regarded me for a moment, apparently waiting for something. Then: "Let me guess." She gave me a playful look. "Down inside you've always wanted to be a blond, right?"

Another bite of the doughnut, and celestial sweetness exploded in my mouth. "What on earth are you talking about?"

"If we're heading back home," Mom said, "we need to do some dye jobs before we leave—you know, so nobody can tell who we really are."

"I think you'd make a cute blond." Jade grinned.

Did I have a choice?

An hour later and much blonder, I returned to the car after using the gas station restroom for the dirty work, and we departed. The doughnuts and coffee refills we'd grabbed (not to mention the Mountain Dew and pistachios I sneaked into the men's room) greatly improved my mood. It wasn't the bleak morning I'd suspected it would be.

Okay, we were on the run, but at least we had full stomachs. And we'd had makeovers too. There'd been no drone attacks in the night after our escape from the cabin, and the sun lit up the sky. Well, at least it made a valiant attempt.

When I glimpsed my mom, I couldn't help doing a double take. With hair blacker than midnight, along with the right styling and makeup, she would have made a rather fetching Elizabeth Taylor. Of course, I wasn't about to tell her the disguise made her look ten times better—not to mention that many years younger.

A tap on my shoulder. "So what do you think?"

I gasped. Jade resembled a younger version of country music star Reba McEntire. Spunky Reba and I had gotten to know each other pretty well. She'd sung "Build a Bridge to Love," one of my pop songs, with me accompanying her on the piano. The song had made number one on the Billboard charts for six straight weeks.

"Wow, you look ... um ... incredible in red."

Don't stare.

"I think so too." She batted her eyelashes. "Hey, thanks for deciding to go back for my dad and my boy. It means a lot to me."

"You would have done the same for me. I hope they're okay."

The emotion swimming in her eyes reflected her uncertainty. "While you were sleeping, I tried calling my dad from a pay phone back at the gas station. There was no answer, which doesn't make sense. He should be at home this time of the morning."

"Maybe he went out for groceries."

"Maybe. But I'm feeling uneasy about this."

As it turned out, she had every right to be.

Several hours later, when we rolled past her dad's house in Iron Valley, the place yielded no signs of life. Yesterday's and today's newspapers had piled on the front stoop. Jade's dad, once a journalism major in college, was a news addict.

Mom drove around the block twice, glancing at the rearview mirror and out the side windows, searching.

My stomach fluttered at the prospect of Galotta being close by. Police cars could spring out of nowhere and surround us within seconds.

No sign of the police or Galotta. But no clue of Mr. Hamilton or Henry either.

I hoped the puppet master and his drones were looking for me hours away from here. Of course, even if not, it would be tough recognizing me with my platinum-blond hair, whiskers, jean jacket, black sunglasses, and Green Bay Packers baseball cap. I hate the tight, restrictive feeling of baseball caps—always have—but sometimes we must make sacrifices.

"Something's wrong." Jade's voice, high and tight, made me think of a violin string about to snap. "I suppose Dad's van could be parked in the garage, but he almost never closes the garage door."

Could the puppet master have taken them away? But if so, why?

He's going to use them to get to you, Landon.

"Now hold on," I said when Mom let the car idle in front of a tired-looking bungalow two blocks away. "Maybe your dad's holed up in the house and *wants* people to think he's gone. I think we need to take a closer look."

"There's no *we* about it." Those tennis-playing guys in Jade's head engaged in a frenzied feud. "Galotta and a dozen policemen could be crouched inside that house just waiting for you to walk in. Remember, these people had your house and van bugged."

"Or they could be waiting for *you*," I said.

"But they don't want me. Remember?"

"You sure about that? With you they could get to me."

She blew bangs off her forehead like she used to when a kid. "We don't know that for sure. I'm going in. By myself."

"But what if it's a trap?" Mom frowned.

"I have no choice. I have to check on Dad and Henry to make sure they're okay."

"Maybe your dad got smart," Mom said. "Maybe he realized he needed to get away—for his own safety and Henry's. What did you tell him during your last phone call?"

"Just that I was in some trouble and not to tell the police anything if they asked him any more questions about me."

"Maybe the police kept coming back," I said. "Maybe he decided he'd had enough of the pressure and decided to duck out of sight."

She shrugged. "Maybe."

"Is there someplace he would go if he was in trouble?" I said.

"Not that I can think of. But we did have an agreement that if either of us needed help and couldn't call, we were supposed to leave a message behind a section of loose floorboards in the kitchen. Our 'secret place,' we call it."

Mind made up, she said, "It's too much of a risk for you. I need to go and check. Alone. There's no other way. Besides, nobody would recognize me in this getup."

True. In the blue jeans and black leather jacket we'd picked up at Goodwill, she nearly looked like a biker.

I turned to my mom for guidance. This was a democracy, not a dictatorship. I hated to admit her maturity often offered wisdom I didn't possess. She said to Jade, "I'd do the same thing if I were in your shoes. But Jade, please be careful. Take the handgun."

"Of course." Jade opened her door. "If I'm not back in ten minutes, then you'll know something's wrong and that you need to get out of Dodge." She aimed a steely look at me. "Promise me, Landon, that you'll drive away. For your own safety."

"Of course." But I couldn't leave her to the wolves that easily. If I discovered she was in trouble, could I really abandon her?

***

I've never seen ten minutes crawl by so slowly. My stomach knotted when the deadline came and went, with Jade nowhere to be seen. What could have gone wrong? Had the house been a trap after all?

Maybe Jade just needed more time, though I couldn't imagine what could be delaying her. Perhaps something had happened to her dad, and she'd had to provide medical attention.

Then just call an ambulance.

We ignored the agreement and waited twelve minutes. Fifteen.

I honed in on Jade's closest exit route in case she raced to the car at any moment. We needed to be ready to speed away.

C'mon, Jade. Where are you?

My right leg jittered. My mom hated this nervous habit and grabbed my knee. "Do you mind? You're shaking the whole car." The tension in her voice mirrored my own.

Stilling my leg, I blotted sweaty palms on my jeans. She bowed her head and closed her eyes, lips moving soundlessly. What a study in contrasts. While I worried, she prayed.

A minute later she looked at me, eyes hard. "She should be here by now."

"You think?" Sarcasm can be an easy crutch.

"We need to drive away. Now. That was the agreement."

Yeah, right. And who made Jade in charge?

My gaze ping-ponged from house to alley, to house, to main road, and to garage. Jade must be on her way—she had to be. Invisible steel bands tightened around my chest; I couldn't take a deep breath.

The makeup didn't mask the stark concern flashing across Mom's face. "We need to go, Landy. She said we should leave if—"

"I *know* what she said."

"Then you know what we need to do." She started the engine, put the car in gear, and touched the gas. The car inched forward.

"Don't." I grabbed the steering wheel, and the car squeaked to a stop. "Just a few more minutes. Please."

She put the car back in park. Threw up her hands. But left the engine idling.

Jade, where are you?

I cursed under my breath. This shouldn't have happened—I should have been counterintuitive and gone with her. I could have hung back. Waited behind a tree. At least been there to ensure she entered the house safely.

Yeah, and then the puppet master would've gotten both of you—two for the price of one.

"Landy, if Galotta's nabbed her, he knows you're nearby. We need to go. Jade's giving us a chance to get away."

She so excelled at stating the obvious—she infuriated me. "We can't just drive away and leave her here."

"But Galotta could be prowling the streets right now, looking for us. It could be only a matter of—"

"I don't care!" My fist pounded the armrest. "I can't leave her."

Her voice softened. "I know why, and I think you do too."

Our eyes met.

Her gentle motherly gaze probed. "You still love her, don't you?"

Blowing air between my lips, I glared at the street. Couldn't believe she wanted to have that conversation at a time like this.

"I've seen the way you look at her."

Mother, please.

"We're not driving away." I reached for my door handle and swung my head toward her. "You coming?"

She nodded, lips firm, resolute. "Two are better than one. That's what Ecclesiastes says."

Getting out, I went for the guns in the trunk, my scrutiny raking the street. From what I could tell, nobody watched us when I shoved one of the loaded handguns, a Beretta 9mm, under my waistband and slung the backpack over my shoulder. I handed her the Ruger Single-Six, and she casually slid it into her coat pocket, as though repeating a ritual we'd done a thousand times before. I could only imagine how out of her depth she must feel right now.

Jade hadn't yet shown her how to use the gun, but at least it could contribute to a show of force.

I closed the trunk and faced the empty street. On a nearby porch, Halloween pumpkins grinned at me, their jagged-tooth smiles both playful and menacing. That's right—today was Halloween, and we'd even dressed for the occasion.

We had two minutes on foot to reach Jade's house. Two minutes to worry about what awaited us in the great unknown. It was Halloween after all. Did Galotta have a trick in mind?

Chapter 42

Isn't it strange how a place you've seen all your life can instantly morph into a location from your worst nightmares?

Pointing the loaded Beretta toward the ground, I approached the yellow single-story ranch from the alley, then crouched and followed the privet hedge, like I'd reverted to a kid playing spy games in the woods with Jade.

But this scenario resembled no childhood fantasy. I would have been a fool if I didn't understand the big risk we must be taking. Unless I *wanted* Galotta to catch me, this had to be one of the last places I should visit right now.

But we didn't really have any choice, I told myself, trying to sneak when I had a hard-enough time walking without my cane. I never should have involved Jade, but good intentions are never enough. I should have fled the country alone. Hid away somewhere in Siberia so no one else would get hurt. Just me, my signal jammers, and an endless supply of AA batteries.

The blinds at the rear of the house had been drawn shut like so many closed eyes. Nope, no signs of life; Jade had apparently vanished into thin air. She was probably inside, checking the answering machine, and had lost track of time.

Maybe.

On the other side of the garage, a dozen dwarves crowded the back-yard, straight from *Snow White*. Those three-foot-high, multicolored cement guys, with round, roly-poly faces, long beards, and merry smiles were just a tad too cheery. Jade collected them, but I'd never understood why. Oh wait. Hadn't she said something about a trip to Disney World with her mom? Their last happy day together before the separation.

I motioned for Mom to follow me, then walked-crouched from the privet hedge to the garage, reaching for the siding to steady my wobbly balance. Rising, I peeked into the rear garage window.

Mr. Hamilton's green van had vanished, but in its place stood a motorcycle. A Harley.

Did anybody I know own a Harley? Nope.

Somebody had to be here, but the cycle wasn't Jade's dad's. He despised motorcycles ever since Carter Van Dyke, a high school classmate, high on pot, had driven into a logging truck one moonlit night when Jade and I were sophomores.

Mr. Hamilton certainly couldn't be anywhere nearby. If he had been here, by no means would I have gotten this close to his house without a confrontation. Ever since Vietnam, he guarded the perimeter of his yard like the Vietcong were just waiting for his one lapse of judgment so they could invade his peaceful existence. I'd often fantasized that his backyard might be booby-trapped.

Time to find out.

Mom crouched low behind me, panting. Could that be actual sweat glistening on her forehead? Heading toward the front of the garage, I peered around the corner, fixing my sight on the back door, gun at the ready.

It hadn't occurred to me until now that Jade had the house key. If she or someone else had locked the door behind her, how would we get in? Knock on the door? Imagine my embarrassment if Jade showed up at the back door with a questioning look.

I'd contemplated our predicament no more than ten seconds when the back door opened inwardly as if by magic. A gaping rectangle of darkness beckoned.

Jade edged stiffly into the doorway, a mix of defeat and embarrassment etched on her face. Her hair hung, disheveled, like she'd been in a struggle.

Something was wrong. At first I didn't understand what it could be until …

A hand appeared, pointing a gun at her head.

My heart swelled against my ribs.

"Toss your gun to the ground," said a man's gravelly voice.

"I'm sorry," Jade mouthed.

"Do it now!" the man said. A vibration in his low timbre betrayed an edge of anger.

I didn't recognize his gruff, demanding voice. Could he be one of Galotta's deputies, parked to keep an eye on the place in case anybody of importance showed up? Would the police materialize out of thin air and pounce on us? Nope, no sign of the cops.

Could this guy be acting alone? A vigilante?

"Do it now or she gets hurt."

Okay, I've seen my share of movies, but never once have I seen a cop put a gun to a civilian's head to get the bad guy to come out, hands up. Then again, hadn't Galotta recently held a gun to *my* head? The rules didn't work for us.

A glance at Mom. Her grim look confirmed what I'd already concluded: we didn't have a choice. But I delayed too long.

The handgun's nose jabbed Jade's head. She shrieked.

Throat constricting, I abandoned the cover of the garage and hustled toward the door. Hands in the air. "Hey, hey, hey! Don't hurt her!"

Jade whimpered.

"Not a step closer!"

I froze, hands still raised.

The look on Jade's face fileted me from the inside. She bit her lip, trying not to cry—and she didn't cry easily.

Had he roughed her up? Or done worse? A tight, electrical burn hummed its way down to my toes. "Have you hurt her?"

The man ignored my question. "Toss the gun to the ground."

I hesitated.

"Do it now. I'm so not kidding."

Gun, not *guns* plural. I caught the nuance. Didn't he know about Mom? Maybe he hadn't seen where she crouched behind me beyond the garage's corner.

If Mom had brains, she'd stay out of sight, where she could do the most good. Which must be what exactly? She didn't even know how to use the gun.

"Do it! Now. Drop it."

Grudgingly, I tossed the Beretta to the grass.

My mind leaped to worst-case scenarios. Our lives were over. Uncle Jed hadn't come through in time, and now we'd all be eliminated execution style. We knew too much about the crime network. How could we be allowed to live? Unless Mom could help somehow … *if* she figured out how.

The hand, the gun, and Jade disappeared into the dark house. But the doorway stood open before me, a yawning entrance into the dragon's throat.

"Come inside," the voice called from deeper inside the house. "But don't try anything stupid. I've still got the gun to her head."

The suggestion of what awaited me in the dark proved less than inviting, but he'd assumed control. Harsh images flashed in the corners of my eyes—even when awake—of him crushing the jammers, then executing Jade before me.

Mom served as our only lifeline now—she had to realize this. But would she do the right thing? I sought to place myself in her shoes. Think like her. The empathy proved far from reassuring. She didn't have a deer-in-the-headlights clue.

My shoes crunched across the leaf-strewn lawn, and I eased toward the back door, eyeing the handgun when I passed it. So tantalizingly close, but it couldn't be worth risking Jade's life.

Angry bees swarmed in my stomach at the prospect of entering the house without first evening the odds. Frantically, I studied the back door, the sidewalk, and the withered flower bed to my right.

No duct tape. Therefore, no MacGyver inspiration.

Realization slowed my steps. He hadn't said a word about the jammers or the backpack full of money. Maybe he didn't know about those either. The fact was, I didn't know anything about this guy. Perhaps he wasn't one of Galotta's cronies after all. But if not, who else could he be?

I lowered the backpack and dropped it into the shriveled flower bed. Taking a half breath, I ventured into the black hole of the entryway.

Leaves crunched behind me.

Mom.

If the stranger didn't know about her, why would she be coming into the house after me?

Maybe she had a plan. More than once, her ingenuity had surprised me.

The dark house held its breath, every drape drawn, every blind lowered. The aroma of bacon and onions salted the stale, tension-filled air. Someone had enjoyed a hearty breakfast—and not long ago. Perhaps Jade's dad and Henry had been here earlier. But where could they be now? Tied up and gagged in the basement?

At least I had one fact working for me. I had this house memorized.

To my right lay the small, galley-style kitchen. Directly ahead of me, stairs descended into the dark basement, where Jade and I had played countless games of Stratego. To my left, a hallway crossed the rear of the house and led to two bedrooms, a bathroom, and the newly remodeled living room/dining room, also accessible from the other side of the kitchen.

The man's voice—calmer now—beckoned from the hallway. "In here. Move."

I shot a look toward the kitchen. A knife. Maybe I could grab one before—

"Stop stalling." The voice rose, a few decibels louder. "You've got ten seconds to get in here. I mean it!"

Or what? He'd kill her?

None of this made sense.

My heartbeat pulsed in my ear lobes. No time remained for me to come up with a feasible plan.

When I inched into the hallway, Mom darted into the kitchen behind me, feet whispering across the linoleum. Hope inspired by whatever she had up her sleeve mustered a speck of optimism.

Blinking a few times, I let my eyes adjust to the thick darkness and eased down the hall toward the other side of the eerily quiet house. To the monster who had Jade's life in the palm of his hand.

Chapter 43

Friday, October 30
Iron Valley, Michigan

S enses pinging on high alert, I passed an open bedroom doorway. Could someone be in there, hidden in shadow, ready to sneak up behind me? Floorboards creaked and popped beneath my feet, giving away my location like a GPS. A Winnie the Pooh nightlight emitted a ghoulish glow just beneath a wall collage of framed photos of Jade positioned at eye level.

"I'm coming!" I called, hoping to buy some time.

No answer.

Think, Landon, think.

Sweat dripped down from the baseball cap, stinging my eyes. Someone had cranked the thermostat, making the house uncomfortably warm. The hat and coat made the heat worse, but I dare not shed them. Perhaps the man with the gun didn't know my identity yet.

Of course he does. Why else this song and dance?

The photo collage riveted my attention when I passed it, a sort of monument to Jade's life. Jade when she'd been a baby—a dimpled grin, a yellow ribbon in her hair. Jade on her first bicycle with the bell she'd never ceased ringing; the sheriff had finally warned her about not disturbing the peace. One of Jade's senior pictures. Cheesy grin. Big eighties hair. Burgeoning womanhood. She resembled a young Martha Stewart.

Okay, maybe I *did* love her.

I glimpsed the end of the hallway, with the yawning opening to the living room. What awaited me—and Jade—in the shadows?

Sucking in a deep breath, I flared around the corner and eased into the cave-like living room, hands raised, back damp with perspiration. The air, faintly tinged with the scent of potpourri, thrummed with tension.

My gaze swept across the void, at first unable to distinguish the threat from shadows created from what ambient light leaked from the edges of curtains. They'd been drawn across large picture windows overlooking the side yard. Familiar furnishings hulked in the dimness: the upright piano nobody played except me when I visited, a brown couch, a rocking chair, end tables. I ventured farther into the room and froze.

The man held Jade in a headlock with one arm while the other jammed a handgun against her right temple. Her arms angled out to either side like she might sprout wings and fly away.

Too dark. I still didn't recognize him. Slight of build, as short as Jade. Not Galotta. Not anyone I knew.

"Okay, I'm here." My shaky voice sliced the silence. "Please. Don't hurt her."

The stranger shoved Jade to the floor and trained the gun on me, using two hands on the grip. Advancing two steps toward me, he pointed the muzzle only inches from my face. I flinched, eyes stinging from sweat I dare not lift a hand to wipe away.

He dropped one hand. Frisked my coat, front pockets, back pockets. Finally, apparently satisfied, he backed away. "Jade, turn the light on."

So Jade knows this guy?

She rose from the floor and clicked on a lamp stationed on an end table. The room blazed with light. I surveyed my captor, a scrawny man I'd never seen before.

A mop of messy brown hair. A gaunt face. Deep-set mahogany eyes appeared almost empty in their sockets. Several days' worth of stubble peppered his cheeks. A green Green Bay Packers T-shirt hung loosely on a too-thin torso. Tattoos of snakes and dragons covered his arms. Probably a metabolism that no doubt burned nearly everything he ate fueled his thin frame. A toothpick protruded from one side of his mouth.

My tight neck and shoulders relaxed a tad. This wasn't the imposing adversary I'd expected. Whether he worked with Galotta, I didn't know. The way he held the gun told me he'd been taught how to use it, but something about his face—

He brought his nose within inches from mine, invading my personal space. His breath reeked of onions, his focus probing my face until his eyes widened.

Suddenly he lowered the gun and tossed his head back with a hoot. "Oh, man! I almost didn't recognize you with that goofy disguise, but it's you, all right. I can't believe it. I done nabbed me Landon Jeffers!"

I gaped at him, mind whirling. For an instant, I suspected he embodied some deranged example of the I'm-your-biggest-fan variety. Or maybe a camera crew at any moment planned to jump out of the shadows and tell me they represented some TV reality show about pranks.

"Oh, man!" He thrust his scrawny arms into the air—one hand still wielding the gun—in a gesture that smacked of victory or delight. Or some sort of deranged happy dance. He, the conquering hero, and I? … the fatted calf?

"I can't believe it!" he cried. "I just won me twenty-five *thousand dollars*!"

I turned to Jade. "What's he talking about?"

She perched on the couch, head in her hands, not sharing in his victory lap. An odd feeling stole over me that she might be somehow complicit in this foolishness. She rose and faced me with a weary-eyed expression. "Landon, let me introduce you. This is Dillon Cripe, Henry's dad."

Ah, Dillon, the lowlife Mom had told me about, the loser who couldn't hold a steady job and had used his fists on Jade a few too many times before abandoning her while she was pregnant with Henry. He'd skipped town after losing umpteen jobs and making too many unfulfilled promises about marrying her and settling down. Classic bottom-feeder. But what did he have to do with any of this?

Jade must have sensed my bewilderment and decided to put me out of my misery. "Landon, there's a bounty on your head for anyone who knows your whereabouts."

"*What?*"

"It's true. When I showed up, Dillon was here looking for my dad and Henry. He said he saw us on the news, fugitives on the run together. When I wanted to leave, he pulled a gun on me and made me stay. Knew it was only a matter of time before you'd show up looking for me."

She shook her head, lowering her voice. "I *told* you to drive away if I wasn't back in ten minutes. Why didn't you do what we agreed?"

"You mean, what *you* agreed."

"Okay, enough talk." Dillon switched the toothpick to the other side of his mouth as if he'd developed some new Olympic skill: toothpick acrobatics. "Tie him up, Jade." He jerked his chin toward a bundle of coiled rope conveniently stowed in the corner of the room. Yep, he'd been waiting for me, all right.

Jade glared at Dillon. "Now hold on. Just give me a minute."

Dillon once again trained the gun on my head. Tempted to brush the nozzle aside, I hesitated, not knowing him well enough to anticipate what he might do.

231

"Look." Jade pulled me aside, pupils rocking. "Dillon's been out of work for a while, so he's pretty desperate for cash right now. He *just wants money*, if you get my meaning."

Maybe an easy way out of this situation lay before us. I just needed to speak the language simpleminded people like Dillon understood.

I faced him. "So the reward is twenty-five thousand dollars, right?"

He lowered the gun to my chest. "That's right and not a penny less. I get the bounty fair and square."

"How about I give you *thirty* thousand in cash to forget you ever saw me."

He blinked. "Say what?"

"You heard me. I'm willing to pay you the bounty plus a bonus. That's my offer. Take the money and go. If anybody asks, pretend you never saw us here."

He stepped closer until our faces were only inches apart. Until I could smell his breakfast again. The unnatural closeness of our proximity made my skin crawl.

Bewilderment seized control of his vocal cords. "What are you into, man?" The way he gestured wildly with the gun—wasn't it loaded?—made me cringe. "You must have stepped into some serious doo-doo. I mean, thirty grand is a lot of dough."

A look of adulation gleamed in his eye, conveying respect. Almost worship. My level of deviance apparently enthralled him.

From outside the house, the distant rumble of an engine drew near. Brakes squeaked. Somebody had parked in front of the house. Had Gordon returned?

Dillon backed off like he'd snapped out of a trance. Eyes trained on me, gun never wavering, he said, "Jade, see who that is."

She parted the navy curtain just enough to peek out. "It's the cops."

Chapter 44

Friday, October 30
Iron Valley, Michigan

M y instincts screamed at me to run or hide, but I could do neither. Not with Dillon's gun stuck up my nose.

His glazed eyes held me in place. "I want thirty-*five* thousand."

A drop of sweat trailed down my temple. Soon a cop would ring the doorbell. "You got it. Thirty-five thousand."

"Where is it? I wanna see it."

Of course you do. Otherwise life would be way too simple.

"It's just outside the back door in a gym bag." I strained my ears for any telltale sounds from the kitchen. Mom must be hearing all this too, right? Maybe she'd mistakenly called the police in hushed tones from the kitchen, thinking it might be the lesser of two evils. If so, she'd made a terrible mistake. The police possessed Dillon's ticket to the twenty-five grand *and* my arrest.

But I offered more. Our future rode on my skills for persuasion.

"It's a lot of money, Dillon." I cocked my head. "More cash than you've ever seen. I can have it in your hands within thirty seconds if you just let us go."

Outside, a car door slammed. I drew in a shallow breath, muscles tense and ready for fight-or-flight. Which would it be?

Dillon studied me with those brown, ferret-like eyes. "How do I know you're telling me the truth?"

"I've seen the money, Dillon." Jade pressed her hands together like in prayer. "He's not lying. You've gotta believe him."

The doorbell rang.

I stiffened. It must be a cop with a direct link to Galotta. Or maybe Galotta himself.

"Dillon, this is *Landon Jeffers*." Jade tugged on Dillon's arm. "C'mon, he's *loaded*. You know he's—"

"Just let me think!" Dillon cried.

"—good for the money. Please, take it and let us go."

Sweat beaded Dillon's forehead.

The doorbell rang again.

"*Forty* thousand." His gaze locked on mine in a staring contest.

"You got it. Forty thousand."

He lowered the gun with a crafty smile like he'd outsmarted me. "Okay, man, you'd better find a place to hide."

I followed Jade, knowing where she'd take me, because we'd hidden there countless times as kids. She opened the hall trapdoor, revealing pull-down stairs. Voices drifted around the corner from the front door at the same moment I scurried after her into the hot, stuffy attic.

She pulled up the stairs and trapdoor behind us, and darkness embraced us like a suffocating, prickly blanket. We crouched amid boxes of Christmas decorations, mouse droppings, and who knew what else.

My heart pounded away like bongo drums. I removed the hat and unzipped the coat too late, already drenched in sweat.

The indistinct drone of voices seeped through the floor. If Dillon wanted his money, he'd have to do some smooth talking to put the cops at ease.

Could Mom still be hiding in the kitchen? If the cops found her, what would she say? They'd surely be looking for her too.

The house creaked. Floorboards whined.

I took a deep breath, but it didn't help dull the serrated throb in my temples. A few more minutes of this heat, and I just might pass out.

Finally, the trapdoor opened, and Dillon's head popped into the bright opening. "Okay, they're gone. You can come down now." A smug, self-satisfied look lathered his face. "You better not be kidding about that money. Or so help me—"

"Dillon, please," Jade said. "Have I ever lied to you?"

"You'll get every penny," I said. "I promise."

Descending the steps, we returned to the living room, frigid compared to the upstairs sauna. Dillon paced the living room like a little boy in need of an unavailable restroom, gun fixed on me. Based on my instructions, since Dillon wouldn't let me out of his sight, Jade headed to the back door to retrieve my gym bag. When she returned with it, Dillon's face lit up.

My hand reached for the bag, but Dillon beat me. He yanked it out of Jade's hands, panting and giggling like somebody half crazed. Unzipping the bag, he spilled the cash on the floor. Thankfully, the cash cushioned the jammers, which Dillon ignored.

He jerked his head up and fixed a wounded expression on me like I'd betrayed him. "Hey, what's going on here? There's a lot more than forty grand here."

"Forty thousand was our agreement."

With two steps he thrust the muzzle toward my head. Déjà vu all over again.

Backing away, I raised my hands. "Okay, I've had about enough of this. Get that gun out of my face!"

Playfulness glinted on his face. "Don't worry. I'll be gone soon, but I'm taking all of it with me."

Jade gasped. "Dillon, no!"

"The agreement was forty thousand. I'm not giving you another cent."

He grinned. "You may not be a-givin', but I'll be a-takin'." While one hand trained the gun on me, he crouched to the floor and tossed everything back into the gym bag, including the jammers. If I didn't think fast, he'd take the gym bag with all my money *and* the jammers and—

Movement blurred from the kitchen doorway. Mom barreled into the room, both hands clutching the Ruger. She pointed the gun at Dillon's head. "Drop it! Now!"

Wow. Could that be my mom? The ruse worked, and just like that, the standoff ended. Dillon cowered on the floor like a three-year-old about to wet his pants. Meanwhile Mom, who didn't even know how to load a gun, kept it trained on him.

Unable to hide my admiration, I gave her a congratulatory smile. "Good job. You came in just the nick of time."

"But there aren't any bullets in here," she whispered.

"Not so loud. Did *you* call the police?"

"What choice did I have? I thought he was going to kill you and Jade."

"What did you just tell the cops?" I asked Mr. Bottom Feeder. Jade had grabbed Dillon's handgun from the floor, and at any hint of resistance, she jabbed him in the head, in the side, and in the thigh. Punctuated by his agonized cries.

"Just that I was—that I was looking for Gordon and Henry," Dillon said between ow's. "They searched the whole place yesterday when I was here looking for you."

When we'd been on our way to the cabin in the woods.

"And just now, I told them I didn't know where you were, just like you asked," he said. "They're long gone."

I reached for the rope. "Tie him up, Jade. Tight enough to keep him busy for a few hours."

"I'd like nothing better." With a smirk, she rolled Dillon onto his belly and began hog-tying him.

"Jade, no!" Dillon cried. "You—you can't do this to me."

"Oh, she can't, huh?" I got down on the floor so Dillon and I were face-to-face. "You were about to run off with all my money, you greedy little thief. What did you expect?"

Veins bulged in his red neck. "Hey, man, I'm really sorry about that. I was—I was just kidding. Seriously. You can ask Jade here. She knows me pretty well. I was just fooling, wasn't I, Jade?"

She scowled at him and tightened one of the knots until he yelped. "What on earth I ever saw in you," she muttered, "I'll never know."

"Then again, we did have an agreement." I counted out the forty grand and tossed it onto the floor beside his head. "Remember our bargain. This means you never saw us—got it? I don't want to hear any more complaining. I think I'm being more than fair."

"Aw, man." Dillon scrunched his brows. "C'mon, I was just joshin' you. I'm sorry you took it so seriously, and here I was hoping we might be friends. I play a pretty mean guitar"—he pronounced it *gee-tar*—"don't I, Jade? Tell him about my guitar playing."

Jade rolled her eyes.

"The two of us could go places—the famous Landon Jeffers on his piano, me on my guitar. Why, it would be fate."

Yeah. A fate worse than death.

"Dillon," Jade said, "shut up."

"I don't want to hear another sound from you"—I shook a finger at him—"or I'll start taking some of this money back. Since you were about to run off with all of it, you broke our agreement. I could just as easily take it all away."

My threat did the trick. It stunned Dillon to silence.

"But I'm not going to do that," I said. "I'm going to show you mercy."

A glance at Mom caught her approving smile.

Dillon remained silent, apparently wising up.

When Jade finished tying him, she scurried off to the kitchen and left Dillon lying there, the quietest he'd been in the last twenty minutes. I found Jade hammering away with her fist at a section of uneven hardwood flooring near the breakfast nook. A floorboard popped up, and a piece of paper lay concealed in its hiding place.

Jade grabbed the paper. Holding it an inch from her face, she read it, lips moving soundlessly.

She grinned at me. "Just as you predicted, Dad got tired of the cops watching him and didn't trust Galotta. He and Henry decided to sneak away last night. I know where they are."

Chapter 45

Friday, October 30
Iron Valley, Michigan

The motel sprawled on the outskirts of town, well off the beaten path and needing some serious updating. The door opened to a flurry of hugs and tears. Gordon Hamilton hugged his daughter.

A towheaded boy of six or seven hugged Jade from behind and glared at me with icy-blue eyes. In one arm he hugged a stuffed lion, Simba from *The Lion King*. A forehead cowlick sent his bangs fluttering in all directions.

Lowering myself, we met at eye level. "Hey, buddy, I'm Landon Jeffers, the piano guy. I don't think we've ever met."

He shrank away like I personified the boogeyman.

So much for being best buds.

I decided not to take his rejection personally; perhaps recent intimidation from the local police made him distrust unfamiliar men. Hopefully, the poor kid would outgrow it, and I'd find some one-on-one time to win him over.

"I've been worried sick." Gordon held Jade tight. "At least you're safe now."

Mentally, I wagged my head. Gordon Hamilton thought we were safe in a rundown motel in Galotta's backyard without protection? I better bring him up to speed in a hurry.

"Well, how do you think *I* felt when we went to the house but nobody was there?" Jade said. "Thankfully, I remembered our secret place in the kitchen."

Mom and I looked on from inside the open doorway. Then it occurred to me that standing within visual distance of the parking lot and other doors might not be the smartest move. We eased inside and closed the door. I turned the dead bolt, ill at ease, and searched for any other entry points.

Crossing the room, I appraised the view out the window overlooking a tree-filled lot. If worse came to worse, this would be my exit.

They'd just eaten lunch, but plenty of order-out supreme pizza remained. Gordon invited us to help ourselves, and we didn't hesitate, though I picked off the black olives and had second thoughts about Gordon's culinary standards. Pizza didn't score on my approved diet list, but when had we given much thought to it lately while running for our lives?

Even Mom, who didn't normally eat pizza, dug in. After she finished, barely saying a word during the meal, she stretched out on the second bed and settled her head back, eyelids closed. Meanwhile Henry turned on the TV and watched *Clone Wars,* oblivious to danger or anything else. Though too keyed up to think about sleep, I reclined next to Mom and leaned against the headboard, pondering our situation while Jade and her dad chatted.

On the other bed, Gordon draped an arm around Jade and studied me with more than a hint of suspicion. A big-boned, hearty man, Gordon has distinctive Native American features, particularly his cheekbones. Years ago, an unashamed rebel of the sixties, he walked an aisle at a Billy Graham crusade and put his trust in Jesus.

His main regret about his rebellious years remains his past drug addiction, which did its share of damage. Mood swings describe the hallmark of his personality disorder. He can be up one minute, down the next—approving one minute, displeased the next. When I was a child, I always feared Gordon, never knowing whether he might bark at me one minute or smile the next.

Now I mulled on where he stood in the context of our dilemma, which affected him too. His life had been disrupted and his daughter, his only child, placed in danger.

He exhaled and looked at me. "I see that you've brought my daughter back to me in one piece. I suppose for that I should be thankful, but what I don't understand is why you put her in danger to begin with."

"No, Daddy, it wasn't like that." Jade shook her head. "Cops were swarming all over your house. Landon gave me the choice to get out of the car, but I chose to stay. So if you want to be mad at somebody, be mad at me."

Gordon ignored her. "And because of you"—his piercing look drilled into mine—"we abandoned our home and now must stay on the run. Do I got it about right?"

Mom had apparently drifted off and offered no help. I clasped sweaty palms between my knees. "Until we get some help, that's what I recommend, yes."

"Until when?" He tilted his head. "Are we supposed to run forever?"

"No. Just until this problem is fixed."

"And how exactly is that supposed to happen?" That I-can-peer-into-your-soul look made me squirm.

I hiked my shoulders. "I don't know."

Lately, keeping Mom, Jade, and me alive had ranked as my top priorities. We'd been living defensively, not offensively; I acknowledged that. Sure, we'd discussed long-term options at the lake, but I'd had little time or clarity of mind to settle on an ultimate solution to our problem. Getting protection through Uncle Jed had appeared to be a sound short-term solution, but he'd been taking his sweet time while our situation became only direr by the second. What if he didn't come through for us?

Gordon Hamilton smiled. Unpredictable, to say the least. "Well, I *do* know. My brother, Jed, called me yesterday and told me your story. That was after I called him because of what Jade said when she called me from his cabin."

I eyed Jade, who flinched and looked away. "Jade, you mean you told—?"

"She told me enough." Gordon pursed his lips. "At first, I didn't understand why my daughter was involved. She appeared to be in danger only because of you, and I was angry."

This remained a sore point between us.

"But, Daddy, like I said, it wasn't like that. The cops were swarming all over your house and—"

"No, Jade, *you* don't understand." Gordon cupped her face in his meaty hand. He swiveled his attention back to me. "Jed looked into your story. Even got the FBI involved. There's more truth to your story than you realize, but a lot's been shielded from the media, so hardly anybody knows about it."

He paused as if carefully choosing his words. "There've been all sorts of unusual homicides by people who don't even remember committing them."

"Let me guess." I cocked my head. "All those folks wouldn't happen to share an incident in their medical history, would they?"

He nodded. "Brain surgery."

"I didn't think Jed believed me."

"Well, he's a believer now. I must thank you from the bottom of my heart for protecting my daughter. You did the right thing by taking Jade with you and keeping her safe."

Eyes that rarely saw tears glistened as he turned to his daughter. "If they'd hurt you, I don't know what I would have done." He pulled Jade close.

Glancing away, I didn't desire to intrude on their private moment.

The people you love. That's the people they hurt.

I couldn't imagine anyone hurting Jade either. If they did, there was no telling what I might do too.

"They could have hurt any of you to get to me," I said finally. "That's why we had to come back for you."

"Jed told me to get out of the house," Gordon said. "That's why we snuck away and came here. He's hired some protection too."

"For us?" Hope flared.

"No, for himself. He knows too much now, he said, and somebody else somehow knows that he knows. He's now being watched."

"But what about us?" Jade said. "We're in danger too."

"Jed has plans for us."

"Plans?" I studied him. "I'm not sure I understand."

"You will." Gordon's enigmatic eyes glinted in the half-light. "Let me tell you all about them."

Chapter 46

Friday, October 30
Iron Valley, Michigan

With my dough, Gordon rented a second room adjoining his. After my first hot shower in two days, I stretched out on the bed—the first time I'd been alone in how long.

My mind spun in a thousand different directions, Gordon's words still fresh. Could the FBI's plan put an end to our problem?

A knock on the door bolted me upright. Who could that be? Jade would have knocked on the adjoining door if they needed anything. Had Galotta somehow discovered my location?

Peering through the peephole, I relaxed. It was the thirtysomething guy from the front desk, the one with the unibrow. I'd spied him bringing Jade more towels for my mom. I cracked the door. "Yes?"

"Oh, sorry. Just wanted you to know we're having some sort of weird problem with our Wi-Fi. Nothing to worry about. We'll get it fixed as soon as we can."

"Okay. Thanks."

Back in bed, I groaned. Maybe the guy had recognized my face, and here I'd asked Gordon to pay for my room so nobody would see me.

On top of that, I'd disrupt everyone's Internet while I remained here. The only other option appeared to be turning the jammers off and letting Galotta know my location—*Come and get me!*—which wasn't happening.

Perhaps I should stop being a coward. Maybe I could turn off the blasted things and face him like a man.

That's what the FBI wanted to do: shut down the jammers, do reverse tracking through the implant, and hunt down whoever monitored me. The fascinating but dangerous proposition would essentially make me bait, a prospect I didn't particularly look forward to. But I had some time to mull over the situation; the FBI required a few days to send the necessary equipment and personnel to Iron Valley before game time.

Yep, more delays. More danger.

My new normal.

In the meantime, they expected me to sit tight without protection; the local police force had been tainted, and they had no idea how far the corruption went. Meanwhile, I found myself trapped between four walls with nothing to do but worry about our future and predict the odds of this grand scheme turning into a terrible mistake.

But hey, we had the FBI on our side now. So why didn't this news encourage me?

Mom's recent words echoed back.

God can help us too, you know.

Glancing at the Gideon Bible on the nightstand, I spanned the room to the sizable window above the rattling air-conditioner. The wooded lot behind the motel still offered the best exit if the bad guys showed up before the FBI did.

I checked my gym bag. Still plenty of batteries, thanks to another gas station stop on the way. The disrupted Internet service at least confirmed that the jammers were doing their job. But the drones at the cabin pointed to the possibility of the puppet master using some other means to track me.

Why this sneaking suspicion that he'd been a step ahead of us the whole time?

Maybe a call to Wade, Jade's techie cousin, would put my mind at ease. Perhaps he could suggest some unusual way the puppet master had tracked us down at the cabin, restoring my confidence in the jammers.

Sitting on the edge of the bed, I slid my head into my hands, knowing I should rest but feeling too wired even to close my eyes. My watch came into focus. 2:42.

The prospect of lingering in one place, especially when we were still in danger, made my stomach gurgle uneasily. With eyelids clamped shut, the vision flashed in the left corners of my eyes: the three of us back on the road, the countryside sliding past. If wheels hummed beneath me, setting life in motion, no one could waltz into my motel room and put a stranglehold on my life.

My attention settled on the ceiling gadget for the sprinkler system. Could someone be watching my every move through a hidden camera? My chuckle sounded hollow in the room's silent embrace. How much did therapists charge to treat this elevated type of paranoia?

My thoughts wandered back to Dillon Cripe. He'd surely escaped from the rope by now. Would he honor our bargain or run straight to Galotta? Keep my money *and* get the reward?

An open palm smacked my forehead.

Of course.

Sixty-five grand was a lot of dough. Could anyone be that much of a creep?

Absolutely.

Thanks to Dillon's tip, Galotta could be combing every motel in town right now.

Unless he knows exactly where you are, Landon. And he's just waiting for the right time to corner you.

Breaking into a cold sweat, I hugged my skull with my fingers. This waiting around for help was ridiculous, like counting the months for my brain cancer, if still growing, to eat my life away. Worse, my mom, Jade, Gordon, and Henry must be in danger too—and all because of me. *I* was the one Galotta wanted. Jade had said so herself.

Wait.

Taking a deep breath, I stilled; realization rippled across neurons. None of them experienced safety because of me. In fact, if I took off on my own and the puppet master couldn't communicate with me, no reason remained for any of my loved ones to get hurt. Ever.

An uncommunicated threat equaled no threat at all.

I swallowed hard, unable to ignore where my logic took me. What if this whole deal with the FBI proved to be a joke? Just a way to keep me stuck in one spot until another drone could pounce on me and finish me off?

I should just walk away. Now. Jade's with her family—she doesn't need me. And Mom's safer with them anyhow.

If more danger reached out to me from the dark unknown, I would face it on my own.

On my own terms. Like a man.

But if the FBI trace proved legit, how could I walk away now? Hadn't we been seeking their help all along?

Besides, where could I go? Not back to Mom's house, a place surely under constant surveillance. And I couldn't return to Jade's house, not after the encounter with Dillon. That left few places where I could hunker down and decide what to do next.

I'd be a fool not to give the FBI's plan a chance, but why waste precious time? Maybe I could find somewhere else to sleep tonight to keep the others safe.

In fact, now that I'd returned to Iron Valley, the graveyard of so many boyhood ghosts, another unresolved matter deserved to be settled once and for all.

If Jade wouldn't tell me the truth about Joey Bartholomew, I'd have to discover it on my own. But that meant revisiting a place I hadn't seen in years, where a classmate had tragically fallen to his death.

Chapter 47

Friday, October 30
Iron Valley, Michigan

It was almost too easy to drop by Gordon's hotel room and slip Mom's keys, lying on the bedside table, into my pocket. She'd drifted off to sleep anyhow—she'd never miss them. A while later she'd wonder why I hadn't returned the keys and speculate about where I'd gone. I hated to worry her, but I couldn't very well tell her what I had in mind, because she never would have let me go.

Though I shouldn't have been driving, I soon found myself behind the wheel and cruising familiar streets, keeping my attention on that line to the right to be sure I stayed in my lane.

I drove until the houses thinned out, replaced by trees and a change in elevation. The sedan ascended small hills here and there until the houses disappeared, and I found myself alone on a gravel road that wound up familiar Drummond Hill, where I'd hiked many times as a boy. I rolled down the window and breathed in the fragrant, woodsy autumn air.

Parking the car on the shoulder, I turned the key. The cooling engine ticked while I lingered, second-guessing my plans and wondering about the mystery that had drawn me thanks to the magnetic pull of place and memory. Typically a planner, I'd recently learned that careful planning can sometimes be a mistake. If I didn't know where I'd sleep tonight, maybe the puppet master wouldn't either.

I exited the car and scanned the dirt road, tinted rust from the iron-ore deposits mixed into the gravel and littering the shoulders. To my left, the road wound down the hill and curved out of sight. To my right, the road continued its ascent to the top of Drummond Hill, the ideal location for many TV and radio station towers.

The nippy breeze tousled my hair while I took in my surroundings. I appeared to be alone, but could I be deceived? A voice in the back of my mind whispered that I'd never be safe again, no matter where I went, unless Uncle Jed signed me up for the witness protection program.

A row of boulders, intended to keep ATVers out, blocked the mouth of the familiar trail that split the woods like a seam and meandered into cooler shadows beneath sun-dappled maples, oaks, birches, and pines. I took the trail, which hugged the northern boundary of a six-foot-tall, rusty, barb-wired fence bearing ominous signs: DANGER: KEEP OUT and NO TRES-PASSING.

My knees weakened at the realization that I'd come back after all these years. A line of long-forgotten dialogue from Joey Bartholomew whispered in my ear.

C'mon, there's this cool place where we can go swimming without anybody knowing.

The signs represented the perfect Pavlovian illustration of human nature. Anything that determined to keep people out would surely arouse reverse psychology in others.

Why stay out? What could be so dangerous?

Inquisitive minds wanted to know.

Now I cursed reverse psychology. Cursed anything that had inspired me to climb that rusty fence with Jade and Joey on that hot summer day so many years ago. Because the fence stood here for an important reason.

Drummond Mine—or the Devil's Icebox, as locals referred to it—saw its heyday in 1887 when mining iron ore was the thriving industry in the region. After the turn of the century, however, the prosperous vein dried up, and miners moved to more productive digs elsewhere. Eventually, the abandoned mine fell into disrepair.

Now I peered through the rusty fence and refreshed my memory of what I'd seen years before: a bowl-shaped depression, roughly the size of a couple of city blocks, carved out of the earth. Over time the mine had collapsed, and the pit indicated where one of the largest caverns, or stopes, had been. The place resembled a quarry more than a mine—all earth tones and rocks and ancient dust.

Sure enough, the old barbed wire still revealed a few places where someone had pulled it down, giving easy access to adventure seekers or downright fools, depending on how one looked at it. I spied the crushed section of fence Joey, Jade, and I had frequented and crossed the line from safe to unsafe. From cautious to unwise. The promise of easy death for the suicidal lay only twenty feet away.

My hands moistened, and my breath came in quick, unsteady gasps. I'd suffered the fear of heights for many years, thanks to what had happened here.

Of course, Joey had gotten too close to the edge, slipped, and fallen to his death. It had been an accident, right? My mind tripped back to words Jade had said only a few days ago.

You forget that I was there that day and saw everything. And I've kept our secret all these years, just like you asked me to.

What secret? What had she been talking about?

A white pine, taller now than memory served, towered just a mere foot or two from the edge. I eased toward it on unsteady legs as if the whole planet might suddenly tilt and I better have something certain to hold onto. Though my memory couldn't be trusted, I could trust this tree. At least to get me closer to the edge, to the spot where Joey's life had slid into the waiting arms of eternity.

You forget that I was there that day and saw everything.

Saw everything.

Everything.

With each inch I eased closer to the cliff's edge, my stomach clenched tighter. I broke out in a cold sweat, though the temperature had to be in the low fifties. It dripped from my hairline and stung my eyes.

I reached the white pine, which rose maybe a dozen feet into the air. My grip around the closest limb couldn't have been tighter.

There I stood a mere foot from where Joey Bartholomew had slipped to his premature death almost three hundred feet below. Here, so close to danger, my gaze plumbed the depths of the sunken mine. Nothing but orange-tinted boulders, playthings in the hand of a giant, lay strewn in a jumbled mess. And here was no gradual descent; the sheer edge, resembling the lip of a cup, plummeted straight down.

Animals had the brains to avoid this place. So why had Jade, Joey, and I come here that day? Did youth bring such arrogance, such assurance that we could cheat death?

I couldn't get Joey's voice out of my head.

C'mon, there's this cool place where we can go swimming without anybody knowing.

Of course, if we'd told his mom or mine our plans, we never would have set foot past the fence that day. Our mothers would have forbidden us. But we'd told no one.

Creeping to the edge, I peered down to a depth good sense—and my knees—would allow. The pile of rocks down deep offered no hint of water. Certainly no pool deep enough for swimming. But perhaps the droughts over the last few decades had dried it up.

Then I glimpsed something I'd missed moments ago.

Only feet away, a white pillar candle and a small, golden-framed photo of Joey Bartholomew perched side by side, a mere foot from the edge.

So someone else cherished the memory. Who else but Joey's mom? The woman who thought she knew the truth about that day and had hated me ever since.

You forget that I was there that day and saw everything.

But what had Jade seen? If only I could marshal those memory trips at will.

For some inexplicable reason, the candle drew me like a moth to flame. I longed to touch it, to wrap my fingers around its roundness. Perhaps because it was a memorial to Joey, a symbol of all we had left of him beyond a grave, photos, and dusty memories.

Kneeling on weak knees, one hand still clutching the tree limb, I reached the other toward the candle. Wrapped my fingers around its solid whiteness.

My hand burned like boiling water scalded it. I cried out, but for some reason, I couldn't wrench my hand away.

But the fire didn't burn my hand. It blazed in my mind.

And I was trapped in an inferno of truth with no way of escape. Trapped in another memory I couldn't deny.

Chapter 48

Saturday, August 24, 1985
Iron Valley, Michigan

"Don't do it, Jade." I crouched beside her. "Please."

Sitting a mere foot from the edge, Jade pulled on special shoes for rock climbing. Joey tested the rope they'd tied around the white pine. They even wore cool gloves for finding evasive handholds in the rock.

Could I be the only one who saw the madness of their plans? "Jade, please. Don't you see how dangerous this is?"

Fear glinted in her eyes. She couldn't hide it from me. She perceived the foolishness of what they were about to do. So then why go along with it? Why didn't she stand up to Joey and tell him off?

Joey inserted himself between us, hands on his hips. "The lady can do whatever she wants, so why don't you just butt out? Better yet, why don't you just leave? I'm sure you've got some Rock-man-ee-of you need to practice."

He always threw piano playing in my face, intending to be insulting. He had no idea how close I was to getting a full-paid scholarship to Juilliard.

Rising, I faced him. "Why are you doing this, Joey? So you learned about rock climbing at camp a few weeks ago. Great. But this is no place for beginners."

Black peach fuzz covered his upper lip. "A beginner, huh? You don't know what you're talkin' about, Chopin." His sarcastic nickname for me.

His bloodshot eyes, not a little wild, bore into mine. Everybody knew Joey had his occasional drug problem. Public school friends constantly pushed it at him. Lately, he'd insisted that he was clean, but his eyes and the irrationality of what he intended to do were a dead giveaway.

I held his gaze. "I thought we came here to swim. What are you trying to prove?"

"I'm not trying to prove anything. If we climb down a ways, there's an easy cleft that takes us down to the pond."

But they had the climbing equipment, so I'd be left on my own. "Okay, fine. Do whatever you want. But Jade doesn't have to go along with this."

He glared at me. "What? You think I'm *making* her? I wouldn't make my girl do anything she didn't want to."

My girl?

A sick feeling uncoiled in my gut. Everybody knew Jade and I had a certain chemistry—we'd always been best buds. But lately Joey had been hanging around her a lot. My mom had warned me about possible trouble. Why this blindness to problems she could spot a mile away?

I swung back toward Jade, and the sun glinted on some metal.

The ring on her finger. Joey's ring.

She bent forward to tie her shoe, and my locket, the gift on her twelfth birthday, should have swung out of her T-shirt. But it didn't. Not today. Joey had displaced me.

I lowered my shaky voice. "Jade, what's going on here? Why are you wearing his ring?"

Joey's contagious attitude had apparently infected her. She rolled her eyes. "Good grief, Landon. Why do you gotta make such a big deal about everything?"

"What do you mean?" I grabbed her arm. "I care about you, and I don't want to see you get hurt."

She yanked her arm away, eyes sharper than daggers. "Let go of me!"

"Hey, hey, hey." Joey shoved me away from her—two hands planted against my chest—and I tripped, landing on my backside. Mere inches from the cliff's edge. I scrambled away from it, my knocking heart shoved somewhere between my knees.

Rising, I got in Joey's face until our noses were only inches apart. "What do you think you're doing? Trying to kill me?"

I shoved him back. Hard. Toward the fence.

He lost his balance and slammed onto his back, almost snagging his head on where the barbed wire fence had been trampled down.

Jade's voice barely registered on my radar. "Hey, you two. Cut it out!"

My pulse throbbed in my ears. I couldn't believe it. I'd actually pushed Joey Bartholomew down.

A steely look flashed across Joey's face. He charged me, but in a rare moment of dexterity, I swung away just in time.

He grabbed my leg and brought me down hard on my side. Pain shot up my arm. I leaped up.

We wrestled in the dirt. Gasping. Sweating.

Joey straddled me and pinned my left arm down, his stinky breath blasting me. He struggled to control my right arm, but I had years of piano on my side and amazing strength. Who could have predicted that Chopin might come in handy during a fight? I struggled to push his weight off me, but he didn't budge.

Seemingly miles away, Jade yelled at us to stop.

Joey drove his fist into my gut. For a second, I couldn't breathe. Black dots danced in my vision.

When he raised his fist again, I reached for the ground. Threw dirt at his face.

He rose and staggered back, wiping his eyes. I leaped up and faced him.

Charging me again, he tackled me hard. The wind rushed out of me. For a few seconds, I panicked. Couldn't breathe again.

Anger thrummed across my veins. And something else.

Something dark and deadly. Rage took possession.

I rose and launched myself at him with a roar. Gave him a mighty shove.

Inertia can be a friend or an enemy. That day it turned out to be Joey's worst enemy.

On any other day, he would have staggered back a step or two, with plenty of space between him and the cliff's edge. If only he'd grabbed the white pine to stop inertia in its tracks.

He might have been okay if the tree root hadn't tripped him and sent him rolling over the cliff's edge.

Chapter 49

Joey clutched the cliff's edge with both hands, body dangling in space. Jade and I sprinted to the edge and grabbed his arms, yelling at him to hold on. We strained to lift him. Sought to save him while panting and sweating and crying and praying.

Boyish disputes over a girl had vanished. We were instantly friends again.

Lying on my belly, I hung over the edge, trying to maintain my sweaty grip on Joey's wrist. My heart hammered, each beat like the bang of timpani in my ears.

Don't believe movies. Movies lie.

We held on for a long time, but we lacked the strength to save Joey. More help was needed. But how could we get help if, by holding him, we maintained the status quo—me on one side, Jade on the other?

"Jade, go get help!" I cried.

"No!" Hysteria surfed the wave of her tears. "You can't hold him up by yourself."

"Get help!"

"No!"

"Hold on, Joey!" Panic and fear soured inside me.

Joey continued to hold on, but the situation had become a stalemate, and he knew it.

He didn't cry or plead or lose his cool. He just looked up at us wordlessly, face red and sweaty, bloodshot eyes accepting while perhaps his last few breaths shuttled through his lungs. Tears carved trails across his filthy cheeks from the dirt I'd thrown in his face.

His eyes said he was sorry for the initial shove. His eyes said he didn't blame me. His eyes said an eternity of somethings in just that instant: how he'd wanted to finish high school and make something of his life; how he loved Jade, even though they were too young to be serious.

Without anyone saying a word, the realization dawned on me that we couldn't hold on forever.

But I couldn't let this happen. Something that fed on adrenaline rose inside me, something more powerful than my body could contain. I had to let it out.

My mind flashed to a favorite TV show, *The Incredible Hulk*. All I could think of was Dr. David Banner getting mad, turning into that green guy with the muscles, and lifting a car to save someone's life.

Joey and I had role-played that scenario many times in my backyard, but this was now—this was real. And I lifted Joey.

His eyes widened. Uncomprehending.

I giggled, amazing even myself. This was going to work—I could save him. Where the strength came from, I didn't know. Didn't care.

Jade stared at me.

Rising to my knees, I lifted Joey to his waist. The distance should have been enough to swing him clear of danger. At the very least, I should have grabbed the tree for leverage. Because in that split second, fate reversed itself like a fateful roll of the dice.

My sweaty hand slipped, and Joey slid free.

Jade screamed, and Joey flew.

He'd always wanted to fly, but not like this.

Chapter 50

Present day
Friday, October 30
Iron Valley, Michigan

Vomit lapped the back of my throat, ripping me back to the present. All the visceral emotions from that day, once trapped behind scarred brain tissue, hurtled back like a grand mal seizure.

Could I be having a stroke? My mom had worried I might. Perhaps that's what all these daymares were—ministrokes leading to the granddaddy of them all. The one that would end it all for me, a solution to all our problems.

If I died, then nobody could control me, and nobody could endanger my mom, Jade, or her family.

On my knees, I threw up on the ground once. Twice. Dry heaves sapped me of whatever strength remained.

Most people grieve over the span of weeks, months, and years. But I did it all in just a few minutes in a sucker punch that left me crying and shaking and sweating.

The terror of slipping off the edge and drinking of Joey's bitter cup thrust me toward the tree, and I grabbed ahold of it, trembling. I hugged that white pine like a drowning man clutches a life preserver.

And wept. Wept because I was a sinner in need of grace. Mom's words from the past slammed into me.

Our sovereign God has a purpose for every event under heaven, whether you want to believe that or not.

Even an event like Joey's death and my role in it?

Perhaps past trauma had short-circuited the synapses to that particular memory, but now that it had returned, I wasn't sure what to do with it. It was like holding the lit fuse to a bomb that might explode.

Should I toss it? Run away? Let it blow me to kingdom come?

The wind whistled over me, my shirt drenched in sweat. I'd earlier been overheated, but now I trembled, glad for the jean jacket. The daymare had drained me of almost all strength, leaving me just enough to grasp the tree.

The grief of Joey's death still roiled in my gut when something shifted behind me, an almost imperceptible trace of movement. A voice spoke, one I hadn't heard in years.

"I never expected to see *you* here."

I whirled toward the voice. Though I didn't expect to see her, I'd found clear evidence that she'd been here before. Joey's mom, Sharon Bartholomew, had come for her private moment with the portrait and candle.

She stood about a dozen feet away, just inside the fence in a pink T-shirt and navy jacket. Hands tucked into the front pockets of her faded blue jeans, she beheld me with a smug look. "So, you came to see where my boy died, huh?"

"Something like that." I could hardly breathe, never mind talk. The emotional rush had abated, leaving nothing behind. Nothing but a soul-sucking emptiness.

"Well, better late than never. It's about time you came to visit this place."

Until today I'd never set foot beyond the fence since the tragedy, not even on the night of the candlelight vigil the evening after his death. Then the place had been lit up like a shrine with pictures, flowers, and lots of candles—not to mention tears and singing for those who could get through the song, "Bridge over Troubled Water." Few of us had been able to sing Joey's favorite song all the way through. To this day, I still couldn't.

She ventured a few steps closer. "Came to thank God it was him and not you, huh?"

I didn't know how to answer her. If I hadn't lost my temper, Joey might still be alive today. Probably married with kids, a good job, and a steep mortgage.

If she wanted me dead, she'd never found a more opportune moment. Here I sat, sapped of strength, and she stood between me and the fence, the only way out. And the cliff's edge lay only a few feet behind me.

"I'm sorry," I said.

Her head jerked toward me, the movement furtive, birdlike. "What did you say?"

"I said, I'm sorry."

She eased closer. "Sorry for what? Sorry that you pushed my son to his death?"

That was what she'd told everyone across town—that I'd murdered Joey because I wanted Jade all to myself. Which was half true. I *had* wanted Jade to be my girl but not at the expense of Joey's life.

"I didn't kill your son intentionally." I might have said "Joey," but I couldn't bring myself to say his name. I longed for some emotional distance right now.

"You're a liar. I know all about it."

Would contradicting her do any good? She'd believed the lies so long, they'd become her truth.

She lifted her chin. "Jade talks in her sleep. Did you know that?"

How would I know that?

The wind whipped up and tossed long strands of sun-damaged, dirty-blonde hair across her face. In a voice husky from chain-smoking, she said, "She was in a cabin with my girl at Bible camp that summer. Lord knows why she was there. Maybe to ease her conscience. She kept repeating Joey's name and saying you were sorry, that you hadn't meant to do it."

"Of course. I was sorry he died."

"No, she was guilty. That's why she was having those dreams. She knew the truth."

"Jade didn't do anything wrong."

"Oh no? Wasn't she the one who told lies for you? Said my boy just got too close to the edge and simply lost his balance?"

I turned my face away.

"But she told the truth in her sleep. You didn't know that, did you?" She leered at me, and I queried whether she might be on drugs, like Joey had been. How ironic that the local sheriff's wife took weed most of the time, if decade-old rumors could be true.

"It's true, isn't it?" She bridged the distance and paused only three feet away, her pain-wracked eyes like probing lasers. "She lied for you during the investigation. Just say it!"

Why compound lies with more of them? I'd become weary of the whole charade, especially after all these years had passed and now that I'd relived Joey's death in a strange sort of virtual reality.

I nodded.

Something inside Sharon Bartholomew shattered. She fixed her watery eyes on me. "I knew it all along, you little liar. I knew all these years that you killed my son."

Rising to my shaky feet, I faced her. "No, that's not what happened. It *was* an accident, but not—not like we said."

Her right cheek twitched. "Then tell me the truth for once. Tell me now."

So I did, more truthfully than I ever had before. When I finished, she lifted her chin. "And you expect me to believe you after you've lied to everybody all these years?"

"I don't care if you don't believe me. It's true. He tripped on the tree root right there and went over the edge. Jade and I tried to pull him up, but … but we just weren't strong enough."

"But you pushed him. That's what you said."

"Yes, but he pushed me first. I didn't mean for him to trip and go over the edge. Blame the tree root for that."

"Why didn't you tell anyone about this years ago?"

I hesitated. That's where things got dicey. If we hadn't lied and a judge somewhere had sent me to juvenile hall for involuntary manslaughter, then the piano scholarship I'd been about to receive might have been yanked away. But I couldn't say that; it sounded too shallow and self-serving compared to her son's life. But she was a smart woman. Maybe she could look back and figure things out for herself.

But the scholarship had been only part of my motive. I wet my lips. "Everybody knew there was friction between Joey and me over Jade. People would think I purposely killed him just so I could have her for myself."

She tucked her chin. "A lot of people thought that anyhow."

"Besides, with your husband being the sheriff and Joey's dad and all, well, we knew it would be awkward. A conflict of interest. He knew about the friction between me and Joey. He might not have believed the truth. It was easier to make sure our stories matched and just say Joey lost his balance and fell."

She edged closer, and something dark and frightening entered her eyes. Or perhaps it had been there along. "I don't believe it! Jade knew you intentionally pushed Joey over the edge. But she preferred you over Joey. That's why she lied for you."

"But that doesn't make sense." I backed away, ever mindful of the cliff's edge only feet away. "If you look back, you'll remember that things were never the same between me and Jade after that. The lie tore us apart. If the deception was all about having Jade for myself, how come I don't have her now?"

She paused. Then: "I don't believe any of it. You were a liar then, and you're a liar now." If her eyes had wielded knives, she would have shredded me to pieces by now.

I braced myself. Would she attack me? Wrestle with me on the cliff's edge where Joey and I had so many years ago?

She balled her hands, and her voice broke, a hysterical shriek on the wind. "You murdered my son!" She lurched toward me with fists raised.

A gunshot rang out.

My body jerked, and Sharon Bartholomew moaned.

Before I could whirl toward the source of the sound, she rushed at me—not to strike me but to stumble to her knees and clutch my arms for support.

"Mrs. Bartholomew?"

"Help me. Please." Her voice, barely more than a wheeze, had never sounded so pitiful. The defiance on her face vanished, replaced by—what? Desperation?

Just then my eyes took it in. The blood covering the front of her T-shirt.

Chapter 51

Death delivers an ending few of us forget.

Sharon Bartholomew's grip weakened. She let go of my arms and flopped onto her back with a gasp. Her watery eyes fixed on a faraway point in the sky, and she was gone.

I shrank away, stomach squeezing. If I hadn't already lost my supper, I surely would have now.

My heart thundered. Somebody had shot her, and that person could shoot me too.

Flattening myself on the ground beside her corpse, I reached for the gun tucked in my waistband, the gun I'd forgotten until now.

I frantically searched the far side of the mine's edge. Given the trajectory of the gunshot, the bullet must have come from—

Galotta.

His profile flashed between two trees. A rifle clutched in his hand.

My breath caught in my throat. He must have shot her. By why?

It didn't matter. He must be coming for me.

Get up. Run. Get out of here.

Panic nipped at my heels. With newfound and surprising strength, I leaped up and scrambled over the fence at record-breaking speed. Shoving the gun into my waistband, I limped down the forest path toward my car, keeping my balance by grabbing passing limbs.

Even in a good sprint, Galotta required a few minutes to reach my position. I found just enough time to hop in the car, toss the gun on the seat, and crank the engine.

The tires slid in the gravel until they grabbed hold, and I sped away, a cloud of dust billowing behind me.

I checked the wireless jammers in the gym bag. The green lights glowed; the jammers still worked.

But how could Galotta have known my location? Had Dillon told him for the reward? Possibly. But how would Dillon have known where I'd be?

A fever of urgency forced me upright, and I clutched the steering wheel while my pulse began to slow.

An image flashed in the corners of my eyes: Mrs. Bartholomew's sightless eyes and the blood ... so much blood ... I peered down, dismayed to see so much of it had transferred to my hands and shirt. My stomach heaved again, but it offered nothing left to expel.

Why had Galotta killed her? Because he anticipated she might do me harm? Because the puppet master still had plans for me? His past words flashed back.

It's time for you to be the person you're meant to be.

What could he have meant? Why couldn't he just leave me alone? Why had I become so important?

Because you're a killer at heart, Landon. He knows it, and you know it. He wants you to embrace this identity.

But Joey's death had been an accident. I hadn't meant to kill him. But in that split second of fury when I'd shoved him, maybe I *had* wanted him dead.

Focusing on the road, I eased up on the gas. Having the cops on my tail now wouldn't have helped matters. But wouldn't Galotta be coming anyhow? He'd search the whole town now that he knew I was in the vicinity. And knowing Galotta must be after me, I couldn't abandon Mom and Jade and her family. They might be in danger too. They better pack up and get out of town.

Unless he'd already gotten to them.

Fingers tightened around the steering wheel, and I raced to the motel. Should I call the police and report the shooting? But Galotta *was* police. Why report something he already knew?

It didn't matter. I needed to tell someone.

Finding a pay phone, I made my report short and sweet, not giving away my identity. There. I'd done my civic duty.

At the motel, I pulled the sedan into its spot, my sapped body and tattered emotions longing for rest. A few more cars and SUVs filled the parking lot, probably vacationers needing a place to sleep before heading to parts unknown.

No lights illuminated the windows in Mr. Hamilton's room. In fact, the door stood ajar. Spiders crawled up the back of my neck when I nudged the door open. Only darkness greeted me.

"Mom? Jade?" My voice intruded in the unnatural silence.

Nothing but blackness beckoned.

Had Galotta killed them just as he'd murdered Sharon? Could he be on a killing spree now, determined to take out everyone I knew?

Panic thrust my feet into the darkness past the threshold. I reached for the wall switch, dreading to see mangled bodies on the floor.

My tense muscles relaxed. The light revealed no more than an empty room. Empty except for a stray stuffed lion. Henry's Simba lay in the middle of the floor, forsaken.

I closed the door behind me, turned the bolt, and pressed my back against it. Why had they left? And where had they gone?

With a look out the window, I checked the parking lot. Gordon's green van still occupied a parking spot in the rear corner, where it had been earlier. I passed the dark, windowless bathroom on my way to the rear of the motel room. Nope, no sign they'd made a hasty exit through the window there.

My fears mounted by the second. No signs of an abduction or struggle. No discernible gunshot holes in the walls or ceiling. It appeared they'd been "raptured," a word my mom liked to use ever since she'd read a popular series of Christian novels about the end-times.

Perhaps they'd felt threatened and left. But why leave on foot? And why be in such a hurry that they'd left Simba behind?

The facts made sense only if they'd been taken.

Galotta had somehow known about my visit to the old mine. Perhaps he'd come here first, looking for me but finding them instead. Had he taken them to use for bargaining later?

Maybe believing I'd been under his radar had been a myth all along. But if he'd been tracking my movements, why this game of cat and mouse? Why not just take me?

None of it made any sense.

Maybe I should go to the front desk. Perhaps they'd said something to the checkout guy before leaving. Maybe—

Someone knocked on the door.

I froze and held my breath. Had Galotta somehow tracked me from the mine?

Fingertips brushing the gun in my waistband, I stepped toward the door, then peered back at the rear window in indecision.

Should I pretend I'm not here?

Another knock.

"Landon Jeffers?"

An unrecognizable man's voice.

Not Korovin or Galotta. And if he was with the police, he would have said so. But who could he be, and how did he know I would be here? My name didn't appear on the motel registry.

Another knock, this one more insistent.

Nope, no more taking chances. Spanning the room, I opened the rear window, climbed into the wooded lot, and closed the window behind me. I circled the motel's rear to the parking lot and peeked past the building's edge.

A tall stranger in khakis and a baby-blue polo knocked on the door again. A shiny, black Lexus, which hadn't been there five minutes ago and rested beside Uncle Jed's clunker, bore a Pennsylvania license plate.

Might this guy be from the FBI? Or could this be Uncle Jed, come to see for himself what all the fuss was about? Too bad I hadn't spotted any photos of Uncle Jed at the cabin to confirm identification.

Though my instincts screamed otherwise, I decided to give the guy a chance. I had to trust somebody eventually. Besides, he might know where Mom and the others had disappeared to.

I emerged from hiding. "Are you looking for me?"

The man swiveled. Salt-and-pepper hair. Rail thin, though he bore a slight resemblance to Matt Lauer. "Landon Jeffers?"

Approaching him and keeping my right hand on the shape of the gun, I said, "Yeah. Who's asking?"

No weapon I could see. He had a Roman nose and piercing black eyes that widened when I drew closer.

I followed his gaze to my bloody shirt. "Oh, sorry. I can explain."

The man shifted his focus to my face, uncertainty flickering. "I heard you were in some sort of trouble."

"Yeah, you could say that." I approached him tentatively. "You seem to know who I am. Who are you?"

"I'm Brady O'Brien, a brain specialist, here on behalf of the FBI. I've come to help."

Chapter 52

Friday, October 30
Iron Valley, Michigan

Back in my room, door locked, Brady showed me a badge from some brain center in Pittsburgh. The text beneath his mug shot confirmed his words. His boyish, honest-looking face matched a portrait of him with a pretty, black-haired woman and two small children—twin boys, I guessed, based on appearances.

"My family." He returned the photo to his wallet, the aroma of Polo cologne drifting my direction.

He was working extra hard to gain my trust, but why the insecurity?

Maybe because you're paranoid and don't trust anyone. And he knows it.

Perched on the edge of the desk chair, he gave me plenty of space. "The FBI sent me on ahead to verify this, um, implant or whatever it is that this Dr … uh …" He paused to check his notepad; if anything, the illegible scribbles alone verified they came from a doctor.

"Dr. Korovin?" I offered.

"Yeah, that this Dr. Korovin allegedly put in your head."

Allegedly?

So the FBI hadn't bought into my story after all. They wanted his verification that I wasn't weaving some wild tale before sending in the cavalry.

Spirits sagging, I excused myself for a moment so I could change out of my bloody shirt. These doubts and delays didn't help our situation. The FBI needed to be here now, not only to protect me, but also to find out what had happened to Mom, Jade, and her family.

"I'll call and look into it," Brady said after I told him about their disappearance. "No need to worry. I'm sure they're okay."

Why such certainty in his words? Maybe the doctor didn't fully understand the gravity of my situation. But if he'd come to help, hadn't the FBI thoroughly briefed him on the situation?

At least I'd found my chance. If the FBI wanted proof, I lived and breathed it. And didn't this option match what Jade, Mom, and I had discussed at Uncle Jed's cabin—getting an expert to verify the implant in my head?

After a little prompting, I told Brady the whole story: about the brain surgery and Dr. Korovin, about the encounter with Galotta and what he'd told me about the implant, and about the nocturnal crimes I couldn't explain beyond mind control.

The talk was therapeutic. Maybe I just needed to talk to someone who could help carry the weight of my situation. Either way, I couldn't hide my elation; the FBI, an agency that could end this nightmare, had sent someone to listen to my story.

The importance of this development couldn't be overstated.

When I finished, Brady nodded, appearing to have already grasped everything I'd said, and abruptly changed the subject. "I need to take you to your local hospital so I can get some brain scans. It shouldn't take long."

"You mean, right now? You can just waltz in there and do whatever you want?"

"Sure. The FBI called ahead and made the proper arrangements."

I wasn't about to argue with him, especially when he offered supper on the way and escorted me to his flashy car. Out of habit, I grabbed the gym bag and mentioned the wireless jammers.

He shook his head. "You don't need those."

"Uh, yeah, I do." Hadn't he heard a word I said?

"Okay, fine. Whatever makes you happy. But you seem to forget you're in my custody now under the authority of the FBI. If this Galotta guy shows up, I just show my credentials, and he's gotta leave us alone. Or, believe me, my contacts at the FBI will have his head."

Maybe he humored me to a degree, but his tone stank of condescension. Didn't he understand what I'd been through over the last few days? And this whole trip to the hospital didn't quite add up. The FBI had told us to stay out of sight for a few days while they trekked to Iron Valley and set up personnel and equipment. If they planned to show up and do reverse tracking, why would I blow my cover to the puppet master now? Until they arrived in town, the jammers still offered protection.

Brady took us through the drive-through at a fast-food joint, where we parked and supped on burgers and fries that had never tasted so amazing. But when I accidentally dripped some ketchup on my hand, my mind hurtled back to the bloody crime scene at the old mine.

How could I stuff my face when Mrs. Bartholomew had died in my arms only a few hours ago?

Brady must have sensed my anxiety. He even gripped my shoulder the way a buddy might. "Hey, everything's gonna be okay—believe me. You just need to relax and eat up. You look like you need it. Sorry. I promised you a phone call about your missing friends. Let me see what I can find out, okay?"

When he pulled out his cell phone, I told him the jammers would block any calls he attempted to make. He shrugged. "No problem. I'll just need a pay phone. Any idea where I might find one?"

I did.

After the call, he returned to the sedan and flashed a big smile. "Not to worry. Your family and friends are doing just fine. I apologize for the lack of communication. One of my agent friends took them into custody a while ago for their own safety. They're in a safe house on the other side of town. That's why they were missing from the motel."

"Really? They're okay?"

"Yeah. I'll take you to see them after we're finished at the hospital."

But again, how did this development fit the FBI's plan?

Maybe Gordon had been mistaken on a few key details.

***

At the hospital, Brady whisked me through several doors and corridors simply by flashing his ID. Personnel had apparently been expecting him, and nobody gave him any flack; in fact, they gave him a wide berth, probably due to the whole FBI jurisdiction thing.

He led me to a small pale-blue room near radiology with the usual charts covering the walls and a wheeled steel examination table occupying the majority of the space. When he gestured to the typically paper-thin gown on the counter and said he'd step out while I changed, my antennae perked up.

I'd been to this hospital for scans before. Usually I simply emptied my pockets of any keys or change, went to the MRI room, lay down on the mechanical bed that would usher me into the round tunnel, and wore headphones so I wouldn't have to listen to the machine's deafening bangs, clicks, and beeps.

"But I don't usually change my clothes for a scan," I said.

"We should do a general exam first—you know, check your vitals, your blood pressure. That sort of thing. Get it all down on paper. That way you won't sue me later." He winked and headed out the door, closing it behind him to give me some privacy.

He *had* come to town on behest of the government, after all, and they had regulations for just about everything. Probably to cover their fannies in case something went wrong.

After changing, I perched on the edge of the table and swung my legs to give them something to do. Goose flesh covered my arms from the air-conditioning. Why did they always keep these rooms so cold?

His explanation made sense, but something off in his manner failed to put me at ease.

C'mon, Landon, you're just paranoid. Face it. You have to trust someone.

A red-haired nurse with a beak-like nose knocked on the door and entered with a murmured hello, exuding little warmth. With barely a word, she took my vitals, recorded them on a clipboard, and vanished. Brady returned a few minutes later, wheeling a gurney into the room.

"What are *those* for?" I eyed the leather straps in his hands.

"Could you lie down on the gurney? I'll need to take you to another room for the scan."

I complied. "So now you're going to strap me down without explanation?"

He avoided eye contact while his hands worked. "We need you to lie completely still for this one."

"But I've had MRIs before. This isn't how it works. They never strap me down, and—"

"Did I say anything about an MRI?" His hands stilled, and he met my flustered look with a patient sigh and a humored smile. "Landon, look. I know you've been through a lot, but you need to trust me here, okay? Please, you need to just lie still and do what I say."

"You really need to strap me down?"

"If you want my help, yes. And you do want my help, don't you?"

"Of course. It's just—"

"Look, I'll get this over as quickly as I can and take you to see your friends, okay? You're probably worried sick about them."

He must be right. Time to calm down and trust him.

"Okay, here's how it works. Once I confirm what's in your head, the FBI will get the green light to help you and your friends. You want this nightmare to end, don't you? Of course you do." He gave my arm an affectionate squeeze and flashed a smile.

"I'm sorry."

"You're forgiven. And really, if I were in your shoes, I'd probably be paranoid too."

"I guess I don't understand the straps. What kind of test is this?"

"A brain scan like I said. But this one's much more detailed than an MRI. You have to lie completely still, and I can't sedate you during the procedure because your brain needs to remain active for the duration."

I took a shot in the dark, nothing more than a Hail Mary pass, a final test to remove all doubt. "So when exactly are the FBI coming—if you confirm what's in my head, I mean?"

He shrugged. "I really can't say. I'm not aware any specific plans yet, but I'm sure they'll be in touch."

But the FBI had been in touch with Uncle Jed. They planned to arrive in Iron Valley in only a couple of days.

His story didn't match theirs.

By now he'd strapped my chest and arms to the gurney with large, heavy-duty buckles. But he hadn't tightened them yet. I worked one arm free.

He grabbed it. "Landon, what are you doing? I explained what I have to do. Why are you—?"

"You're with Galotta and Dr. Korovin, aren't you?" I seethed.

No denials from him, which further confirmed my fears. I wrestled with him until he gave up.

"Fine. Forget the straps!" He cursed, all pretense at warmth gone. "I've had enough of you. If you aren't going to cooperate ..."

When Brady turned his back to me, I slipped my other arm free and began working on the buckles, hands trembling.

C'mon, move!

My right thigh burned like a bee had stung me. I looked down just in time to see Brady withdraw the syringe. He peered deeply into my eyes. "Take a good look at this face, Landon Jeffers, because it's the last one you'll ever see."

Chapter 53

Friday, October 30
Iron Valley, Michigan

Somebody had left the faucet on, and all my energy—not that I'd had much to begin with—dribbled onto the tile floor in an invisible but substantial flow.

I leaned my head back and pictured the poison traveling through capillaries, veins, and arteries. But Brady had said he couldn't sedate me for this test. Another lie piled on a mountain of them. There was no test. Never had been.

Now Brady—if that was even his real name—pushed the squeaky-wheeled gurney down a long corridor. A steady stream of ceiling fluorescent lights shuttered past, methodical and hypnotic. Somewhere in the distance echoed the name of a doctor being paged over the PA system.

The signal jammers—he'd left them behind! Galotta would know my location.

Landon, does any of that matter now? This has all been part of the master plan. Brady's probably taking you to Galotta right now.

Brady's rubber soles thumped against the floor in a steady beat, a much slower cadence than the staccato of my pounding heart. My muscles began to relax despite my racing mind. Eyelids grew heavy, my tongue unresponsive.

I fought the drugs even while my mind acknowledged that I fought a losing battle. The promise of blissful sleep appealed more than the struggle to stay awake. But I *had* to stay awake. I needed to fight this. I wanted to be free.

Do you want to die, Landon? Wake up!

Mom, Jade—I must find them. Could they be somewhere in this hospital, too, being prepped for tests like lab rats? Maybe they'd been scheduled to get brain implants too so they could be enlisted in an army of drones, heads shaved like Holocaust survivors.

This is the last face you'll ever see.

Brady intended to kill me. What else could his words mean? Too much of a problem for the puppet master; termination must be the only logical choice.

"Wah ah ooo tay keen may?"

Ceiling lights silhouetted Brady's face. He impatiently bit out the words. "Brain scans, Landon. I already told you."

"Ooo go win too keel may?"

He ignored me.

More fluorescent lights beamed past on this runway to oblivion. People strolled by, some in street clothes, some in lab coats—not looking, not caring. After all, I must be another patient on my way to a routine procedure. Why should they think otherwise? Just another happy day at the hospital.

Do something, Landon. You gotta fight this.

My right arm still worked, though it had apparently been encased in cement. Even the tiniest movement required amazing effort. Gritting my teeth, sweat beads popping out on my forehead, I reached out for someone. Anyone.

Fingers grazed the lavender sleeve of a passing woman with curly black hair. She bent over me with compassionate Italian eyes. "Are you okay, dear?"

"Hep may." I clutched her sleeve as hard as I could.

"Does he need help?" the woman said to Brady.

"Hep may. Heeez go win to keel may."

"Sorry." Brady pried my fingers away. "He's been sedated. He doesn't even know what he's saying."

With a sympathetic nod, she spun away and abandoned me to my fate, heels clicking and fading. Like the steady ticking of a clock. Time running out for me.

She vanished, and I had no one else to turn to.

Wait.

That wasn't true.

Oh, God—Jesus—if you're there, please help me. I haven't had much time for you in the past, but I really need you right now.

The wheels commenced their squeaking. In the blind left corners of my eyes, red pixels swarmed like angry bees driven to sting someone. The memories couldn't be happy either. They wanted out of my head too, desired to be free, but this man planned to erase them forever. Pull the plug on Landon Alan Jeffers.

Brady slowed the gurney and slid me into a crowded elevator. People sandwiched me. The doors closed.

So tired. Sleep knocked on my door, but I turned him away. Forcing my eyelids open required nearly every ounce of energy I could muster.

"Hep may," I croaked out to no one in particular.

"Don't mind him," Brady said to anyone who listened. "He's been sedated for surgery and doesn't even know what he's saying."

Surgery? Blood whooshed in my ears. Surgery for what?

Surgery for your malfunctioning implant, silly. They'll get it right this time, Landy. And then you'll never, ever know what you're doing. You'll be a real drone. Killing people without a thought to call your own.

In the corner of my right eye, someone watched me. Somehow I strained my head a fraction of an inch. A vaguely familiar blonde woman stared at me with rounded eyes. Where had I seen her before?

Our gazes met, and she covered her mouth with her hand, whimpering. "It's him! Oh my word, it's *him!*"

An adoring fan? Nope. Horror and anger, instead of adulation, spilled over her features.

People are wonderful when they love you, but when they hate you, they can do more good than they realize. Gray matter channeled information from memory cells to recognition cells.

The music is so loud, she can't hear me. She doesn't realize I'm coming up behind her with the knife.

She's the mark, and I instinctively know what I must do.

I raise my arm. Slash downward.

She jerks her head around. Screams. Crumples to the ground.

The memory slid into place with the suddenness of a thunderclap.

Chapter 54

Friday, October 30
Iron Valley, Michigan

"H e's the man who stabbed me!" The woman shoved others aside and forced her way toward me.

Yes.

She'd call security. The opportunity to halt this hellish trip to my execution lay in her hands.

I forced words between numb lips with a force I didn't know I possessed. "Hep may!"

She lurched toward me, fists raised, eyes laser sharp.

Brady faced her. "Ma'am, please, just calm down." He grabbed one of her wrists to hold her at bay. "I think you've mistaken him for someone else."

"No, it's him—I know it is." Her voice quaked. "I'd never forget that face. I almost died because of what *he* did."

Louder this time: "Hep may! *Please!*"

Elevator doors whooshed opened. Brady turned his back on her and hurriedly wheeled me out, pushing me away at a fast clip.

"Hey, wait!" the woman called. "Stop!"

Brady didn't slow, but her shoes pounded the tile floor in pursuit.

"Security!" she yelled, her words nearly trapped in a sob. "Someone call the police. That man on the gurney—he stabbed me!"

He cursed and swung the gurney around a corner.

Dizziness smacked into my head. With one hand, I gripped the railing with what little strength I had left.

Her thumping heels closed in. A hand grabbed the gurney's railing beside my head, and we slowed. A wedding ring gleamed on her finger.

"I need you to stop," the blonde said to Brady. "Just wait until security gets—"

A grunt.

He must have slugged her. The woman groaned, and her body slid to the floor with a thud.

I gritted my teeth, longing to help but finding myself powerless. The words exploded out of me. "Hep may!" But of course no one but Brady could hear.

He shoved the gurney forward at a run, his shoes smacking the floor. The wheels squeaked double time.

Behind us a man's voice rang out. "Hey, you with the gurney. Stop!"

Brady cursed again and pushed me at a sprint. Other distant footsteps punched the floor, edging closer.

He swung wildly around a corner at breakneck speed, almost losing control. My world tilted. The gurney must have gone up on two wheels before correcting. Thankfully, the straps I so despised held me in place.

"Hospital security!" the man shouted. "I'm armed. I'm warning you to stop."

Brady didn't. But, slowing the gurney, he reached for something at his waist. A gun? He left me rolling and whirled. Swung his arm toward the corridor.

BAM!

My body jerked. At least my reflexes didn't sleep.

In the distance rang returning gunfire.

Gasping, Brady clutched a big gun with a long barrel. Aiming it at the guard down the hall, he fired it again.

BAM!

More returning gunfire.

Something thudded into Brady's body, and he grunted. He slammed into the gurney and leaned on top of me as if he'd lost his balance. His weight knocked the gurney on two wheels.

It tipped. It tottered. Brady tilted too.

I braced myself, gritting my teeth. The gurney tipped and clattered to the floor on its side. Though jarred, I was okay, thanks to the straps.

Brady lay on the floor, facing me, an ugly red blossoming at his mid-section. He coughed blood onto the floor. Resigned, bloodshot eyes fixed on me.

A spasm rippled across his face, and he stared through me to the great beyond.

Voices echoed in the distance. A man shouted. A woman yelled words I couldn't make out. Had the security guard been shot too?

The straps that had kept me safe hadn't been tightened enough to trap me. I had to get out of here. But how long before the drugs turned down the dimmer switch of my brain? I blinked and gave my head a shake to stay alert.

In the distance buzzed the static of walkie-talkies. People drew closer. Someone would call the police. Galotta must be on his way.

C'mon, Landon. Move!

Fighting the drug-induced stupor, I slid my dysfunctional hands to the buckled straps and persisted, grunting and panting. I could do this—I had to. Thankfully my arms had already been outside the straps. I worked on the buckles.

Seconds later, straps loosened, and I crashed to the floor, mere inches from Brady's stare and an ever-expanding puddle. Finding my legs unresponsive, I used my arms and started crawling on my stomach toward a closed door I prayed might be unlocked.

So little progress. My hopes flagged.

I'd never get out of here unless I could run, but I couldn't even walk.

A hand from nowhere grabbed my arm from behind. My head swiveled toward the face.

Gordon Hamilton. How could he be here?

He knelt, slung one of my arms around his neck, and lifted me to my rubbery legs. "I can't explain now. Just trust me."

"Wha ... wha?"

"Shhh. I gotta get you out of here. Jade wanted to come after you, but I wasn't about to let that girl out of my sight this time."

"Wire ... wire ... wuss. Jam ... jammah."

"It's okay. I grabbed the gym bag and your gun out of your examination room." He led me awkwardly through a side door into an adjoining office. My legs slid like dead things. "So glad I was a janitor at this hospital for a while. I know all the exits."

What happened in mere minutes seemed like hours. Gordon led me outside, helped me into a sedan I didn't recognize, and drove us away.

I listed against the door, stunned yet thankful; whatever strength remained drained away. My eyelids wouldn't stay open, and I slid ...

... into a dark place without doors, without light. Without hope. Would I ever wake up again?

Too tired to care, for better or for worse, I gave up the fight.

Chapter 55

Friday, October 30
Iron Valley, Michigan

Sometimes just when you think the story is over, it isn't. Someone patted my face, but I ignored the sleep disruption.

Another pat. Harder. More like a slap.

My face stung. Pushing the hand away, I groaned.

"Landon? You gotta wake up."

That voice. Gordon's rescue hadn't been a dream after all.

Clawing my way up, I broke the surface. Gasped. Opened my eyes.

Bland walls. Musty smell.

I blinked and rolled to my side on a bed, filling my lungs. "Where am I?"

"Best Western on the south side of town." Gordon's tense voice came from my right. He paced the room. "I didn't know where else to take you. I used an alias and some of your cash. Hope that's okay."

Whatever the cost, it had been worth every penny to get away from that hospital and Brady.

I sat up too quickly. An unseen hammer drove nails into my skull. Gasping, I gripped my head in my hands and waited. The pain lessened by degrees, but the ache remained. Could this agony be from the drugs or the cancer? I could no longer distinguish between the two.

"I don't understand." I squinted at him. "How did you know where I'd be?"

"Jade sent me after you."

"She and my mom are okay?"

Gordon waved a hand. "I'll get to that." He perched on the edge of the second bed, hands clasped between his knees. "But it wasn't so easy. We didn't know where to find you."

The trip to the mine had been a colossal mistake. I should have told them about my intent before vanishing. Of course, they'd been worried.

"I have some bad news." His face registered sad tidings. "Uncle Jed is dead."

"What?"

"Yeah, it's the strangest thing." His Adam's apple bobbed. "His car went off a bridge down in Washington, DC, right into the Potomac River. Nobody knows what happened."

My stomach roiled. The puppet master had gotten to him. "Does Jade know?"

"Yeah. The call came from my sister right after you disappeared. Jade was really broken up about it. She was worried about you, but then we got this bad news. Only then did we realize we were in danger and needed to run."

"What do you mean?"

"Jade noticed a little black box, apparently a GPS tracking device, under the rear bumper of my van."

"How did you know what it was?"

"Jade's cousin, Wade—he came over and identified it. We couldn't take my van because of the GPS. And you'd taken the other vehicle, so Wade gave us a ride here and let me use his other car. We got out of there fast."

That explained the hurried exit and the left-behind Simba.

Guilt slapped me hard. If I hadn't taken the car, I could have helped them escape. They'd been in trouble, but I hadn't been there when they needed me.

"After we got out of there, Jade was desperate, almost hysterical. She asked me to try to find you and listed several places where you might be. So I went looking for you and left them here in an adjoining room."

I shook my head. All because of my decision to go solo. But that was what I excelled at, wasn't it? Just me, going it alone while others were in danger or dying around me.

Gordon said, "I went back to the motel, hoping you were there, so I could tell you where Jade and the rest of us were. I arrived just in time to see you get in the car with that man who drove you to Burger King and then to the hospital. He didn't smell right to me, so I followed in case you needed help."

"You have better instincts than I do." Combing fingers through my matted hair, I studied him with new respect. "You saved my life, Mr. Hamilton. Do you realize that?"

He ducked his head shyly and couldn't suppress the grin.

"So where are they? My mom, Jade, and Henry?"

He sobered and swallowed hard. "That's the thing. Henry's here, still asleep in this bed." He gestured to the rumpled blankets behind him. "He wanted to stay with me. But I don't know where your mom and Jade are."

"What do you mean?"

"Like I said, they were staying in the room next door. While driving you here from the hospital, I stopped at a phone booth and tried calling Jade's room to let her know I'd found you. No answer. When I brought you here, they were gone—all of them except Henry, that is. He was watching TV in here. Something must have happened to them while I was looking for you."

My stomach clenched while I waited for the rest.

"I didn't know what to do at first. Then a little while ago, a clerk knocked on my door. Said some man had left special instructions. A message was to be delivered to you."

Some man?

Gordon handed me a business-size envelope. A typed name graced the front of it. My name.

Fears confirmed. Everything had been planned down to the letter.

God, please. Would you please just end this?

His eyes rounded. "Weird, isn't it? It's like somehow they *knew* you'd be here."

"They" knew everything, didn't they? When Brady's mission had failed, they'd apparently set plan B into motion. If they couldn't get me through Brady's ruse, they'd get me the old-fashioned way.

By taking hostages.

I tore the envelope open. Inside lay a white piece of paper, folded into thirds. The letter, addressed to me, had also been typed. Five paragraphs glared at me. I rose, steady for the first time in a while, and turned toward a lamp for better viewing.

All along, because of the wireless jammers and our prohibition of cell phones, the puppet master had lacked a direct connection and been unable to bargain for anything. Reading this letter could be a big mistake. When technology had failed, he'd resorted to the oldest, most dependable form of communication.

Words typed on paper. Addressed to me.

And now Mom and Jade had vanished.

I couldn't run away from this one.

Stalemate.

Sucking in a deep breath, I began to read.

Landon,

I have your mother and Jade. They're fine ... at least for now. But they'll stay that way on only one condition. It's time for you to come out of hiding. It's time for us to meet again.

I know there are many things you may not understand about yourself, about your past and your memories. What I hope you will understand is that everything you've ever done in the past is inextricably linked to who you are today. You cannot run from who you are, nor from who you are meant to be. You should embrace it. No matter how hard it is for you to remember, you must. Then you will see for yourself.

I want to help you remember.

The place for our meeting was not chosen randomly. Remember, the past, the present, the future—they are all intertwined, as you will soon learn. I probably know more about you than you do, but you will soon see the truth about yourself. Embrace it. You are destined for greater things than you realize.

The old school. Midnight. Come alone if you want to see them alive. Call the FBI or the police, and you will never see them again. Remember, we're watching.

Ray Galotta

***

I read the letter twice, three times.

My watch snagged my gaze. 10:43 p.m.

Pressing my eyelids closed, I pictured how it must have happened. Due to her albinism, Jade would have detected a man's shape but been unable to recognize Galotta, if she even knew his identity, until he stood only three feet away. By then, notions of escape would have come too late.

I wiped my mouth against the back of my hand. The thirst for something much stronger than a Mountain Dew teased me.

Why not just come and get me if you want me so bad? Why lure me to the old school?

Because it had been the scene of the school shooting. Because my history there still lacked clarity.

My subconscious, through the memory trips and daymares, had hinted at as much. But the details still lay hidden behind the wall of repressed memories. That wall needed to come down for me to understand any of this.

But at what risk?

I drew another deep breath. Blotted sweaty palms on my jeans.

This couldn't be happening.

I couldn't run, but if not for Gordon, I would have been alone with this.

Well, not according to my mom.

Our sovereign God has a purpose for every event under heaven, whether you want to believe that or not.

According to her, I could even smash the signal jammers against the wall and reject anything the puppet master directed me to do.

I didn't consider myself ready to tempt fate or test my faith. At least not yet.

Getting up, I hunted down the jammers and my gun.

Part 4
Blood in the Snow

Chapter 56

Few experiences are creepier than visiting a place in the dead of night that is intended for a crowd and finding it empty. Or at least it appeared to be.

The redbrick walls of Iron Valley Christian School hulked in the streetlights before me: colossal, Victorian, and dark. Bracing myself against the biting wind, I pulled my jacket's collar tighter around my neck with one hand while the other patted the Beretta tucked in my waistband.

Galotta hadn't said a word about leaving the signal jammers or gun at home. I'd brought them in the gym bag, but would they be enough?

My presence here startled me. The man responsible for Mrs. Bartholomew's murder only hours ago had summoned me, and now I would probably walk into his trap. But what choice did I have?

You don't have to do what these evil men want. Sin no longer has the power to control you, Landy.

Reaching the top of the concrete steps, I shot a glance back at Gordon across the street. He watched me from the car's open window, knowing his instructions. If I didn't return in an hour, he'd call the cops but make sure he talked to someone other than Galotta. With a nod, he drove away.

One of two intricately carved wooden-framed glass doors yielded to my pull and silently swung open. I passed a second set of glass doors and lingered in the dark, empty lobby, partially lit from streetlights.

Unsure what to do next, knowing I must be early, I checked my watch. 11:42.

Still plenty of time to look around. Maybe I'd recall something important before Galotta came calling. Wasn't that what all this was about? Remembering the past I'd forgotten?

Straight ahead stood the closed door to the school office, where my mom had slaved away for so many years. One long hallway continued to my left at a ninety-degree angle and disappeared. A doorway off that hall led to the cavernous gymnasium. To my right, flanked by classrooms and lined by old, gray dented lockers, continued another hallway.

At the end of the hallway to my right, in the last classroom, the one with the windows facing the playground, critical events leading to the shooting had begun so long ago. I swallowed hard, heart revving in my chest, nerves wire-tight.

What am I doing here, God?

An unseen voice, whether from God or my subconscious—I couldn't tell—whispered back.

Remember, Landon. Remember all of it. Your memories hold the key.

But the key to what?

Even if the events from that terrible day leaped back to instant recall, what did any of them have to do with the puppet master, this GPS in my head, and the disappearance of my loved ones? I couldn't comprehend how any of this fit together, but Galotta's letter had implied a connection.

The wind moaned just outside the entry doors. In the distance, down an unseen hallway, something clanked. I spun. Could someone be coming?

Nothing but silence welcomed me.

I desired to race away from this place. But I couldn't, not if I wanted to see my mom and Jade again.

A familiar sound shattered the silence, raising the hairs on the back of my neck. The echo of a bouncing basketball drifted from the gym doorway.

Pulling out the Beretta, I eased closer and entered the cavernous place. The lights were off, but streetlights and the moon partially illuminated the gym through high windows. In a single beam of light, a bouncing basketball at the farthest court slowed to a gentle roll, then stopped.

Spinning around, I gripped the gun and searched the emptiness. "Hello?"

No answer. But somebody must have set the ball in motion.

"Is anybody here?" My voice echoed eerily.

Again, no response.

The puppet master enjoyed playing games with me. He'd lured me to this place—and now what? What should I make of a bouncing basketball?

A basketball.

The familiar sensation of an incoming daymare swept over me again, as if someone lingered behind me, only inches away, hot breath gusting on my neck. What came next, I knew, would be inevitable. I hated it and longed for it all at the same time.

The agony drove me to my knees, head in my hands. Memories hurtled toward me like a drug hitting my bloodstream.

Chapter 57

Monday, December 13, 1982
Iron Valley, Michigan

From the open gym doorway drifted the echo of the bouncing basketball, the only sound in the empty hallway. No, not quite. Outside the front doors, the snow drove down in a way I'd never seen before—three inches per hour, if newscasters could be believed. Only moments ago, I'd said goodbye to classmates before they pulled on snowsuits, grabbed metal lunch pails and books, and trudged through the snow toward the yellow bus.

School had let out early, and I'd been left behind. Abandoned instead of belting out cheery Christmas carols with my buddies during the treacherous ride home.

I found my mom in the school office, of course. Where else would she be? She hung up the phone and met my frustrated gaze with a patient look. "I know, Landy. I want to go home just as much as you do."

"Couldn't we just fit them in our car and give them rides?"

"We'd never fit everybody in the Opel. Besides, it wouldn't be safe, and then how would those parents know where their kids are, huh?" She shook her head. "Sorry, but we just need to wait until their folks call me back."

Mr. Archibald, the principal, breezed into the office, his long, tan raincoat swishing around his legs. He brushed past me like I didn't exist, woodsy cologne so strong it made my nose sting.

"Any word on the last few kids?" he said to Mom.

"Yeah, Lance's dad's on his way, but that still leaves three kids. We can take Jade home, as usual, but the other two girls still need a parent to come and get them. I left messages, but nobody's called back yet."

"Well, keep trying to reach them. I gotta go. Wendy got our van stuck in a ditch."

"Oh no." Mom pressed fingertips to her cheekbones.

He waved a dismissive hand. "We'll be fine. A tow truck's out front, waiting for me. So you'll stay and man the ship until those parents arrive?"

"Of course." A pained smile. She'd been left holding the bag. As usual.

"Thanks, Sandra. You're a godsend. I gotta go. Bye." He headed out the door.

"Drive safely," Mom called after him, always polite even in the most trying of circumstances.

I shadowed Mr. Archibald into the hallway, where he pushed through the glass doors. Moments later, he seemed to step into a cloud, the whiteness swallowing him whole. Scotty from *Star Trek* had apparently teleported him to the starship *Enterprise*.

The empty hallway smelled faintly of Pine-Sol. Once ringing with boisterous laughter and loud, playful voices, it now lay quiet and empty of life. Creepy, in fact.

The sound of the bouncing basketball returned to my ears. Lance Sternham, one of the remaining four, was probably showing off his layups. I hated basketball because I stank at it, and just seeing how Lance excelled at the sport only intensified my conviction of being a loser. But my mom had said to me more than once, "He can't play Beethoven's 'Moonlight Sonata,' now can he?"

Speaking of piano, I decided that with the delay I should probably work on that new competition piece for the spring fine arts competition. But a blast of cold air interrupted my plans. Two scruffy-looking men entered through the glass doors, stamped boots on the snow-encrusted rug in the lobby, and blew into bare hands.

One of them studied me with brown eyes above a scraggly beard. His long, green coat stank of cigarettes and other repulsive things I couldn't place. The dirty orange knit cap hugging his head failed to conceal brown hair that tumbled to his neck in greasy locks.

"Hey, kid!" His face bore a lean, hungry look.

Something told me neither man could be a parent who'd arrived to give my friends a ride home. "Hi" was the best I could manage.

The second man, clad in a black leather coat and burgundy-and-green plaid pants, surveyed me with distrustful, icy-blue eyes. Blond, messy hair fell from beneath a baby-blue cap and framed pimply cheeks peppered with a few days' reddish stubble. The strong aroma of Everest cologne filled the space between us.

He looked past me and peered furtively out the glass doors through which they'd come, anxious about something. Maybe he just worried about the weather.

The men reminded me of an episode of *Gunsmoke*. If we'd relocated to the Old West and supplied these two strangers with leather vests, cowboy hats, and big six-shooters, they would have fit right in.

"You all alone here?" Brown Eyes said.

Before I could answer his odd question, someone touched my back.

"Can I help you?" Mom's gentle voice shaved the edge off my unsettled vibe. "Quite the storm we're having today. I hope you haven't slid off the road."

Brown Eyes nodded wearily. "That's exactly what happened. Our truck's stuck in the ditch out front. Mind if I use your phone to call a tow?"

I studied my mom. Could I be the only uneasy one in the presence of these strangers? But if their presence concerned her, she put up a good act.

"Sure, no problem." She gestured toward the office. "I'll show you where the phone is."

All kindness. No annoyance that a parent she'd been trying to reach might call back while the stranger hogged the line.

Great. Another reason why we'll be stuck here the rest of the afternoon.

Brown Eyes followed Mom toward the office while Blue Eyes lingered at my side and continued blowing into his hands. He scanned the empty hallways again.

"This place sure is quiet." He eyed me like I was somehow to blame. "So where'd everybody go?"

"They let school out early because of the storm."

"But if everybody left, what are *you* still doin' here?"

The usual spiel slipped off my tongue: about Mom, the school secretary, being unable to leave until the last stragglers had found their rides.

"Too bad, kid. So how many are left before you can split?"

"Three, I think, after Lance leaves. His dad's on the way."

"Three. Then you and your mom. Anybody else?"

The oddness of this question didn't occur to me at the time. "Nope. Just us."

"Well, I bet you won't be stuck here for too long." Kind eyes creased at the corners when he smiled; maybe the man had kids at home and missed them. Strong fingers mussed my hair. "Tough luck, kid. I know what it's like to get left behind. It's no fun, no way, no how."

The echo of the bouncing basketball drew the stranger toward the gym's doorway. I followed him, figuring he simply had time to kill while waiting for their tow.

Like I'd guessed, Lance did layups while two high school girls I didn't know worshipped from the bottom row of the bleachers. They squealed each time Lance made a basket like he was God's gift to basketball.

Jade sat apart from the Lance worshippers—something like a private island with her nose in a book. Literally. The problem was, when she read this way, she couldn't possibly be aware of what occurred around her.

Apparently, the stranger didn't care about basketball because his attention fixed on the girls. In fact, the way his gaze lingered on them, especially Jade, sent a ripple of uneasiness rolling up my spine.

He jerked his head toward me. "So this is a Christian school, huh?"

"Yeah."

"What does *that* mean?"

"Well, it means we believe in Jesus and the Bible."

"Oh yeah. Thanks for reminding me, kid." He pulled out a cigarette and lit it with a lighter.

"Uh, mister, smoking isn't allowed here."

Ignoring me, he pressed the cigarette to his lips. Drew in deeply. He granted me a full connection of the eyes as if daring me to defy him. Two plumes of noxious smoke shot out of his nostrils, resembling a fire-breathing dragon.

Stepping away, trying not to cough, I glanced toward the office. What could be taking so long?

Brown Eyes appeared and strode down the hallway toward us. "Jerry, the truck's on its way. Should be here in five minutes."

"Okay, sounds good, Rusty."

Good. They're leaving.

Deciding not to waste more time, I headed to the piano. If Mom needed me for some reason, she'd figure out where I was.

If only I'd lingered to be sure the strangers left.

If only I'd known about the gun hiding in Jerry's pocket.

Chapter 58

Gasping, I staggered to the front row of the dusty bleachers and collapsed. Resting the gun on my thigh, I allowed myself a moment to calm down, the memory so fresh I could almost taste it. With the back of my hand, I smeared sweat off my forehead and wiped it on my jeans.

So Jade *had* been here on the day of the shooting.

The memories had chosen to make a comeback. With patience, what else might I learn?

So keep remembering. Retrace your steps.

Getting up, I studied my watch. Still time to visit the storage room. The unused classroom had become a depository for unneeded chairs and desks.

To my amazement, the piano still awaited me, an old antique upright with chipped, yellowed keys. The cover had been left open, the keys coated in several layers of dust. Perhaps I'd even been the last person to touch them before the instrument had been abandoned to time and neglect.

Something magnetic pulled my fingers to those keys. With the contact of my skin to ivory, the past whooshed back.

Chapter 59

Monday, December 13, 1982
Iron Valley, Michigan

I paused from my playing, fingers aching, back throbbing from sitting too long in one position. Forty-five minutes had passed without any word from my mom. Surely the other rides had shown up by now.

In the hallway, silence. Wind-driven snow lashed against the lobby's glass doors. Another inch had accumulated during my practice.

Sheesh.

If we didn't head home soon, we might get stranded and have to spend the night here. Pausing just outside the school office, I listened.

No bouncing basketball. Nothing. Where had everybody gone?

I stepped into the office. Lights still on, the door strangely ajar. "Mom?"

No answer. Nobody inside.

The skin on the back of my neck puckered.

Near the back of the room, a small safe had been positioned on the floor under a table, invisible to anyone who might walk in. I wouldn't have thought twice about the safe if its door hadn't hung open on its hinges, the empty cashbox lying on the floor. The previous week, I'd overheard a conversation between Mom and Mr. Archibald. The cashbox had been full of tuition for the next semester, due before Christmas break. Mom had been tasked with taking the money to the bank.

But now somebody had stolen it.

Knees weakening, I backed away. My thoughts leaped to the two strangers. If they'd taken the money, they would have needed my mom to get the safe open.

So where could she be? Lying in a classroom somewhere, hurt? Or worse?

Call the police.

Chest tight, I searched for the telephone. Didn't see it anywhere.

Tinny voices drifted from the back corner of the room, causing my body to jerk. They were being broadcast from a radio of some kind.

On the back desk, next to various paper cutters and staplers, squatted a radio-looking device with various switches, buttons, numbers, and a microphone. The number twelve glowed on the display. The moment I figured out what the device must be, a voice burst from the classroom PA system's speakers. A woman's.

"Please, just let us go." *Mom.* "You've got all the money. I don't know what else you want from me."

At least she sounded okay.

"Just be patient, lady," Jerry said. "We can't let any of you go until our ride shows up."

"When he shows up, we'll be out of your hair," Rusty said. "But until then, we just gotta hang tight."

Somebody was crying but not my mom. Who could it be? One of the two high school girls?

Could Jade be there too? Where else would she be? We supplied her ride home.

What about Lance? Had he left with his dad? If they'd corralled everyone into classroom twelve while waiting for their ride, surely Lance would have stepped up and been the man.

Not a word from Lance. They'd probably waited for him and his dad, a possible threat, to leave before pulling out their guns.

Studying the PA system, I puzzled over how I could overhear the conversation. I'd never observed the system working from this end. In a classroom, a teacher simply pressed the call button while speaking to transmit his or her voice to the office.

Maybe Mom leaned against the wall and pressed the call button without being detected.

She's hoping you'll hear and send help.

I scurried around the room until I found the telephone, but the line was dead. From the storm or cut phones lines? Didn't matter. Hanging up, hand trembling, I tried to think of what to do.

This can't be happening.

A burst of static made me jump.

Rusty: "Hey, where's that kid we saw earlier, the one in the lobby?"

Jerry: "Yeah, the one with the curly black hair."

Silence. I swallowed hard.

Rusty: "Hey, lady, I asked you a question."

Mom: "Please … stop …" She gasped. "You're hurting me."

I clenched my fists. What could they be doing to her?

Rusty: "I'll let go as soon as you answer my question. You know, you're kinda cute when you're scared."

Mom sobbed. "I don't … don't know where he is. Please, don't hurt him."

A familiar voice: "Don't you dare touch Landon. If you hurt him, you'll be sorry."

I grinned. That was Jade all right with her usual spunk.

Rusty: "Shut up, you. You've got a big mouth. Jerry, go see if you can find that kid. He might be trouble."

Jerry: "Whaddya mean, Rusty? He can't call nobody, and if he tries to leave the building, he won't last long in this blizzard."

Rusty: "Don't make me ask you again."

Jerry: "All right, all right. I'm going!" He cursed.

Mom: "Run, Landon!"

Chapter 60

Monday, December 13, 1982
Iron Valley, Michigan

Mom's warning propelled me to action, but it also served as a homing beacon.

Jerry would check the office first. I had to get out of here and find help. But the school had been built at the end of a long driveway, surrounded by farmers' fields. At least a quarter of a mile in the snow and cold separated me from the nearest house.

But what other choice did I have?

Racing down the hallway, I paused at my locker long enough to grab my coat and boots. I hustled to the south entrance and pulled everything on, suspecting Jerry would be hot on my trail.

Hands against the crash bar, I shoved the door open against a snow drift and exited into a blinding world of lashing snow. The wind hurled flakes at my face and exposed hands, stinging my eyes. The cold jolted my system and stole my breath away.

I paused to pull the hood on and reached into my pockets for my gloves.

Gone. Where could they be?

No time. I gritted my teeth and thrust my hands into my armpits, heading across the parking lot.

A glance back at the school through the white fury confirmed my suspicions. No sign of Jerry yet.

My legs slogged through a foot of snow, face throbbing, lungs aching. In the parking lot, only our car remained under a great mound of white.

With a jolt of determination, I pushed myself into a jog, wended my way in the disorienting blindness. I ducked my head, shielding my face from the wind, and squinted through the thrashing flakes, searching for the parking lot entrance. The sky resembled a nasty bruise, the light fading fast. Close to four o'clock by now, it would be dark soon.

Sure enough. A pickup truck, half buried in snow, rested crookedly in the ditch near the entrance. Rusty had told the truth. Perhaps the men had come to steal the tuition and hadn't counted on getting stuck. Or maybe they'd gotten stuck and taken the opportunity to get some fast cash while in the neighborhood.

The moment I passed the truck, a vehicle on the main road slowed and turned into what I guessed must be the driveway. Snow didn't cover the red pickup.

Whoever drove it could help me.

I'd mistakenly strayed from the driveway. Correcting my path, I planned to hustle toward the truck and wave to get the driver's attention. But two steps toward the driveway, I slipped and fell in a snow bank, only a dozen feet from where the truck would pass.

On hands and knees, I looked up when the truck flashed by, the driver's profile a silhouette against the opposite window.

Lucius.

What could *he* be doing here?

Had he sent those men to rob the school? But that didn't make sense. Lucius was loaded.

That left me with only one remaining suspicion.

Jade!

Chapter 61

Outside the storage room, I leaned against the wall and clutched the gun, pausing to catch my breath. The throb in my forehead faded, along with the usual wave of nausea.

Memories came alive now. The men hadn't come to take the school's money. Lucius's buddies had been eager to make a fast buck, but the theft had been a cover for something else. Something bigger.

I clamped my eyelids closed and struggled to bring the memories back. Tried so hard my head ached. No use. The mental brick wall still rose, tall and formidable, though certain to crumble soon.

If Jerry and Rusty had done Lucius's bidding at the school, maybe they'd helped him with other tasks too. Jerry had smelled strongly of Everest cologne, the same aroma I'd whiffed when the shadowy figure elbowed me on the night he'd stolen Jade's locket. Perhaps Lucius had paid the men to terrorize Jade on his behalf.

Peering down the hall, I spotted a mop leaning against the wall.

And a new memory hit me afresh, this one of Louie Clover, the school janitor.

I rushed to the school kitchen, just beyond the eerily empty cafeteria, and resisted the urge to flick on a light, which would have given away my location.

A quick glance at my watch. Almost midnight.

Though I didn't have much time, I couldn't help myself. I needed to check one more location for affirmation that I must be on the right track.

In the kitchen, streetlights filtered through windows. They cast beams across several stoves and a commercial-size refrigerator. I neared the pantry, lit by the soft glow of moonlight, dreading what I might see—

No way.

My eyes widened at the sight of the Savage 30-06. Louie's hunting rifle lay on the stainless-steel shelf just like it had so many years ago, brought to impress me. Louie had been long dead, and now I stood here alone so many years later. Yet in my mind he spoke to me, his voice accompanied by the strong odor of Vicks VapoRub.

It has to be our s-s-s-s-secret. You c-c-c-can't tell n-n-n-n-nobody.

I blinked and took a deep breath. And realization dawned.

The bouncing basketball. The strategically placed mop. The shiny hunting rifle.

Pure manipulation.

Landon, have you forgotten who you're dealing with?

They'd been dropping clues along the way. Visual triggers. For once the puppet master and I shared the same goal.

He wants you to remember that day.

But why?

Checking my watch, I winced. No time—and I inched so close to the truth now.

I returned to the lobby, craning my neck to listen and gripping the Beretta. Where could Galotta be? An unnatural, festering silence shrouded the place. Only one last place left to visit.

Classroom twelve. Maybe Galotta awaited me there.

Trying to breathe, I fingered the Beretta's safety off and eased down the corridor. Moisture vanished from my throat and mouth.

Closed doors flashed past on either side, their small windows bright from streetlight-illumined classrooms. If any of those doors opened, I'd be ready.

Then came the moment I'd been both dreading and anticipating. The back of my throat itched.

The headache rushed on me like a storm system about to unleash a drenching on the world. My brain discerned what to expect and prepared me to relive what I'd forgotten. Either that or it intended to kill me in one massive stroke.

Time to remember, Landon. All of it. Time for the truth.

Nausea squeezed my gut. I paused and leaned forward for a breather. And at that moment …

… the commercial gray carpeting of the present morphed into checkerboard floor tiles. The same hallway at another time.

Chapter 62

Monday, December 13, 1982
Iron Valley, Michigan

Straightening, I pressed on with measured breaths. I passed a trophy case and caught the reflection of a much younger Landon.

Ready or not, here I come.

Hadn't we called those words to each other—me and Jade and Joey—during our pretend battles in the woods with BB guns?

No game now, and there wasn't time to find help. If Lucius was involved, I had to do something. What had Jade told me?

If anything should happen to me, tell the police it was my stepbrother, Lucius.

Did he plan to kidnap Jade? Or worse?

Six classrooms away.

Five. Four. Three.

Someone grabbed my arm from behind while a hand clamped over my mouth, muffling my shriek. I whirled.

Dad? Where did he come from?

His voice cracked with fear. "What's going on? Where's your mother?"

I pulled him into the nearest classroom, where in a hushed but frantic voice I told him everything, including hearing the voices over the PA system and seeing Lucius in the pickup. His gaze fell on the hunting rifle I'd grabbed from the kitchen.

Dad's gaze measured me with a look of accusation.

He'd recently taken me hunting and gotten a big buck. Then he'd showed me how to use his hunting rifle to get my own buck someday. Said I proved to be an excellent shot. In the absence of help, I'd grabbed Louie's rifle from the pantry without thinking.

No time to explain. Dad grabbed the rifle from my unsteady hands and faced the door. Motioning me behind him, he cracked the door to the hallway.

Loud, angry, and impatient voices rang nearby.

Jade's voice: "Don't you even think about touching me. No!"

Jerry: "You're coming with us."

Mom: "Hey, leave her alone. What are you doing?"

Rusty: "Jerry, just grab her, for crying out loud. Don't let her get away." He cursed.

Mom: "Hey, you've had your eye on her the whole time. She's the reason why you came here, isn't it?"

Jade: "Let me go! I'm not going anywhere with you. No!"

She screamed.

Chapter 63

Present day
Saturday, October 31
Iron Valley, Michigan

I leaned heavily against the wall and struggled to breathe, my knees so weak I doubted they could hold me up.

And voices—*I can't believe it*—came from classroom twelve again, just like they had so many years ago. My mom's voice and the voice of an older Jade. They tried to reason with someone.

With my eyes clamped shut, my mouth watered. I could do nothing but surrender and step back into 1982.

Chapter 64

Monday, December 13, 1982
Iron Valley, Michigan

We eased into the hallway: Dad first, me second.

Think, Landon, think. You have to make sense of this.

Why would Lucius be here, in the middle of a snowstorm? He'd killed Jade's mother, Jade had said, leaving the wealth to her and her stepdad. But where would the money go if Jade died?

This wasn't about a theft or even a kidnapping.

Lucius had probably parked outside in the getaway truck, waiting for his hitmen. Paid to do the dirty work.

"Dad," I whispered, my throat so tight I could barely speak. "They're going to take Jade and kill her. I know it!"

He nodded, but I wasn't sure whether he'd grasped what I had.

Dad eased toward the closed door while I peered around him. Shadows danced across the door's frosted glass and dappled the tile floor. Moments stretched, strained.

My gut rebelled. I was going to be sick or wet my pants. Or both.

More muffled voices thrummed through the glass. Angry. Terrified.

Jade's voice. "No!"

Muscles tightened. What could Dad be waiting for?

Mom shouted. Then came the loud slap of a striking hand, and Mom groaned.

Jade yelled, "No, no! Don't touch me!"

Dad twisted the doorknob and barged into the room. Lifted the rifle with both hands.

Beyond the threshold flared a slow-mo video clip of images and sensations my brain took only seconds to process.

The icy room. The window flung open to the dark, snow-filled night. Snowflakes swarming in like angry albino bugs.

Jerry grabbing Jade and wrestling her, shrieking, with legs off the floor and kicking, toward the open window.

311

Mom lying on the floor, hand pressed to her bleeding nose.

Rusty pointing a handgun at her head to keep her in place or about to finish her off.

Two high school girls huddling together in the corner.

Time sped up.

Rusty swung toward Dad, eyes widening. The handgun swung toward Dad at the moment Dad brought up the rifle and fired.

BAM!

Dad missed, but Rusty didn't.

My father fell to the floor and reached for his bloodied shoulder. He writhed and cried out, the rifle clattering to the floor.

I stared at him, frozen in place.

Jerry hustled Jade toward the window while her heart-seizing shrieks begged for somebody, anybody, to do something.

Rusty swung the gun toward me, wild eyes fastened on my stunned face. Instead of blowing me away, he chose to help Jerry instead.

Together, they forced Jade through the open window, followed her, and began leading her across the deep snowdrifts of the playground and the lashing blizzard. In the parking lot on the other side of the playground, Lucius waited in the red pickup. Headlights glimmered across the sparkling snow, two glowing eyes.

All this happened in mere seconds while I watched, too numb to move.

Don't be a coward, Landon. Do something. She needs you.

Jade twisted away from Rusty for a nanosecond and shot a look back at the open window, wild eyed. "Landon! Help me!"

Chapter 65

Present day
Saturday, October 31
Iron Valley, Michigan

Blinking, I awakened to the present. To the cry of my name. Mom lay on the floor, nursing a bloody nose.

Déjà vu.

Across the room Galotta shoved Jade through the open window and into the night, a gun pressed to her head.

"Landon!" Jade cried.

"Move!" Galotta shot a look at me. I stared at him numbly. "Is any of this coming back to you now? Don't you see what this is all about?"

In that split second, a red-hot poker drove into my cranium, shoving me to my knees.

Chapter 66

Two men dragged a shrieking Jade through the snow.

Heart drilling through my ribs, I grabbed Dad's arm. "C'mon, Dad, we gotta help her! Please, you need to get up."

He leaned on me and rose on unsteady legs. I reached for Louie's rifle, where Dad had dropped it, and we shuffled toward the open window. I pressed the gun toward him.

The three were illumined under streetlights. "Dad, you gotta do something! You gotta save her. They're going to kill her if you don't."

All color had leached out of his face. He toppled into me, my arms breaking his fall. I eased him to the floor just as he shoved the rifle into my hands.

What?

I eyed the rifle, and a barrage of memories flashed in my gray matter like a slide show.

Jade standing her ground against the posse in the playground.

Jade climbing the monkey bars and pretending to be Nadia Comaneci, arms extended, toes gripping the bar like she was on the high beam. Arms cartwheeling, her cry slicing the air.

Me rushing toward her imbalance, arms outstretched, determined to catch her.

Me sprinting toward her falling body in slow motion. Unable to reach her in time.

I'd missed her that day, and she'd broken her arm. The experience had piqued her interest in nursing. The past, the present, the future—all linked.

But today I couldn't let her fall. She counted on me. To not catch her today meant her certain death.

God, please help me.

There was still time to save her. Somebody would find her body in a ravine somewhere, strangled, if I didn't do something.

Swallowing hard, I rushed to the window. Squeezed through.

A snowbank broke my fall. I struggled to my feet, icy wind and snow lashing my face.

The wind shrieked. I should have been freezing, but, drunk on adrenaline, I kept going.

The men dropped Jade. Maybe they'd glanced back and seen me with the rifle—I don't know. But they'd left Jade in the snow and decided to run.

But Lucius would send them back. He'd make them finish the job.

Oh yes, he would.

They couldn't so easily run away from this, and everything depended on me to end it. I couldn't let them come back. If they returned, Jade's life would be over.

I lifted the rifle without hesitation as if I were hunting deer.

Remembering my dad's advice, I took a deep breath and aimed at the two men. Exhaled. Pulled the trigger.

Once.

Twice.

Chapter 67

Present day
Sunday, November 1
Iron Valley, Michigan

A slap across the face brought me back, though I found myself still stuck halfway in the past, wallowing in the truth of what I'd done. *I'd* killed those men. *I* bore the responsibility for their deaths. Not Dad. Never Dad.

I'd been so wrong, hating him all these years when he'd been the innocent one. Why had he taken the fall for me?

Squeezing my eyes closed, I still stood in the snow. Rusty and Jerry lay facedown at my feet near snow-shrouded playground equipment. Gaping, oozing wounds in their backs glistened, their freshly spilled blood steamed in the howling wind.

My stomach jolted. I was going to be sick.

But Galotta wouldn't let me. He slapped me hard again.

I straightened, face stinging, and looked around. Winter had vanished, the bodies gone. I'd been yanked back to the present, standing amid leaves after midnight, illuminated by floodlights.

Reality won the battle over disorientation. Evil still lingered, this time in the form of the gun Galotta pointed at Jade's head. She cowered a mere five feet away to my right. Those tiny tennis players in her head fought a death match.

"Do you remember now?" Galotta glared at me, veins bulging in his neck. "You're a natural-born killer, Landon Jeffers. That's who you are."

I returned his glare, still processing the truth, brain sluggish.

Joey Bartholomew's death had occurred partly due to my reckless, anger-driven push. Though I'd defended Jade's life, I'd also blown two men away with a hunting rifle.

"Do you see now why you had to remember?" Galotta said. "Why we had to play this little game of long, long ago? Do you see now why what you did back then is so important to who you are today?"

You're a natural-born killer, Landon Jeffers.

You're evil. You're worthless. People are dead because of you.

Galotta reined me in with his bloodshot eyes. "You were chosen, Landon, because you have a gifted brain and because you've killed before."

They've known about me all along, even better than I've known myself.

"We've been watching you for a long time, waiting for just the right moment to enlist you to our ranks, but you weren't so willing, were you? We had to hold up the mirror so you could see the true Landon, the evil Landon. Now do you understand? You're one of us now. You just didn't realize it."

An assassin? That's my calling?

Shivering in a cold sweat, I willed someone to wake me from this nightmare.

"Don't listen to him, Landon." Surprising confidence rang in Jade's voice. "He's just trying to poison your mind. God has only good plans for you."

I looked at Jade, at the fear in her eyes she tried to hide. I'd have to sort all this out later, but first … where could my gun be?

The Beretta lay at Galotta's feet. And something else too. My backpack lay open in the grass. Apparently while I'd wrestled with the daymares of memory, he'd stomped on the signal jammers, shattering them.

No.

If Galotta had the puppet master's controls, he could make me do anything he wanted.

"Lose something?" Galotta grinned. "There's no hope for you now except your destiny. Landon, it's time for you to be the person you were meant to be. And only death and supreme sacrifice can initiate you to the path of greatness."

Death? Sacrifice? What could he be talking about?

My scalp tightened. The puppet master had made Galotta kill his mother. Now it would be my turn to prove my worth, the reality of my situation like ice water freezing in my veins.

Fall leaves crunched behind me.

"Stop right there!" Galotta swiveled the gun away from Jade and pointed it at someone behind me. Just over my right shoulder.

"Landon, don't listen to him. Choose the path of life, not death."

Mom.

"Don't come any closer!" Galotta shoved Jade, and she stumbled toward Mom, who grabbed her arm and righted her. Now they stood side by side and faced Galotta, barely visible in my right peripheral vision.

With his foot, Galotta pushed my gun through the leaves toward me. "Pick up the gun, Landon."

"Don't do it, Landon." Mom's voice quavered. "You don't have to obey him. You answer to a higher power. Remember?"

"Shut up!" Galotta slid his free hand into a pocket and pulled out something resembling a silver smartphone. He fiddled with it. "Take the gun, Landon."

My hand now had a mind of its own. I bent and reached for the Beretta. Gripped its cold steel.

God, help me. I'm truly a drone now.

Chapter 68

Sunday, November 1
Iron Valley, Michigan

I studied the gun, a sucking sensation in my stomach. On my last mission of violence, I'd stabbed a blonde from behind, taking her by surprise.

At least then I'd been blissfully unaware of the control in real time. Now I resembled a puppet, and in the back of my mind I considered—

"Landon, listen to me," Mom said. "Remember what I told you. You have to remember."

Struggling to focus, I turned my head toward Mom.

If you're a true child of God, Satan can't control you. Only God can.

"Landon"—Galotta gave the orders now—"don't listen to her. Not a word. Do you understand?"

Mom's mouth moved, but with the press of a button, Galotta had deafened me. Not even my rib-slamming heart registered.

Tears streamed down Mom's cheeks because she grasped that I couldn't hear her even if I'd wanted to. She slid to her knees—hands folded, head bowed.

But I didn't need to hear her to grapple with the choice before me. And to remember …

Signal jammer or no signal jammer, you don't have to do what these evil men want. Sin no longer has the power to control you, Landy. Even without the batteries to block the signals, you can say no.

If you're a child of God.

Was I a child of God?

Apparently not. Galotta still wielded control for evil purposes. That repeating of the sinner's prayer when I was little—it must have been nothing more than fire insurance. Something I'd done because my friends had.

I *needed* to be God's child. Lives depended on my choice.

"Landon, point your gun at Jade."

No!

My arm moved at Galotta's command. I mentally fought every centimeter, but my arm didn't even tremble in resistance. Jade appeared in my

321

sights. I didn't have a prayer of thwarting his commands, not in my own strength.

But wasn't that the point?

This can't be happening. God, you've gotta do something!

Tears glistened in Jade's eyes. She lifted pleading hands toward me, toward the barrel pointed at her face. Panic blared from her vocal cords.

She said something I couldn't hear.

Didn't she comprehend I couldn't help myself?

"I'm so sorry," I choked out in a sob. "I can't help—"

"Not a word." Galotta pressed a button, and my voice vanished, though I still mouthed the words.

"I can't help what I'm doing."

The stark realization of his ultimate control made me shudder.

Squeezing eyelids closed, air rushing through my lungs in explosive gasps, I prayed for deliverance.

On the mind screen in the blind corners of my eyes blazed snapshots of Jade and me together. Swinging from ropes at the treehouse. Running through the woods with our BB guns. Creating a Tolkien-inspired secret code in dog-eared notebooks. Sharing a private moment in the school playground. My handing her the locket. Jade kissing me and dashing away while I stood there, hand pressed to my cheek, eyes stinging.

I opened my eyes. Tears pooled unbidden though my arm lagged not a scintilla.

Don't make me do this. Please don't make me do this.

Jade charged at Galotta.

He swiveled his gun—while I screamed, "No!" in my mind—and shot her in the thigh.

Jade collapsed on the leaves, moaning and writhing, clutching the wound. Blood in the leaves. Just like …

Blinking, I gasped.

… just like the blood in the snow.

My fault. All those years ago, I'd been the one responsible, but I'd blamed him. Blamed my father for my own transgression, which he'd willingly carried in my place.

Forensic experts had testified that he unnecessarily shot Jerry and Rusty in the back when they'd been running away. Said he should have called the police, but he'd taken justice into his own hands instead.

He'd gone to prison for second-degree murder. In my place.

A memory flared: Dad prying the rifle out of my numb hands, wiping the barrel clean of my fingerprints, and taking the rifle in his own grip. Just before the police arrived and arrested him as the shooter.

Standing before the judge, he'd paid the price for *my* sins. Just like Jesus had done for me on the cross so long ago.

Are you sitting in the chair, Landy? Are you trusting in what Jesus did for you?

Galotta said, "Landon, shoot her." Somehow I could hear him but not the others.

God, please, no. Not Jade. Please, God. Help me! Save me!

Sweat beaded my forehead, stung my eyes. I peered down at Jade, but no longer did terror veil her eyes. Something else glinted there, even while she clutched her leg.

Peace.

Gently, I began to squeeze the trigger.

"I love you, Landon," she mouthed through her tears. "This isn't really you. I forgive you."

She forgives you, Landon. Just like Jesus forgives you.

Sit on the chair, Landy.

Sit. On. It. Now.

I squeezed my eyes shut.

God, please forgive me. Thank you, Jesus, for paying the price for all the terrible things I've done. I trust you now—

"Shoot her, Landon. Shoot her in the head. *Now.*"

In my mind, eyelids still clamped shut, I yielded control to the only One who deserved it. But my finger squeezed the trigger a little more, even when my mind screamed at my hand not to.

Sin no longer has the power to control you, Landy. You can say no.

I pulled the trigger, but my arm went wild. The bullet zipped into the leaves.

Jade's wail of relief met my ears.

My eyelids sprang open. Could it be possible?

Galotta cursed and lurched toward me. Pointed the gun at my heart. "Kill her. Now. Or you die."

The gun swung around at *my* command, and I aimed at his heart. "Not on your life!"

Righteous indignation flared in my eyes. How dare he think he could control me. How dare he assume he could make me kill the two most important people in my life.

Thank you, Jesus. I'm free! He doesn't control me anymore.

Galotta's cheek twitched. "Put the gun down, Landon."

"No." My voice worked fine now.

New emotions flickered across his face. Confusion. Bewilderment. Anger. "Then you leave me little choice." He sighed. "This wasn't how your story was supposed to end. You have incredible gifts you don't even realize." His arm stiffened, finger tight on the trigger.

"You don't have to do this. I know they've made you do terrible things, but you don't have to play their game any more than I do. You have a choice, Ray. Join me. You can be free too. We can be free together." I offered him an open hand.

Galotta's face reddened. The gun in his hand jittered. "I'm going to kill you."

I struggled to breathe. "Go ahead. Pull the trigger, and we're both dead. I'll go straight to heaven. But where will *you* go?"

He jerked his head in defiance. "I'll—I'll go to Sylvia."

"Are you sure? At least in heaven I know I'll see my loved ones again. Do you have that assurance?"

He swallowed hard.

"She's all you live for—admit it."

Sweat trickled down his forehead. "Okay, I admit it." He dragged his tongue across his lips. "All right, fine. Let's see if you're right. On my count we'll—"

Thwop.

My torso jerked from the impact.

I looked down at the round, bleeding hole in my shirt. Teetered on unsteady feet.

Galotta hadn't done this.

A man. Thirty feet away. Gun at arm's length, now aimed at Galotta. Another drone?

A second shot rang out. Galotta crumpled to the ground with a groan.

The moment I fell, strength vanishing from my legs, I glimpsed the hooded man running back to his car. Tires squealed. With both of us eliminated, the puppet master could still win.

No, God, please.

The grass tickled my face. My life poured onto the playground, where Jade and I had once played marbles and argued about who'd get the cat's-eye.

Chapter 69

Jade crawled to Landon's side, dragging her throbbing leg like dead weight, and studied his wound with a shudder. So much blood.

Landon's eyes glazed over. He breathed erratically. "It ... hurts."

A blanket of ice wrapped around her heart. "I'm sure it does. Just hold on, Landon. Hold on!" She winced, trying to ignore the agony.

"He's going to be okay, isn't he?" Sandra said in a panicky voice.

"I don't know."

"Are *you* going to be okay? You're hurt too."

"Don't worry about me. Call an ambulance! Hurry."

"But we don't have cell phones, remember?"

Jade shot a glance at Galotta, whose vacant gaze embraced the moon-lit sky. He was gone. "Search him. Hurry!"

Jade cupped Landon's blanched, stubbly face. She sought to ignore waves of panic. "He's cold. He's going into shock."

"J-a-a-a-de." Even his blink had become sluggish.

"It's okay. I'm here."

So much blood. He's not going to make it. God, no.

"Landon, I'm here. Hold on!"

Sandra discovered the "Landon controller" in the grass. Discovering it couldn't be a phone, she tossed it to Jade. Then, searching Galotta's pockets, she found a cell phone. She punched some numbers.

"Hurry!" Jade yelled, voice breaking.

While Sandra practically yelled at an emergency responder, Jade checked Landon's vitals. The heartbeat had become erratic. She needed to stop the bleeding.

"You ... said ... the words." Frothy blood bubbled between his parted lips. He must have been hit in a lung.

"Shhh." She tore his shirt open and pressed down on the wound with both hands. "Just save your strength and stay awake. Do you hear me, Landon? Help is on the way."

His heartbeats slowed. She must be losing him.

No, God, please. This isn't the way it's supposed to end.

He coughed. "You said … you loved me."

She forced courage into her voice. "Of course, I love you. I always have. Didn't you realize that?"

He smiled. "Our hearts always knew, didn't they? We didn't need … words. We had our own … music."

Could he be going delirious? "Landon, just stay awake. Keep talking to me, okay? I want to hear your voice."

She recognized that dazed look. Dread dragged its claws down her back.

Sandra lowered the phone, her voice shaky. "An ambulance is on the way. They said their ETA is about fifteen minutes. But that's too long, isn't it?"

Jade nodded, unable to speak.

He'll never make it. God, what am I supposed to do?

Jade eyed the "Landon controller" and grabbed it with one hand while the other kept compressing. An app of some kind glowed on the screen. Colored bars. Numbers. What did any of them mean? Systems of the body?

Galotta had used this gadget to control Landon. Maybe …

"Call my cousin Wade!" Jade rattled off the phone number. "Tell him to get here ASAP. If he complains, tell him he can have the whole speaker system if he gets here in five minutes."

Landon's eyelids closed, apparently too heavy to keep open.

"No, Landon, no." Jade willed him to obey her. "Stay awake. Stay with me!"

"Jade, I … love … you. I—"

He heaved a deep sigh, then stilled.

Oh, no. God, please.

She checked his heartbeat. No pulse. No breathing.

Her breath caught in her throat. Heart revving, she started CPR while trying to see through her tears.

"Wade's on his way." Sandra buried her face in her hands, rocking on her knees.

Jade continued with the chest compressions and mouth-to-mouth, but her efforts must be futile. This couldn't be happening.

Gone. And just when we finally understood each other.

A gray sedan raced into the parking lot and screeched to a stop. Wade sprinted to her side. "Um, what's going on?" His eyes widened at the sight of Landon.

She flung Galotta's gadget at him. "He was being controlled through that thing. Can you figure it out? Hurry!"

Wade whistled. "Oh man!"

"Can you figure it out?" she yelled. "His heart stopped. I can't—"

"Check it again."

Shoving strands of hair away from her face, Jade checked his vitals. Her eyes rounded at him. "What did you just do?"

Wade's shoulders hiked. "I think I turned his heart back on."

"Just like that?"

"Just like that."

She expelled a rush of air. "Can you keep his heart going until the ambulance gets here?"

"If this thing keeps doing what it appears to do."

Still compressing the wound, Jade leaned her head back and let the dam of emotion break.

"So I really get the speakers now, huh?" Wade grinned.

She arched an eyebrow his direction. "Are you kidding me? You can have the whole stereo system for all I care."

Chapter 70

Monday, November 23
Iron Valley, Michigan

What had been a dream?
　　　　What had been a memory?
　　　　What had been reality?
At first, I couldn't tell the difference.

And not until I finally woke up could I start sorting out my life. Then for days everything became almost too much to take in: the hospital room crammed with family members, the nurses coming and going, the tubes running from various parts of my body. Then there were the police patrolling the hallways for my safety and the shocking news about how I'd died and been miraculously brought back to life until the paramedics could work their magic.

Weeks after my successful surgery for the gunshot wound, I nervously awaited the results of a recent MRI, fearing what my oncologist had to say about the progress of my cancer.

The FBI had questions, which I answered the best I could. I had plenty of my own. And some didn't get answered until I finally found a rare, quiet afternoon close to Thanksgiving to chat with Jade and my mom.

Jade embraced me. "I'm so glad you're doing okay after everything that's happened." The aroma of strawberries enfolded my nose. The ping-pong guys in her head competed at a leisurely pace today.

She must have detected my gaze on her crutches. "Oh, I'll be fine. My wound's not as bad as yours. I guess you've got me beat on that one."

Mom hugged me too, though not too tightly due to my chest soreness. "There's so much to talk about. I'm not even sure where to begin. So maybe you want to start."

I snatched a deep breath, glad to use both lungs now. "Am I really safe here? That's what the FBI tells me, but it's still hard to believe."

Mom nodded. "Absolutely! And when this is all over, they have a new life planned for both of us—in that witness protection program you've heard about."

Nodding, I sought to look happy, but the offer involved only me and my mom. I didn't know whether I could say good-bye to Jade Hamilton. Not after being together again after all these years and going through what we just did. In fact, if the FBI had their way, I'd have to give it all up— friends, my new music studio, even my career. At least I didn't need to give up Amee; she'd seemingly vanished off the face of the earth.

Uncomfortable silence came next. I expected them to quiz me about the almost exact replay of the school shooting years ago; they must have caught on to the similarities. But so much of my revelation, of course, had been confined to my mind. How could they possibly know my experience without my telling them?

Mom spoke up. "Okay, there's something I need to know. On the day when we met Gordon at the hotel with Henry, why'd you take off on your own?"

"I needed answers."

"And did you find what you were looking for?"

"There are several things I've learned about myself, and … well, this isn't going to be easy to talk about."

Why not just speak the words for all to hear? Why hide anything? We've all been in this together.

"I went up to Drummond Mine."

"Why'd you go there?" Mom said.

"Because something was nagging me, something I couldn't remember about the day Joey Bartholomew fell to his death. But then everything came back to me." I swallowed hard. "Mom, Joey didn't die because he got too close to the edge. He died because I pushed him."

"What?" Her gaze locked onto mine. "But I thought it was an accident."

"It *was* an accident, Landon," Jade said. "Joey pushed you, and you pushed him back. You didn't mean for him to trip on that tree root."

"What tree root?" Mom said.

So I told her everything, including Galotta's murder of Sharon Bartholomew, which I'd now twice reported to the police.

I shook my head. "I didn't mean for him to fall. And then Jade and I agreed to lie and cover up the truth. Right, Jade?"

She nodded, eyes downcast. I explained to my mom about the awkwardness of the timing and the possibility of my losing the piano scholarship. She patted my arm understandingly.

"I also tried to save Joey, with some sort of superhuman strength I didn't know I possessed." Jade's eyes met mine. "I freaked you out that day, didn't I? It wasn't just the lie that drove us apart. It was the truth of my abilities. You were afraid of me."

"I still don't understand how you were able to do that," Jade said.

"Call it adrenaline on steroids. Maybe with this implant, the puppet master could tap into that strength and make me do things no one should naturally have the ability to do."

"And that's why they've wanted you so bad," Mom said in a hushed tone. "Why they won't let you go."

My attention drifted toward the window.

And why the puppet master is still out there somewhere. Watching and waiting.

The FBI had cautioned me that the investigation might take some time before they could track down those in charge of the crime network and shut it down. Dr. Korovin had bolted, his Cyberhealth Clinic now an empty shell; agents had begun investigating his lease, hoping for a lead by following the money trail. So far, they'd met only dead ends.

Even if they found Korovin, he'd been only a pawn in this unimaginable game. Until they apprehended the puppet master, I still carried a heavy weight on my shoulders.

"They've been watching me a long time, haven't they, Mom? Didn't they do some sort of tests on me when I was little?"

A look of disgust crossed her face. "They lied to us. Those people said they just wanted to test your brain aptitude because of your musical abilities, but now I see that they must have been watching you for years."

"One of the men in charge slapped me across the face, didn't he?"

"He said he was just testing to see if you were clairvoyant. He made me so mad. I grabbed your hand, and we got out of there in a hurry after that."

"And now they want to possess me and use me as a weapon. Well, I'm not about to let them." I looked sadly at Jade and sighed. "I'm so sorry about your uncle. I know he tried to help."

"He must have gotten too close to the truth," she said. "But at least we have protection he didn't have."

"Really? I guess I'm paranoid. I can't help it."

"This may help, but it's turned off right now, being a hospital." Jade handed me a small square gadget attached to a wristband. "The signal jammers did their job, Wade said, but this will work even better. Actually, I have two of them, in case one doesn't work."

"It looks like a watch."

"But it does so much more."

"Like what?"

"You wouldn't understand. In fact, I don't either. Wade says we just need to trust him."

Well, perhaps Wade I could trust. Then again, whenever I'd trusted anyone over the last few months, look at what had happened.

I met her eyes. "So what do I owe you?"

She smiled. "Consider it a gift. You forget that I can afford it. I just don't flaunt my wealth."

Hmm. Maybe we could talk more about that sometime. "Okay, but what happened at the cabin?" I said. "The drones came anyhow."

"Wade doesn't know for sure, but he thinks the puppet master must have used heat imaging via satellite. Maybe by process of elimination, he determined we must have been there. Wade doesn't know of any way to shield you from that."

Great.

"I have something else I need to tell you." I looked them both in the eye. "When Galotta lured me to the school, I remembered a few things I'd forgotten about the past."

"The repressed memories?" Mom said.

"Yeah, I remember all of it now. And I know Dad wasn't responsible for shooting those men."

Mom and Jade exchanged baffled glances.

"When Dad passed out, I took the rifle, and … *I'm* the one who shot them."

Jade raised an eyebrow.

Mom pressed a hand to her neck. "What are you talking about?"

I related the events as I now embraced them while they stared at me with rounded eyes. "Surely you already knew this," I said to Mom. Had she been lying to me all these years to keep the family secret safe?

"Landy, I have no idea what you're talking about. Remember, I was lying on the classroom floor with a bloody nose, on the edge of passing out, when I heard the shots. I never saw what happened outside. So you think your father took the fall in your place—that's what you're saying."

"I *know* he did, Mom. I watched him take the rifle out of my hands and wipe it clean of my fingerprints before the police arrived."

Mom leaned back, hand pressed to her forehead.

I turned to Jade. "You were there too. Certainly you remember."

"But I didn't see what happened either. Remember, those men were carrying me *away* from the school. I never saw who pulled the trigger. And when those men dropped me and ran, the wind got knocked right out of me. I just lay there for the longest time. I couldn't even get up. The next thing I knew after the gunfire, your dad was looking down at me. He had the rifle, and he asked me if I was okay. I never saw you again until later at the hospital, after I heard you'd blacked out and suffered some sort of amnesia."

"But I was there, Jade. Are you positive you didn't see me with the rifle? I thought you glanced back at me."

"I didn't even know you were outside the building."

Studying their faces, I determined to find some sign of affirmation. "But that's how it happened—I know it is. I was trying to save you, Jade. Those guys were working for Lucius. They were planning to kill you. Lucius was in the getaway truck, waiting for you."

Jade nodded. "Yeah, we know all about that from Lucius's trial, remember? That was before he went to prison."

Why couldn't I remember anything from the trial? Apparently, some memories still desired to stay in hiding.

"Are you telling me you think your father is a liar?" Tension crackled in Mom's voice. "Why would he lie about something like that?"

"I was hoping you could tell me. Maybe he wanted to protect me. Perhaps he knew I wouldn't have much of a future if I ended up in juvenile hall. I don't know. I figured he would have talked to you about it, but I guess I was wrong."

Mom leaned forward and patted my hand, voice softening. "Look, you've been through a lot lately. And isn't it true that you've seen some pretty bizarre things in your head thanks to those memory trips or whatever you want to call them? Maybe you just need more time and rest to sort things out. Then maybe—"

"But I killed those men. *I'm* the one responsible!" They both jerked in response to my outburst. "I need to call Marshall Doolittle." He was our family attorney. "I need to tell the police what I did. They need to release Dad so he can come home!"

"Whoa, slow down, Landy." Mom gripped my arm with a fierce expression. "First, you need to calm down, okay?"

Perhaps I did need more rest, but that didn't mean—

"Landy, try to understand." She sighed. "Even if what you say is true—and I'm not saying it's not; maybe events really did happen the way you say they did—it takes an awful lot to overturn a murder conviction. I mean, they aren't going to set your father free just because you suddenly remembered something you forgot from over twenty years ago."

Jade asked, "Do you have new physical evidence?"

This conversation hadn't gone at all like I'd planned. "Well, no, but—"

"Landy, the court had a lot of circumstantial evidence against your father," Mom said.

I braced myself, unsure I wanted to hear this.

"Your dad knew those men. Some of his train memorabilia had been stolen, and he suspected they were responsible. We're talking thousands of dollars, and things were financially tight for us back then, if you recall. He had a motive to hurt them. So when he saw them at the school, he just snapped."

"That's what Dad said?" I said.

"No, it's what the prosecuting attorney said, but your father never denied it. Yes, those men were mixed up with Lucius's murder plot against Jade, but that has nothing to do with why the jury found your father guilty. They found him guilty for shooting those men in the back when they were running *away*."

But Dad had been shielding me. He knows the truth of what happened that day.

But if I asked him, would he verify my story? Would he even remember who I was?

Overwhelmed by their words, I just sat there and swallowed. Bottom line: they didn't believe me, and that hurt.

"Landon, there's another possibility maybe you should consider," Jade said.

"But I already know—"

"Just hear me out, okay? Maybe the puppet master *implanted* those memories in your head. Have you considered that?"

Galotta *had* wanted me to accept that I must be a natural-born killer, that I belonged on his team. But his pressure had backfired, and I'd seen my need for God instead.

Surely if God had given me the power to resist the puppet master's direct commands, he would have enabled me to see through his lies as well.

I leaned back, deflated. Talking about my newfound faith and how it had played a role in beating the puppet master could wait. Regardless of what else I said now, would they even believe me? I guessed what they must be thinking.

Poor Landon has been seeing strange things in his head. He needs more rest.

Just when I thought I'd found answers, nothing appeared to be certain anymore.

Chapter 71

Monday, November 23
Iron Valley, Michigan

After my evening meal, my oncologist, Dr. McTed, dropped by to talk about the results of my MRI. "I have some good news and some bad news. Which would you like first?"

"Good news."

He pulled up the nearest chair. More hair sprouted on his face than on his shiny, bald head. "Okay." He took a deep breath and smiled. "You're not going to believe this, but based on the scan and our blood work, I can say with confidence that you're cancer free."

Staring at him, I said, "How is that possible?"

"In fact, Landon, I know this is going to sound bizarre, but I don't see any evidence that you ever had glioblastoma multiforme to begin with."

Silence teased the moment.

"What? I don't understand."

"Without getting all technical on you, let me put it this way: Certain cancers grow with distinctive patterns and leave unique fingerprints, so to speak. Glioblastoma is rather octopus-like. What I see in your head doesn't show the evidence of anything like glioblastoma."

I swallowed. Tried to breathe.

"I know what you're thinking." He paused. "Somebody did a biopsy, right?"

"Yes, a doctor in Denver."

"I'm afraid he was killed in a car accident a few weeks ago."

Did the puppet master get to him?

"I'm sorry to hear that. But what about the scans? No, don't answer that. Let me guess. The hospital burned down with all the records, right?"

He didn't conceal his look of surprise. "Well, not the whole hospital, but there was a suspicious fire in the records room several weeks ago."

Why should any of this surprise me now?

337

He changed the subject, expression turning serious. "I have other interesting news. Yes, you did have a tumor, and it caused some damage, but everything I see would lead me to believe it was benign. Having it removed was wise, especially due to the pressure on your optic nerve, but—"

"We're not talking about terminal brain cancer at all, are we?"

"Absolutely not."

But that's what the puppet master wanted you to think. Maybe he even gave you the tumor to set the wheels in motion. How else were you to meet Dr. Korovin?

I'd have to process all this later. "Okay, what's the bad news?"

He hesitated. "If I were in your shoes, I'd want the implant removed too. But I'll be frank. It's in a very difficult location, and whoever removes it would be taking a very big risk of causing further brain damage."

"But Dr. Korovin put the implant in and didn't seem to have any issues."

"And you probably signed your life away in case something went wrong, right?"

The umpteen waivers. Of course.

"Of course, you're welcome to get a second opinion, but I'll be honest. No neurosurgeon I know is going to want to touch that implant. You'd be placing yourself in considerable risk."

"What kind of risk?"

He spread his hands. "You could be paralyzed from the waist down. Or maybe you'd lose the use of your hands. It's anybody's guess."

More than anything, I desired to have the implant removed once and for all, but I could end up just like my father.

"Are you saying there's no way for me to be free of this thing? Couldn't you maybe pierce it with something and try to—I don't know—disable it so it can never harm me again? You've got Galotta's corpse. Maybe you could study his implant and learn what you need to know."

"Actually, the FBI has his body and the implant now. I'm sure there'll be a full autopsy. I could request information they are willing to share. Sure. It may show us how we could send in a probe, like when we do a biopsy, and see if we can at least damage the implant. But ..." He paused and made a funny face. "This may sound like science fiction, but I'll say it anyhow. From what I understand, so far, the FBI isn't sure who even made that thing. What if the implant has some type of defense mechanism? What if the people who put it in your head don't *want* it taken out?"

"You're saying it could be boobytrapped?"

"I'm not saying that. I just don't know. But until the FBI is able to figure out what exactly this implant is and who's behind it, whatever we do would be a big risk. Are you willing to take that chance?"

Chapter 72

Thursday, November 26
Iron Valley, Michigan

Back in my old bedroom, I opened a dresser drawer and admired my clothes. Accepted the welcome embrace of the familiar. Taking in the street outside my window, to the cop car representing twenty-four-hour guard duty, I pondered my future.

I puzzled over what God could have in mind for any of it. He'd always been in the driver's seat, but at least I acknowledged his control now.

What do you want from me?

So much still didn't make sense, but I'd take life one day at a time and hope for more answers down the road.

Tomorrow, unless plans changed, Mom and I would be ferried off to an unknown location to start a new life with new identities. Nobody would have a clue what happened to Landon Alan Jeffers, and Hollywood reporters would write articles, speculating about my disappearance. An occasional story about a false sighting would make the news cycle.

No more recordings. No more concerts. That life would become history if I wanted to ensure the safety of those I held dear.

It hadn't been much of a choice, not with my mom's recurring screams in the night from nightmares of men hunting her down and killing her after first shaving her head and cutting her head open. She couldn't take much more of this lifestyle, and I would have been heartless to expect her to.

Later, standing in the living room, I held her close and kissed her forehead.

"Thank you, Landon." Mom peered into my eyes. "We're doing the right thing. You'll see."

But were we really? This hiding away also meant I might never see my father again, could never ask him the truth about the school shooting. Couldn't thank him for saving my life in more ways than he realized. Just the memory of his tremendous sacrifice shoved a softball-sized lump into my throat.

Did I even know my father? I'd let so much hate cloud my perception of him. What a waste of so many precious years. God help me, I'd never waste another day.

Mom wouldn't be able to see Dad again either. I suspected she'd chosen to put on a brave face, but could she really live with that separation?

Might there be another way?

***

Mom had invited Gordon, Jade, and Henry over for Thanksgiving dinner, but it became a solemn, strained affair. Everyone understood this was our final goodbye. We might never see any of them again, thanks to Galotta and Dr. Korovin. Thanks to the monsters who'd stolen my life and surely still wanted me dead.

Jade and I exchanged a few awkward glances, and she grabbed my hand under the dining room table. But after giving hers a squeeze back, I had to let go for her own good. Holding onto the hand of the woman who loved me like I loved her hurt too much.

Later, I lounged around the new music studio, too keyed up to go to bed, still thinking about the lives we'd leave behind. With everyone gathered around, I played a few requests. Playing the piano again after being separated from it for so long had become therapeutic. I closed my eyes and let my fingers glide over the keys, remembering familiar chords, rhythms, and patterns by heart. The crowds in big auditoriums had vanished, but at least I still had the music.

Henry lingered in the doorway with a wary expression. He gradually inched into the room while my hands flew across the keys. Eventually, he perched on the bench beside me while I played "Storm," a popular request at concerts. I simulated thunder with my left hand in the bass section while my right hand drew a picture of the sun slipping out from the clouds and showering the wet world with golden sunlight. I concluded by simulating the singing of birds, using twinkling notes in the upper register, their song of joy gracing the wet world below.

When I finished, he giggled. "Play it again, Uncle Landon! Play it again."

Uncle Landon? My eyes misted.

Finally, I had another fan. But didn't I have to leave him too after finally winning him over?

Enough with these regrets. I can't change the past or control what happens next. I can only trust God to guide my future.

What did the verse say, the one Jade had shared with me from Ephesians 5? Something about redeeming the time, of making the most of the minutes we have left. I didn't intend to waste a precious second.

I glanced at Jade, at her smile. Yes, this was how I wanted to remember her.

Later, sitting at my old desk while my mom slept, I found a clean piece of paper and a pen. Surely they'd later realize I'd made the right decision. Before I drove away into the night, slipping past the cop on duty, I left the note on the piano.

> It's better this way. I can't keep putting you in danger because of my problems. It's best that I find answers on my own. Please don't try to find me. I love you all. Landon.

Epilogue

Four months later
Wednesday, March 23
Trader's Hill Campground
Folkston, Georgia

I ran hard through the trees along a familiar trail just as the early-morning sun broke through the forest's edge. No longer dependent on the cane, I pushed myself hard, not glancing back to confirm what I suspected.

The men with the guns. They were coming for me—I was sure of it.

Breaking from the trees, air shuttling through my aching lungs, I dashed up the hill toward the single pine tree standing tall and majestic in the middle of the meadow.

Of course, no one pursued me, but lingering paranoia dogged my steps and propelled me on my new fitness regimen. Panting with hands planted on my hips, I took in the beauty of the place and glanced around to ensure I was alone.

I'd found the meadow of my dreams in Georgia, revisited from a long-ago camping trip. It had been one of the last camping trips I recalled with my dad before the school shooting changed everything. Back when life had been happy and I'd known him like any ten-year-old could.

I rented a site at the campground by the month and pitched my tent only fifty yards from that meadow under the cover of trees. Sometimes I sat and watched that pine tree. It reminded me of another tree on a lonely hill far away and long ago, where someone had paid the ultimate sacrifice for me. A place where I could lay my burdens down.

But not yet. My journey hadn't been completed.

My daily tasks included visiting the pay phone near the ranger's station and beginning my own journey to find the right brain surgeon. I didn't need the FBI's help; I could let my fingers do the walking. Later, after a trip to the camp store for necessities, I'd stroll to the campground chapel, a small A-frame with a white cross perched on top. I riffled the pages of the old Bible lying on the dusty pulpit until I came to the book of Psalms and found chapter 23. Certainly this would be a good place to start.

And in the corner, also dusty, hulked an out-of-tune piano I played but only after closing the doors. Perhaps only the deer listened. I found a hymnal and explored old-fashioned hymns from my boyhood—so simple and pristine. Sometimes the music washed over me, and I paused and wept.

Of course someone still watched me—not the puppet master but someone a wireless jammer couldn't keep away. What could be his plans in all this? No idea. But that fact made life interesting. What awaited me just around the corner would surely be a surprise.

Though I didn't fear for my safety, I of course battled anxiety and paranoia. But when the days passed and the old threat faded into something resembling memory, I gradually let my guard down.

God chose to surprise me one day when I least expected it, just when the days were getting longer and warmer. Returning from the camp store, I came within a dozen feet from my tent and froze, breath trapped in my throat.

I recognized my own tracks, but those weren't mine. The ground revealed two sets of them. My hand reached for the gun tucked in my waistband.

"Hello?" The hair on the back of my neck bristled.

No answer.

Fearing a thief—or worse, a drone—I unzipped the tent and peeked inside to check my belongings, which included boxes of supplies, a sleeping bag, and an air mattress. In the middle of my pillow lay a bottle of salted pistachios.

Heart thundering, I searched the tent's perimeter and forced myself to stand still. I took in the forest sights and sounds in all directions: the breeze on my face, the scent of pine, the whine of a mosquito.

Nothing appeared to be out of place.

I followed the trail to the meadow, gun ready. Still seeing no one, I ascended the hill to the lone pine, chest tight, breaths shallow. Reaching the tree, I scanned the far ridge of trees and feared to hope.

Motion stirred in the corner of my eye, and I turned when a woman and a boy emerged from the trees. I nearly fell to my knees.

Though I should have been annoyed, my heart eased into quiet acceptance. Jade had played Sherlock and hunted me down, even though I'd told her not to. Leaving that old postcard of the campground in the sock drawer had been a mistake.

But how could I be angry? Maybe she brought good news. Their smiles said as much. Could this nightmare finally be over? Surely Jade wouldn't have brought Henry along if they'd been in danger. Gordon would never have allowed it.

In that split second of discovery, my gaze darted to underbrush, to nearby trees. Tensing, I waited for a drone to dart toward Jade, knife in hand.

But no, no one. Only us. And only peace.

I'd missed them so much.

A smile broke across my face while they strolled toward me, neither hesitating nor bursting into a run, like they had all the time in the world. Which they did. For now, God had planned this moment, this one and none others, just for the three of us. At least for now, we would be together and safe.

What he had in mind for tomorrow, only he knew. But maybe it offered a future I would no longer explore on my own.